"MONEY IS POWER, F
THE ROOT OF ALL
BLESSINGS," -C

SHE'S NOT ONE OF US

Ariele Chapman

PROLOGUE

AVA

I haven't been in this house in quite some time, but now, with everything finalized, I'm able to gather my things. It's been almost a year since I've been in my childhood bedroom. I remember picking out the perfect shade of blue for the walls, spending hours deciding on a color. It was between a deep blue and a blue gray. My mother told me it didn't matter, but to me, it did. My room was my safe space, not that this house was particularly warming.

It was anything but.

I sit down on my bed and stare at the cracks along the doorframe. Closing my eyes, I wince at the thought of how I survived this place, the coldness and the cruelness. I stand up and walk toward the wall, my hand gently brushing against the paint that once gave me a sense of calmness. The painting I did hangs on the wall. I gently glide my hand along to the next one, and then another, stopping at the doorframe. My fingers trace one thousand bad memories. My body begins to feel flushed, and the dizziness sets in. I lean against the doorframe for balance.

How has it been so long since I walked into this house, and why was I so eager to come back? It's even more empty than when my *family* lived here, in this overly sized, ridiculously priced estate. I never could understand why someone would want a house this large for a family that didn't even get along.

A few moments pass, and the feeling leaves my body for the time being. It will be back again. I'm no stranger to panic attacks.

At the window, I push back the dusty curtains to let some light in. As much as I hated this house and the memories it holds, I always enjoyed this one spot, where I became the hunter, not the hunted. The balcony overlooks the entire neighborhood. I can see into everyone's homes—the heated arguments, the sex, when they are doing something they shouldn't be. I knew everything. *Almost everything.*

I walk over to my old desk and pause before opening the drawer, pulling out a letter that I longed for, that is now tainted. The ink slowly faded, just sitting in a wooden coffin of memories. I re-read a line of it, the last line, which happened to be the worst part of it.

"I can't love you anymore."

I snap back into the reality of my life—the stepdaughter of a monster, and a daughter of the mother who had no idea. I fold the letter neatly and tuck it into the pocket of my jeans.

Almost everything in my jewelry box is empty. It was full when I left that winter night. I never met an emerald I didn't covet.

My paint brushes remain brittle, dry, untouched. They once longed to be held, to be used, to create a single stroke on any canvas, but here they are, defeated, forgotten. I begin to pack them up. Maybe I'll paint with them again someday, or maybe in another life, a blank canvas.

From the corner of my eye, I notice something, put down the stiff paint brush, and walk over toward the window. Is that a car? It's not *his*. He left already. Has it been there this whole time, and I didn't notice it because I was too busy reminiscing on all the things I left behind when I became this other person? A person who had a reason to live now. Someone who didn't just go through the repetitive motions, like a heart beating.

"Nonsense. You're being paranoid," I tell myself, walking back to my paint brushes and continuing to grab things to put in cardboard boxes. I've always hated the feeling of cardboard, the texture, the roughness, the symbolic feeling of displacement.

I twist off the caps of my acrylic paints and open them up to see if they are salvageable. The luscious cadmiums and the sadistic crimsons are placed gently into the box, along with the calm blues and the overly joyous yellows I used to paint oversized sunflowers on my happier days. I pack up my ink pens and my watercolors, palette knives and whatever else I can bring with me that won't make me mentally relapse to who I was.

Before continuing to the closet, I neatly re-organize each item in the box. I stop dead in my tracks when I hear a single creak from downstairs.

"Hello?" No one answers. I try again. "Hello?"

With a deep breath, I leave my room and walk through the hallway. I hear the creak again.

One by one, I walk down each step of the grand staircase, toward the front door. I could have sworn I locked it, but I give the handle a slight jiggle. To my relief, it's still locked. The noise is just in my head, I'm sure of it. I'll just get some water and head back upstairs.

As I turn the corner to the hallway, something sharp hits my side. I'm trying hard not to close my eyes. All I can see is a shadow-like figure. I try to reach my hand out, it doesn't come near me. I'm feeling so tired.

It's best if I close my eyes for a minute.

Just one minute...

ONE

ALLISON – NOW

I never knew my half-sister. My mother, Victoria, said to never even call her that, because *she's not one of us*. She detested Ava. Everything about her made my mother's skin crawl. The thing she hated most, though, was how my father loved Ava. My sister, Ashley, and I didn't even know about her until our father's funeral. No one ever mentioned her. It's like Ava didn't exist before that day.

I remember the funeral perfectly. A blonde-haired girl, covered in freckles from head to toe, walked in as our aunt was giving a speech. Everyone turned to look at her while she found a seat in the back row. She was with a decent-looking man, but he did not compliment her at all. She was exquisite, and he was bland. Her dress was simple, nothing overly stated. It's like she was trying to blend in, but she stood out because everyone here was in designer clothing, everyone except her.

People began whispering. "We didn't think she'd show," someone said.

"I guess she wanted to make an appearance, in case she got money," another family friend added.

"Where is the rest of her family?"

It was mostly things like that. She knew people were whispering about her the entire time but seemed unbothered by it all, like it was second nature to be shunned by the Brentwood family. I was trying to figure out who she was, but no one would tell me. My older sister, Ashley, was as clueless as I was. Our mother glared at us, and we quickly faced forward, focusing on the speech our aunt was giving.

I wondered if it bothered her that they didn't mention his old life. They wouldn't dare. They never mentioned his other wife, his other daughter. He had a whole existence before this family, but why was it kept such a secret to me?

When the service ended, my immediate family moved into a small room. The priest wanted to give our family a safe space to heal. We put our heads down and reached for each other's hands, and within seconds, tears streamed down my face. They felt hot enough to burn the skin on my cheeks. I attempted to keep them in, but the more I tried the harder it became.

Just as the prayer ended, the door opened and there she was. From up close, she looked like one of us: blonde wavy hair, freckles, green eyes with small specs of brown in them. She walked right up and looked me up and down, taking me in. I felt small and uncomfortable with how close she was to Ashley and me. She looked directly at my mother; I sensed the girl's disdain, noticed the panic in my mother's face, observed the dread of the entire Brentwood family. I've never seen my family like this before. It was like watching lighting hit right next to where we were all standing, the room in static chaos. Electricity pierced through our veins.

The color drained from my mother's already lifeless skin.

"Hi, Allison and Ashley. I'm your sister. It's nice to officially meet you."

I couldn't muster a single word. My heart went numb, and my entire world started to enclose around me. My chest felt heavier and heavier with each second, and I couldn't stop replaying those words: "I'm your sister." All I could do was look around at everyone else's expression.

They were all the same, though.

Ghostly.

The entire family walked out of the room, dragging me with them. That was all she said, and that was all they let her say. Everyone left, leaving her alone.

I wanted to hate her as much as my family did. I wanted to hate her for ruining one of the already saddest days of my life. I wanted to pretend she didn't exist and forget the entirety of the situation, but I was just so curious. Why was I supposed to hate her? I didn't even know her.

If she knew we existed before, why didn't she try to see me? If she knew we existed before, why did she have to do it today, of all days?

Now I'll never get to know her. Suicide, everyone said.

I remember after learning about Ava, I'd drive to her house, park down the street, and just watch her exist. There were so many questions no one would answer. My family wanted to keep me in the dark.

"Being in the shadows gives you more power," my grandfather used to say.

I wonder why she was packing up the house if she wanted to end it all. Why waste her last moments doing that? I heard they couldn't get rid of her blood from the floor, so they had to replace the flooring in the room Ava died in. My mother told me her realtor friend oversees the listing, that it goes up for sale within the next few months or so. I find it odd the house is going on the market in general, but my mother's friend says, "Real-estate can't wait, and a hot market is a hot market. Suicide is no exception."

Honestly, I'm not a fan of my mom's friend.

I find it hard to believe someone who got three hundred million dollars less than a year ago committed suicide. My mother could't care less about her, but I think a part of her is happy Ava is gone.

I grab my keys and head out the door. I think I'll go for a long drive.

TWO

CALISTA – THEN

"Over my dead body," I yell at my daughter, Ava. "You will *not* attend that funeral."

Ava screams at the top of her lungs. "I *will* go to that fucking funeral. If you don't want to go, then don't go." She storms to her bedroom and slams the door shut.

I feel helpless. How can I let my daughter go to a funeral with monsters who would rather it'd been her who died? I can't let her in the lion's den. She's not ready for it. Ava has no idea what I had to sacrifice for her to live this life- *the life I tried to give her. The regret I live with every day.*

I walk to her bedroom and knock on the door, but I don't dare wait for a reply before entering, or I'd be waiting all day.

"They didn't even mention you in the obituary. You don't exist to them. Why would you want to grieve with people who don't want you there?"

There's no need to look at her. I already know those words stung. I just can't bear to see her get hurt like that again. I don't like to be the one to tell her when she can and can't do things. After all, she won't be living under this roof soon. Ava's eighteen years old and will be attending Northwestern University, doing things on her own. Things I wouldn't like if I knew what they were, but at least she won't be far from home. Not that home is any safer these days, but she's close enough to where I can keep watch.

I go to sit down on her bed. My heart breaks with every inch she moves away from me. I try to put my hand on her back several times before giving up.

"Mom, you need to stop," she says angrily.

I get up and walk toward the door, looking at her on my way out and pausing to get in my final words.

"That family is cancer, do you hear me! His siblings have been coming by here all week to check in on us, after almost eighteen years of being absent from your life. Do you want to know what they have really been doing? They've been spying on us, seeing how well off we are. They know that now that your dad's dead, the will reading will be soon. Do you think they actually care about you?"

She looks away from me.

"They might, if they got to know me!" she says, hopeful.

"If they wanted to get to know you, they'd have done it years ago. It's a little too late for that now." My voice shakes.

But that's where Ava is wrong. They don't want to know her. When a member of that family passes, they don't want to disperse their Brentwood fortune to anyone extra, and my daughter? They see her as just that—an extra, taking away from the rest of their inheritances. When my ex-father-in-law, Clyde, died, it was a blood bath. At least, that's what Josh told me.

"Will you at least bring someone with you?" I plead with her.

She nods. I don't know why she is so keen on going. That family

10

dragged us through the mud. We were homeless after Ava's father abandoned us for that witch of a woman. He left us with nothing, put all our belongings on the street, and forced us to find food and shelter on our own. Ava was only two months old at the time. It wasn't until I met my second husband that we finally had a real house to call ours—this empty, castle-like structure surrounded by suburbs for miles and miles. It's a lonely life here, but I had to make the sacrifices I did to put Ava first.

Ava will see that one day. She will, I know it. It just was a sacrifice that ended up trapping us, one I never saw coming, but I have to live with my consequences of believing in happy endings. Bad luck shouldn't strike like this twice. I am a fool, but a fool with diamonds on my neck, large enough to cover my bruises. Ava had to endure terrible things, but she will be free *soon*.

I let her be and run to the store to get a few of her favorite things. With her home, it doesn't feel so lonesome, and I like it. When she leaves for college, it will be just me. I can't bear the thought.

At the store, I walk through the aisles, grabbing flour and sugar to make Ava her favorite chocolate chip oatmeal cookies. As I reach for the semi-sweet chocolate, I notice someone staring at me and whispering.

I glare back at her; she leaves without hesitation. It's been like this all week long, whenever I leave the house. People wondering now that my ex-husband is dead, who will get his millions. I had no idea he had money when we were married…until later. He never showed it. My ex was a modest man, with a modest car, in a small apartment. The only large things about him were his demons, the darkness overpowering him, the lack of control in his life that made him become a monster.

I had no idea his family was basically heir to General Mills. until he wasn't mine anymore, *he belonged to her.*

I ignore the cereal aisle because just walking past it makes me feel uneasy. At the checkout, more bored suburban housewives gossip as each one of my items is scanned by the cashier. To think, I used to be one of those bored suburban housewives when I first moved to the neighborhood. Now I'm just a lonely one. The cashier hands me my bag of groceries, and I walk to my car. The walk feels like an eternity, and I fumble for my keys in my purse.

When I get home, the first thing I do is preheat the oven and begin to mix the batter. From scratch is best.

My husband comes home from work and walks right past me to his office. I married Tanner when Ava was just three years old. She didn't have a say in the matter, but sometimes, I wish she would have. They say children can sense whether someone is good or bad. Tanner walks out of his office, on the phone. He looks frustrated. His almond-shaped, brown eyes tell me everything I need to know. His dark hair is slicked back, and his Brooks Brothers suit is looking a little tight on him. He was in better shape when we first met.

I roll the pieces of cookie dough into the last few neat balls, the oatmeal texture feeling nice against my skin. Tanner sees me making cookies and immediately insults them.

"Don't make them too salty now."

I ignore him. He's been extra intolerable lately, his snide remarks getting crueler every day. Tanner's on edge. He has a new business opportunity in the works, and the stress of it is causing him to take it out on me. He's always been like this, though, very driven and focused on being successful. What people don't know is that his parents bought us this house. He couldn't afford it at the time. I tried to talk him into the cute bungalow down the street, but he insisted we live in this one. Tanner always told me people respect you if you have money. Sometimes, as much as it pains me to say it, he's not wrong. We lived in a modest townhouse for several years before we found the house on Kenilworth, before all his business deals truly took off.

I pour the chocolate chips into the batter and gently fold them in. Tanner walks by and takes a fingerful. He smacks his lips annoyingly.

"Eh, I liked last week's better," Tanner says, walking back into his office.

It's hard to believe I've been married twice in my lifetime, fooled by false love and lies.

I put the cookies in the oven and stare blankly at the wall.

When the timer dings, I get the cookies out of the oven. I left some cookie dough in the bowl, just in case Ava would prefer that instead. I let our dog, Murphy, out to the bathroom and back in before bringing Ava a plate of cookies.

As I head up to her room, Murphy right behind me, I get a whiff of fresh paint as I walk up the stairs. She repainted her room another shade of blue. Every year, it becomes even darker than the last. Right now, it's a dark gray-blue, like murky ocean water that only looks beautiful if the light touches it just right, but it almost never does.

I let myself in her room. She's sitting there on the floor, her drawing ripped into tiny little pieces. I place the plate of cookies down on the ground.

Picking up all the little scraps around her, I start to piece it back together.

"It looks better this way," I tell her.

Murphy runs up and licks her face. She loves that dog. I got him for us during a Christmas that was just the two of us. Tanner was on a work trip. He wasn't pleased with me, but for once in this marriage, I stood my ground.

A faint smile crosses Ava's face for a slight second.

"I didn't like the color I used," she says.

She reaches for a new piece of paper and restarts her drawing. Each stroke is gentle, the opposite of who she is as a person.

Tanner walks up the stairs, passing her room completely without so much as a hello. He slams the bedroom door shut. I haven't slept in the bedroom with him in over a decade. I sleep on the couch, just in case.

It's safer this way.

I'm not sure how to get Ava to avoid the funeral. She doesn't deserve to put herself through that. Instead, I pick up one of her paint brushes, hand it to her, kiss her on her forehead, and tell her I love her. I know it's not much, but that's all I have left to give.

THREE

AVA – THEN

I need to go to this funeral to meet my half-sisters. They don't know I exist, but after tomorrow, they will. I want them to know their mother ruined my life. That their mother is the reason mine ended up marrying Tanner. I want them to know they are offspring to a sociopath.

My mother is yelling about me going. She's trying to make it seem like not going is better, that I'm putting my life in danger. Mom's being overly dramatic for no reason at all.

Affairs happened all the time where I grew up. It's as common as catching a cold during the fall and winter months. My father's affair made him a better person down the line. Not a great person, but a slightly better person. He had his flaws, but to not attend his funeral because my mother thinks his side of the family would harm me is absolutely ludicrous.

She tries to make me feel small by telling me I'm nothing to the Brentwood family, like this will make me want to no longer attend. I'm going to just walk upstairs in the hopes she doesn't follow me.

In my room, I sit on my bed just to think, and when I finally calm down, there she is, trying her hardest to convince me not to go.

It doesn't work. I'm going.

"You aren't allowed to even sit up front with the family. They told the priest. Did you know that?"

I assumed as much, so I stay silent and just let her ramble off reasons why I shouldn't attend. To be fair, they all sound reasonable, and no sound person would want to go, but I am anything but sound.

My mother leaves my room, and I begin painting. I'm unsure what this painting wants to be, so I'll just figure it out as I go.

I text my friend, Easton to see if he wants to come with me to the funeral tomorrow. He's been my friend since I was fifteen. We met the first time I bought weed off him, and over the years, we've grown closer. He taught me how to run a business to make money to get by. I don't do the hard stuff, but lucky for me, a lot do.

Easton helps me escape from this world of suburban housewives, so bored of their own lives that they leech onto the failed hopes and dreams of others.

He texts me: "I'm in... Popcorn, Swedish fish, drinks?"

I look at my painting and feel a rush of emotions. My brush stroke was forceful enough to rip through my paper. Frustrated, I begin to tear it up.

My mother walks in with cookies. I take a bite of one, just to make her happy. Honestly, I haven't been hungry in years. Something about growing up where I did could make you never want to eat again, and not just because every person is rail-thin, but because existing here numbs you. Sometimes, I feel like a player in a video game, and someone else has the controller.

I watch my mother as she picks up the pieces of my artwork scattered all over the ground and let out a fake smile so she feels appreciated. It works. She hands me my paint brush and sits with me for a few minutes before letting me be. I can finally be alone with my thoughts. Although sometimes, I wish they would stop forever.

By the time I finish my painting, it's pitch-black outside. I sit on my balcony and watch the cars go by, watching each neighbor's front porch light slowly turn off. Only one neighbor keeps their light on all night—they are convinced no neighborhood can be safe all the time.

I walk to my bathroom and wash my face. The water's so cold it stings my cheeks. I need to look good for tomorrow, I just need to. Walking to my door, I lock it and push my dresser in front of my bedroom door. It helps me sleep better, knowing if he tried to get in here, I'd have a single moment to prepare myself.

I feel restless, so I take one of the pills Easton gave me for anxiety the last time I saw him. Within minutes, my eyes feel heavy. I begin to fade away for just a few hours.

In the morning, I wake up feeling hungover, walk to the bathroom, and turn on the shower. The room fills with steam before I get in.

I breathe in the hot air and exhale.

I can do this.

Grabbing a razor, I begin to shave my legs. No idea why I bother. My dress is black, long, and plain. I don't want to draw too much attention to myself because me being there is attention enough. A loud thud downstairs catches me off guard, causing my hand to slip. Bright red blood runs down my leg and into the drain. I finish up in the shower and rummage through my bathroom cabinet for a Band-Aid. All I can find is a piece of toilet paper.

After blow-drying my hair, I put on what I think is the correct amount of makeup for a funeral. I've never been to one before, and I didn't expect the first one to be my father's, if I'm being completely honest.

My mother tries to convince me not to go several more times, but when my phone rings, I use that as my scapegoat. I blow her a kiss. She looks stressed, more so than normal.

Easton picks me up. When we first started hanging out, I made fun of him for his car. He calls it his "middle-class car." Easton says drug dealers who have too nice of a car draw too many red flags, and people who drive around in a shit car also draw the same number of red flags, so he drives a silver Prius. He doesn't look like a drug dealer— not that drug dealers have a particular look. His Ivy League haircut suits his chestnut brown hair, and when he talked to you, you can't help but get lost in his honey-colored eyes. He could have been a model—not that he ever would.

We pull up to the church service and have a hard time finding parking. My father's side of the family is very large. He has his mother, three brothers, and one sister. Each sibling is married with kids of their own. I always wished my family was bigger and have been jealous of how large my dad's side of the family is. It's just my mom and myself. My grandparents died when I was one year old.

I walk into the church service halfway through my aunt's speech, if you can even call her that. Everyone stares at me walking toward the back row. I don't dare try to sit up front, knowing I'm not wanted there. Easton takes a seat beside me. Periodically, someone turns around to stare. I see my two half-sisters in the front row. It's not hard to tell who they are. They look like me, their hair blonder, their facial structures more angular than mine. My face is heart-shaped, like my mother's.

My aunt is talking about what an upstanding father he was, but he wasn't. She tells a story about what a loving husband he was. He wasn't. She continues talking about his family and childhood and all he accomplished in this life. I am not mentioned once. I cease to exist in this realm.

Halfway through the service, I get up to go to the bathroom. No one would dare leave a service to use the restroom, but I wasn't raised like most people.

I open the stall door and sit down, digging through my purse and taking a few gulps from a miniature liquor bottle. It stings the moment the alcohol touches my lips. It burns all the way down my throat. I walk to the sink and reapply my makeup in the mirror, taking a long hard look at myself before fixing my dress and stepping back through the door.

The service is over. People begin to filter down the aisles toward the exit. My family—at least, what *used* to be my family, heads into a small room.

This is my chance.

Easton stays seated and pulls his phone from his pocket. He is content texting and letting me do what I came here for.

I'm trying not to shake. If I'm trembling down to my very core, I can't look composed. How will I say it? How will it come out?

I open the door. Everyone looks at me. I can see Victoria, the mistress, his wife…whatever she is. She's terrified of what I'm about to do. Victoria tries to motion to my aunt and uncles to stop me, to force me out of this room, but it's too late. I walk up to my half-sisters, and I let the words fall out of my mouth, like milk being poured into a bowl of cereal. Easy, quick.

"I'm your sister. It's nice to meet you." I look at both of them without breaking eye contact.

No one says anything. They leave the room. I'm alone again.

Just last week, my aunt who I haven't spoken to almost my entire life came over to "talk," to make amends. It made me so excited to connect with more family, a second chance, but in one moment, it was all a rouse. My mother was right. They were putting on a show.

I walk back toward Easton and motion to him that I want to go.

He gets up out of his seat quickly, and we exit out the door.

"Are rich people always so…rude?" he asks.

"It depends if they know you might have access to some of their money."

We get in his car, and I achingly roll down the window to let the sun hit my face. We drive around for what seems like hours, until the night feels more like winter than summer.

FOUR

ALLISON – NOW

Ava's once-beautiful home now seems uneasy. My mother used to drive past this house when I was growing up. I was too young to understand what she was doing—prying information through the large windows of Ava's home, doing anything to get a glimpse of the woman my father loved before her. She used to tell my sister and me she was house shopping. We played along and used to point to which room would be mine and which would be hers. I didn't know it then, but I picked Ava's room.

After parking my car, I peer through the windows. I step on overgrown weeds to get a closer look. Walking toward the front door, I check to see if the lockbox is still on it. To my luck, it is. The realtor my mother is friends with always uses her pet's birthday as the code. I check to see if anyone is watching. In a neighborhood like this, someone always is.

I enter the code, swiftly grab the key, and let myself in. The house has always been immaculate.

I close the front door behind me and walk into the entryway. When the light hits the floor just right, it looks like a shadow of Ava lying in her pool of blood. For a moment, it seems real, and every hair on my body stands upright. I feel like she is stuck in this room, trapped in her personal hell.

The stark white walls are covered in obscure art. I walk up the staircase leading to the main floor of bedrooms. When I get to Ava's room, I pause. Only once before, I snuck in with Ashley, like a game, but I haven't been in Ava's house since *it* happened.

I couldn't bear to bring myself back here, until now. Though I try to tell myself I had nothing to do with her death, I know deep down to my core I might have.

As I twist the doorknob letting myself into Ava's room, I forget to take a breath for a moment. There are dozens of partially packed boxes. I sit down and go through the one with her paint brushes in them, taking my finger and gently playing with the bristles. They feel stiff, like brittle bones.

I walk toward an old painting she did, half finished. It is of an open field with rows of lavender and a little house. I imagine that's the life she wanted, the life she could have had with all her inheritance. *My inheritance.* She had drawn the outline of a young woman having a picnic in the field. I like to imagine that's where she is now, but I know she is trapped inside this house. I can feel her here.

Neatly organized by the year are the birthday cards she saved. Calista always gave her the same Dalmatian card, but its spots were filled in with a different color every year. My mother never did anything like that for us. I look through a few more cards and wonder what will happen to these. Though I try to tell myself to leave them here, I know they'll be better off with me.

Ava's jewelry box sits on her nightstand next to her bed. The mattress I rest on is firm, and I open the box delicately so as not to accidentally drop anything. I'm shocked to find that it's bare. The first time I snuck in here, I knew she was born in the month of May. People say emeralds represent youth, good fortune, and foresight. I used to believe that, but not anymore. If it were true, she'd have seen this coming. She'd have never come back here.

I walk toward another box filled to the brim with love letters, signed by Scott, and I sit down cross-legged, enthralled with every line. I've never been loved like that before. I open a journal, every page filled to capacity. Thoughts overflowing on every page, the kind that if you keep them inside of you, you'd slowly become hollow from the world. Some pages, the handwriting is softer, more delicate. The other pages are bold and blocky. They must have written to each other in this, her trading it off to him so he could read her thoughts late at night when the rest of the world slept. I know I shouldn't, but I can't help myself. I read through them, my eyes swelling up. Scott would like to have these, I think. I pack up a few of her things and place them in a box for him, sure I'll be able to find him, for Ava's sake.

Another one of Ava's paintings hangs on her gloomy blue walls, and I get lost in the brush strokes for a moment. I decide I will take this one for me so I can have a piece of her. Turning it over gently, I wrap it up in one of her towels that was in her bathroom.

A key is taped to the back of the painting.

The tape barely holds the key in place, so I remove it, holding up the key and looking closely at it. I check to see if there are any other keys on the backs of her paintings. One after the other, I quickly take the paintings down from the walls, turning them over and finding nothing.

What secret were you keeping, Ava? What is this key for?

There is a creak from downstairs. I know I shouldn't be here, but I can't leave now. What if someone is in here? I panic, and the blood rushes to my face, making me flushed. Dizziness overtakes me. I know better than to call out for someone. No one can know I'm here.

Grabbing the key, I hurry under her bed, letting the long blankets that drape to the floor hide me. I close my eyes and pray no one walks into Ava's room.

Another creak comes from downstairs. I hold my breath and try to imagine being in Ava's painting, sitting in a lavender field, looking up at the sky. It's sunny, and I pretend there's a beautiful beam of light touching my freckled nose. I'd like to think in that world, maybe we'd like each other. Maybe we could be family there.

Someone is talking downstairs.

A voice I've never heard before.

FIVE

CALISTA – THEN

I've been sick to my stomach all day over the will reading. Having to look at all those people—if you can even call them that—makes my skin crawl. Ava handled herself better than I thought she would. She usually acts out of passion and not logic, not a trait I was endowed with. Ava has the darkness her father had, and if I'm being honest, it terrifies me.

When I was married to Ava's father, his family treated me like scum. Nothing has changed. Any chance the Brentwoods got to make my life miserable, they did. Josh had no backbone to stand up to them because if he did, they would have cut him off dry- *he needed it, every dime.* Sometimes, I wish they had. Maybe we'd have been happier and still together. Money can make people do terrible things, and if you know money is at stake, people will go to unthinkable measures to keep their fortune under lock and key.

I wonder if Ava misses Josh. She didn't shed a single tear when I told her he had died- they were on good terms right before he passed. I worry about Ava, her pain buried so deep within, she's trapped out any light that was left. We were the last to know Josh died. I got a phone call from my realtor friend, who wasn't sure if I'd heard the news.

"Heart problem," she said. She continued, pausing every so often for a dramatic sigh. "Apparently, it got worse with his age. He had a stroke after the surgery. Such a shame. He was so young. You must be devastated. It happened last week…I'd have thought they would have told you by now."

I don't recall what I said back. All I remember is I hung up the phone and cried. I had to let myself grieve first, instead of telling Ava right away. When I did share the news with Ava that night, she looked at me, shrugged, and walked out of the room emotionless.

Josh and I met in high school during our senior year. He was tall, with sandy blonde hair and a smile that could break you. His gaze held a unique intensity. I tried to avoid looking into his emerald eyes—I was afraid that if I lost myself in them, I'd be trapped forever. He was adventurous, loud, overly confident, and liked by all his peers. For some reason, though, he didn't want a partner that was his equal. He wanted me—the shy freshman who hid behind her camera. Josh wanted someone gentle and loving, something he never got at home. He was searching for every quality his family didn't embody. Josh would pass me in the hall briefly on his way to class or baseball practice and attempt to strike up a conversation.

"What kind of camera is that?" he'd ask.

"Oh, this is a Canon E1," I'd say.

The conversations were often short and to the point. I didn't realize he wanted more from me. Back then, I was gangly and too tall, with stick-straight hair. My eyes were wide and my lips full but never accentuated because I didn't wear makeup to school. I didn't want the added attention. It was better to be a ghost, unnoticed, than to be whispered about.

Vivian, his sister, was in my grade, and she made it a point to let people know I was a loser. Every chance she had, she'd whisper to her classmates...things about me that weren't true. That I was a slut, that I was obsessed with her brothers, that I was desperate to be loved. I resonate with that last part now more than ever these days. Tanner never loved me the way Josh did.

When Josh went away to college, we didn't speak, and that was that. He was no more than a quick flirtation, a simple infatuation of the heart. A curiosity I put to rest.

The years flew by. I tried my hardest to be unseen, but being unnoticed was the easy part. Vivian only taunted me here and there, but it was tolerable. I got my diploma and continued trying to be veiled. It was best that way—keep my focus on my education and let my life begin after that, once I accomplished everything my parents had always dreamed about me achieving.

It wasn't until I went to college at Indiana University that our paths crossed again. He was more charming than I could remember... His beautiful olive skin kissed with freckles from his tan, wavy blonde hair he'd often tie back before baseball practice. He was a senior, and again, I was a freshman.

When he asked me on our first date, it felt like, for a single moment, the earth stopped rotating. From that moment on, we were together.

We'd spend our days in the park, drinking shitty beer, eating Chinese food out of the carton, lying on a quilt my mother made me. We'd go to concerts, dancing the night away. He'd brush my long hair when it got wet after a day at the pool. I didn't need to worry about his rude sister, his pompous brothers, meeting his family, or anything of the sort for the time being. At college, we were tucked away in this fragile bubble. Nothing outside of us existed.

While I worked through my last few years of college, he got a job close by, and every day after my classes, he'd pick me up with a dozen red roses, sometimes he would even fill my dorm room with them. I never had the heart to tell him I thought roses were overdone, cliché, but I was loved by someone, and when you love someone, it's best to silence that inner voice because inner voices often come with consequences.

Tanner slams on his horn, and I snap back to reality. I look in the car mirror at the scar on my face. It's ever so slight enough that when the sun hits it just right, you can see it glistening white.

I look out the window, longing to be anywhere but here. My *husband* hasn't spoken to me since the meeting got out. He's been acting unusual the last few months, more so than normal. Tanner used to be someone safe for me, a shoulder to lean on. He enjoyed being my savior. I think he liked the idea of rescuing a single mother— left on the streets, no home, no money, and with a newborn. He must have seen that as an opportunity, for a way to let God forgive him for his sins. I was his way of pretending he was a good person, and that is how I became trapped again.

Tanner turns down the radio. "Can you believe that judge?" His face turns a shade of red I've never seen before.

"I'm sure it's a mistake," I say, trying to calm him down.

"He did this on purpose, that cruel son of a bitch."

"We will talk to our lawyer and figure out the next steps. I know he wouldn't leave Ava with nothing. That's not like him, the old version yes, but not this one." I'm not sure *I* even believe the words coming out of my mouth. "We will get a copy of the will and trust, go over it, and then call their lawyers."

He isn't having it.

"I raised that girl for sixteen years. The least he could have done was leave us a little money, for a thank you," he mutters.

I look at the side mirror and notice Ava driving slowly behind us. She's not paying attention. It looks like she's on the phone, unphased, unbothered by what just went down in that room.

"You wanted to raise my daughter with me out of the goodness of your heart, did you not?" I scolded. "You have all the money in the world...Millions...You look like a leech. When is enough enough with you?"

He pulls over and slams on the brakes. My head hits the back of my seat.

"I provide everything for this family—a roof over your heads, food on the table, education, clothes, you were a sad pathetic thing before me. I didn't make you work. You should show me some gratitude now and then!" he screams.

"I'm sorry." I begin to cry.

I'm not sorry. I'm not sorry at all. I'm only crying because I'm trapped here. I'm crying for me, not him.

There needs to be a way. That money was my way out with Ava. Money of our own. I've never been so desperate to hope fate is on my side for once, that by some miracle there will be a mistake in the last will and testament. Dear God, please, I don't ask for much. I haven't asked you for anything at all.

We turn into our driveaway, in a neighborhood where the houses are big and the people are empty. The longer I stay here, the more of a vessel I become. I'd give anything to be Ava's age again, to make different choices. I'd have chosen myself. I hope she knows better than me, that my mistakes don't haunt her. We pull into the garage and turn off the car. The garage door closes, and once again, the feeling of being imprisoned overcomes me.

SIX

AVA – THEN

The room where they are reading the will is depressing, dingy, and has that classroom-type of smell to it. I'm not sure why this couldn't have been done over the phone. The clock hasn't moved at all since the last time I checked. It's hard to have focus. So much depends on this next hour.

My other side of the family that I don't really know is in the room across the hall from this one. They had to make special arrangements to not be in the same room as my mom, stepfather, and me.

I have no idea why my stepfather is here. He said it was for moral support, but I doubt that. He's not the supportive type. I have no idea what my mother saw in that man to begin with.

A lawyer walks in the room and begins talking about my father and what he wanted. I look at the clock. Only two minutes more have passed.

"We seem to have a bit of a situation," the lawyer says nervously.

My stepfather's face shows sheer panic.

"Although your daughter was left three hundred million dollars, it appears that the trust and the will do not match."

My stepfather begins to nervously pace back and forth,

aggressively running his hands through his stiff hair.

The lawyer continues. "We will have to argue this in court or a possible mediation, as there isn't much I can do beyond this point. Something was not recorded accurately before his untimely death. Although rare, these things happen." The lawyer looks away from us after he finishes speaking.

A defeated look falls over my mother's face. She was convinced my father would have left me something, a testament to solidify he had regrets about leaving us. Maybe my mother needed that more than I did. I was too young to remember everything, and I can't decide if that is a good thing or a bad thing.

Through the window in the door, I see my half-sisters leave and walk toward the elevators with their mother. They knew I was in the room across the hall from them, so close to a blood relative they know nothing about. I can't even fathom what lies my stepmother told them about me.

My mother and father had a quiet marriage. His family didn't know until later. A former acquaintance saw my mother's ring and told his parents. It was after they found out that his mood shifted. Mom said he became unrecognizable.

My father met Victoria at work after being married to my mother for less than a year. He claimed she was *just a friend*.

More times than my mother would like to admit, he'd work late hours and come home in a fit of rage after losing an important sale. Sometimes, he'd scream at my mom, taking out all his frustration on her. My father wasn't very good at keeping jobs, and now, it makes sense. Why did he need to work hard and be the best when he was already set for the rest of his life?

Over time, my mother said he would just not come home at all for days. She had too much to be worried about—a pregnancy that was almost to full term, a child she wasn't sure she wanted anymore. As much as that hurt to hear, I prefer the truth.

When I was born, nothing really changed. Lots of late nights, cruel words thrown around as effortlessly as a baseball being tossed in the heat of summer, and dinners that ended up on the kitchen floor. From what my mother told me, their house wasn't lavish, and their lifestyle was kept plain. No fancy cars, no mansions, and coupons for grocery runs. Mom thought they were barely making ends meet. She didn't find out what kind of money the Brentwood family had until he already had a new life. My father wouldn't even pay child support. My mother tried to take him to court over it, but her lawyers were no match for his. Eventually, she was forced to give up.

Mom never knew his family possessed that kind of old money people dream about having. She had never even been to his house; they lived on opposite sides of town. My mother grew up in a modest family, a small house filled with love. I was always a bit jealous of her for that and wondered what it was like, what it could have been like for me.

When I was younger, I used to imagine my mother making freshly squeezed orange juice while the eggs sizzled on the pan, the bacon getting crisp enough in the oven, filling the entire house with an aroma of blissful Sunday mornings. I imagined sitting eating breakfast with my parents. He'd put down the paper and smile at me, ask me what I wanted to do this weekend, my mother staring lovingly at us. I never got that.

Instead, I got a version of my mother that would have never

existed had she not met Tanner. Often, I think I'd have been a better person if he had never intruded upon our lives. Mom said she met him randomly, but I know that's a lie. I spent countless hours researching him when I got older and found out he used to work with my father.

They knew each other from way back, and Tanner knew my father came from money, I'm sure of it. I think he married my mother just knowing maybe, one day, her child would get some money when my father died. There was this lengthy second child support battle that went down after my mother married Tanner. Out of the blue, my mother decided to try again. Tanner made sure to let Josh know he was there to help my mother through it.

Now, I'm enjoying watching Tanner in a web of turmoil. It's nice to know karma exists sometimes.

The lawyer has us fill out several forms before we can go. Tanner storms out the door first, shutting it behind him before my mother and I even have a chance to walk through. Mom ignores Tanner's behavior, and we decide to take the stairs instead of the elevator.

"Are you okay?" she says guiltily.

"Yeah, I'm fine. I never expected anything, so it is what it is." But deep down, I'm defeated. I was so close to escaping. To finally giving up on my other jobs, the ones that follow me around like a shadow in the heat of the day. The jobs that will never pay enough to start over, to hide, to become someone entirely new.

"Do you want to maybe make dinner together tonight, just us?" she asks, slightly jittery.

"No, I am meeting up with friends tonight." I try my best to not let her catch on that I'm lying to her face.

"You only get so many nights at home until your summer break is done."

"Mom, it just started, like, four weeks ago."

"Okay, well, I'll try to wait up for you tonight. Maybe we can have some ice cream. I can go to the store to get your favorite flavor!" She pretends to be excited, knowing it won't happen.

"Sure." I sigh. It's getting harder and harder to want to spend time together. I try not to blame her for this mess, but sometimes, it gets hard.

The stairwell goes on forever. When we finally get to the door, I give her a half-ass hug. This hurts her, but I can't bear to bring myself to embrace her anymore, knowing she's forced me to live with a monster all these years, because she got tired of fighting back. How does it not bother her to have to reside under a roof with the epitome of evil? I guess if the house is nice enough, people will sacrifice anything.

We get to the parking lot, and I climb in my car as quickly as I can. I need to meet up with clients who are trying to buy, need to make as much money as possible to get out of this house for good. It's unbearable being home for summer, but the move-in isn't for a couple of months. Tanner said he won't pay for my college because I am not his biological daughter. He is more concerned about appearances than anything else. A green lawn in a summer so hot that everyone else's grass is scorched is a sign of privilege and success to him. I think it's more important to blend in at times than to stand out monetarily.

My mother and Tanner are in front of me when I drive onto the highway. She looks like the saddest woman alive, myself coming in at a close second. They take their exit home, and I continue to my destination. I turn up the music, fumbling with the dial to find something good on the radio station.

If Tanner died, would he leave us anything? Or would he take it to his grave? I would not put it past him. He thinks of himself as royalty, like an Egyptian King worshipped by his people and at the end of his reign buried with all his beautiful gold and jewels, honored by all, even after death.

Sometimes, I think about it, about helping my mother finally be free so we can live a life without these dark clouds looming over us constantly. It's a seesaw effect. I go back and forth between being angry with her for her choices, and wanting to sacrifice everything for her, to take away her pain. We deserve a life without physical and emotional abuse, and doors being slammed with so much intensity, the framed photos in the house fall to the ground, leaving thousands of glass shards in its wake. She's good at pretending, but here and there, I get a glimpse of the real her. It breaks me.

The idea of my stepfather dying has my mind racing, and I need to snap out of it. I can't think this way, but it's too late. An idea comes to me, one I don't want to admit. I think it's time I'm finally free from him.

There was a time he spit on me for not understanding my math homework. I was seven, maybe, or eight? And he once shoved me up against a wall and told me not to eavesdrop on his conversations with my mother. I think of the time I saw him and my father talking, the redness in their faces, their veins practically leaping off their flesh. He needs to die.

I pull up to my client's house and ring the doorbell. They open the door just a crack to accept their delivery and hand me a wad of cash I place in my pocket. Only thousands more to go to finish paying for next semester of college, on top of my other three jobs.

I walk back to my car and open the door, careful to not scrape it against the curb. A sense of uneasiness comes over me, and I take a deep breath, unable to shake the feeling someone is watching me. I look around and see nothing but the beautiful brownstones surrounded by elderly trees. A street that has been around to see so much—couples moving into their first homes, passionate fights at three in the morning, even protests that defied all odds. I look around once more, to be safe.

After turning on my car and adjusting my mirrors, I drive off, going back to the house where love and dreams cease to exist. I hope my father's will situation gets sorted out soon, but if I get that money, I'm afraid Tanner will try to find a way to claim it as his. I'm afraid that if I get that money, I'm as good as dead.

How would he try to kill me? I'm sure it would be excruciating. He lacks the compassion to make it quick, this I know. It's a good thing legal battles take time because I might not have much of it left if he gets his hands on the Brentwood fortune.

I think I owe it to myself and my mother. One of us must do something. I just wish it wasn't me.

I think I'm ready now.

SEVEN

VICTORIA – THEN

I'm mentally drained from this legal battle. It's only been one month, but the days seem to slowly drag. It could be a mixture of the excessive heat paired with the ungodly humidity of the intense Chicago summer we've been having. Every bead of sweat drips down my spine and pools at my lower back. I wipe my face with my palm. I hate the summer's here.

There are piles of legal files. I did not sign up for this when I married Josh. It should have been an easy life. I was willing to sacrifice passion, but I never thought I'd be dealing with his ex-wife after all these years. When is enough going to be enough? Her disdain for me is comical. She was never able to get over her grudge for me. I did her a favor! Her home is bigger than mine, her car is nicer than mine, and she got Josh in his prime years. I got him when he was thicker around the middle, lazy, sicker. She wouldn't have been happy with him now, if he were still alive, that is.

I shouldn't need to apologize for having an affair because you can't apologize for something like that. And I don't need to make a martyr of myself. Yes, I did a bad thing, but I don't regret it. I never confronted Calista because what would I say? Sorry for screwing your husband when you were pregnant? Or can you ever forgive me for complicating your life? There is a reason I ignored Calista and tried to move on. Unfortunately, I did not think we'd live so close by. Karma tends to laugh in your face like that.

The phone rings. I ignore it, but its constant buzzing sound as it vibrates irks me. My daughters walk down the stairs, dressed to go out.

"Where are you going?"

"To a friend's house."

They are lying. I'm almost sure of it. Allison's voice breaks slightly enough for me to know.

"Text me their address, please."

They will probably send me a fake one, but I don't care at this point. I have too much on my mind. How could Josh have done this? I made him change the trust, and I watched him do it. I had to make sure that if anything ever happened to him, we got it all. After everything I did for him, I wanted to make sure he knew I was deserving of it all- *not her.*

My phone rings again. It's Erik, the person who drafted Josh's will and trust. He's calling to apologize again. This is the third time today. I walk to the counter, take a knife from its block, and grab the juiciest tomato from our fruit bowl to slice. As the knife slowly makes its way through its skin, I watch seeds cascade along the marble counter. For a split second, I picture Calista, then snap out of it. I can't think like that, not with everything going on.

After grinding some sea salt on the tomato, I bite into it. It wasn't as good as I thought it would be, something that I find happens a lot in life. I take another bite of the tomato and clean off my hands with the dish towel nearby. The old me would never waste food, but walking away from the half-eaten snack gives me happiness. The rich can leave food on their plate without guilt.

I grab the stack of legal papers and head upstairs to draw myself a bath before going through them. Once I put the stopper in the tub, I turn the water on, and it begins to steam. I take a deep breath, trying to center myself. This bitch will not get in the way of my fortune, I want all of it, not just some. I step into the tub, gently lowering myself.

Scalding-hot water splashes on one of the pages in my hand. The information is making my head spin. Why do lawyers need to talk like they are better than you? What's the point? To feel like their years of schooling paid off?

I look at another piece of paper and cave.

It's time I call Erik back. The phone barely even rings before he answers, and I can hear his panicked breathing.

"Hi, Erik."

"Hi, Victoria, I wanted to apologize again for—"

I'm annoyed with just the sound of his voice.

"Look, I just want to know what all of this means. Everything you sent over makes no sense. He changed everything last year, and it seems odd for you to have made such a big mistake, since you get a hefty sum of money to manage his assets and the rest of the Brentwood fortune."

Erik pauses. He mutters something under his breath, but I can't figure out what it is he just said.

"Erik, look. Can't we just argue that he was a sick man and he didn't know what he was doing?" I feel like this has to be a good option to plead to whichever judge is going to be put in charge of this case. "He was on dialysis. He was a sick man with a heart condition, and studies show that when you are on dialysis, your mind can suffer impairments."

Erik sighs. "Victoria, the other side can claim the same thing. You need to dig deeper here. You need to find a way to scare the other side. A judge won't believe anything you say if he finds out Josh was going over to the Maple family's home several times a week before his death."

Erik pauses before continuing with his logical thinking.

"Don't you think a judge will find it a bit odd that he was on good terms with his former family?" His voice shakes.

He had to bring that up. Erik likes to remind me that Josh regretted his life with me. The longer we were together, the further he strayed, right back into his old life. A life that he destroyed the first time around. People don't ever learn you can't get a do over, no matter how badly you want it. The memories don't ever leave you. You can laser off a tattoo, but hints of old pigment sit there under layers of your skin, and in the right lighting, the mistake will still be there.

"Erik, there is no way the Maple family is getting a dime. If you caused this, you know the Brentwood family may as well kill you."

He lets out a gasp of air.

"Is that a threat?" His voice is the slightest bit firmer.

"It's the truth."

"Well, in that case, when their lawyers request discoveries, you better find a way to cover up the one million dollars in donations to a charity that doesn't even exist."

Before I can even get a single word in, he hangs up.

I submerge myself under water and scream. No one is home, so

I don't even know why I am trying to bury my anger. I resurface and slick my hair back from my face, clenching my knees against my chest. Erik is sensitive to how eager I am to dismiss him. I need to try my hardest to be less cruel. He's been in love with me for years now, and sometimes, when I'm bored, I'll give in to temptation. All those times Josh would go see Ava, I'd have a moment of poor judgement. Erik would stop by. It was harmless, really. Adultery is as common as catching a cold these days.

I sit in the tub a few moments longer before reaching for a towel hanging close by.

Looking in the mirror, I get lost in my own reflection. When did I begin to age like this? My skin, dull. I look closer in the mirror and notice my crow's feet becoming more prominent. My breasts saggy, my pooch protruding more, and my skin starting to show my age. I used to be prettier, more sought after. Calista aged better than me, and it drives me to insanity every time I think about her beautiful long golden hair and her slim figure. I'm shorter than she is and a little more plump. As I run my hands through my hair, a large piece breaks off from constant bleaching.

A sudden wave of anxiety overcomes me. I put my towel back on, wrap it tightly around my body, and walk down to the living room to dig through the junk drawer for a pack of cigarettes. Using the candle lighter, I place a cigarette between my lips and take a long puff. When the smoke hits my lips on the exhale, I feel better, if just for a moment. If this legal situation doesn't get revolved soon, my girls are going to know what I did. I'm not sure what would be worse: them knowing how I met Josh, or the fact that I committed a crime, enough to strip the Brentwood family of everything.

As I put out my cigarette, hiding any evidence of it in the house, I grab my purse and fumble for my keys. I'm late for my Botox appointment. But when I sit in the car, I realize I'm still in my towel. Fuck.

My phone rings again. It's Josh's mother. She wants me to come over. I am not one of them anymore. My daughters are, but I am not. They will dispose of me if they have to, if they are left no other choice.

The neighbors stare at me in my car. I'll have to cancel my Botox appointment again. I'd rather inject poison into my face than sit in front of something just as toxic.

As I get back in my car to head out, I get a text from an unknown number. I open it, thinking it's just spam, simple junk mail, nothing too out of the ordinary.

I wish it had been that.

"How do you sleep well at night, knowing what you did?"

I close my eyes so tight I can still see shades of red from looking at the light and pray this is from Erik. It has to be him, I was a bitch to him not even an hour ago. He's trying to scare me.

A lump in my throat begins to form. Everything feels like it's closing in on me. I run a stop sign, my hands shaking.

EIGHT

AVA – THEN

I sit and stare at the four walls that have held me captive these last thirteen or so years. Looking at my closet, I don't know where to start. I go through all the expensive clothes my mother insisted on buying me out of guilt. Most of them unworn, unloved.

My mother felt that if she bought nice things for me, it would ease the blow of living here. She was constantly bringing me lovely gifts, things I never would have picked out for myself. Emerald earrings, pearl necklaces, designer shoes I'd never wear because then the bottoms would scuff. The point of the shoes was a showpiece to sit in your closet. *I* am a show piece. At least, I used to be.

My mother spent my stepfather's money often. I know this because of the constant screaming going on a floor below me. She liked to spend money because she didn't have any in her marriage with my dad. My dad didn't want her working because she had to raise me. It was a different time back then; women didn't work as often. With this *husband*, though, she spends in excess. I think it's how she copes. Because if you're going to be depressed, it helps to do it in designer clothing. At least that's what I've always been told. My mother hides her bruises behind Prada and Dior, it gives her a sense of pride until she's undressed and looks at herself in the mirror.

It's hard to believe that in just a few days, I'll be living in a dorm on my own. I wish I could say this was it, that I can finally cut off ties from this life, but with the legal battle still going on, I have to meet with lawyers and do all this paperwork, sit in countless mediation rooms, and be told over and over again that my father never intended to leave me with even a dime.

Tanner offered to help pay for the lawsuit, which made me uncomfortable. My mother's eyes lit up when he told her that. That he would love to make the Brentwoods pay for what they did to my mother and I growing up, for leaving us on the streets with nowhere to go and nothing to eat. My father made a lot of mistakes, but I know in my heart that that was his biggest regret, leaving us.

Tanner told my mother that he'd pull money from his accounts to help foot some of the bills. I honestly couldn't care less about getting any money at all. There's no need. I've been working random jobs for the last six years—some legal, some not—and I have just enough for some of college with my scholarship. Tanner has alternative motives because he told me he wouldn't pay for college, yet he's willing to help pay the lawyers for this lawsuit, a lawyer who is an old buddy of his. I wish I could tell the lawyers I don't want any money, but I'd be as good as dead if I pulled that card, this I know.

After putting my underwear and socks in cardboard boxes, I take out an oversized Sharpie and label them. Next, I make my way to my art studio and take out just a few of my favorite color paints to bring with me to school. The dorms don't offer too much space. Only the essentials will come with me: the drawing pads, the watercolor Prisma pencils, some ink pens, and a few drawing books.

The jewelry box is my next task. I only grab a strand of pearls my mother gave me when I was six, each pearl's sheen incomparable to the next. The grit on each pearl reminds me of when my mother gave them to me. She said if you put the pearl between your teeth and you feel the grittiness on them, that's how you know you have a good one.

I put the pearl necklace in a padded box and place it in one of the cardboard boxes. Rummaging through more of my items, I grab a few books I have been meaning to read.

The doorbell rings. I look out my window to see who it is and let out a loud sigh. It's one of the lawyers. I don't really like him. He reminds me of a snake, the way his jet black hair slicks back with his gangly limbs. His suit is oversized—any respectable lawyer would know to dress even the slightest bit better.

I open my door just a crack to hear what Tanner and his lawyer are talking about. My mother went to the store to get dinner for this evening, and by the timing of it, I know this was planned. Tanner must not realize I'm home. I've always tried to be quiet in this house.

Several moments pass before I open my door wider to try to hear what they are talking about. I walk down the stairs carefully, avoiding every spot that creaks.

The chair in the living room screeches, and I now know they are sitting at the table.

"This needs to be quick," Tanner hisses.

"I didn't want to text you this over the phone. I could get disbarred," the lawyer says.

"Well?" Tanner asks eagerly.

"I'm willing to cut you a deal, if you can promise me one-third of what Ava is supposed to get if we can find a hook in this case. I can charge more in legal fees, and then you can keep the rest. No one will have to know anything. And then we can pocket millions. It's a win for both you and me, and when we are done, we will dispose of the girl and her mother. It will be like they never existed. You can say the daughter had a drinking problem, pill problem, and the mother killed herself from losing her daughter. Whatever your heart desires."

Screams cook within my lungs, but I say nothing. I feel like porcelain being smashed repeatedly until you can no longer tell I used to be something real, something whole.

There's no way I can get this money. I just can't. Surely, there is no loophole. I hope my father meant to give me nothing, I hope that to my core. After making it back to my bedroom, I'm cautious to not slam the door behind me.

Regaining composure, I reach for my nightstand and take out a letter, staring at it before reading it several times. I shouldn't take these with me, should let the past stay in the past, not dwell on failed love. Lying down on my mattress, I let my bed swallow me whole.

Sometimes, I wonder if Scott thinks about me. I wish he never found out about some of the things I had to do. Maybe it's good he's not around anymore. As I stare at my blue walls, like a fish swimming the same race a million times, I count to ten. I start over again until I can regain composure, but all I can think about is Tanner covered in a pool of blood, my reflection looking back up at me as I look down at him, lifeless.

Through my window, I can see my mother's car pull into the driveway. The garage door closes just as quickly as it opens. I wonder if every time she walks into this house, she realizes she's just as caged as the animals in the zoo, if not worse. They are admired by children and adults who visit them, who pay money to see them. These animals are well taken care of, rehabilitated, yet never well enough to go back to where they came from. Tanner likes to make my mother feel like a prisoner, and I resent her for letting him.

Mom will do anything to survive, to feed me, to make sure I'm clothed, to make sure I have the right books for school, but she was afraid she couldn't do it all on her own. Tanner manipulated her into marrying him, to giving her a safe place. The day she said, "I Do," was the day it all changed, the day he knew he had her and she couldn't go anywhere. My mom told me that on her wedding day, my father showed up there. He kept trying to tell her something. She wouldn't have it and asked him to leave. I wonder if she ever found out what he wanted to tell her. My best guess is maybe just a simple apology. That's the least he could have done.

My mother unbags the groceries, as I join her in the kitchen. She places each item in its own container in the fridge, and I watch her organize everything compulsively. I find that this helps her cope. She has little to no control over anything, but the small things make her feel better.

As she unwraps a juicy piece of steak, I watch the blood seep out of its sides. The knife moves back and forth, piercing its flesh, as she cuts it up. Tanner is sitting in the living room, ignoring my presence. He must have thought I went with her to the store.

Tanner's phone rings, and he quickly rushes toward it on the counter. I can't get a good look at who is calling him.

"Work emergency. I'll be back late." He leaves in a hurry, grabbing his briefcase that sits on the kitchen chair.

The air suddenly becomes breathable.

"Looks like it's just us tonight," my mother says, her smile genuine. I wish I could tell her that it *will* just be us again soon.

Before dinner is ready, I take Murphy for a quick walk. On the way home, I notice a car several houses down. I walk toward it to get a better look. It doesn't appear to be any car I've seen on this block before, and I see everything from my balcony at all hours of the day. Before I get closer, it drives off. Whoever it was didn't want to be seen.

As my mother and I sit down at the large table meant for ten but has only ever dined two people, I stare at my meal. She made the same thing for my father the week before he died—a giant steak with his favorite side of thinly sliced russet potatoes layered with a cheddar cheese and chives garnished on top.

He had been coming over for weekly dinners for the last couple of years before he died. My Father knew he was sick, and it was making him become a better person. He knew time was something you couldn't get back. I loved that he'd started coming over for two reasons: one being that Tanner loathed him; two, it was nice to see what a life would have been like if my mother and father had never split up. Watching them banter and laugh brought me hope. It's hard to believe he used to be so deplorable. Regret over time can change a person, and I had a front row ticket to that show.

I wonder if my mother told Josh about how unhappy she truly was. Doubtful, because my mother would never let on that she was still unhappy. She wanted him to think she had won, that he was the loser in this game.

It was a breath of fresh air to sit across from my father and mother, eating dinner and telling them about my day, about what a waste of time high school was. Whenever Victoria would call during our hangouts, he'd send it to voicemail. It made my mother smile.

All I could think about was what his other family was doing when he was at these dinners with us. I could picture Victoria calling her circle of friends, telling them what a wench my mother was, criticizing everything about her, and when she had had enough cruel words to say, she probably moved on to me.

I know my father meant for me to have that money; I know it in my bones. If only he had known Tanner would kill for it…

Tanner will be gone until late, like most nights. I know my window of opportunity to go into his office and search around is small. My mother never dares to go in there, and Tanner knows it, so he assumes I wouldn't indulge in such thoughts.

My mother finishes her second glass of wine and slowly dozes off on the overly priced designer sofa Tanner had to have to scratch his balls on while he watches football. I walk toward his office door and quietly open it, shutting it gently behind me. Tanner is hiding something, I know it. Why would he need millions of dollars? When is enough enough with him?

His office is an organized mess. I'll start with his desk. Though I fumble with each drawer, they are all locked. I search for a key, in hopes that he has one lying around somewhere.

The clock on his wall is minimalistic and modern. It makes it hard to tell the exact time, and that makes me uncomfortable. I look through more of his shelving and come across letters from the bank. Taking my phone out, I snap as many pictures as I can, then place the bank statements back in their folder and keep digging. I sit down at his desk and rest my head upon the smoothness of the glass top over the wood.

That's when I see something unusual sticking out from the corner of the glass—a small silver key sandwiched between the glass top and the wood.

I grab a pencil and try to maneuver it through the crack to the key.

The door slams.

He's home. I panic.

Crawling under his desk, I'm grateful at how spacious and deep it goes against the wall. I don't dare take a single breath. The door handle jiggles slightly before it opens. He sits down at his desk, and my heart is in my throat. I can hear him turn on the computer, clicking through things, his grunts becoming more revolting every time. It feels like in one minute, ten hours have passed. He reaches for his phone in his pocket and begins to call someone. I can hear it ring, and a muffled voice on the other end answers.

"Hi, Bill," Tanner says, irritated. That must be the lawyer who was over here today.

"I wanted you to know, I did some digging about who the judge would be, and there may be a way to sway him a little bit too. He's an old golfing buddy of mine, really loves money," Bill says eagerly to get Tanner's approval. It's working.

"The girl and her mother have no say in the matter since I'm paying for it. Her mother wants to make the Brentwoods pay for what they did to her, so no need convincing her to hire you on as the lawyer for the case, she can't exactly pay for one herself," Tanner gloats.

I hate how he refers to me as "the girl." My stomach is in knots.

"You think this case will go our way, right, Bill?" Tanner asks, needing confirmation to soothe him.

"Yeah, he was on dialysis when the will was altered, so we can plead a strong case."

Tanner reaches for his pocket and puts the keys on the desk. He turns off his computer, gets up, and shuts the door.

I don't dare move, listening for the creaks on the stairs as he walks up, his large-framed body holding the weight of every step. The upstairs door to his bedroom closes. I sit back at his desk, the seat warm, and look at the keys. Taking every key on his ring, I fidget with every lock to see if there's a match. After several tries, one of the keys finally slides into the lock, and I can hear every single mechanism turn. I open the drawer and pull through files and files of trust documents, unpaid bills, and letters from his brother, who has been estranged from the family for years. I read through them.

"If you don't give me the money that is rightfully mine, I will have no choice but to get the courts involved. You know that half that money was mine, and by you not turning over our parent's trust documents and proof of the money that was in those accounts, you'll be forced to turn it over in discovery. I know you spent almost every drop of their millions from their accounts. You are the only one in charge of it. I'm not sure how you convinced them to do that. You let our parents rot in a nursing home, and their bills haven't been paid in months. They are threatening to ask them to leave. You have one week."

That was ten years ago.

I look through more of the folders in the drawer and take pictures, continuing to look for anything else to help us get out for good, to help me have no guilt when I kill him. Rummaging through dozens more manilla envelopes and swiftly flipping through each one, I pause for a second, noticing something stuck together between two pages.

It's a photo of Tanner and Victoria.

I take the photo and fold it up, putting it safely in my pants pocket. Then, I tidy up his office to make sure it is exactly as it was. He won't know this is missing. Who would look for that anyway?

My mother is still lying on the couch, eyes delicately shut, her mouth slightly open as air passes through her lips. I watch her chest as it lightly moves, take a blanket from the other side of the couch, and cover her with it. She doesn't sleep in the master bedroom with Tanner; she hasn't for years now. It feels safer down here on the couch, safer near a door where she can escape. I get it, I really do. It's my fault she's stuck here with him. She just wanted to raise me somewhere safe, but by the time she realized who he truly was, she couldn't get out, so she bides her time. I turn off the TV and kiss her forehead. She lets out a small sigh.

As I get settled back in my room, I push my dresser in front of the door. I sleep best this way. At the balcony window, I watch everyone. It's the same as most nights: a daughter sneaking out of her house toward her boyfriend's car, a husband coming home from work, a pool boy sneaking out of the backyard right after he kisses his employer's wife. All these people know I know their secrets. They all hate me; I can tell by how they pass me on my walks. It's not *my* fault they can't hide their secrets like me. *I own their husbands.* I can't trust any of these people, and they can't trust me.

Before I close my balcony doors, I explore the darkness carefully one last time, looking for anything, something, but all I see is a single streetlamp flickering, it's light slowly fading to blend in with the hollow night. I close my windows to shut out the small world.

I take out the picture of Victoria and Tanner and place it in a Georgia O'Keeffe book. He'd never look there. He hates art.

NINE

ALLISON – THEN

I wonder what it's like inside Ava's house, how many bedrooms it has and what the color of her bedroom walls are. My mom let me paint my walls for my fifteenth birthday last year. I spent hours at the paint store, looking at hundreds of paint chips. When I found the color, I just knew it was the one—a soft French blue, gentle, welcoming, and feminine. Lately, I've been wanting to go for a little bit of a darker blue, nothing too drastic. I just think I've outgrown the shade. It seems more of a childish color to me now, less elegant and not as grand as I thought it would make the room feel.

Rolling the windows down slightly, I take in the fresh air on Ava's street. Kenilworth has this faint scent of cut grass mixed with fresh lavender. Our neighborhood doesn't smell anything like hers; ours smells like nothingness. I wish we lived on this block instead.

When I was around seven, I remember begging for a brand-new doll house. As I pleaded with my parents, I grew tired of the overwhelming emotions running through me. My father told me that just because we have money doesn't mean we need to spend money. I think Ava's stepfather feels differently about that.

Everything about their house is luxurious: their driveway lined with peonies, large apple trees along the sides of their home. Every brick is perfectly placed, and the gold trim along the sides radiates when the sun sets on it. Every shingle changes colors over time, as it should.

I watch Ava through her window. She seems pre-occupied, gazing at an empty canvas. I watch as she holds clothes up to her body, folding some into boxes while others get put back neatly in their places. Ava walks toward the other side of her room, no longer visible. I wish I could get to know her more than just through her window.

Time has escaped me. I haven't been sleeping well the last couple of months. My eyelids feel like paperweights, but as I close them, I feel a slight bit of relief.

The sun has gone down when I open my eyes. How long was I out for? I turn on the ignition, panicking as I speed off, hoping no one noticed my car here. The people on this street know everybody's business. My mother always talks poorly about it. She thinks living somewhere where your neighbors would kill to know about the gossip on the other side of the steel gates is a personal kind of hell. My mother said it was fitting for Ava's family.

Now that the secret is out about my father's past life, all she does is talk about her hatred for Ava and Calista.

I think my mother is jealous.

I know she is.

I am.

TEN

CALISTA – THEN

It's a lovely day for gardening. Tanner thinks I shouldn't get my hands dirty anymore, says that's what the help is for. He doesn't understand the feeling I get raking through the dirt, pulling the roots out from the ground when something is dying and I know it's too late to give it aid. Watching the things I've planted slowly bloom, just like clockwork every year, gives me a sense of peace.

When we first looked at this house, all I could think about was how vast the backyard was, a little escape. When we bought it, I thought this was the place where Ava and I would make memories together. I'd braid her hair in the backyard while she looked at the freshly bloomed roses. We'd spin in our dresses until we were dizzy and sneak cookies before dinner, watching the sun set behind the tall trees.

I couldn't have been more wrong.

Things didn't always feel so desolate. Every year, it became worse, though. I remember the first time I knew I had made a terrible mistake in marrying Tanner but had no money to get out...

Ava was so young when I met him. Being a young mother with no job and no money was challenging, to say the least. Josh's family made sure we never saw a dime. We were bouncing around from friend to friend, sleeping on couches, and I was trying to produce enough milk to feed my newborn. A friend of Josh's, Brett, reached out and offered Ava and me his guest room when he heard what was happening. He had always liked me, but I could never do that to Josh, no matter how badly he had hurt me. I tried to say no, but he insisted.

Brett's neighbor Tanner saw me and came up to me to ask me out. He appeared to not mind Ava, and he seemed like a nice guy at the time. Brett insisted he'd watch Ava for the night, he knew I'd never end up with him, so he gave me away. I agreed to it, but every day of my life, I wish I hadn't.

That's the sad part about divorce. It costs hundreds and thousands of dollars, and the more money the person has, the longer that person likes to drag it out. People will always tell you just to stay, live in your nice house, turn a blind eye, reap the benefits. I tried that. It hasn't worked for me, and certainly not Ava, but she was warm, and she was fed. I have to keep reminding myself that if she didn't have this life, there's no telling where we would be. My nursing degree was of no use since it had been so long after studying. I could no longer take my exams. I had no job, and working at a department store making minimum wage wouldn't pay rent, bills, and keep Ava's stomach full. We made do with the life I didn't mean to create, and I would do my best to protect her.

Tanner and I moved into this house several years after getting married. It seemed too large for our small family, but he insisted we'd grow into it. He wouldn't take no for an answer, and by the next day, he was signing paperwork on it.

When I walked into the house for the first time, my jaw dropped.

The immaculate height of the walls…The floor-to-ceiling windows. The second I saw the yard, I was already planning all the types of flowers I was going to plant here, in my forever home. Peonies so wild and bold you had to stop and smell them every chance you got. Hydrangea bushes lining the sides of the house, and gardens of rose bushes everywhere, sprawled all over my own five acres of land. I'd put a swing on the oldest and sturdiest tree on the property.

That first year in the house, everything seemed fine. Tanner was much happier back then. Ava would run around the yard while we'd sip on Sangria. He used to smile at me and put his hand on my lower back, tell me things like, "We need to have another child, to make this family complete." Things that made me feel like I'd finally made it. I was finally safe. He would roll up his sleeves after a long day at work and help me dig up dirt to put new plants in. I remember him grabbing my face, getting soil on my cheeks, while he pulled me in for a kiss. Tanner used to love it out here with me, but now, he's too good for it.

No one is too good for getting their hands a little dirty with honest, hard work. It was all an act to him. We were pawns.

Ava was about six years old when the first incident happened. She was sitting on the steps upstairs, and I was outside gardening, when I heard a loud scream and ran into the house as quickly as my legs would carry me, thinking the worst.

Ava's tears violently streamed down her flushed little cheeks. Tanner was hitting her, and my blood boiled. I shoved him off her, but he was double my size. He pushed me to the ground, I hit my head so hard that the room began to spin, I didn't care though.

"Don't you ever hit my child!" I screamed at him.

He got up and looked me in the eyes. "She's *my* child now, and I'll discipline her as I see fit."

My body began to shake.

Ava's face was swollen from her tears. It broke me. Tanner let go of her, and she ran to me, sobbing.

"Why did you hit her?" I pleaded.

"Because she asked when she could go see her dad," he said, emotionless.

"You beat Ava because she asked a simple question?" I was at a loss for words.

"I want her to know the kind of pain that comes with that name."

My mind was unable to comprehend the words leaving his mouth. I gripped on to Ava as long as I could. All I could think about was how had I been so blind?

As I tucked Ava in, it was still light enough to see the shine from the fresh coat of French blue paint she had chosen for her bedroom. I kissed her forehead and apologized for what happened. She started hysterically talking.

"All the kids at school talked about their daddies on their family tree." She squeezed Bunbun, her raggedy old bunny Josh had gotten her the day she was born. She saw him once in a blue moon as a toddler. He tried his hardest to stay far away from her.

My heart sank. I never knew pain could cut so deep to my core like that. When Josh left us, it hurt me, but to watch Ava go through it left a dark mark on my soul.

"I'll see if we can call Daddy this week, okay? I love you very much." I kissed her forehead.

When the door shut behind me, I knew the answer already.

Victoria wouldn't allow Josh anywhere near Ava. I had tried to get ahold of him, but Victoria controlled his phone. Josh was busy with *their* two little girls running around, she'd never allow it.

The kitchen needed to be cleaned. The dishwasher didn't get the nitty-gritty out of the plates the way an old-fashioned scrubbing did. Tanner walked up next to me and kissed my cheek to initiate an apology.

"I'm sorry for what happened today. I just lost control of my emotions for a second. Work's been so stressful. We lost a potential investor today," he said, pleading for forgiveness.

I wanted to take the sponge and scrub every surface of my skin he just touched.

"Let's plan a family day at the zoo this weekend," he said.

I nodded. He kissed my forehead and walked toward the staircase to head up to bed.

Why did we even need to go to the zoo? I had realized I was the caged animal; it doesn't matter how big the enclosure is, a cage is a cage.

The next day, I searched to find someone selling a specific plant for my garden. Flowers can make everything better.

The past taunts me, but as I admire over a decade of hard work, I breathe in the fresh peonies. I always stop to take them in, look at the tree swing, the rope falling apart. There's no point in repairing it. There's no point in repairing anything.

The sharpness of the sheers slice through the stems. I place them gently on the ground to bring inside later and walk to a few other plants to check their growth. The tomatoes are ripe and juicy. Perfect for dinner tonight.

Tucked away past the bushes of hydrangeas, deep in our backyard, is a plant I've been growing for what seems like eternity. The soil is moist and cool to let the plant that will free me thrive.

The purple helmet-shaped flowers, standing a foot tall, stare back at me. It's so cruel to those who desire it, to hold it, to smell it. It's beautiful.

Soon, it will all be over.

It will be done.

I know what he did to his brother, and I know what he did to his parents. He thinks I don't, but he's wrong. Every night when he sleeps soundly in bed, I go into his office and go through every file in his drawer. I had keys made after he left them on the counter once when he went golfing with his buddies.

Tanner stole money from his parents. His brother sued him to see what was left of it, but he died suddenly one day. All those business investments were never real. Tanner was stealing money and investing it poorly. Now it's coming back to haunt him. He needs to put it back where it came from, before people coming sniffing.

Tanner thinks I'm a dumb housewife, but I'm more than that. I'm a mother who has been imprisoned for the god knows how many years. I'm a mother feeding my young, trying to find a way out of the exhibit of our lives. I'm exhausted being nothing more than a show pony, a picture-perfect family Tanner can parade in front of his friends, not that he really has any now. They all stopped coming around some time ago.

I need him to get this money for Ava because without Tanner's pretend money, I couldn't take on the Brentwoods. They need to suffer. I owe it to Ava, and once it's a done deal, I'll finally be able to kill him. Just another couple of months, I tell myself. There is no way the Brentwoods want this to drag on because their secrets might just spill, and if that happens, there's no telling who they'd come for. I set the table for dinner. It will just be Ava and me tonight. Tanner will most likely make an excuse to go out.

When dinner is ready, I call for Ava to come downstairs. She's been packing to leave for school. Ava's worked so hard to pay for college, and I want her to feel special tonight.

As Ava sits down in front of me, I see the strong and independent woman I raised. I hope she doesn't hate me for what I've done to her, for being weak and not getting out when I could. Maybe she can forgive me one day, that after Tanner is gone and she knows I did it, she'll hug me again, like the kind of hugs she used to give me, the kind that make your blood warmer, the kind that makes everything in the world melt away.

After dinner, I walk to the couch, holding my wine. Harnessing all this hatred inside is exhausting. The bitter red wine engulfs me.

A warm blanket drapes over me, and I smile. This is how Ava shows she forgives me. I know this because she does this every night.

I can't wait for it to just be Ava and me again.

Just a little bit longer.

ELEVEN

ALLISON – NOW

Lying on my stomach under Ava's bed, I stare closely at the fibers of the comforter, Ava's bedframe my only shelter. I panic, thinking the worst and trying to remain as still as possible. Maybe it's just the realtors figuring out what needs to be updated before they can put the house on the market. Who gets the commission on the house since Ava's mother and stepfather have been missing for almost two years now?

I remember the day my mother came down the stairs, her mood elated. For breakfast, I had made a bowl of oatmeal with thinly slice bananas and honey drizzled on top. It felt like a delicacy. I accidentally knocked over my bowl when my mother squealed.

"They are missing." She smiled.

"Who is missing?" I asked, concerned and confused.

"Ava's ratchet mother and stepfather."

At the time, I held my composure so my mother wouldn't suspect I was visibly upset by the news. Just because you don't care for someone doesn't mean you should be happy if something happens to them.

"How long have they been missing for?" I asked, too sick to eat.

"I'm not sure. Maybe a few days?" She pulled up a chair and began to peel an orange. My spilled cereal began to drip on the floor.

"I heard Ava is a suspect. I wouldn't put it past her. She's a monster, takes after her mother," she said.

Walking to the sink, I rinsed out what was left of my food. I hated being wasteful.

"Why would Ava want to kill her own mother and stepfather?" I asked, genuinely concerned. I didn't really know Ava too well, except for the handful of times I'd watch her through her window. She didn't seem like the kind of person to hurt someone, not that I could sense.

"People just do things, Allison," my mother said sharply.

"In that case, what have *you* done, Mom?"

Her mouth fell silent. She finished her orange and walked out of the kitchen. That was the end of that. I couldn't help but think, what had my mother done?

When I walked up to my bedroom, I heard my mother on the phone, talking with her friends and gossiping like giddy schoolgirls, laughing at the misfortune of others. I couldn't believe this was the woman I had been left with and wished she had died instead of my dad.

The guilt pangs me when I think things like that. How could my dad marry someone so villainous? I didn't really notice who my mother truly was until that very moment. She hated Calista so much, hated that we had to give up some of the Brentwood fortune.

My mother needed the Brentwood family to support her. She liked feeling untouchable, and now that my dad was gone, she feared the family saw her as nothing but a termite, eating away at the foundation that took so long to build. I would always be a Brentwood by blood, but not her. She was as disposable as flowers after

Valentine's Day—one day of beauty, two at most, before you notice the delicate petals beginning to fall off, one by one, until they are swept into the trash.

Did my mother get so desperate that she harmed Calista and Tanner? She'd been acting different lately, barely taking care of Ashley and me. Her mind had been elsewhere, and she seemed on edge all the time—taking secret phone calls in the middle of the night, going outside for a cigarette to calm herself as she paced back and forth, barely cooking for us, ordering takeout a lot. At the time, it didn't seem like the usual grieving people talk about after a loss. It was like a secret beginning to grow roots that live so deep within you, it eats you from the inside out.

I peak my head out from under the bed, attempting to hear the voices better. The footsteps sound like they are getting closer. I quickly slide back under the bed. The door to Ava's room opens, and my stomach twists and turns.

This is it.

This is the way I die.

A voice begins to speak, more mature, one that when up close sounds familiar, but I can't remember where I've heard his voice before. I can't put my finger on it, but I'm certain I know it.

"Did you check everywhere for it?" the familiar voice asks.

"Yes, I've turned this house upside down. I can't find it." This voice sounds younger, angrier.

"Did you check the paint cans, the jewelry boxes, the office?"

A pair of feet stop at the bed. I cover my mouth, doing my best to hide my hysteria.

"If we don't find it before the house goes up for sale, she'll kill us."

They hurry out of the bedroom, slamming the door behind them. I wait until I hear footsteps rush down the stairs and the front door to shut. Emerging from under the bed, I sit with my legs crunched tightly against my chest. It takes me several minutes to catch my breath, to feel the blood evenly distribute within my body, to let my adrenaline settle down. I inhale and count to five before exhaling, then take out the gold key and feel its grooves.

This is what they want, but where do I even start?

The balcony window allows me to see if anyone is watching this house. There are some nosy neighbors strolling past, staring at it, wondering what happened here. Another neighbor is walking with her friend while she pushes a stroller. The new mom leans in to tell her friend a rumor she heard about this family.

They probably are wondering what this house is going to sell for, probably wondering who wants to live in a house where a young girl died. They might even be saying it's haunted. I shut the curtains. I don't need anyone else gossiping that they saw a girl in the window of a home no one lives in anymore. Everyone loves a good ghost story, though.

Suddenly, being in Ava's room feels wrong, taking things of hers. I hold out one of her love letters, and I know I still need to go find Scott. Maybe he'll be able to tell me what the key goes to. He shouldn't be too hard to find; no one really is anymore. Social media makes it simple.

Taking her painting, I adjust the towel slightly to cover more of it. The flowers in her drawing are soft, delicate, yet uninviting. The way the purple helmet of each flower is perfectly shaded, the way they pop out of the painting, so real I imagine the softness of the petals... I'll tell my mother I got it from a friend. She probably won't even notice. I walk over to Ava's other painting of a flower. In this one, half the flower is alive, flourishing. Dew drops sit on each petal of a peony. But the other half is wilted, lifeless. They are intertwined.

I grab the journal she shared with Scott and a single pearl that sits on her nightstand, putting it in my backpack and walking toward the door. Stopping there, I stare at the cracks going along the doorframe, so deep in the drywall that it became a pattern in time. I walk down the stairs, making sure to not accidentally turn on a light switch.

When I get to the kitchen, I decide to sit at the table. I should go, but I can't yet, so I admire the beautiful gold pendants staggered over the island. The kitchen is breathtaking—the black marbled walls, the dark wood floors meant for hiding dirt...and now secrets. I stare at the beautiful stove, a deep forest green, that matches the garden view from the kitchen windows. This was Calista's favorite room, I bet. It's one of mine.

Staring at the empty seats across from me, I wonder why my father enjoyed being at this table more than ours the last few years of his life. Did he feel remorse leaving his old family for a new one? People always say regret eats away at you like cancer. If you're lucky, it's quick and painless.

My mom used to tell my sister and me my dad had business meetings, work events, or that his doctor's appointment was running late. She always seemed in a bad mood, easily agitated on those nights. I noticed her making call after call, but none of them were ever answered.

After the funeral, my mom found out my dad was sneaking over to see Ava. I guess my mom's best friend's ex-husband moved to the same block and saw my dad getting out of the car, smiling, giving Calista a warm hug before walking inside the house.

Someone had to have heard something in this neighborhood the night Ava died, or the night Tanner and Calista went missing. This town gossips too much for a night to ever be truly silent.

As I leave the house, I quickly lock up and make my way down the driveway, constantly checking to see if I'm being watched. I walk down the block to my car and place Ava's painting on the passenger seat, along with a few of her other things.

Soon, I'll come back here. I need more answers. But first, I need to talk to Scott. I wonder if he's heard about me. If he hasn't, maybe it should stay that way.

TWELVE

VICTORIA – THEN

Brooks Law Firm is who the Brentwoods hired to fight the Maple family. They ask question after question, but at least I don't have to pay for it. The digging and the prying make me irritable. I tried to cover my tracks the best I could, but I fear it won't be good enough.

The opposing side had hundreds of pages of documents that made my mind spin. They wanted me to turn over receipts, trust documents, stock information—our entire life from the last decade. They want to see what it would have appreciated to, all things that are out of my wheelhouse. If I had just let Josh pay the child support he owed to Ava's mother, maybe she wouldn't have come for me so hard. She blames me for their failed marriage, which to a degree is fair, but it takes two to have an affair, the last I checked. He could have said no.

As I sift through more documents, highlighting different items, I come across something that stops me dead in my tracks. They want to know why half a million shares were sold last year for General Mills. If I lie and they catch me, that's it, game over. I'm as good as dead. The Brentwoods would murder me. I'd never be found again. They'd bury me somewhere on their ten acres of land, within their 15,000-square-foot compound of pure emotional anguish.

Josh's parents spent their entire life trying to be disgustingly rich, and a scandal like that would destroy the monarch of the family. If it wasn't at my expense, I'd probably enjoy watching the shitstorm. Who wouldn't?

If you want to really get to know someone, you need to learn where they came from, how they grew up, and what their relationship is like with their family. It's like stalking your prey—you need to know when to go in for the kill, when they are at their weakest. I knew Josh's family was his frail place.

I studied Josh because I knew what I wanted and had to figure out how to get it. My friend, if you could call her that, dated one of Josh's brothers in high school for five weeks. She was bragging about how Luke bought her a diamond necklace for dating for thirty-one days. I really think she got it because she'd blow him in the locker room after his football games, but to each their own. If I wanted to be respected, to be feared over being liked, I needed to carry the Brentwood last name. I had to bide my time, though, because he was in love with the awkward shy girl from his school and, to my misfortune, ended up marrying her after college.

Being a Brentwood is a waiting game.

Tick Tock.

The mound of paperwork feels like it's replicating. I pick up a piece of paper—dates of every time Josh went over to Calista's for family dinner the last couple of years. My skin feels like it's shedding, like a snake, wanting to hide.

This list of dates is as if Calista was keeping score, a form of retaliation. I bet she was laughing, taking pleasure in writing every fucking date down. He missed our children's birthday parties. He missed Valentine's Day last year. He even missed half my birthday dinner with our closest friends, rushing in late and claiming he had a business opportunity come up. After everything I did to help keep him alive, he did *this* to me. I bet she even cooked him his favorite foods.

Fuck her.

The possibility swirls in my mind that maybe he was having an affair with Calista, even after everything he did to her, partially on my behalf. Calista's moral compass never steered her wrong. She was honest, loving, and conscientious. Calista would never take him back. It was the one thing he had no jurisdiction over. He had hurt her, and she couldn't move past that. Josh left her with nothing, not because he wanted to, but because he was so afraid of what his family might do if he defied them. And because of me.

So, he chose who he was over who he could have been. Calista was left homeless, with no food, no job, and an infant. She did fine for herself after that. She should have thanked me.

At the time, Josh wasn't making enough money. He tried job after job to be successful, but nothing panned out the way he expected, and the money he made he was spent on drinking and recreational drugs, trying to numb the emotional pain of his life. Josh needed his inheritance so he could feel successful, and also to stay alive. I don't fault him for that because some people can find fulfillment with love and family, but like him, I was not that person either. After all the things he did to mess up Calista with his own personal battles, he decided to listen to his family, to abandon her, and to come home to find someone more suitable for him. They gave him no choice.

The thing about Josh, was his life was controlled. Every single aspect of it. Who his friends were, what sports he played, because if he didn't do everything right, he'd be cut off, forgotten. He had to be perfect, get good grades, not embarrass the family, and when he met Calista, he knew they wouldn't approve of her—an ordinary middle-class girl who was raised by a kind family, with no understanding of how the one percent lived. Her clothes were always brandless. I think maybe she owned one designer purse he bought her for a maternity gift. She just never cared about those things, which is ironic because she's with Tanner now, and to say that man is materialistic is an understatement.

Josh's life was stressful. There was no excitement in it until he fell in love with Calista, defying his family's wishes. He never brought her around them, not because he didn't want to make her uncomfortable, but because he knew if she met them, she might not have stayed. She wasn't as strong as me. Josh's sister told me she used to bully her for shits and giggles in high school, and the last thing Josh wanted was Calista to feel unwelcome, not just by his asshole of a sister, but the rest of his family.

He kept Calista apart from them until they got married. I think the pressure of Josh's family got to him. It's not that Josh could have done better; it's that Calista was too good for him, too pure. Pure doesn't make a Brentwood.

Most people wouldn't have known Josh was disgustingly loaded, the children had to remain that way until their father died, that was rule, no bragging. His father made the children practice quiet luxury, their mother hated that, she wanted to show off every chance she got. They had to ask for everything. Josh's mother was the matriarch of the house. She was bitter and viscous, like a bee sting to the tongue. If Josh did anything wrong, his mother would make a fool of him, beat him, bully him, threaten to take away his future money. Afterall, it was his parents' fortune, not his. They thought they were being gracious by putting a trust in his and all his siblings' names, but with their finances came strings, and the kids were just the puppets being controlled by their handlers.

Josh's lack of control made him impulsive and reckless. He was so desperate for the attention of others and thrived on attentiveness from other women. Josh liked to feel wanted, needed. Having affairs was how he licked the wounds that had been salted over and over again by his godawful parents. It gave him a sense of control, that he was in the driver's seat finally, after all these years of being trapped. He had cheated on every girl he had ever been with, except me, I think. That's the thing, though. No one really cared because if you're a Brentwood, you're untouchable. I'm pretty sure Josh's dad cheated on his mother, but when you have an eight-carat diamond on your finger, you tend to turn a blind eye.

I ended up living in the same city as Josh after college and found out he was working for a new startup, so I made sure to get a job there, to wiggle my way into his life. He'd come into work with bloodshot eyes, like he'd been up crying.

One night after a holiday party ended, Josh and I decided to go out to the bars to get another round of drinks. Calista never came to work functions. She seemed to always be with Ava, taking proper care of her.

Josh seemed upset about something. He knew he messed up, but he never really told me what he had done. From the looks of it, it was shameful. This was my opportunity, and I took it. I had the bartender pour him shot after shot, until he could barely stand up straight. I leaned in, feeling his five o'clock shadow graze my cheek just so slighty before he kissed me back.

We had an affair for about a year. He'd send Calista out to get groceries, and I'd come over while Ava slept in her crib. We'd have sex while I stared at the popcorn-style ceiling.

I met Calista a few times when I'd babysit for her. Josh said it would be better if Calista trusted me. She was so innocent, it made me sick.

Ava would cry non-stop when I watched her. It was like she knew what I was doing. Children can sense people who are evil, and she helped me realize who I really was. I was *not* a good person. Josh used to tell me he'd leave Calista for me, but he was always hesitant. He loved her, but he just didn't know how to love someone the right way.

Calista never saw how broken Josh was, how his ego had been shattered and constantly stomped on by his family, until the point he was nothing more than grains of sand along the beach. Josh used to send her hundreds of roses to her door when she was in college, Calista told me one day when I came over to help with Ava. He never once bought me flowers. Josh even learned to braid her hair for her. When she was sick, he brought her crackers and soup. It made him feel like he was a good person, deserving of her love. He obsessed over all things her, until he couldn't remain the person he was trying to be.

No one can.

I didn't need him to love me like he loved Calista, and I didn't want a naïve love. Calista should have known it was too good to be true.

Everything is.

I'm not proud of what I've done sometimes, especially when I look at my two daughters, hoping they don't turn out like me. It's just that I wanted to give myself a better life. To give them the life I never had, I had to fake it. I still do.

Creating this personification of who I am supposed to be was a game. I changed the story of my upbringing, made my voice softer, and even bleached my hair. A Brentwood woman must always be blonde. I became who his family wanted so it was easier for them to approve of me. You alter yourself to be a Brentwood, not the other way around.

Calista was never meant to be a Brentwood. Her soul had no shade in it, just pure light.

As I sit, drowning in a sea of ink and figuring out how to forge a few things in my notes, I pick up the phone to call Erik. He'll know what to do. He's part of the reason I am in this mess. When Josh married me, he swore that if anything happened to him, I'd get his inheritance, and my girls. He swore Calista wouldn't see a dime, to prove his love to me. I was there when he filled out the forms and updated the trust. Erik oversaw everything. I believed Josh because he gave me no reason not to. The trust did not match.

During the will reading, Ava's name came up. Everyone in the room was silent. I thought it was an error. I wasn't worried until I saw the look on Erik's face. Josh knew what he was doing. Ava was to get one third of Josh's money.

Wine splashes on the counter from my glass as I fill it to the brim. If Karma could talk, it wouldn't be words, but sounds of laughter, a constant ringing of agony echoing all the way down to my eardrum. I lean against the kitchen countertop we remolded last year—with his parent's approval since the trust bought the house we live in—and stare at our family picture on the wall.

My daughters are going to grow up without a father. No one to walk them down the aisle or tuck them in at night. Josh's heart condition, no matter what the family did for it, wasn't fixable. It was damaged from the start. Did he know he was going to die when it happened? He was doing fine until that last dinner he had with Ava and her mother. His checkup seemed like he was on the mend, that his procedure had worked, all thanks to me. I circle the date on Calista's time sheet.

In a moment of rage, I rip up the paperwork asking me to share all my finances with them. I sit down to finish my wine in what little sense of peace I have these days.

The front door opens, and in come my two not-screwed-up-yet children.

"How was your first day back at school?" I attempt a fake-enough smile, trying to keep it together, trying to not let them think anything is wrong.

I love them, but sometimes, I resent them. I gave them the life I should have had growing up.

THIRTEEN

AVA – THEN

The college campus is breathtaking. I never thought I'd live to see this moment. I walk through it and admire the old buildings covered in ivy. I think of all the things these buildings have seen and heard, the words that have been spoken inside of them. If brick could talk, it would tell tales of caution and stories of power and wisdom.

I keep a low profile and try to avoid anyone who would know me from high school. These buildings have heard my name spoken inside them before I ever got to step foot across their thresholds. Although only a few of my peers from high school are attending the same college, it only takes one person to tell your story before you get a chance to do it yourself. People are drawn to gossip because they'd rather be talking about you than themselves. People who gossip are boring. It's really that simple. Small-minded people who can't converse about the world talk about others.

Before I realize it, I fall to the ground. My palms are burned and bloody. I notice things fell out of my backpack and quickly check around for the photo of Tanner and Victoria. One by one, I pick up pencils and my charger. I place them in my bag and brush myself off, replaying the letter Tanner's brother wrote him as I walk to class.

I told my mom I'd come by for dinner tonight, where they will go over legal mumbo-jumbo and I'll pretend I'm starving because the college food is horrific. It will make my mother feel better. I'm positive she's been in the kitchen cooking since seven in the morning. It's how she handles her stress. I'll brush my plate around to make it look like I ate more than I did, and she'll hug me, while Tanner will eat in silence, glancing at the sports on the TV and completely ignoring any real conversation.

While I'm back there, I'll be able to do more digging. Tanner's parents died a few years ago and his brother shortly after. Did he kill them? Did he know it was the only way out of his mistake? He has no one but my mother and me, but even then, he doesn't really.

The bell dings just as I head into my art class, where I'll be criticized for my brush strokes and lack of craftsmanship. Art is meant to be messy, to be wild, to let your subconscious take over. I find a seat toward the back and take out my notebook, pretending to write notes on Monet. Listening to my teacher speak, I jot down the pros and cons of dying instead. Seems less boring.

I learned about Monet my junior year. We both shared the mindset of wanting to commit suicide and the love of painting landscapes. Monet's father tried to control him. His father wanted him to continue being a grocer, but Monet didn't listen. He did have financial issues, but he prevailed and ended up with a beautiful garden to show for it. I liked Monet because he didn't listen to his family. No one should have to.

No one likes to have their entire life be reduced to that of a puppet attached to strings so fragile, if you make one wrong move, you collapse. And if the fall is bad enough, the chances of getting back up are slim. Sometimes, it feels like my strings are being plucked one by one, and at any moment, I may fall. Not all puppets are made of wood. Some are made of porcelain.

My teacher calls on me for something. I pretend I don't know the answer, even though I do, preferring to remain silent, to watch my classmates around me eager to please and impress, their hands reaching so high. But no one likes a know-it-all, or so I've been told.

After the never-ending lecture, the professor tells us we have two hours to start on our painting, to find a landscape that resonates with us, one we dream about when our eyes roll back inside our heads. I pull up picture after picture and try to imagine myself anywhere in the world. Though I begin to lightly sketch a lavender field, I have no idea where this is going. I just need to put pencil on paper and see where this takes me.

Looking out the window, I see a familiar face but try to look away before he spots me. It's too late. Scott's green eyes remind me of the first few days of spring, when everything slowly comes back to life. I stare at his tanned skin, kissed by freckles on his nose. His soft blonde hair gleaming with the sun hitting him just right. He quickly puts his head down, pretending the moment never existed at all.

I wish we weren't at the same school. It's been several months since we talked, but it feels like an eternity at the same time. I'm nothing more than a memory to him, a painful, aching memory, the kind that makes you wake in the middle of the night in a cold sweat, gripping your sheets to hold onto the reality you woke up in and to escape from hellish dreams.

Class is finally dismissed, and like Monet, I am relieved. Monet was never well liked, considered to be a selfish man, but I think it's the other way around. People bothered him because he knew most people to their core were evil and the only true beauty is in nature. Nothing matters but the flowers, and I agree.

Before I go to my mother's tonight, I need to make my rounds. Easton gave me some items to move earlier in the week, and I could use the extra money right now. The schoolbooks were more than I expected them to be, and I'm running out of a few of my more expensive watercolors.

People think I am the richest of the rich. The irony.

I rummage through my backpack, checking to make sure all the product is there. Several of these bottles have to be sold by the end of the week. The shoulder strap of my backpack begins to fall gently down my triceps, and I grip it tighter.

A random person smiles at me. I watch her as she walks effortlessly to her class. She seems happy. I wonder what that's like.

I hop in my car. Nothing too flashy, but it gets me from point A to point B. I worked three jobs to save up for this piece of scrap metal, and I love that it's mine, that I earned it, that my mom didn't need to feel guilt. Tanner would have said I didn't deserve a car within seconds of handing me keys. He'd have gotten me a Mercedes, or something even more obnoxious. I look at the steering wheel, noticing the leather slowly coming undone, and turn up the music so loud it's like I'm in a different multiverse, one I'm happy and unfragmented in.

Driving around town and dropping off people's pills to them used to make me paranoid, but no one would ever suspect someone like me doing something like this. That's where people are wrong. It's always people like me who do this. People with broken families, lies, deceit, people who want an out, to make a better life for themselves. I am the *exact* person who does things like this.

My flesh begins to feel warm, and a bad memory seeps through my pores. I touch my skin, remembering all the hands that have done the same. It's better than what I used to do. Anything is better than that. I close my eyes and let the moment pass, taking a few seconds and checking my mirrors before driving to a place I've never wanted to call home.

The gates to the front drive close behind me, and I pull up to the house I was forced to live in. I tried to research emancipation, but every time I brought it up, it resulted in nothing more than laughter. Tanner would never emancipate me because I came with a large payout for him. It all is starting to make sense now.

My mom sees me pull up to the driveaway and walks out the front door to greet me. I put my car in park and unwillingly step out of it. The door squeaks when I shut it. My mom gives me a hug so tight, I can answer the question for myself on how she is doing. I don't really like getting hugs from her, not because I don't love her, but because, for a single second, I'm deprived of oxygen, and it reminds me that no one ever let me breathe here, that breathing is something you can only do if you feel safe. I'm reminded of the life she didn't mean to put us through, and it makes me feel sad all over again.

Mom offers to take my backpack, but I politely decline. She rushes me into the house, straight into the kitchen, where I'm greeted by Tanner and his lawyer, Bill.

"Have a seat," Tanner says, leading me to the kitchen table.

"Thank you." I try my hardest to not let on that I know what is going on here.

"We thought it would be a good idea for Bill to come over for dinner. Something less formal," he says.

Tanner loves to remind my mother and me that he's funding our lawsuit. One I didn't even want or care about. It's like Tanner tries to convince himself he's a hero, that we should all lick the dirt off the bottom of his shoes. Bill reaches for my hand to shake it, and I pause for a moment, really taking him in. He looks about mid-fifties, his teeth blindingly white when he smiles. I don't know why, but his slicked-back dark hair reminds me of the bullies from the Outsiders. He looks average, nothing nice about him, except his designer suit. I reach for his hand and firmly grip it when I shake it back.

"Hi," I say, not even looking at him.

My mother watches the exchange go down from the kitchen island, where she is preparing a type of pasta dish she got out of a magazine article. "A Pasta Dish Better than Venice" was the title of it. She sent me a picture this morning, saying this is what she might make for dinner.

Mom gently grates a fresh block of parmesan, each shred of cheese falling like snow into the bowls. She sets one down in front of us, and the steam moves upward toward my face. It feels good.

"So, how are you liking school?" Bill asks, looking at Tanner instead of me.

"Oh, it's wonderful. I've been enjoying the atmosphere of college. Being away from home has been really nice too." I dart my eyes to Tanner. My mother's disappointed in my answers.

If I don't respond better, Tanner will take it out on her tonight. I have to remind myself to behave because I don't know how much more of this she can handle.

"How's law?" I ask, not waiting for anyone else to eat before taking a bite of my food.

Bill doesn't answer. I continue, wanting him to know who he is dealing with.

"What makes someone want to be a lawyer anyways? It's such a dishonest profession. Kind of scummy, if you think about it. I mean, you have to represent people who are guilty of horrific things, people who pretend to be innocent in the court of law, but they are anything but. What made you want to be one? Is it a family business? Were you forced? It's weird how *lawyer* and *liar* sound eerily similar." I take another bite of food, making sure to talk with my mouth full.

Tanner's face turns red. It's as if the blood isn't flowing anywhere else in his body.

"I mean, I'm sure you're a great lawyer, and a wonderful person, but I've never met a lawyer who was a good person to their core. Except environmental lawyers. They are in a different category." I pause to take a sip of my water.

My mother looks at me, pleading with her eyes for me to stop. I need to try harder, for her.

"You make an excellent point, Ava. We all are scummy, but that's how we will win your case. We need to be better at it than the other side. If you want to win, you need to get your hands dirty." Bill takes a bite of food, his lips smacking as he eats. I hate him.

Tanner looks unwell. He doesn't eat my mother's cooking but instead walks to the pantry and takes out some pork rinds and then reaches in the fridge for an iced tea.

"My stomach hurts, so I'll just eat this. It looks great, though," Tanner says without remorse, my mother accepting it.

I need to eat my full dish now, even though I'm not very hungry.

Bill pats his mouth dry with his dinner napkin and continues talking about the lawsuit.

"I know my fees are hefty, like most of the lawyers around here, but I'm a hell of a trust lawyer. When you live in an area like this one, there's family suing family left and right. Your stepfather already paid to have me on retainer, but I'll get you that money. It's rightfully yours. You are lucky to have Tanner as your stepfather, who practically raised you as his own. He's willing to pay hundreds of thousands in legal fees just to fight for you, not that it costs that much currently, but it could get to that fee, if this drags on. But the goal is to make it short and sweet."

I look at my mother. She knows I want to get up and leave, but I'm glued to my seat until this dinner is over. It's the least I can do for her.

Bill continues. "Plus, I'm friends with the judge, so it will help to have a little extra persuasion on our side." He winks at me.

Acid comes up from my stomach, burning my esophagus and causing me to gag. This man makes me uncomfortable, not just because I know what his true plans are—to overcharge us and to split the fees with my stepfather if we win so there's no paper trace of him taking our money—but because of his general sliminess as a person. Bill will also probably be the one to kill me too. I'm sure he'll charge Tanner more for that...Nothing surprises me these days.

My mother seems impressed. She really thinks this lawyer is the real deal. I wonder what it's like to live in a delusional world. My mother takes another bite of her lovely homecooked meal.

"Better than Venice," she says, smiling.

I've never been, but anywhere is better than here.

"I have no choice in lawyers because I don't have that kind of money. Not yet at least," I say, laughing, wanting Tanner to feel like I am oblivious to his plan.

Bill helps himself to a glass of red wine that is sitting on the table beside his food.

"What kind of lawyer fucks up a trust and a will? Especially for the Brentwood family. It's a unique case because it was either on purpose or a mistake, and both look bad for the other side."

Bill reaches for another mouthful of food.

"This case will be one that could get studied in school. There hasn't been a mistake this big in ages," he says.

I don't talk the rest of dinner. Instead, I just listen to Tanner and Bill talk about the potential legal roadblocks they may hit during the case, the amount of time these things take, etc. I tune out the world for minute and think of how Scott looked at me today when he saw me, like I was nothing more than a sin surrounded by flesh.

I wish he would hear me out, I wish I never told him anything. I regret telling him anything at all. Some things are better kept in the dark.

When the dishes have nothing left on them, I help my mother clear the table, gently rinsing each dish with soap and letting the scalding hot water burn me. It feels good, reminds me I'm present in the moment. But my mother rushes to the sink and changes the water to a more moderate temperature.

"Your skin," she says, watching it turn bright red, like meat thawing.

"Thanks," I say, not wanting her to worry. She'll have enough to worry about soon.

Mom finishes cleaning the kitchen, then walks toward her garden to prune her plants, the sun slowly dropping below the tree line.

Quietly, I walk up to my bedroom and go sit on my balcony, letting my legs dangle. The Jaspers directly across from us are arguing in their kitchen, probably about how their daughter was inappropriately dressed at school. I look at the house three doors across from ours on the right. Kids are watching TV while their parents have sex upstairs in their bedroom with the curtain pulled just slightly back, like they wanted to be watched.

Pressing my head against the cold metal rods that keep me safely in place, I glimpse down into my neighbor's backyard. Mr. and Mrs. Eden are digging something up. It doesn't look like a flower bed; it looks more like a grave? A cold breeze catches me off guard, the kind that gives painful goosebumps, the ones where every hair stands up on your arm.

I poke my head through my balcony and try to get a closer look at the Edens.

My mother knocks on the door, and I quickly get up to let her in. She sits on my bed, aging slightly more every day.

"Thank you for being here tonight. I know it's not easy for you," she says with sadness.

I sit down next to her.

"It's really not a big deal. It's just rich people fighting with other rich people. Tale as old as time." I pretend I'm unphased.

"Most people get to grieve their parent's death, but now add a lawsuit and lawyers telling you your dad didn't love you and that he wanted nothing to do with you...It is a big deal," she says remorsefully.

Her gaze lingers on my ceiling, and she stares at the glow-in-the-dark star remnants above my bed.

"I know your dad did that on purpose. I know he did. He wanted to make up for all the awful things he did to us," she says, certain in her mind.

I nod, hoping this gets my mom to stop talking about it.

"Hey, Mom, um, did someone die next door?" I ask, hoping she knows the answer.

"No, why?" My mom seems taken aback. She looks puzzled.

"Mr. Eden looked sad today. I saw him when I pulled up to the house."

"He seemed okay when he asked me for a shovel to do some gardening work in their yard earlier today. I think he is planting a new tree of sorts."

A feeling of dread comes over me. That most certainly is for a body.

"Will you spend the night tonight? This house feels so empty without you," she asks, with sadness in her voice.

As I nod, my mother kisses me softly on the temple to wish me goodnight. I go back to my balcony when she leaves and watch the Edens. Something is not right. I've never seen them plant anything in their yard, they don't own any pets, and they certainly don't do manual labor themselves, because they hire people to mow their lawn. Maybe I'll go over there tomorrow morning with something my mother baked.

The air turns crisper, and the evening becomes darker. I close my balcony windows and walk toward my door, locking it and placing my dresser in front of the door again—my bedtime ritual ever since I was about thirteen.

May 25, 2013.

The exact date I started barricading my door.

It allowed me to fall asleep feeling secure, like I had a chance.

I had just come in from playing with my friends down the street, and I was about an hour late. Because I didn't have a phone, I couldn't check in with my mother or stepfather, so I figured it was no big deal. If they needed me, they could just walk over to Lauren's parents' house. I had even left a note stating where I was.

The air had that first day of summer nostalgia, this distinct smell of the start of warmth. It's indescribable, but from the moment I stepped outside, I knew, and all the memories of summertime flooded back to me on an endless loop.

I walked home and went through the front door, where I saw Tanner holding my mother's hair. He was screaming at her for how much she spent on groceries using his credit card without his permission. Though I was unaware at the time, my mother had to get approval to provide homecooked meals for the family. I was nervous but knew I had to do something, so I rushed to the block of knives adjacent to where they were standing in the kitchen and held it up to Tanner.

"Let her go, or I'll kill you," I whimpered, shaking with every word.

Tanner let my mom go and charged at me, but I held my ground, holding a six-inch blade by my side. I wanted to run, but my legs began to feel like concrete, hardening by the second. He took my knife from me with little force. I was nothing compared to how stout he was. The knife left my hand. The handle was warmer and smoother, but the razor-sharp blade against my neck felt frigid and cold.

"Don't you *ever* tell me what to do again. *I* provide for this family.

My money, my rules, or would you and your mother prefer to be out on the streets again?" he yelled, his spit landing on my face.

I wanted to cry, but I couldn't. My body tried to fight back. The blade touched my throat just enough to draw a single drop of blood. My mother stood there, afraid for what would happen if she got near me.

"If you ever try to intervene again and pull a weapon on me, in my house, I won't hesitate to push this blade into your narrow little neck," Tanner said coldly. He slowly pulled the blade away and placed it back in the block with the other knives, my blood still on it. Tanner grabbed his briefcase and slammed the door shut behind him.

Motionless, the only thing holding me up was the kitchen wall. I was void of all thoughts, completely empty. The emotional abuse, the screaming, the occasional hitting for my bad behavior…I was used to that, but I wasn't used to the idea of death at my age. My mother sat down beside me, staring at nothing and everything at the same time. I noticed her look around at the beautiful high-end appliances, the floor-to-ceiling windows, the shiny marble countertops, the gold trim along the counters. Then she looked at me, defeated, the lavish living suddenly no longer worth it.

"I'm so sorry," she said. A single tear touched her warm face.

"Can we leave?" I reached for her hand.

"It's not that simple," my mother replied, holding back a flood of tears.

"But he isn't a nice man, and he hurts you sometimes, and what if he hurts me worse than he already has?" I was trying my hardest to get through to her.

"We can't leave because we won't be safe if we did. All our friends are Tanner's friends. They wouldn't believe me if I said anything anyways." The game was already lost before she even had a chance to sign up to play.

"Can I get emancipated? I can go live with Scott. He always tells me that his mom really likes me, and I'm welcome anytime." I stared out at my mom's garden, unable to look at her.

"It doesn't work that way honey."

She never gave me a shot to play in the game either.

"We can ask my dad for help!" I begged with hopefulness.

"You get a small amount of child support a year. A few hundred dollars a month, you know, just enough. That's all your father can afford to give. He has a new life, a new family to provide for." Her answer was weighed down with a type of sadness I'm slowly learning about.

"When I'm eighteen and you're forty, we'll run away, start somewhere fresh, a new state, and we'll work whatever jobs we need to, live off the land, eat dirt if we have to," I said, knowing it was a pipe dream.

She'd never leave. Mom was too afraid. Abuse was simply a regular house guest to her.

"Okay." She reached for my hand, attempting her best to give me a smile. "Okay," she said again, convincing herself we'd make it five more years.

Later that year, I learned my mom couldn't go to the police because all his friends were in some type of law enforcement or politics. Tanner donated a lot of money a year to the police department, regularly letting them come over for dinners my mother spent days preparing. It was a lot of effort for no reward. She was feeding her captors.

It wasn't as easy to leave as we thought, and trust me, she eventually tried, a lot. My mother knew, without money he'd find us. He could make us disappear so easily, but he was holding out. She knew deep down, waiting is what would keep us from harm. So that's what we did. We bided our time, no matter how slow the clock ticked.

It all makes sense now why he had to force my mother with violence and threats to stay married against her will. If I am still his stepdaughter and my mother is still his wife, if I get money, it will become his, all of it. No matter what type of lawyer I find to protect my money, it won't matter. He'll always find a way around it. There is no peace with him.

Crawling into bed, I regret agreeing to stay overnight, but I do it for my mother. I am it for her, her only reason to exist these days. How could someone like my mother be so easily tricked into a bad marriage? How could someone who just wanted to give love and get love in return end up this way, stuck, with nowhere to go, hopeless and afraid? It breaks my heart, watching her, chained without the chains to this house, to her life.

When I was thirteen, I decided I'd never trust anyone ever again. I'd rather be unlovable and unwanted than anything else in this world. Being unwanted would help keep me safe.

Right when my eyes begin to close, my phone dings. It's from Easton. He's been around for the last five years of my life, helping me get out of the mess my mother accidentally created for us. I started selling drugs the day after everything happened, but I waited a couple of years more before selling my innocence to the men around town. If it's one thing I know, it's that you don't need to be in love to have sex. You just need to be desired with no intention of wanting to be loved—love is the part that ruins you.

I let my body sink into the mattress, feeling my eyes begin to close. Tomorrow is another day, one day closer to figuring out how I will get rid of Tanner. Maybe I can use the Eden's makeshift sinkhole.

If the price is right.

FOURTEEN

ALLISON – NOW

My eyes begin to focus just barely enough to see the flashing red on my alarm clock sitting on my desk. Forcing myself to sit up, I press the snooze button. I've been having a hard time sleeping these last few months. The lawsuit has slowly started to catch up to me emotionally. I went from being one of two daughters of my father's to three.

The alarm goes off again, irritating me. I walk to the connecting bathroom Ashley and I share and turn on the shower, letting it get just warm enough before I step inside, the steam filling my lungs. I've always enjoyed long showers, where my skin feels raw after, but the worst part is when you are done cleansing your body, only seconds later to feel pain when you step onto the cold tile, your wet hair dripping down your back, stiffening your muscles and joints. Everything good comes with its set of bad, even something as simple as a shower. I go to turn off the shower and see blood all over my hands, I panic, but then suddenly, it's gone, *nothing* is there. I take a deep breath before getting out.

The mirror fogs up, and I wipe it down. With each stroke, a part of myself is revealed. I begin my morning ritual. First, I start by lathering my skin with lotion that smells of sweet milk, then apply an exfoliate. Once that's done, I put on toner and begin to brush my hair, giving myself a fishtail braid. I slowly work my way into my makeup, putting a little bit of blush on and then mascara before hanging my towel to dry. Downstairs, I greet my mother and sister. Ashley wakes up at five in the morning to begin her routine.

My mother won't stop talking about the Maple family. It's become the only thing she focuses on since we settled the case. She holds a grudge against Calista, but Calista can't help that my father loved her first. It's about timing. No one should be at fault for that. People are allowed to change their mind and love other people. It's life. Calista isn't even around. She's missing. Ava is dead. My mother already won.

Ashley eats her breakfast in silence. She acknowledges me but then focuses on her phone. I pull up a chair at the table and pour myself a bowl of cereal. My mother is getting ready for a date, which makes me happy because I want her to feel loved again one day. I think for her to move on will help all of us feel some type of normalcy again.

This afternoon, I'm supposed to have high tea with Ashley and my grandmother. My mother is not invited, and she shows no interest in wanting to attend either. I grab my coat because the weather is changing, and as the leaves begin to cascade from their branches, I smile and step outside into the beginning of Autumn.

Ashley doesn't come with me because she was keen on staying home this morning to watch her favorite shows. She said Mom will drop her off later and to text her when I was heading that way. We seem to spend less time together these days, now that everything is settled. Ashley won't forgive me for willingly signing away millions of dollars to Ava. My mother has learned to deal with "my betrayal," or so she calls it.

The parking lot near the coffee shop by our house is full, but I manage to find a spot. I sit there, endlessly scrolling on Facebook, looking up hundreds of Scotts before finding the right one. I'm certain this is him.

When I click on his profile, Ava is in none of the pictures, but I'm sure Scott has his reasons for whatever happened between them. It's easy to find someone these days because almost everyone wants to be found. If they didn't, they'd stay hidden from the world. Scott looks happy, healthy, his eyes a beautiful shade of green, his tanned olive skin glowing while he sits on his motorcycle, his helmet neatly placed by his side.

I notice his college was the same as Ava's. They probably avoided each other. You can't pour your heart out in letters like that, sharing the love they did, and then sit in the quad across from each other while you both eat sandwiches, talking to other people. It doesn't work that way, not even in the movies.

I look at any clues for where he may work but don't find any information. Maybe he doesn't need to work? I check his Instagram. It's set to private. I debate following him for a split second but decide against it. What if he knows who I am and he wants to avoid me? But he also may not know who I am at all. I can't decide what's worse.

Maybe I'll go to Northwestern and try my best to see if anyone knows him. I'm sure someone will. Everyone always seems to know a beautiful boy like that.

Eventually, I get out of my car and walk inside the coffee shop.

The line moves quickly, and my adrenaline makes it hard for me to stand still any longer. I get to the cashier and place my order for an iced coffee with a small amount of cream in it. They call out my name. I grab my coffee and head out the door. It's not a long drive to Northwestern, but it will feel like one. The trees slowly fade from green to red and yellow. There is comfort in the beauty. I think how cold the water of the lake would feel against my skin, the current pulling down on me as I gasp for air.

An hour passes before I arrive at the campus. It's quiet for a Sunday. Everyone is probably still asleep from their wild night out, their hangovers keeping them glued to their blankets and pillows. I've never been drunk before.—I'm trying to wait a bit, with everything going on in my life, besides, I was told it's better to drink when you're happy to become happier, because when you drink when you're sad, it will just make it worse. I don't think I'll ever drink, if that's the case.

The campus is beautiful—brick buildings as old as the city when it first began, aged trees with chestnuts falling, the squirrels playing along the branches. Large stone benches to sit on along the quad, to gossip and catch up with friends. I love it here. It's like a world inside a bubble, impenetrable.

A group of girls pass by, their makeup smudged, hair disheveled. I gather my thoughts and myself and walk up to them.

"Hey, have you guys seen Scott? He left, uh, something at my place last night." The words nervously come out of my mouth.

One of the girls looks at me, slightly bothered that I interrupted her conversation with her friends.

"Scott, who?" she asked, peeved.

"Scott, he's a junior, local." I pretended it was just a one-night stand, whose information I forgot to get.

"All juniors live in that building, unless they are off-campus. In that case, we can't help you, sorry." The girl points to a beautiful ivy-covered building. "Deckham Hall," she says before walking away, like our interaction never happened.

I hope Ava was nothing like the people who go here. And I'm certain she wasn't. It's what I want to believe.

The door to Deckham Hall is locked, so I jiggle the handle a few more times, thinking maybe I'll get lucky. There is a pull on the handle from the other side. At least whoever comes out will let me in.

When I look up, I realize it's Scott. The universe is throwing me a bone.

"Hi," I say.

"Hi?" He's confused. His lips are full, chapped, and the dimple on his right side makes me blush. "Have we met before?" Scott rubs the back of his neck.

"No, I, uh, am transferring here, next semester," I say anxiously.

He adjusts the strap on his backpack and gives it a hoist higher up on his shoulder.

"I was just about to get some coffee. Want to join me? I'm not the best tour guide, but I can give you some advice about classes to take, teachers to avoid…if you want. What year are you?" His smile melts me.

"Sophomore. Transferring from IU."

"Right on. Well, avoid the dorms. They suck."

"Even the one you're in?"

"I was visiting a buddy. I live closer to Wilmette. I like it better there. Less hectic." He sifts his hands through his dirty blonde hair. "What's your name?"

I panic and look around campus for an idea. The mistake falls from my lips as soon as the words come out.

"Ivy," I say.

"Scott." He reaches out his hand toward mine, a simple gesture, yet I am frozen.

I don't know why I lied, but I can't undo it and decide that to Scott, I am Ivy. Maybe it will be easier this way, to find out about Ava. Everyone else around me is a liar, so I guess now it's my time to start.

We walk toward a coffee shop several blocks away from campus. The streets aren't lively yet. Everyone is still lounging in bed, thinking the world will wait for them to wake up.

Ava will never get to do that again, to spend a night out with friends, feel her head pounding—a sign she had a memorable night out. I think of all the firsts she never got to have and the lasts of everything she did. My heart aches for her.

When we arrive at Brigg's Coffee, Scott opens the door for me. Several college kids are sipping on lattes, reading, some jotting notes down quickly as they study their schoolbooks. It's not like other coffee shops I've been to that are brightly lit, the ones that are more loft-like and sterile, that seem to have a million plants inside to make people think it's a calming, nurturing environment. This coffee shop is dark and dimly lit, the walls a strange plum color. There are used books everywhere, every corner of the pages bookmarked, only a single plant inside, and couches that look worn down and have seen many late nights. I prefer this one—the one that's lived in versus the one you go to just to snap a photo of your coffee, take four sips of it, toss it, and post a picture online.

The cashier takes our orders, and Scott says the drinks are on him. I smile nervously. We wait at the counter for our drinks before finding a seat on a dark brown couch which reminds me of what a normal grandpa would have in their home next to their television for watching Sunday football.

Scott watches me carefully blow on my drink before taking a sip.

"So, what's your major?" Scott reaches to take a drink of his black coffee with cream and two sugars.

"Art," I say, feeling another lie fall from my tongue.

"What medium?" he asks genuinely.

"Painting, and I'm a business minor too. Better to be well rounded, you know." I avoid eye contact.

"I'm just a business major in general. Nothing special there, but you can do a lot with it. The possibilities are endless."

People who study business are people who want money, nothing less.

He sips his coffee. I watch him take his tongue and lick the corners of his mouth. All I can think about is how beautiful he is. For a single moment, I forget I am here for Ava. I've never felt more guilty for my thoughts, knowing how Ava pined for him.

In her final moments, I wonder if she thought of Scott.

"Do you know anyone who is an art major here?" I ask, trying to get back on topic.

"Not really. I mean, sort of, but they don't go here anymore, so it would be hard to connect you both." His tone changes, becoming more somber. He takes another sip of his coffee.

"That's okay." I'm trying not to sound nervous.

"If you can get through the pretentious students and the professors who are only professors because they failed at their dreams, so they wanted to teach others instead"—he pauses—"then you'll like it here. It's a good education, and you can't beat the connections. The other stuff is all...just sort of there." He barely makes eye contact with me.

I don't want to keep prying, I really don't, but I need answers. I need to know what he knows, what became of Ava. Maybe with his help, I can piece together her last few days. I want it to make sense. *I need it to make sense.*

I stare around the coffee shop, watching students slowly trickle in to get a caffeine fix. Every girl who enters looks the same—perfectly waved blonde hair, riding boots with their jeans tucked in, and a North Face jacket to keep them warm as the weather changes. All the girls start to blur together. It seems like being in a bubble might not be such a good thing, every person and every day the same, a routine to drive someone mad. Every Sunday, you wake up late after a night out and work on any assignments that are due Monday. You sit in class four to five days a week with the same people, the same professors, going over new topic after new topic, until it all feels like a carbon copy. You eat when you need to, you sleep when you can, and for approximately four years, every day is a Xerox copy of the day before that. It seems vastly unappealing to me, but this is what is expected.

I am a Brentwood. New blood.

As an heir to the Brentwood fortune, my legacy is to go to a good school, which will be brought up at parties later by my family.

Paraded around for my genius, they'll embellish me. They will want me getting into a ritzy school, like my last name had nothing to do with any of it. None of it is real.

As I cup my mug, I settle in deeper into the couch. Scott understands my body language and sinks deeper into the couch with me. The more we talk, the less I remember I'm nothing but a lie to him.

"So where did you grow up? Are you from around here…or?" I ask.

"I actually grew up about thirty miles from here, around Willowbrook. I sort of enjoy being close to home. My mom is a single parent and raised me by herself. So, I like to be able to stop by for dinner here and there. It makes her happy."

He glows as he talks about his mother. It must be nice.

"What about you?" He gets closer to me on the couch.

I don't want to pull away from him, even though I should. A part of me likes it. I keep reminding myself it's for Ava, the guilt slowly looming over my head like a cloud with a storm that has no end in sight.

"That's really sweet you get to see your mom so often. I'm sure she's elated whenever you drop by. My mom would probably be thrilled if I never came home for dinner again. Cooking is her downfall, so she'd be relieved. She prefers fancy dining establishments," I say, laughing.

For some reason, I blurt out that I'm from Woodburry. The words taste like acid as I say them, and I immediately regret it.

When the words slip out of my mouth, his lustrous smile begins to fall slowly from his face, like the leaves on the maple trees outside, ready to die in this life and come back later, when things aren't so bleak. His eyes begin to lose their spark, but only for a mere second. He snaps out of it quickly.

"Okay. It's not *that* bad of a place," I tell him, hoping to lighten the mood.

He pauses, struggling to find the right words. I see his mind searching, racing for the right thing to say, but there isn't one.

"Sorry, I just knew someone from there. They passed away." He looks away from me when he says it, his wounds still fresh, but mine are even more open.

"Ava, right? I heard. It's so sad," I say, playing it off.

"Yah, Ava."

The silence is deafening, and all that needed to be said was told to me with just one look. I check the time on my phone and realize I am going to be late for my high tea with my grandmother. Getting up as quickly as I can while still attempting to be polite, I try not to make things feel any more awkward than they probably do.

When I get up from my chair, Scott immediately stands too. The words take a second to come out of his mouth, but I am patient because, lately, I haven't had the right words either.

"Would you want to maybe meet up again some time? Go for a coffee again, or something? Maybe dinner? If not, it's cool."

His words cause a pain to my chest, as if something locked onto my heart, making every beat feel like, at any moment, I'd combust. I hesitate for a few moments, and we lock eyes. Is this how Ava felt when she was with Scott? Did he make her feel like everything was going to be okay? Does he feel like he failed her? Because nothing was okay.

His eyes turn from a fern green to a deep emerald color when the lights in the coffee shop dim even more. I start to count the freckles on his nose but lose count. He is both an answer and a distraction. I think of all the letters he wrote to Ava, how much he loved her.

No one's ever loved me the way he loved her. I feel an overwhelming sense of guilt because I know I should say no. This might cause him more harm than good. Maybe it will connect us somehow, make me understand her more, and I can get the answers I need from Scott.

Please, forgive me Ava. Please.

"Yes." My voice is shaky as the words leave my lips.

He smiles, and I watch the freckles dance on his face.

"Okay, cool. What's your number? I'll give you a call later this week, if that works, and we can figure something out."

I give it to him and grab my bag.

"I'm running late to see family," I say, not wanting to leave but know it's for the best. No one is late to see the Brentwood matriarch.

Scott and I walk toward the door to leave. He holds it open for me.

"Have fun," he says.

I look back at him as I walk in the opposite direction and catch him staring back at me.

I'd have kept every love letter he wrote me too. I'll give him those letters later. I need answers first.

After unlocking my car door and getting in, I turn up the heat and sit back, closing my eyes for a mere moment. The guilt is spreading through my body like a cancer. It's tumultuous.

I turn on the radio and let the sound drown out my thoughts. What music did Ava like?

After driving for a lifetime, I get closer to the suburbs where my grandmother resides. Their neighborhood's trees are the most mature in their area, they encompass Windsor Lane. It's hard not to notice that every home is bigger than the next. The houses compete without even knowing it. Every home begins to blur together. A white exterior with a large white fence around it…A tire swing to show off that the home has children in it, yet no one ever uses the swing…It's just to signify the American dream. Every home has several expensive cars parked on the driveway, without a single scratch or piece of dirt in sight. They aren't meant for driving.

The homes on Windsor Lane remind me of Ava's house on Kenilworth—large yet isolating. Every time I pass them, I am overcome with a feeling of coldness. My mother and father's home is nothing like these ones. Theirs is a modest size, about four bedrooms and three baths. It doesn't boast marble floors and staircases like these ones do. The cars parked on the driveway at our home are simple, cars that get you from point A to point B but look a little extra than the average sedan. I think of my father's car sitting in the driveway, untouched, the battery life dissipating.

I miss him.

The start of the driveway is about a mile long, not a single bump on the way. I press the speaker button at the entrance and wait for the dial tone before punching in the code. They do a good job of keeping people out.

Once through the gate, I pass by luscious roses that line the driveway, the grass freshly mowed, the rows still prominent from the morning's cut.

The Brentwood Mansion is unlike any other home I've ever seen.

The house is around twenty thousand square feet, giving the palace of Versailles a run for its money. The stone siding of the house makes it feel like a fortress. I stare at the molding and carvings along the exterior, which make it seem like this house was from the ancient times or a palace housing royalty.

I step out of my car to walk inside.

It always felt like gods lived within this home, but it was just my grandparents and their children. Everyone always wonders who will get this house one day, when my grandma dies. My grandpa passed a few years back. My mother hopes it will be us. She has never let us miss an afternoon tea ever. Ashley is probably already inside. My mother likes to make sure we are no later than five minutes early.

The front door is made of African blackwood, a type of wood so rare and nearly impossible to work with. My grandparents refused any other type. They said gold was too easy to get, and they wanted something much rarer to make a statement. What they want, they get.

In the Brentwood home entrance, marble lines the floor, and pillars hold up the ceiling covered in frescoes. The light hits dramatically through the grand hallway as I make my way to the sunroom for high tea. I wish I felt like I belonged here, but this home is for the pretentious, and even though I was born into this family, I don't seem to fit.

The sunroom is immaculate. Cherubs dote the walls in a stunning mural, a beautiful view to drink tea to. I walk toward the table and make eye contact with Ashley. She looks annoyed because I am exactly on time. She scuffs at me when I say hello. I walk toward my grandmother and curtsey, kiss each cheek. She's cold as if she is already dead. I take my seat beside her.

My Grandmother CeCe is in her seventies. She had children on the younger side, which isn't as common anymore. CeCe is a petite blonde with broad shoulders and long beautiful legs, but what she lacks in size, she makes up for in dominance. She has a sweet side to her, but only toward the grandkids- the ones she likes. Her legacy lives on through us. At least, that's what she tells us after she polishes off a bottle of Romanee-Conti 1945.

Reaching for the tea pot, I graciously pour my grandmother her tea first, then Ashley's. I've always enjoyed watching the steam pour out of the spout.

"How have you been, Grandmother?" I ask, rummaging through the bin for an Earl Grey tea bag. I find one and dip it into my scalding-hot water.

"The same as last month, dear child." Her cracked lips purse together, blowing on her tea to cool it down before taking a sip.

I look at Ashley and picture her turning into our grandmother, someone who sees life's values by materialistic possessions. A fantasy unobtainable by most of society.

The delicate teacup made of the finest porcelain is covered in lush water-colored peonies, just like the one's outside of Ava's home. My heart sinks into my gut just thinking about her.

As I sip on my tea, there is a taste of bergamot orange, with subtle hints of lemon and grapefruit. I've always preferred the black teas. My mother hates tea. She's more of a coffee person, and if I'm being honest, she's been more of a vodka person these days. I grip the delicate teacup firmly without realizing it.

Mustering up all the courage I have, I decide I'll start with my grandmother for questions.

"Did Ava ever come for high tea?" I ask softly.

My grandmother takes a sip of tea and leaves the table. She walks toward a painting of tulips.

"Ava has never been to this place," she replies.

"Why?" I ask, excusing myself from the table and walking toward the painting she has become lost in.

"Your father made a few mistakes in his life, and his first wife was one of them," she says coldly.

I look over at Ashley. Her eyes are begging me to stop, but I don't want to.

"How come no one ever mentioned her around here?" I hope for a real answer.

"Your father had a choice to make, and he choose correctly. That's the simplest answer I have to give you, darling. Family politics are complicated. You're too young to understand." She pauses before gathering more cruel words. "Because of his mistakes, this family is out hundreds of millions, and all to that girl who died. That money will never come back. No one can find it. It's as dead as she is." My grandmother remains emotionless.

The words burn.

How can someone just not acknowledge their own flesh and blood? What choices could my father have been given, besides money or love. Isn't love what keeps the axis tilted? The thing that people write sonnets about, movies, books, the thing that creates passion and drive? A sense of shame falls over me, knowing my father picked the money. It seems Brentwoods always pick money. I feel less than adequate here.

My grandmother walks back toward the table, and I follow her, like a lamb to slaughter. She reaches for a scone, so I copy. I place mine on the matching peony plate.

My mother always told me that my grandmother is the kind of woman who can cut glass with a single word. I sit at the table, watching her eat, unbothered by the loss of a grandchild.

Ashley talks my grandmother's head off about her ballet class and the new moves she is trying to master. This pleases my grandmother. When Ashley finishes talking about her exceptional grades in school and how all the children in her class want to be her friend, the conversation moves toward me again. I don't want it to. I'd rather sit and listen while my mind runs elsewhere, free to roam with my thoughts.

"Have you been keeping up with your ballet as well?" CeCe asks.

"Yes, but with college applications due, it's been harder to focus," I say.

"All Brentwoods go to an Ivy League school. Your last name will be enough. Focus on your ballet. Boys like a thin physique," she says sternly.

I put down my scone. It seems I have lost my appetite.

And all to that girl who died plays continuously in my head.

Ava wasn't just *that* girl. She was my sister, but to everyone in this family, she was a mistake. They are happy she is gone, even with their hundreds of millions. The millions I signed off on. Even my mother agreed to it strangely, as much as it pained her. Ashley did not want to agree to it. Everyone was so stressed out about the money. It was what everyone talked about constantly. There was and still is plenty to go around, but to the Brentwoods, every penny counts. *Every single one.*

Ashley and I did not agree with each other on that topic. She thinks the money should've stayed within the Brentwood family. Ashley's been brainwashed by my father's family, feeding into their propaganda. I hope she realizes that in our entire life span, there is never going to be a need for that type of money.

Excusing myself from the table, I tell CeCe I need to use the restroom. She scolds me for announcing it publicly.

"A woman never speaks of such things, especially at a table where people eat. Who raised you? A barn animal?" She blots her mouth with a napkin, careful to not smudge her bright red lipstick.

I walk down the grand hallway toward what used to be my father's room, but I can't bring myself to go in. Instead, I find myself near the basement. It was never finished. My grandmother insisted that finishing a basement was useless, that guests deserve to be wowed the second they walk into your home on the first level and that having them have to walk below the earth was defacing everything she believed in.

The door is usually locked, but today, it's cracked slightly open. I carefully look around before opening it more.

After turning on the flashlight on my phone, I look around. The contrast from this place to the one inches above me are vastly different. With each step, the stairs wobble beneath me. it smells rotten down here, and it's making me feel unwell. A single cabinet stands out to me, the handlebar reflective from my light.

I'm drawn to it.

There are hundreds, if not thousands of pages of paperwork, and stock information. I move to the next drawer. A jar of human teeth makes me stop dead in my tracks. Then I see another, and another…

A wave of sickness overcomes me as I pick up one of the jars to examine it. The teeth do not belong to a child who is waiting for a few dollars from the tooth fairy. These are large. I dry heave several times before throwing up all the acid left in my stomach.

Taking a few pictures of the jars, I place them back gently, holding my stomach as I do. I close the cabinet drawer and sprint up the basement stairs as quickly as I can, not looking behind me.

When I resume my place at the table, joining the family I was born into, my grandmother hands me another cup of tea.

I look at the tea cup and notice blood on the handle. I set it down, panicking. I look all over my hands, they are *covered* in blood. The room spins.

"You mustn't let your tea get cold. These are the finest herbs money can buy, darling," she says, smiling at me. I look at my hands again. *Nothing* is there.

I smile back at her, nodding.

I try to sip my tea, but I begin to shake uncontrollably, my teacup chattering on its dainty plate.

How could I ever come back here, a house of horrors disguised with gold trim and luxurious furniture? The fear begins to set in, and I realize I am trapped at a serpent's table. A snake in Chanel. I sit through the rest of high tea, silently nodding, my mind stuck on the jars of teeth below.

Who do they belong to?

FIFTEEN

CALISTA – THEN

Ava hasn't been home in over a month. With every day she's gone, my heart slowly breaks, but a piece of me is finally free because she gets to live outside of these walls for the both of us.

The last time she was home, we had a dinner with Bill. Just the thought of it makes me feel uncomfortable. Ava seemed pre-occupied with everything going on, and Tanner thinks I'm too dumb to realize what he is doing, so I sit there and look hopeless. It's not hard to pretend, though, because that's how I often feel.

I go into Ava's room, untouched, and sit on her bed, staring at the dark shade of blue on her walls, so close to black. Her bedroom, a canvas to her emotions for years. Every time Tanner would break down her door, or hit one of us, she'd decide to paint the walls a new shade of blue. She'd tell me, "Life goes in phases, just like a color wheel." We'd go to the paint store and spend hours comparing swatches. Life was easier when her walls were a soft French blue.

There is a slight breeze outside. I can hear the whistling sounds from the wind. The weather is getting slightly cooler out, and the days are growing shorter. I take a deep breath and exhale, pausing for a moment and realizing my days are growing just as short.

Tanner is away on business, but I know he's really meeting with Bill, staying downtown at one of Bill's extra condos in the city. The kind of place that lacks any color, concrete walls, floor-to-ceiling windows looking out into a city…Where for a mere second, the person looking down on everyone from thirty stories up feels like a king.

When Tanner went to the bathroom last week, he left his phone on the counter, and I went through a few texts as quickly as I could. I only got as far as Bill offering Tanner his condo and going over lawsuit strategies, but that was enough for me to piece things together. Phones give everything away. It's why I delete my messages, and I will never leave my phone unattended. That is, if I had people to talk to. Tanner got rid of all my friends.

Ava's bedroom begins to feel colder when the sun sets. The more time I sit in her room alone, the worse I feel.

The clock strikes seven. I quickly leave her room and rush downstairs.

I need to be sure no one sees me.

I need to meet with them in private.

From the corner of my eye, I notice a hint of frost gathering upon the window. I walk to the closet and grab a jacket and hat, putting them on and embracing the soft wool lining wrapping my skin in warmth before walking out of my backyard door. Tanner doesn't believe in cameras in the house because it could incriminate him if he ever did something wrong. He only believes in sensors, to know when the door opens and closes. I know I am safer because I cannot be seen yet, at the same time, still in danger.

Toward the very end of the yard, I push back the branches of the giant oak tree. There lies a small opening to our neighbor's backyard, a small tunnel of security.

Years ago, when we moved into the house on Kenilworth, the Edens were the first to greet my family. When they rang the doorbell, I opened the door, eager to meet someone new. It's indescribably lonely here.

Mrs. Eden is a lovely elder woman with silver hair. She was holding a beautiful wicker basket, standing next to her husband, his kind eyes hiding behind overly worn glasses. He looked a few years older than her, with hair to match. They introduced themselves as Paul and Aletta. Aletta was insistent that I try a bite of her muffin right then and there. Although I wasn't hungry, I wanted to make her happy. I could tell she put so much love into her baked goods. She handed me the basket, and I reached inside. It smelled like everything could be cured with this one insatiable bite. The blueberries gushed, the muffin moist and delicate.

The Edens used to spend a lot of time in their backyard on the days that were warmer, when the air would begin to smell like summer and mischief. When kids would be free from the confinements of education, sneaking around late at night, getting into everything they shouldn't have but were supposed to all at the same time. Every year, the Edens would spend less and less time outdoors because they could hear the beratement and punishment from Tanner's cruel mouth. Each time Tanner yelled, it became louder and louder, and with every argument, the Edens windows began to close one by one, until I never saw them outside anymore.

They were lucky to be scared for me without shared walls. I envied them.

One day, after a violent screaming match, Tanner shoved me and I fell, smacking my face on the counter, giving me a black eye. Tanner said it was an accident, but I knew better. Ava walked to school alone that day because, even with makeup, the sadness would seep through. It was useless. I waited until Ava got to school to let myself cry in my empty home, not wanting to subject her to any more unpleasant memories. I carry that guilt with me enough as is. Tanner was doing an investment meeting, so at least I could be unaccompanied for the day.

When tending to my garden later, I saw a small note tucked into the old oak tree in the yard: "The oak tree branches should never be trimmed because all shelters need to remain hidden."

I inspected each and every branch and noticed there was a crack in their fence. The family who used to live here before us, in a small house before it became a teardown, had a teenage daughter who would sneak out of her yard and into the Edens's backyard. Eventually, she married their son. I miss love like that.

Moving the branches back carefully, I walked into their yard, like they had been waiting for me for years. The second I stepped onto their grass, I knew I would be okay here because I was hidden from the gossip of the other neighbors. The neighbors who loved to hate us because of the power this house had on the block. The neighbors who wanted to be our friends in hopes of getting something out of us. With money came users and liars.

I kept myself away from most of the people on this street because I did not trust them. I still don't, living in fear of one of the nosy neighbors spreading rumors and secrets about us. It feels better to be unseen, out of the public eye. All you have to do is look my name up online and see who I used to be married to, the legal cases, the custody battle, everything. I preferred to be a mystery, letting people think I was an uptight bitch rather than a mother terrified of every new sunrise because I didn't know what the day would bring.

From the window, Aletta was watching me. She opened the back door to let me inside and herded me into her home, like a lamb being rushed into its pen by a dog.

Aletta made me a hot cup of tea and gave me ice for my eye. Paul was sitting in his worn-down leather recliner, sipping on a cup of hot coffee, the steam disappearing into the air as he stared at me. I could tell he was worried about saying the wrong thing.

Aletta guided me to a seat on the couch next to Paul. Her home was cozier than ours, still large but filled with fondness. The walls a lighter color, with family photos on every inch of wall space. Farmhouse chic would be the way to describe her style. I preferred her home to mine. Aletta sat down on the couch, her face somber yet warm-hearted.

The candlelight flickered, and I watched the flame dance upon the wick as they began to talk.

"Calista, what happened?" Aletta asked.

My secrets would be safe with her, but I was still hesitant to say anything for fear of it getting back to Tanner.

"Paul is a retired police officer. You can talk to us. We won't say anything. We understand that people with money get a slap on the wrist, that their law is different than most," she said, her voice soft.

"It's nothing, really. It was an accident. I fell." I hoped my lie would be good enough for them to stop prying.

"Look, guys like that will kick you when you are down. They'll stomp on you until every bone is broken, until you are nothing more than dirt under someone's shoe. I've seen this a lot, and nine times out of ten, the wife can't leave because it's more dangerous to escape than it is to be complacent. You and your daughter have a safe place here if you ever need it. We will be here in the shadows, and whatever happens will be between us, okay?" With every word Paul speaks, I'm reminded of my father—a gentle and kind man, one adored by his family and friends.

Careful not to burn my tongue, I blow on my tea before taking a sip. There is only so much more pain I can take.

The only walls to know the full truth are within the home of Aletta and Paul, and in case anything ever happens to me, they agreed to take Ava. Later that month, I drafted up a will, just to be prepared. Though I didn't have my own money, I had a few special things I wanted her to have. I felt like a fool being married to two different men, both demonized by what life had to offer them.

The security I got from Paul and Aletta over the years meant everything to me, and the only time I had much of an appetite was when Aletta would make her famous muffins. She noticed my bones showing more through my clothes, my collar bone sharp enough to cut through my cotton T-shirts. Aletta would give me food and draw a warm bath for me at her house. She'd rub my wounds with a soft washcloth, letting the water drip down my spine with every stroke. Aletta wasn't just my neighbor, but a gentle reminder of my mother who had passed.

In my bones, I knew they would protect Ava and me, and they kept true to their promise because they knew men like Tanner would never stop if I left him.

As I step foot into their yard now, I head toward their back door. I have memorized every step to the asylum their home brings. The door slides open, and I step inside.

Paul and Aletta have aged over the years, but their spirits remain young, and with every year that passes, they get more kind, which is hard to believe when the world around us is so cruel. I sit down on their familiar couch and am handed a warm muffin and a hot cup of tea, as per usual. We sit in silence for several moments before anyone speaks.

I decide to go first because I am trying to be brave.

"Will it be ready next month?" I pray to God it will all be over soon.

Paul looks at me, placing his hand on my shoulder.

"We dug up enough space in our yard. When the first snowstorm happens and everyone is forced to be stuck inside, cuddled up on their couches with their fireplaces going, too preoccupied with their own lives and day off from work, we will do it, and not a moment before." Paul's voice sounds more assertive with every detail.

Aletta stays silent, sipping on her tea. I can feel her guilt about hiding a man's body in her yard, and I assure them I will be able to frame Tanner for all the money he stole from his enemies, that I will tell a convincing story. After the first few court meetings, I knew this was the only way, and Paul and Aletta agreed, making me firm in my decision to act soon. I filled them in on everything, no secret left unheard.

Paul walks me through all the steps on how to get away with murder, on how to be the victim, the grieving widow, to let the people have sympathy for me because no one like me could ever kill someone. The woman so spineless and small, no one would ever suspect me of killing. Of course, there would be some women in our area who would say I did it for his money, but Tanner has none. It's all a rouse. We are broke, and he won't sell our home for cash. Status is everything to him.

"Thank you for everything," I say.

"No one good deserves to be stuck in Hell," Aletta replies.

I walk back to my house that night through the yard, brushing aside the branches, and stop to stare at my plants, slowly wilting with the chilled air. Silently, I pray for the first storm of the year to hurry. The lawsuit is moving quicker than I'd like. We have another meeting soon about the next steps in the case.

The Brentwoods are putting up a damn good fight. When the time is right, I'll submit the evidence proving Josh wanted to give Ava money, the proof showing he really did love her. I turn up the heat to the house, unsure if it feels cold because of the lack of love inside, or if the air turning is the reason behind my bones feeling frozen.

Walking up the stairs, I head straight to Ava's room and crawl under her comforter. Wrestling with my thoughts, I hug the blanket around my frail body. If I tell Ava about my plan, there wouldn't be a way to protect her. If she has no idea, she can't tell the police anything- if and when they question her. She'll be at school, sitting in art class, and then I will call her and tell her the news myself.

I stare at the deep cracks along her doorframe and close my eyes, trying to remind myself I am not a bad mother.

I wish I believed myself.

SIXTEEN

AVA – THEN

The car ride to the courthouse seems longer than usual. My mom and Tanner picked me up from campus to all go together. Tanner stares at me from his rearview mirror, his eyes scheming. Bill said this could be a longer process than expected, and I'm sure he's benefiting on this whole thing being drawn out. I tug at my gray sweater; the turtleneck is suffocating me. The heat trapped inside me becomes too much. I roll down the window, but Tanner rolls it back up immediately.

We pass by the concrete jungle that is the city, one large skyscraper after the next. I peer into strangers' windows, with the possibility of someone looking at me as we drive by. I imagine a different life for myself with every new block we pass.

Finally, we arrive at a building with no character, simple and boring. The way I wish my life was most days. A nice doorman opens my car door. I look around to see if my half-sisters are nearby, but the street is empty. The air is more chilled now, and I can feel winter approaching, like a slow painful death. The wind brushes against my skin, and all the hair on my body stands upright. It hurts.

My mother steps out of the car, joining me as we walk into the building, Tanner follows quickly behind us, ignoring the doorman's simple greeting.

Bill says hello as we approach the elevator. Being trapped in one with both Tanner and Bill is insufferable, and I anxiously watch the numbers go up one by one as we wait to exit onto the tenth floor. Bill leads us to a small room, where a grueling mediation will begin. I look Bill up and down, studying his facial expressions, his mannerisms, any chance to catch him in a lie later. He looks smug in his suit from Nieman's, which doesn't look good on him at all. That suit is for a real man, not a con artist.

A shorter man with silver hair, about sixty years old, walks into the room, no greeting, no nothing. He clears his throat and sorts through paperwork, licking his fingers and looking through each one after the other. He nods. The sounds he makes become clear to me. He has to re-study the case for a few moments before we begin.

I glance over at my mother, who looks restless, her blonde hair out of place because she ran her hands through her hair too many times in the car ride over here, her makeup soft but dark enough to cover her bruises. My sweater begins to bother me again. I take both hands and stretch it out, but it still feels as if I'm asphyxiating.

The fact Tanner is here makes my blood boil, but there is nothing I can do since he is paying for it. Bill should be disbarred.

The Judge stands up and introduces himself.

"Hello, I'm Judge Howard," he says.

We all stand up and introduces ourselves. This feels worse than every first day of class I've had to endure. Once he sits down, we follow suit.

"The point of mediation is to reach a settlement without this having to go to court. This has proven to be an effective manner in reaching a resolution that both parties can walk away from, knowing it is the best possible outcome," Judge Howard says confidently.

Bill and Tanner whisper something to each other, but I'm sitting too far away to be able to pick up any hint of a word. My mother is holding on to something firmly in her hand, a small crinkled-up piece of paper.

The judge walks over to the board and writes a number down.

"This number is not to be spoken outside of this room, is that clear?" The sternness in his voice is absolute.

Everyone nods.

On the board, written with a red-colored marker, the color of a clown's nose, is the number eight hundred million, with a dollar sign before it. I had no idea the Brentwoods were worth that amount of money, and that was just Dad's portion. We knew they were rich later, but I had no idea they had that amount of wealth. *Billions.* Dad didn't want their money for years. He tried to not need them, tried to live a smaller life with me, but he went back to what he knew.

The room falls silent. I look over at Tanner. He has a smug smirk on his plump face. I can feel his heart racing from the other side of the room. I bet my mom felt like a fool for trying to get five hundred a month from them for child support.

It's no wonder Tanner wants me dead. Eight hundred million dollars. I keep repeating the number to myself over and over again.

Bill adjusts his tie and stands up to present the judge with his findings.

"Given the amount of wealth written on the board, my clients and I want to have a moment to discuss the amount of money we'd like to ask for," Bill says, confident he will have the judge eating out of the palm of his hand.

I wouldn't touch that man with a ten-foot pole, and I've touched a lot of men in my life.

Tanner stands up and tells the judge we want half, without even so much as a discussion. Bill nods. My mother and I look at each other, already knowing this will never happen. Bill and Tanner are living in a pipe dream, and all they can see are shades of green.

The judge writes that down in his notes and asks if there's anything else we'd like to tell him before he goes to the other side to mediate.

My mother shakes off her nerves and hands something to the judge.

"I noticed this during the discovery. When Victoria Brentwood turned over her spending from the trust, there seemed to be an error. I went and looked at the stocks, and they did not dip one million dollars in a day. It never did. I looked over the documents relentlessly, and something isn't right. Money was pulled for no reason. They may be pulling money and gifting it to each other to try to hide more of their finances, so I just thought maybe you should know that, before heading into the next room." She's proud of herself for her findings.

Bill's and Tanner's faces light up. I really wish they would leave.

The judge nods his head and walks into the room next door. I wonder who is in the other room. Is it Victoria the homewrecker and my two half-sisters, or just Victoria so her kids won't have to find out their mother is a conniving bitch?

The mediation room is lifeless, the walls a bleak gray color, sucking the souls out of anyone who has to spend time trapped inside of this box. Mediation seems so pointless. Both sides are stubborn, wanting nothing more than to stick to whatever it is that they think is right. I have no idea how this is going to go, but all I know is, whenever this is done, my plan will be set in motion.

An hour goes by. The judge has still not returned. He is probably being bribed in the room next door. Nothing is illegal if you have enough money, everyone knows this. Tanner and Bill leave the room to discuss things in private, while my mother nervously looks at her notes, all the information she gathered about the Brentwood family from years of torture.

She is ready.

She has been ready for this for half of her life now.

My mind starts to wander, and I think of Scott. I try not to, but my mind won't allow me to think of anyone or anything else. He'd laugh at the thought of me stuck in a boring, colorless room. The outline of his face branded into my memory. I miss his voice; I miss how everything felt possible with him. He wants nothing to do with me, though.

The clock looks like it stopped working, but I know it hasn't. It's an illusion. Apparently, mediations can often go on for fifteen hours at a time and sometimes last months. I leave the room to go to the bathroom, not thinking I needed permission for something so small.

The hallway is dimly light. The walls begin to feel like they are narrowing in on me. I walk into a stall, sit on the toilet, fully clothed, and take a few deep breaths.

The faucet turns on.

Quickly, I exit the stall and wash my hands. I glance at Victoria looking at herself in the mirror, trying her hardest to ignore me. We haven't been alone together almost ever. It's hard to believe she tried to steal me from my mother once.

The sound of the water splashes against the porcelain sink, the faucet not loud enough to drown out the sound of our hatred for one another.

She finishes lathering her hands with soap, making sure all the residue is off her skin. I don't even wait for her to grab a paper towel. I want to catch her off guard.

"Isn't it wild to think you knew my stepfather, before you married my dad?"

Her face turns stark white. She ignores me, and watching her pretend I don't exist satisfies me. Victoria reaches for a paper towel and begins to dry her hands.

"It was the weirdest thing. I was trying to find a stapler for my essay and came across a photo of you and Tanner together, taken years before my mother ever married him. Very odd. Two people who are so money-obsessed now stuck in mediation rooms, arguing over my father's family's fortune?" My voice is strong enough to intimidate her.

Victoria begins to walk out of the door, but before she has a chance to escape, I get in one final thing.

"I wonder what your own daughters would think of you, if they really knew what you did?" A small smile accidentally emerges.

Victoria slams the door shut behind her.

As I stare at myself in the mirror, I let my skin seer under the hot water of the bathroom's sink. I grab a paper towel and dry my hands, feeling the roughness of the material against my paint-stained palms. Pulling at my turtleneck once more, I yank it enough to hear the fabric stretch. I open the door and walk back to the mediation room.

Upon my arrival, everyone is sitting silently, waiting for my return. I grab a seat at the far back and wait for the judge to speak.

"The other side said they would be comfortable giving Ava one hundred thousand dollars. That is it. They feel they are being generous, as she was removed from the trust over a decade ago, and that is more than a healthy amount to start her own life with," Judge Howard says.

Although the offer is atrocious to Tanner and Bill, it fills me with joy to see the light flash before Tanner's eyes. His face is becoming a shade of red I could never replicate with paint, no matter how hard I tried to mix them. It is the color of distress, an agony so severe, death is the only option. The color looks wonderful on Tanner. It suits him well. He starts to pull his hair and yell, pacing back and forth.

"Those piece of shit bastards!" he yells.

The judge has seen this plenty of times, I'm sure of it.

Bill walks over to the judge, places his hand on the back of the chair, and whispers something to him. They both nod in agreement.

The judge looks at me, nobody else.

"Ava, how do you feel about this offer? Do you feel it would be in your best interest to take it, or would you like to give them a counteroffer?"

I know the judge doesn't really care about what I think. The court system is corrupt enough as it is. Every hour the judge is here, he gets paid over eight hundred dollars an hour, just to listen to people complain over money. The job, although easy, seems like torture. I look over at my mother and know we need a little more to start a new life somewhere, but if I say anything less than eight million dollars, I'm not sure what would lie ahead for me. Tanner would most likely get fed up and try to kill me while I lie sound asleep in my dorm.

There is only one answer everyone wants to hear from me, so I say it. Not what I really want to say, which is that I just need enough for a small cottage in the middle of nowhere, painting during the days on the street as a local vendor, working my way up to owning an art gallery, and riding my bike to my mother's house a few miles away in the evenings for a quiet dinner. I wanted to say one hundred thousand dollars is everything I could ever need.

But, I can't say any of that.

"I am one of three daughters, which means I want one-third of the total number."

My mother nods at my statement because she, too, knows there is no other answer Bill and Tanner will settle for.

The judge sighs. He knows we will be here all day, sitting in the same clothes, picking at the same warm turkey club sandwiches, staring out the one window, where we can see the outside world continue while we remain in this realm.

Bill gets a phone call and excuses himself, rushing out of the room. I see him nod several times through the small window in the door. He hangs up and walks back in the room, smiling.

"Your honor, it seems that the discovery the other side gave us and the reports of the stock and their value were a lie, and it has increased tremendously since then. They showed us ten year old reports."

The judge takes this in carefully.

"We'd like the other side to know that we aren't playing their games and that we no longer wish to mediate today, until we can get every receipt over the last sixteen years to prove that they live lavishly and have more than enough money to give to Ava, the first daughter of the late Joshua Brentwood, your honor."

"Very well," the judge says.

He leaves the room to tell the other side we will not be negotiating anymore today. I watch Victoria through the tiniest window in the door. She storms off, her bleach-colored hair bouncing behind her. A man follows, hurrying to comfort her.

My mother's gaze is stuck toward the gross sum of money written in red, the years we struggled when the Brentwoods wouldn't give us a dime for food or a place to stay. That number isn't even the full amount, just my father's portion. Each sibling is worth that, if not more, and then the parents probably double that. I used to watch Mom cry about how she failed me as a mother. Her tears were my oldest childhood memory. That money would have helped us never meet Tanner.

She used to tell me my dad wouldn't let her work when they were together because he wanted to take care of her. Everything that was his was hers, until it wasn't.

The Brentwood family kept their money close to them, and not a dime out of their accounts went unnoticed. I find it strange how one million dollars is not accounted for. They are hiding something. Maybe they bribed the judge, or maybe Bill is in on it? That would be the most logical answer.

The same man who my mother used to hate for what he did to her, for his addiction, his drinking, his violence, was the same man who, over a decade and a half later, would come over for dinner for his weekly visitation with me. It was almost like he wanted to be a better father because he knew he was going to die one day, that his heart condition wasn't going to get any better, unless a miracle happened. Dad didn't want to die a bad person; I don't think anyone does. His reason for being a better person seemed almost selfish, but I watched him change, and it helped my mother's wounds slowly scab over, still there, still visible, but in a new phase of sympathy.

Every week, my dad would come over for dinner, and when he would leave, he slipped us each one hundred dollars. At first, my mother kept it a secret from Tanner. Whenever he'd be away finding new investors for his new companies that never seemed to happen, my dad would come over for dinner. My mom would work hard in the kitchen before the occasion, but she never told me, in case he cancelled. I'd come home from school and there he would be, sitting at the table ready to eat a homecooked meal with us. Dad didn't say much about his other life, but whenever the phone would ring, he would silence it.

He chose us.

It didn't take me long to forgive my father for everything he did—the homelessness, the starving on the streets, sleeping at strangers' homes until my mom found us a safe place.

My grandpa had spent all his money on cancer treatments for my grandma, having to double mortgage their house, and could barely keep up on paying their bills. So when everything was going on with my mom and the divorce, they could only help so much. In the end, their debt became her debt.

In the beginning, we had a warm bed to sleep in and a home filled with loved, but once my grandma died from breast cancer, my grandpa died of a broken heart. Everything was gone. They say that's how you can tell two people are truly in love—how close in time they die together. After that happened, my mother and I had nowhere to stay. The bank took back my grandparent's home. Anything they owed on bills, we paid off with what little we had. We were on the street with a suitcase and a plastic bag filled with cheap gas station food.

Sometimes, my mother's friends took us in. My mother would try to work whatever job she could, but it was never enough money because no one wanted to hire a single mother to a newborn, who had to leave work to pump or who didn't have enough experience in her field.

My mother could barely afford her legal bills from the lawyer who represented her, and she used what little money my grandma had given her in secret to help her with her case. The Brentwoods forbid my father from paying any child support to my mother because we were undeserving of the title. My grandmother—if you could even call her that—made sure to give the judge extra money for an early retirement. There was no competition, and there were no rules when it came to the Brentwoods.

The Brentwood lawyer claimed my mother married my father solely because of his last name, that she had planned the entire thing from the start as a high schooler. Their lawyer, although convincing, was grossly wrong because my father pursued *her*, not the other way around.

All the girls were madly in love with my father. He was charming and had a contagious laugh. My mother said he was talented in giving someone the world…and then crashing a meteor into it.

My dad didn't find out about his heart condition until he was in high school, but I think maybe he thought that if life was short, he needed to do everything he wanted to do, no matter the repercussions of who he hurt, including my mother and me. I did have sympathy for him, which is why when he started coming around for dinner to make amends, we gave him a chance. My mother thought it would be for the best.

She said back then, his drinking became so excessive and his anger scarier with every sip. Soon, the drinking turned to drugs, and the drugs turned to manic episodes, to the point where she stopped going out with him and would stay home to raise me. Dad had affair after affair, desperate to be wanted, for people to adore him, but he was too naive to realize he had that all at home.

My dad knew something most didn't—how much time he had. Things like that can change a person.

Every day, my mom thanked God that I was too little to remember everything that happened. She wanted to leave him, but like every fool, she loved him just enough to try to help him.

When I got older, my mother told me things I couldn't piece together from my childhood. She promised to always be honest with me; however, she wasn't honest with herself. As we would sit and eat brisket and mashed potatoes at the table not meant for this original family, my mother and father sharing a meal together, we just ignored how we got here in the first place. My mother thought it would be best if we just moved on and only focused forward. She said we should forgive people for their past because if we don't, we'll be stuck there with them forever, in a vicious cycle of bad memories. If we dwelled on those, we'd get stuck down the rabbit hole, with no hope to crawl out of it one day.

When I get home that evening from the mediation, I walk into my dorm room paid for by the copious amounts of drugs Easton had me sell for him and lay my head down on the pillow, melting into its feathers. The world we lived in is so fucked up, people, places, things, just existing, making other things cease to exist.

Staring at the ceiling, I look at the glow-in-the-dark stars left by the person before me slowly beginning to unstick from the cheaply made popcorn ceiling. I watch the smallest corner of one of the stars curl just so slightly.

In the morning, I get ready for my class before a full day of dealing and meeting clients. I walk to the mirror and brush my hair with a fine-toothed comb, feeling pieces of my hair get stuck between the teeth. A chill spreads all the way to my spine when I wash my face with cold water. I apply mascara, my lips pursing slightly open with each stroke, and grab jeans and a flannel to wear for this beautiful fall day. The colors melt onto the ground, crunching beneath my feet as I walk to art class.

Today's agenda will presumably be learning about tortured artists. The rest of the class will be bored, but I'll be enthralled, learning about how these artists survived, what got them through their demonic habits, their mysterious lives.

Just as I arrive to the building my class is in, I lose focus when the wind picks up, and my paper on top of my book flies off, landing a few feet away. I go to get it but feel a hand on my paper. When I look up, I see everything I missed.

Scott.

He hands me the piece of paper without realizing it is me at first. We hold each other's gaze for a while before quickly walking in the other direction. I haven't known pain like this before, not until him.

He was the person I told everything to. Now it's bottled up inside me, the pressure causing a catastrophe.

All through class, the teacher rambles on and on about Picasso. The students are half asleep because everyone knows Picasso was as mad as they come…until me.

SEVENTEEN

VICTORIA – THEN

The mediation did not go as planned. Running into Ava in the bathroom made me want to pull every hair from my head. I don't want her to have a single dime of the Brentwood money. Josh promised me after I told him I had a way to fix *his* problem, that in exchange he'd write Ava out of the trust, but that bastard two-timed me and knew exactly what he was doing.

I grab a glass of wine and melt into my couch. Erik needs to figure out a way to make up for that missing million dollars. The Brentwood family now knows something is not right because their lawyers will get a full written play by play of everything that went on in mediation today.

I'm expecting a phone call later, screaming my head off about where that million went. Everything we buy, even if it's a bottle of shampoo, must be approved by the Brentwoods. I have no idea how Josh lived like this for so long. Granted, they controlled him because, without his special medication that practically costs the price of one Rolex every week, he'd have died years ago. Josh's organs started to slowly fail him, and then it became daily dialysis.

I finish my glass of wine and walk to the kitchen to pour myself one more, when I get a text with an address. I thought we were done with this.

In a moment of rage, I throw away the bottle and walk with my glass up the plush carpet stairs that were put in a few months ago, a present to myself for being a grieving widow. Josh never wanted white carpet, but he's not here anymore. The Brentwoods approved the carpet because they felt bad my husband died.

At the end of the upstairs hallway is the bedroom we used to share. Now nothing is left of him in that room. Both nightstands are mine, the room decorated however I so please. I place my glass down and walk toward the closet. In the very back, I reach for a box and pull out a few stacks of cash. Josh and I have been saving money here and there from the trust, hoping no one would notice a small amount of money missing in the grand scheme of their almost multi-billion-dollar fortune. To them, though, one million is twenty million over the course of several years with the right investments. The Brentwoods would have never approved of this, though, even if they have done much worse. I made sure Josh told me everything, in case I needed it one day, because blackmail is the only way to stay in that family.

The Brentwoods' past haunts them like an old friend, desperate to sabotage them, secrets wound so tight that a single thread out of place could make their entire family burst at the seams.

The aroma of cotton and ink seep into my nose. I take a hundred thousand dollars more and place it on the bed, then dig in the closet for a subtle purse to place the money in. Nothing too flashy that would make someone assume I have more money than I do. I head out the door, my glass in my hand. There's no time to put this back in the kitchen. *She* is growing impatient with me.

As I leave our main street and drive toward the poor side of the city, I think of my childhood, how I tried so hard to escape that life, only to wind up back where it all started. My obsessive urge to be wealthy, to be somebody, the conning I had to do to become Victoria Brentwood...I didn't just burn the bridge I took to get here; I demolished it.

Upon my approach to Englewood, I hear gunshots in the distance. I stopped ducking from the sounds when I was around five or six. The houses are decrepit and falling apart. All the windows have metal gates on them, and the doors have multiple locks. I wish I could say it felt good to be home, but it never has. I wanted a bigger life, and I got it, the strings still attached.

The houses are small, filled with two families in about four hundred square feet. Kids are playing basketball in the street, while their parents sit on their lawn chairs, having a beer, celebrating making it another day. I pull up to a house. The windows are boarded up, and the roofing looks like, at any moment, it will collapse. I park my car on the side of the street and don't even bother locking it. If someone really wanted something, they'd do a smash and grab.

Kids on the block are staring at me. I know what they are thinking; I once thought that too. After knocking on the door, I wait for Marla to answer. I look at my reflection in the glass, broken up by the metal bars. My skin has aged a lot the last few months. My roots need a dye, and my crow's feet are too prominent to look at these days. Being a widow has not been kind to me, but keeping this secret has practically dug my own grave.

Marla comes to the door quickly, shushing her four children, all under the age of sixteen. She's a short, plump woman who has never had a spa day in her life. Marla wipes the dirt off her face with her shirt, exposing her midriff. She does not greet me with a smile as she unlocks the bolts on her door.

Marla rushes me into her house, if you can even call it that. She sits me down at the table. I watch her reach for a pack of cigarettes. She takes her lighter and places her hand over the flame, lighting one. Marla takes a puff of her cigarette before speaking, as if to gather her thoughts.

"Did you bring it?" she says sternly.

I nod. "Yes."

I take out the money from my purse. It smells fresh, the dollars crisp and packed together.

"Where is the rest of it?" she asks, quickly skimming the stacks.

"It's all there, one hundred thousand," I say, confused.

"The way I see it is that you lied. This trade we did was not fair, and my poor children are going to have to suffer now, and that is on you." Marla points her finger at me, just barely touching me in the chest.

I begin to feel uneasy. It was supposed to be simpler than that. It was a done deal, but with the news of everything, they found out. People in the neighborhood I grew up in, they live vicariously through others because when you're trapped in hell, all you can do is survive by living in a fantasy.

"I want another mil."

The pit in my stomach begins to churn. My money is connected to the Brentwoods. Whatever I spend is approved by them, even my daughters' money. Everything goes through their trust lawyers. Erik will need to find another loophole in the system, better than last time.

"A deal is a deal," I say firmly, trying to hold my ground.

Marla reaches for something in her back pocket and slams it down on the table. A blade, thick enough to cut flesh, stares back at me.

"You have two weeks, or I'll go to the press," she says, without so much as blinking.

"No one will believe you." I excuse myself from the table, clutching onto my purse tightly.

"Hospital and coroner reports don't lie. I may be poor, but I'm not dumb. You of all people should know this." She taps her fingers on the blade. "I'll see you soon." Her words are patronizing.

I hurry back to my car, the windows still intact, not that it matters. All of this was done for my family, and look where it got me. I should have known that if anything went wrong, I'd be forced into giving Marla and her family more money.

The tires of my car screech when I speed off. I want to get home as quickly as I can. Erik will know what to do. He usually does. I'll want to talk to my daughters first, but I need to find a way to tell them what I did. They'll forgive me. I did it for them. And they will see that; they have to. Now that their father is dead, the Brentwood money goes to them, not me. The children get the money, slowly over time. The money is never given to anyone a Brentwood leaves, and those are the rules. The key is to hold on long enough, even if a Brentwood wants to leave you, so you can get your payout. Having kids helps the fortune continue through a different family lineage, like mine.

I reach for the glass of wine in my cup holder and gulp it down, not even caring if I get pulled over. It would be the least of my worries.

I stop at the liquor store and grab another bottle of wine, a bottle of red, just in case I get home and realize there is none left, plus another pack of cigarettes. My lungs crave the irritation the smoke causes, my blood thirsty for the nicotine to enter it.

I'll tell the girls what happened at mediation this morning. The lawyers advised that they not be there for the first one, in case they found out about the adultery, in case the Maple lawyer played dirty, which I wouldn't put it past him. All lawyers do.

Ashley, the spitting image of me, she'll throw a fit about the money that is rightfully hers. She'll cuss and stomp her feet and say things like, "Our dad isn't her dad," and, "She has her own life; why does she want to bother us in ours?"

Allison will want to give money to Ava. The child that is least like me, she constantly wants to do right by others. I look at her, confused how I gave birth to someone so virtuous. She reminds me of Calista sometimes, and it makes me feel sick. God gave me a piece of Calista so I'd have to be reminded of what I did to break up that marriage.

I pull up to the house and walk inside. The girls are watching a movie in the living room, eating pizza, glued to the fluff of romantic comedies that are nothing more than a lie. They'll learn one day there's a reason real life isn't like that, but I'll let them enjoy their film for now.

The stairway back to my room feels longer than it did this morning, my legs seemingly heavier with each step. I make it to my bedroom and walk toward my closet again, rummaging through the box and counting every dollar bill in my possession. All that's left is thirty thousand, everything else has been given to pay off Marla.

I don't want to ask *her* for more money. She already is covering most of the legal fees. I can't owe her.

So, I curl up in bed, staring at the ceiling until I fall asleep on my silk pillowcases, a luxury I used to dream of having when I was growing up.

EIGHTEEN

ALLISON – NOW

The house on Kenilworth looks more discomforting with every season that passes while it remains empty. The only warmth inside of it has been a few realtors walking through, doing house inspections for prospective buyers who aren't even phased someone died in that house. The people who want to live on this street make excuses for those types of things that would usually detour others from wanting to buy a home here, but to live here is to be admired. I still don't know how they can sell a missing persons' home.

I wish I could stop forcing myself to come back. I wish I wasn't addicted to knowing Ava, to wanting to know every detail of her life.

Taking the key out of my pocket from Ava's room, I fumble around, feeling the smoothness of the sides and the roughness of its teeth along my finger. I haven't had much time to figure out what this key belongs to, and I have no idea where to even start. It frustrates me.

My car keeps me warm for only a few minutes longer after I shut off the engine, but I can't bear to leave its safety. I feel sick to my stomach for what I know I need to do now. Zipping up my coat, I try to take in as much of the heat as I can before stepping outside into the cold afternoon. I close my car door quietly and quickly cross the street.

Reaching for my notepad, I write down each address I plan to stop at. I'll begin at the house at the end of the block first and make my way down to Ava's neighbors. Someone is hiding something; rich people love to know everyone's business. Half the time, that's what high tea is for, to talk about other people and their shortcomings and failures.

The first house is more of a modern farm-style home, decorated with pumpkins on the porch and tacky-looking spiders on the wall, the size of a large dog. I ring the doorbell; I feel like I'll freeze up if someone answers. No one comes to the door, so I try again. Nothing. I walk to the next house, a large modern Tudor home, and anxiously wait after I ring the doorbell. No one comes. Just as I am about to walk to the next house, I hear a creak, and the door slowly opens. A beautiful suburban soccer mom answers the door.

"Can I help you?" she asks. It's hard to tell if she's nice or if it's just an act.

"I'm Allison. Um, I was wondering if you could answer a few questions for me? I'm taking a survey about the area, for the local high school paper." I hope my lie is adequate.

"Oh, sure. Go Ravens!" she says, opening the door wider and signaling for me to come inside. She leads me toward the living room.

The interior of her home is decorated very dark. The only brightness is the last light from outside, entering through the windows. The lady walks toward her kitchen and grabs a fresh plate of cookies and some hot cocoa. She gently sets the plate down in front of me, insisting I try one.

"I'm Noreen, by the way." She reaches for one of her own cookies, takes a bite, and smiles.

Noreen isn't the kind of woman who looks like she eats sweets, her body frail and her black hair tightly wound up in a high pony, without a single strand out of place. She puts the cookie back down on the plate.

I was right. It's an illusion that she would eat something with calories.

"What year are you? Sorry, I can't remember if you told me or not," she says.

"Oh, I'm a junior." I reach for a cookie to try one. The cookies smell fresh. The hints of cinnamon are pleasantly surprising when I bite into one, and the chocolate melts in my mouth. They are store-bought, but I don't care. I'll eat this whole plate, since she won't.

Noreen perks up. "My eldest is a freshman in college, and my other son is a junior. Maybe you know him?" She looks excited. Noreen is the mom who tells people her son is popular, but he's probably a bully.

"I just moved here a couple of months ago, so I don't know too many kids yet. It's why I joined a few clubs, so I could meet some people and stuff."

"Of course, of course!"

I take out my notebook and try to think of a survey quickly, but nothing comes to mine. Trying to stall, I reach for another cookie.

"Would you mind if I ask you those few questions now?"

"I'm ready when you are," she says, her hands neatly folded on her lap.

"Okay, I'm taking a survey if more money should go toward the art program at the high school versus the sports teams. Many students feel that their extracurriculars aren't properly funded because everything goes to the local football team." I pray this sounds half believable. In every movie I've ever watched, that is usually a thing students are upset about.

Noreen's Botox makes it nearly impossible to tell what she is thinking when she begins to speak.

"The sports teams bring in a lot of sponsors and scholarships, so I think the money is in the right place."

Her kids are obviously both student athletes.

"I appreciate your candor, Noreen. I also think sports funding is so important." It pains me to speak such falsehoods.

She smirks.

"How do you like living here?"

I use this as my moment, while I am in her good graces. She likes me because she's the kind of woman who likes anyone who agrees with her.

"I like it a lot, but a lot of the kids at school…They've been gossiping about this Ava girl that I think used to live around here, or something?" I answer coyly.

I watch Noreen's lips purse together. She's calculating all the different ways this conversation can go. I hope her lips leave a loose enough crack to let the secrets spill out of them. She takes me for one of those types of women.

"Oh, well, um…" She pauses, reaching for her drink again.

"Sorry, I shouldn't have asked." I'm hoping she'll feel guilty and tell me something.

"You're fine. I'm surprised kids are still talking about the incident and all, but when you live in a house like that, in a place like this…"

She waits a few seconds before finding the proper words for a child to hear.

"She was troubled, so I'm not surprised she…you know…She was sleeping with several of the men around town, the *married* men, mind you. My husband would never. He's not like that, thank God." She takes a deep breath. "They paid her well, but she probably just couldn't live with herself anymore. I mean, to be a call girl at such a young age, when you have all that money at your fingertips? It's abysmal, on top of all that family drama. I mean, it's a lot to live with."

I nod.

The walls in her house begin to slowly close in on me. My chest feels like someone is ripping through skin and yanking at my heart, slowly squeezing it. I am in disbelief.

"Are you okay? You look pale." Noreen walks to her kitchen to get me a glass of water. She comes back, hands me the delicate glass, and watches me closely as I take a sip.

"Thank you, sorry. I have asthma, and the weather has been making it act up a bit. I'm not used to seasons. I moved from Florida."

"You'll get used to it," she says.

I muster up enough mental strength to continue my search for answers.

"Did she, like, have a secret meeting place or something? How did people find out about it?" My interest is skyrocketing through the roof.

"We love to talk around here. You'll come to learn that secrets in Woodburry don't die with you. Especially when it gets cold outside.

There isn't much to do but gossip." She winks at me, and I feel nauseated.

"Was her family aware of it? Was it, like, this big scandal through the town?" I ask, awaiting more information, like a drug I can't stop taking.

"Oh, it didn't come out until after her death. There was a note that she left. It was upstairs in her room. It had a list of all the husbands and a dollar amount next to each one of their names. She was a good little bookkeeper apparently." Noreen looks out the window, checking to see how much light is left in the day. "If you start to hate her, you'll fit in more around here. Trust me."

I thank her and give her a hug, but her touch makes me want to rub my skin with bleach.

"Welcome to the area. Let me give you my son's number. You're cute and petite, so he'd probably just adore you. He's a strong football player. All the girls fawn over him. He's a real looker."

Noreen hands me her son's number on a piece of paper, her handwriting dainty. I'd expect nothing less.

With a wave, I walk out the door and make my way toward the next house. I am in disbelief of what I just heard. It can't be. That Ava was a call girl? It makes no sense. Why did she need all that money? Their house was the nicest one on the block. Everyone wanted to be a Maple—even me when I first learned about her.

The next three houses go unanswered. I slowly walk back to Ava's and try one of her neighbors. The house next to the Maple home is small, the tiniest on the block, a single-level home you can tell has been here since the street first came to be. I wait a few minutes after ringing the doorbell, hoping someone will answer, and to my good fortune, a little old woman does, her husband by her side.

The husband clears his throat before answering.

"Can we help you?"

"You sure can," I say, unsure if I'm ready to hear anything else that may break me. I don't know how much more I can handle, and I'm starting to question myself.

This couple's home is quaint, the kind with cute sayings on the walls that others often make fun of. I begin to think maybe Ava really did kill herself, that I am chasing nothing but ghosts.

"We are Greg and Shari, and you are?"

"Allison."

They sit me at their kitchen table, old and sturdy, nothing flashy about this couple. I'm sure if they sold their home, it would just be bulldozed for the land, another mansion going up in its place.

"What survey are you taking today that we can assist with?" Greg asks, his hand holding his wife's.

"Oh, I'm taking a survey about proper funding for afterschool education and the effects the sports funding has on the art programs." My lies are slowly becoming more real the more I tell them.

"Lovely," Shari says, clasping her hands together in excitement. She lights up when answering my question.

"I think more money should go to the arts. I mean, the school gets a substantial amount of money because the property taxes are a fortune in this area, but don't get me wrong. It benefits the students tremendously. I think that the money should be split equally. There are a lot of differences, though. Sport safety costs more than a paint brush." She laughs at this.

I let out a slight cackle, which makes her face twinkle. She is a people-pleaser.

Greg and Shari walk me toward the front door to see me out, but before Greg has a chance to turn the handle, I blurt out a question so fast, it stops him in his tracks. The door remains open.

"Were you there the day it happened?" I ask, my voice jumpier with every word.

They look at each other with hesitation, trying to find a polite way to tell me to mind my own business and what's done is done.

I stare at them blankly, hoping for something.

"We think it's best you leave," Greg says.

Shari nods, standing beside him.

"Please, I just—" The door is open behind me, and the breeze chills my bones.

"All you need to know was that that family was cursed. It's no secret the father had some anger issues, and the girl struggled with depression, but we can't help you. Unless you are the police, we aren't going to answer any more of your questions. Her death has taken up too much of our time already…and lowered the property value of our home. Best of luck with your school survey."

The door closes instantly. Walking back to the sidewalk, I pass by the Maple house, losing momentum in my search. I ring the doorbell of the Maples' other neighbor, and another couple answers quickly.

"Hello?" the man says, curious as to what I'm doing there.

"I need help." It's the truth this time.

The nice man quickly escorts me into his house, and his wife seems puzzled when I walk in. He quickly takes my jacket and seats me next to the fireplace, their dog is sound asleep enjoying the warmth,

"I'm Paul, and that over there is my wife, Aletta. Are you in danger?" he asks, his words soothing me.

"No, it's not like that. It's…"

I look around at their cozy home, the pictures on the wall, and notice a drawing in similar style to the ones Ava did. The brush strokes mixed with a palette knife, the colors alternating to form more depth in her landscapes, I can tell it's hers. I've seen several more like this in her room.

"I'm Allison Brentwood," I say, without a single drop of confidence in my voice.

Aletta drops the cup she is holding, sending shards of glass everywhere. She bends down to pick it up piece by piece, making sure nothing is left behind.

Paul looks at me. The smile on his face is long gone.

"What are you doing here?" he asks, his voice stern.

"I…I never got to know her, and I just…well…She's gone, and I…" The tears won't stop forming in my eyes, and I can't control my sobbing. My cheeks are wet from every teardrop falling on them, and my lips are covered in my own snot. I try to gather myself.

Aletta rushes over and puts her arms tightly around me. I melt into her shoulder, weeping. Paul looks at me, sympathetic but unsure how to approach this.

"There there," Aletta says, making a shushing sound and rocking me in her arms, side to side.

I look at her and wipe my eyes with my long-sleeve shirt, now stained with makeup.

Paul sits down on the sofa, waiting until I gather myself enough to be able to speak in a calm manner. He waits patiently for me and doesn't try to tell me to stop crying. He lets me have this moment.

I collect myself and try to muster a few words, hoping it's the right thing, but there really isn't a right way to say anything in these types of situations. Not that I've ever been in one like this before.

"I'm so sorry to bother you. It's just…I…nothing feels like how it did. I can't focus. Just breathing feels like something entirely new. I figured since you lived next door, you might be able to tell me what happened?"

The fire cackles, making the quietness of the room feel less empty. For this, I'm grateful.

"We are so sorry for your loss," they say one after the other.

Words that cause me nothing but anguish and bad memories since my father died. That's all I heard for months at a time. "I'm sorry for your loss," or "My condolences." But secretly, everyone is glad it happened to me and not them.

I nod at their responses, staying quiet so they will know I'm ready for them to continue.

Aletta grabs my hand. "Look, sweetheart, I wish we knew more, but the truth is, we told the police everything we know. The day she died, we weren't home. We were visiting our grandchildren."

Aletta looks at Paul. I can tell they are trying to decide if they should say anything more.

Paul takes over for her while Aletta walks over to me and rubs my shoulders.

"Ava was a very troubled young girl, and her family life was rather difficult. It's a shame that her parents are missing. It truly is." Paul gets on his knees, sitting beside me and holding my right hand.

I don't deserve the kindness these strangers have to offer. I point to Ava's picture on the wall, and their gaze follows.

"Why do you have her artwork on your wall?"

Paul lets out a loud sigh.

"Ava gave us one of her paintings, before she went to college. She was cleaning out her room and said she thought we'd appreciate this one and give it a safe home," Aletta says.

"It's best if you just try to remember her in a positive light," Paul adds.

"I can't remember her because I don't know her." I wipe my face again, get up, and head toward the door. "Thank you for your time." The salt seeps into my chapped lips.

"Anytime, sweetheart," Aletta says, unlocking the front door.

Frantically digging for my car keys before I exit their home, I drop the contents of my purse. I'm not sure how it happened, but I quickly go to pick everything up. Aletta bends down to help me, handing me each item that is strewn all over her hallway.

Aletta pauses, holding the key I found in Ava's bedroom. She studies it quickly before handing it back to me. Her eyes seem lost in the tongues and grooves of the key, like mine when I first found it.

"Wouldn't want to lose that. Keys aren't something to misplace," Aletta says jokingly.

Paul and Aletta look at each other from down the hall.

I think they know what that key goes to. I don't believe them anymore. I don't believe anyone.

As I run to my vehicle, the rain starts to come down. I sit inside my car for a moment before driving around the corner and parking it. I throw my coat over my head and run toward Ava's house. I don't want my car on the side of the street where the neighbors can pry. Being seen is not something I want.

The lockbox is still on the door. I fumble with it, my hands more slippery from the rain, until it opens.

The house is dark. The only things living inside are the demons of its past. I run up the staircase to Ava's room. She needs to have left more clues.

The door to her room is open, and everything is turned upside down. Her artwork was thrown on the ground, her paint leaking on the beautiful hardwood floors. Her school notes are scattered all over the place, covered in water and dirt. Her room did not look like this when I was last here. It was over-picked, and things were missing, but it looked nothing like this.

Someone's been here again.

Was it Paul and Aletta?

In the dark, her room looks black. The power to the house has been cut, while a new buyer waits to hear if they got the house that a girl died in. A fun story to tell over a cocktail night, pretending it's haunted, making ghost sounds. While the couple's friends laugh at someone's misfortune, they'll say, "Anything for a good school district," and other things like that.

My phone has enough battery left in it to turn on its flashlight. I take a quick glance at her room in case I missed anything. Sitting on the ground, picking up each piece of paper after the next, I place them back in Ava's dresser in a neat pile, examining each one. Her notes are one-lined poems and short stories. Some I've read the last few times I was in her room. The rest of it is just notes about color theory and art history.

I walk toward her nightstand and notice everything inside it is gone. The love letters from Scott that I left behind aren't on the ground either with the rest of the piles of notes. In fact, they cease to exist. All the words carefully picked out for Ava are no longer. Who would possibly want to take that?

I think back to the voices I heard the last time I was here. Maybe it was the men she had affairs with looking to clear their names or family members of theirs, ashamed, making sure there wasn't another list of sorts. It slowly begins to make more sense to me now. A town that gossips doesn't have ghosts; it has demons, desperate to remain hidden in large homes and bank accounts.

My heart tells me it was a suicide. I'm finally trying to stop being in denial. I stare at her balcony and picture how she was the day it happened. Her mother and stepfather, no matter how dismal he may have been, are gone, missing, presumed dead. The rest of the town thinks she did it, the local whore, ruining marriages, galivanting around town with her boyfriend, keeping secrets from him.

I think about how she felt like she never fit in in this world, that in another life she would be free. Her paintings were her way to call out for help, her art her suicide note, a way for her to tell the world, "Don't forget me, even though you detest me." She wanted to remain on the walls of those who loved her, but who loved her?

The rain outside becomes louder, my thoughts competing with the sound. I think about my father and how Ava is selfish, to be able to spend more time with him in the afterlife. That is, if one even exists. My cheeks become heated, and I think of all the times he went over to her home for dinner while he neglected his new family, the one he chose over Ava's. Me.

Taking the palette knife sitting on her nightstand, I stab one of her paintings repeatedly until the rage begins to leave my body. I scream as loud as I can, letting the neighbors know this home is haunted with the cries of a young woman. Both her and me.

The key I'm holding so tightly begins to indent into my flesh. I put it back into my purse and run out the front door. The rain is heavy now, beating down on me and making it hard to see. I wipe the rain from my eyes and walk quicker toward my car, but the streets are beginning to flood. After falling, I get back up, sopping wet. I'm so close to my car. I just want to go home, even if it hasn't been the same since my dad died. Maybe I need to cancel my plans with Scott…I just can't.

Everything is *not* fine, not in the slightest. I reach for my phone and begin to text my mother that I'm on my way from a friend's house. The rain picks up, and I put it in my pocket. I'll finish texting her when I get inside my car. Barely able to see in front of me, I wipe rain from my eyes several more times, checking to make sure no cars are coming. The rain hurts my body, like Mother Nature warning me to go home, to stay away. That good things don't happen to people who live on this street. I'm listening to her, and I won't ever come back.

As I get to the middle of the road, my body falls to the ground, and I hear tires screeching. I lay in the cold rain, motionless. I've never felt a pain like this before. My body is completely numb yet on fire at the same time. I look around with what energy I have left. My gaze stops. I can make out the outline of the castle-like silhouette of the Maple home, it's architectural feature the most prominent on the block, a beacon of death. It's the last thing I see before everything starts to fade to black.

NINETEEN

CALISTA – THEN

On days Josh joins us for family dinner, I become a bit neurotic. A part of me thinks it's because I can show him what a life would have been like with us if he'd stayed. I fix up the couch where I find myself sleeping, close to an exit incase Tanner is in one of his moods, and fluff each square pillow into shape, smoothing out the couch cushions.

Ava will be home from school later. She'll be pleasantly surprised to have her father over for dinner. He is finally on the mend since he had his surgery a few months ago. Josh has needed a lot of surgeries over his lifetime, so I don't even bother asking what this one was for. I can tell it upsets him.

Tanner will be home tonight, but he'll sit on the living room sofa and ignore Josh's entire existence, something he has no problem doing. Sometimes, I wish I'd listened to Josh on the day of our wedding. Instead, I scolded him for what he did to me and for how angry I was about how my life was turning out. I had every right in my bone to speak my truth. I listened to him when it was too late. My bed so tightly made, that you could suffocate yourself with the finest Egyptian cotton.

I wipe down the crumbs on the kitchen counter that you can only see if the light hits the marble just right; otherwise, it's hard to notice something is there. It's a lot like lies, easily overlooked.

The door to Tanner's office isn't locked today, so I crack it open and peer inside before entering. I've been rummaging through his desk a lot the last few years, my suspicion growing that we are broke. The credit cards have been declined when I buy groceries sometimes, or when I try to pay the cleaning company at the house. He cancelled the new appliances he wanted for the kitchen, his excuse being that things aren't made how they used to be. His behavior has been growing more hostile toward myself and Ava, resulting in the constant repairs of the holes in the walls before a visitor arrives. A house I tried desperately to make feel like a home, but it never took, so a house it stays.

As I walk into Tanner's office, I stop and look at myself in the mirror on the wall. I've aged, not just because of the years that have passed, but for every year that had no love in it. It ages someone faster. I rummage through his drawers and re-read the lawsuit from his brother. Tanner saved his replies in an email and stapled it next to his brother's letter. His brother was suing him because he wouldn't show him what amount was left in their family's trust. Tanner said his brother isn't capable of having access to it whenever he wants because he's a loser with no direction. He gives him a certain amount every month, but his medication is more costly. Tanner berates him on his lifestyle of smoking weed and living in a shack by the beach.

It sounds simple...nice.

I put back the paperwork exactly as I found it, not a corner creased, nothing out of place, and type in the password to his computer. Only a narcissist would use their own birthday as the password. No one else is as important as him. His email was left open, and I see dozens and dozens of emails from a lawyer about his family trust. It looks like it's been drained. Millions…gone.

As I scroll through more, I stop at an email from a lawyer advising him the money needs to be put back, that over two hundred million is missing. How is that even possible? He has all these new investors for his new company, so where could all his money have gone? I lean back in his leather office chair and look at the pictures hanging on the wall. Never one of Ava or me. We never made the cut. His office walls are for only his achievements.

My mind starts to wonder about Tanner's parents' money. They are elderly and in a home, depending on that money to be taken care of until their deaths. I feel awful for thinking it, but the people who raised Tanner are some of the most brash and rude people I've ever met. It makes sense. They used to dine with the Brentwoods at the country club. The Maple family always wanted to one up the Brentwoods, but they never could. They were never going to be in the same league.

The clock reads one in the afternoon, and the day is getting away from me quicker than expected. I rush out of his office, leaving the door the exact way I found it, the thought looming over my head that we are broke. Sure, I could get a job, but who would hire a mother with no work experience and a college degree from two decades ago? The best I could get is a cashier job, but ten dollars an hour would barely pay the car payments, or school for Ava, let alone feed us.

Everyone always says the kitchen is the heart of the house, and they are right. This is the only place I find comfort. I walk to the refrigerator and pull out the fresh produce I picked from my garden earlier in the day. It will make a nice stew for dinner. I find the beautiful Damascus chef's knife Tanner got for the house, not because he liked to cook, but because he said it is the best of the best. Like everything in our house, it had to be the finest money could buy. It's no wonder, with a mentality like that, our money is gone.

The juice and seeds pour out from the sides of the ripest tomato, bursting when I slice through its flesh, the knife so sharp it makes me uneasy. I finish dicing up the tomatoes and move onto the carrots. Josh sent me an e-mail what the doctors told him he could and could not eat. He'd be easy to kill with how sick he was, but no one knows about his disease, except for his own family and myself.

I can't imagine what it's like to be born with an expiration date, to have doctors tell you you'd be lucky to live until high school and, after high school, you'd be lucky enough to see the Cubs win a world series one day. I try my hardest to forgive him for being such a horrible person to me for all those years, for the trauma he caused. All the times he came home drunk, angry, swinging at me, I knew he was suffering, but he never got help. His family thought therapists were scam artists, and that if the price was right, they'd spill their secrets.

Looking back at our relationship, I should have noticed his darkness early on, brought on by a lack of control in his life. Josh wanted to be desired by everyone because it made him feel good. He wanted a sense of control over his life, wanted to feel normal and do the things healthy people did—drink excessively, party all hours of the night—but he also wanted a family, kids to read to before bedtime, to have family breakfast with. Josh did end up getting it, just not with the person he wanted.

My eyes begin to burn as I slice through the onion, the layers scattered all around me. I rock the knife back and forth, mincing each section. *Chop, chop,* the sound soothes me. I take the cutting block and bring all the vegetables toward the stove, scrapping them in and listening to them sizzle in my pot. After rinsing the knife off, I put it on the counter, back in its block, its home.

The house smells homey whenever I cook, which is why I try to make fresh meals every day. It's the only time the house becomes slightly alive, lived in.

While the stew cooks, I walk to the pantry and grab a rolling pin to start making a pie crust. I let the crust sit while I go pick some fresh berries from my garden. The wolfsbane still thrives, hidden among the flowers, and I stare at it longingly, praying for the day I can use it and end this miserable cycle of the life I've been tricked into. Once, I tried to pack a bag for Ava and myself with things we'd need to survive for a few months until I could figure something out, but Tanner told me if we left, he'd make sure our lives were hell. So here I am, cooking stew and pretending everything is perfect.

The Brentwoods let me go in peace. I may not have gotten child support for years and years and been left homeless, but they wanted nothing to do with us, which gave us our safety. The Brentwoods do all things in order to have control. Tanner does things to try to be powerful. They are not the same.

Each blueberry I pick for the pie looks perfectly ripe, and I fill my basket with enough to make two pies before walking back into the house. I put butter in a bowl with the freshly picked berries, sugar, butter, cinnamon, and a hint of flour and mix it all together. The bowl is now stained with a deep red color, its smell reminding me of how close summertime is. As much as I love summer, it saddens me that Ava will be gone, that she'll be leaving me. That I'll be alone again, something I hate more than anything in the world.

Tanner comes home from work as the pies finish baking in the oven. He doesn't even stop to smell the fresh pastry, just walks right toward his office. He's yelling on the phone behind the thick wooden doors, audible even with the heavily insulated walls. Tanner's in there for hours and doesn't resurface until the doorbell rings. He answers the door without so much as a word, just staring at Josh.

I quickly rush Josh inside. Having him for dinner is worth all the screaming Tanner will do later. I want Ava to know what it's like to have dinner with her parents, who love her. I want her to feel like, despite everything, we have her in common, that we can make up for the past by focusing on the future. Ava always saw her dad as a tragic type of hero, and I never wanted to take that from her.

Josh sits down at the kitchen table with me, gawking at the fresh pies I made.

"Do you want to see what Ava is working on upstairs?" I ask, excited to show him her newest piece.

"Of course," he says, truly appreciating her talent.

He sets his briefcase on the table and walks upstairs with me. Tanner comes toward the kitchen, and we pass him by in the hallway to the stairs.

"Pie smells good." Tanner's putting on a show for Josh. Whenever Josh is here, Tanner pretends to be someone else. If only it were real.

Josh doesn't buy it, not for a single second. Evil recognizes evil, is what Josh always tells me. That is what he told me the day of my wedding to Tanner, "Don't marry him, he isn't who he says he is."

Josh was holding a single photo of Victoria and Tanner together. It was a coincidence, nothing more, I thought it was just a photo, a one-night thing. The women around town were crazy about him. He dressed very Wall-Street-like, had well-manicured nails, a full head of hair, and drove a sexy red corvette. Tanner had his eyes on me, though, the girl in the label-less clothes, with breast milk stained on my T-shirt half the time. I used to think, why me? Now I think, *why…me.*

Victoria and Josh were already married by the time of my ceremony with Tanner, but Josh came across the photo about a month before my wedding and decided to tell me the day of. I remember a pounding on my door as I was getting ready. My friend was smoothing my dress of any crinkles and creases. I chose a slim-fitting dress made of crepe, with a sweetheart neckline. Nothing flashy.

Tanner and I did a simple chapel wedding, no fuss. I didn't feel like I deserved anything elaborate, and the only people I really wanted there had passed on. It was just Tanner, Ava, myself, and our two witnesses, both of whom we no longer speak with. Tanner had a falling out with my friend's husband over some business deal, but after looking at his finances, it seems obvious it was not my friend's husband's fault after all.

As Josh was let into the room, the photo in hand, he looked distraught. My friend tried to slam the door on him when she saw who was pounding on the door, and I had to convince her that it was okay, that I was okay, but I was frazzled and angry that, out of all days, he chose this one. He kept pestering me that I needed to listen to him, that I was making a mistake, that Tanner was a bad guy. That his friends didn't trust him, that there were ulterior motives.

Josh kept saying, "Please, please, don't marry him. I know I've been a total fuck-up. I'm the biggest piece of shit on the planet for what I let my family do to you, but don't marry this guy." His tone was desperate.

"He loves me," is what I told him.

"But do you love him?" Josh asked.

I remember his face, forlorn.

The truth is, I felt comfortable with Tanner, safe. I didn't love Tanner in the same way I loved Josh, but I felt I could give Ava a better life, and Tanner loved me. People always say that, over time, love can grow stronger, that just because the spark isn't there doesn't mean it won't be ignited one day.

The fact is, I would never love anyone how I loved Josh.

"Yes," I said to Josh, breaking his heart. I knew he didn't love Victoria. He made a mistake, and if you make a mistake in the Brentwood family, you can see it through or get cut off.

Josh didn't love Victoria, but he liked her enough to make it work, especially because he got her pregnant. Victoria threatened to tell everyone the Brentwoods were forcing her to get an abortion. At least, that's the rumor I heard. When his parents found out about his affairs, particularly the one with Victoria, they gave him an ultimatum. The Brentwood family told Josh that if he didn't leave me and marry her that they'd no longer pay for his medical bills, and his job didn't cover his finances. His own family was willing to let him suffer and let his heart fail rather than to tarnish their purebred name. So, they painted me as the worst woman in the world, and she became his lighthouse.

The saddest part about it wasn't that Josh chose someone else; it's that I didn't choose me either. Truth be told, I've never chosen myself. Now, I choose Ava because she has so much more life to live. A life the Brentwoods prevented me from giving her.

I reflect on all of Josh's late-night words when he drank, the drugs he took to fight off his torments, and think how miserable it must have been for him to pick between his life or mine. He kept everything bottled inside, and he never let me truly in. I tried to help. God, I tried.

He may have cheated on me, but to be wanted by others, to be loved by others, that was the only control he ever had over his own life. Josh just wanted to be in the driver's seat for once. He didn't know he'd soon lose control over the car.

We are in a better place these days. It took a while, but we got here. Josh and I have been getting along, ignoring the past, and trying to move forward, especially for Ava. He won't admit it, but Ava is his favorite.

Ava's room is covered in art projects. Her newest landscape she's working on is of a lavender field in France. Josh admires it, envious of her talents, proud to be her father. He's grateful she accepted him back after everything. That is something he doesn't take for granted. I watch Josh examine the stroke work on her painting, the meticulous attention to detail every piece of lavender has.

Josh walks around her room, staring at the pictures on the wall. He makes a comment about the lack of pictures with friends displayed anywhere.

"Should we be concerned?" he asks, beginning to snoop through her things.

"She keeps to herself."

162

Even though her disconnect from the world saddens me, partially because I know I did this, I know staying with Tanner hardened her spirit. I wish I could rid us of him, I wish we could leave, but he made it very clear we are his dolls, to be kept on a shelf, untouched, a simple prop in a showroom. I've tried sneaking out in the middle of the night, bags packed, stashing money for months at a time, lying about the grocery bills, doing cash back every time I went to the supermarket. There was only one time that I had the courage to try to disappear into the middle of the night with Ava, but the scar along by spine is a reminder to not try it again. I had a walker for a month, telling everyone who asked that I slipped on ice on the driveway.

"Ava is wise beyond her years," Josh says, smiling and looking through some of her scribbles.

She'd kill us if she knew we went in her room when she was at school, but it's a secret Josh and I have.

Walking down the staircase that has seen more fear than laughter, more frantic running up to a room to barricade ourselves within our home than playfully walking up the stairs, I stare at Josh and picture what our life would have been like.

My mind wanders back to the picture he showed me on the day of my wedding, the same photograph Tanner hides in his desk. The words taunt me, and I remember the sentence Josh said on that day.

"Don't make the same mistake I made," Josh pleaded with me, his eyes swollen from fighting back his tears.

"I'll be better off this way," I said firmly. What a lie that was.

The image of Josh is seared into my brain, his brow furrowed, his lips pursed tightly, his eyes red.

"My friend said this guy is bad news. You don't have to like me, but you need to listen to me," was his final attempt at stopping me.

"I don't need to listen to you. Why would I ever take advice from a man who cheated on me, got another woman pregnant, married her, and abandoned all responsibilities for his firstborn while we starved and had nowhere to sleep?" I felt a weight lift off my shoulders.

He couldn't even look at me as I spoke to him.

"If you want me to listen, start sending child support." I paused.

"I warned you," he said.

We didn't talk again until the first time Tanner beat me. Josh saw Tanner and I out to eat one day, my oversized sunglasses hiding my face indoors. He just knew. Josh started sending money every month for Ava after that. It wasn't much, but it's what he could get from his trustee without it being obvious where the money was going. I used to never understand a life where you had to ask someone for money to do the most mundane things, like eat or buy new deodorant, that was until I married Tanner.

We pass the dimly lit hallway toward the kitchen. Josh sits down, and I join him shortly after, pouring us each a glass of water. We play a game of cards to pass the time until Ava comes home for dinner. It should be any minute now. Josh reaches for his briefcase and takes out one of his prescriptions. I can't make out the label, but I know without those pills, we wouldn't be sitting at this table, laughing, enjoying each other's company, in leu of mistakes that are seared into our skin, like a calf branded for slaughter. Josh reaches for his glass of water to wash down his medicine, and I'm grateful this surgery gave us more time with him, for all the years I was robbed of before. Do-overs can be unexpectedly nice.

Tanner emerges from his office, smiling, overly jolly. I don't know why, but it makes me uncomfortable. He sits down at the table next to us, something he's never done before.

"Don't get used to coming around anymore, since Ava will be gone soon," Tanner says, laughing.

Josh ignores him and reaches across for a piece of freshly made pie.

"Victoria says hello!" Josh watches Tanner's face turn purple before Tanner storms off.

I keep my smile to myself because Victoria doesn't know Josh comes over. Josh likes to play it off like she does so Tanner has no reason to blackmail him with his second option family.

For the first time in months, my appetite is back. I take not one, but two pieces of pie.

The front door to the house opens, and I can hear Ava make her way toward the kitchen. She rushes toward her father, throwing her school bag and her art portfolio to the ground, and gives him a big hug.

I may have only had one child, but that's good enough for me. Watching as they embrace, I thank God for the strength I had to abort Tanner's child when I found out I was pregnant. I could never love Tanner's child as I do Josh's.

The table is filled with momentary love. Ava takes her place, and we dig into our meal. I notice Josh holding his chest, and he can see the concern in my face.

"Are you all right? What's wrong?" I ask, watching him brush it off.

Ava rushes to the sink to give him a fresh glass of water.

"I'm fine, I promise. It's probably from the surgery I had. Cleaning some old things out for some new parts and what not." He laughs it off. Actually, if you have Tylenol, that will help with the pain."

"Are you positive? I can call 911…" I know this wouldn't end well for him if his other *family* found out.

He rubs his chest a few more times before forcing us to compose ourselves.

"If you have Tylenol, that will fix me up."

As I get up from the table to get some, Tanner waves at me from his office that he will go do it.

"We are out of the ones down here, I'll get more from our bathroom," Tanner says.

I sit back down. He is trying to show off to Josh. Look at what a *good* husband he is.

Josh reaches for some more stew.

"See? I'm good enough to eat." He takes the ladle and serves himself another bowl. "So how is school coming along?" he asks Ava.

It brings me joy to watch her eat so much in one sitting. We live in a constant war zone, where our appetites are suppressed, but not today.

Tanner walks over to Josh and hands him medicine. Josh cups the pills in his hand and throws the pills back, washing them down with water.

Tanner walks over to the couch in the living room and puts on the sports channel, his grin still glued to his face, playing the perfect husband. I try to not think about what he'll do to me tonight. There's no use in worrying right now. For now, I'm with the dreams of my past.

TWENTY

AVA – THEN

The streets have a light dusting of snow. Everyone is anticipating a large snowstorm this winter.

Easton is supposed to pick me up today so we can make our rounds together. He thinks I shouldn't be alone right now, not with how everything has been lately. I wait for him by my dorm room, angry that I'll need to spend the next six weeks at the house of hell. The campus shuts down completely during winter break. The only positive is I won't see Scott around campus for the time being.

The horn beeps, and Easton pulls up. He reaches across the console and opens the passenger door to let me in. Easton wanted to drive me home, to catch up, since it's been a while since we've talked.

The drive looks prettier when the branches are bare, the tree bark chilled to its roots, knowing it will pass and they, too, will bloom again. The cycle of the seasons always inspires me because I try to imagine myself being in a permanent spring one day.

As we drive past suburb after suburb, I look out the window. So many people are trapped in a life they want to escape from. I can relate. Every day is the same for them—the wives kiss their husbands goodbye, the husbands go to work, the wives take their children to school before stopping to get coffee, and then they go to their hot yoga class. There's always one mom who's left out of the friend group, like my mom, feeling ostracized. She's better off, though. Half the moms workout as a front but buy copious amounts of cocaine to stay thin. Whenever a doctor denies their child Adderall but it's really for them, they do the next best thing.

When we get closer to my home, I decide I want to pick up a few things at the store.

"Can we stop off to pick up some stuff?"

"Yeah, whatever you want." Easton smiles.

We pull up to a small family-owned grocery store, the staple of our town. I open the car door and quickly run inside.

As I walk through the aisles, trying to find a tea flavor my mother and I would enjoy, I feel a tug at my jacket.

"*Whore!*" this woman yells. "*Whore!*" she screams again.

Everyone in the store stops to stare at the only exciting thing to ever happen around here. I ignore her and keep browsing for tea. She yanks me again, and as I turn around to tell her to calm down, she sucker-punches me in the face. Though I wish I could say it hurt, it's nothing I'm not already used to. I do nothing because out of everything someone can do, doing nothing is the most terrifying.

Everyone in the store looks at me, and I calmly walk to the checkout. I hand the cashier some money and walk out the door. It took me all my might to not tell that woman her husband helped me pay for my art supplies for college. I walk out the doors, Easton waiting for me.

"How did you get a shiner here?" he asks curiously.

"Who knew Noreen could throw a punch?"

I'm genuinely surprised, but I don't feel guilty because these men have insufferable wives. What I do feel, though, is filthy, ashamed about what I did to survive my household, to save up money for my mother and I to start a new life somewhere. But remorseful? No. I didn't know there was money in my future, had no idea everything I did to survive wasn't necessary, but that's my catch twenty-two. So, I remind myself I'm nothing like Victoria. She had a plan. I'm just trying to make it out alive. The clock is slowly ticking.

Every mediation has been the same. Bill and Tanner make an offer, and the other side storms out of the building, claiming they need a break. We have a final mediation in a few weeks before it goes to trial. I've been stalling, knowing my days are numbered if the money comes through. Though I've been agreeing with the lawyers asking for higher amounts, I know the other side will never agree to it. Most teenagers get to hang with their friends after school, go to a dance class, but I get to sit in a mediation room for hours on end, being told countlessly how my father didn't love me. Not even I love me.

We pull up to the house, and Easton drops me off. As I walk toward the front door, he cracks down his window.

"Are you gonna be all right?" he asks, even though he knows me well enough to know I'll lie to him.

"Yeah, what's another six weeks" I say, laughing.

I walk into the house. The lights are off. It's so quiet I can hear my own heartbeat. I listen to it pitter patter and walk through the hallway toward the living room.

"Hello? Mom?"

No one answers me.

I don't bother turning on a light switch, just in case it's supposed to be this way. After texting my mom, I wait for a reply. Maybe they went out to dinner? Or maybe they got kidnapped because of Tanner's shady business practices…

Tanner's office door is cracked slightly open. It's enticing me to go through his office once more, to figure out any more clues about the secrets he keeps deep within. I'm not sure how much time I have, but I'll take whatever it is I can get.

Going through his drawer, I look in the same spot as last time, at the letter his brother wrote him. I look for a loose sheet of paper and a pen and write down dollar amounts, in case I'll need to recall the information later. Then I look through his paperwork to see if there's any more handwritten letters—there's just one.

You don't know me, but I know you.

Reading it sends chills down my spine. The handwriting looks eerily familiar. I brush it off and decide to turn on his computer to go through his emails. Everything is neatly organized into a folder—work, family, future, business propositions, all folders that would seem sane if this were anyone else. But Tanner doesn't care about family, so I know what folder to begin my search in.

Within it are hundreds of emails from trust lawyers Tanner is corresponding with, on top of his lawsuit with his brother. I click through each one, trying to read everything as quickly as I can. Tanner's brother is dead, and I know he killed him. Otherwise, why would the correspondence stop? His brother wanted to know where all the money went. Some of it was his, but not all of it. Their parents had dementia, so they signed away everything for Tanner to oversee, which makes sense now why we live in the house we live in. The house is the compilation of all the money his parents made from hard work and the reason why the town thinks he is someone he is not. He is cubic zirconia in a sea of diamonds.

I click through more of the family folder and stop at a picture, clicking to enlarge it. The child in the photo confuses me. I can't put my finger on it. It sort of looks like Allison with a bowl cut? I exit out of the picture and continue rummaging through his emails, hoping for something to blackmail him with. In case I can't go through with killing him, I need collateral. Every email is worse than the next.

I decide to dig around in his spam and find countless emails about all the money he owes investors, so I write down every name and dollar amount and add it up. There must be three hundred million in money he owes. I'm playing with fire by being in here for this long.

No one is home yet, so I walk toward my room and lie down in my bed. As I close my eyes, trying to gain clarity of everything I read in Tanner's office, I start to piece together the dots.

My mind jumps to dozens of conclusions. Tanner knew Victoria, and Victoria wanted my dad. What if Tanner and Victoria had a deal and then were going to split the money when my dad died? Maybe the deal went bad—Maybe she actually loved him? It seems too easy, so I know that that isn't it. It was always odd timing, how Tanner showed up at my mom's most vulnerable stage in life, how he whisked her off her feet, how he knew I had Brentwood blood. But would someone really want to wait all this time to inherit money from me once my dad was dead? And what if my father didn't die for another decade or three? Has this always been a waiting game?

I open my eyes and walk toward my dresser containing all my notebooks and look for a blank one. It feels like I should write down everything, from start to finish. Everything must be documented—when the abuse started, the yelling, the holes in the walls, the lying and stealing. I need everything to be concrete, to take him down in case something goes wrong. But I'll need to write my sins too. Everything can't always be one-sided when revealing the truth.

Staring at each blank page seems daunting. I don't want to remember the start of my misery. Words never seem good enough, so instead of writing everything down, I'll draw some of it. In place of turning on the light, I walk toward a candle whose scent is like what I imagine a pleasant Christmas Eve smells like—a family full of love, presents that aren't thrown in your face when you do something wrong one day. Reaching for the lighter next to it, I flick my thumb and gently place the flame to the wick. The wick slowly burns, and I get lost as the fire dances, gently swaying side to side. I used to think about setting fire to this house, watching everything in it and all of Tanner's possessions go up in flames. That would bring me peace.

The ink bleeds into the fine-toothed paper in my notebook. I begin to draw the secrets that have been contained within these walls for too long. The first time my mother told me how she met Tanner…With every stroke of my pen, it's becoming clearer. Tanner was in this scheme for the long haul. Every year my father lived was another year the trust accumulated more money. Tanner just saw it as long-term investment because he was desperate for more money, to be wealthy, to be feared.

I switch over to my watercolors and let the murkiness of the ink blend in with the soft pastels. That's how life is, the dark mixing with the light, damaging its very essence. I feel sick to my stomach, knowing Tanner probably never loved my mother, a rouse. He probably even killed his own brother to hush him when his brother found out he couldn't pay him back. The last email was a couple of years ago. Nothing would surprise me these days. Anyone who gets in the way of wealth, he'll destroy. I turn the page and copy down the amount of money he owed people from what I wrote earlier. One by one, the lines on the page begin to fill up.

An overwhelming thought crosses my mind, one I don't want to believe. Could Tanner have introduced Victoria to my father, knowing about my dad's infidelities and his desire to be in control, knowing Victoria was after the life Tanner craved too? Was this all planned from the start? I know if I write down my thoughts, it's permanent, but the more I wonder the timing of everything, the more I am certain. This was all some type of scheme. Victoria could seduce my father. She'd trap him, and then she'd get the money. Tanner would reap the benefits for a finder's fee, but then Victoria realized it wasn't so easy to get money from the Brentwoods. Everything had to be approved of and signed for, and by then, it was too late.

I think of the rage Tanner must have felt knowing only she was able to succeed, to birth another Brentwood. So what if Tanner decided to go for my mother because of me, another heir. It was risky because what if I got nothing? I am a Brentwood by blood, but that doesn't guarantee me anything. The picture is all making sense now.

The paper needs to dry before I can turn another page, to record everything swimming around in my mind, like a fishbowl made of mirrors, circling over and over again. The reflection is exhausting.

Every page slowly fills with stories of my torture, my mother's entrapment. A memoir I don't want to remember. When my hand grows tired, I close my ink pen and place my book under the bed, allowing it to dry with privacy. I forget to barricade my door shut, like I've done every day for almost my whole life, but this time, my eyes are heavy. A thirty-minute rest is all I need, and then I'll keep going, keep writing, keep logging everything I know, in case I need it one day.

When I wake up, the pressure on my neck is excruciating. I cannot breathe and open my eyes. Tanner is strangling me. I try to resist the urge to fight back because I know he can't kill me. He won't dare try until the money is transferred. I need to be alive.

"You listen here, you bitch. You are going to do exactly as I say."

My neck begins to burn, the bruising already taking place. I stopped hiding my bruises because it became exhausting finding the right shade to cover them up. My mother still spends a substantial amount of time hiding hers, trying to hide her shame for a failed marriage with a failed person.

"You are going to ask for no more than three hundred million at the next mediation, do you hear me? If you don't, I'll kill your mother right in front of you."

His hand is covering my mouth, so all I can do is nod, my eyes wide.

He releases me. I gasp for air and hold my neck. It feels like my bones are becoming powder. He walks to the corner of the room by my door, and I see his shadow in the darkness.

"Welcome home," Tanner says, slamming the door behind him.

I run to my bathroom connected to my bedroom, holding my neck, and stare at myself in the mirror. Turning on the sink water, I let it run, the sound drowning out my already soft cries. The faucet is loud enough to scream for me, so I melt onto the cold tile. I am angry with myself for forgetting to lock my room, to keep only my demons within my walls, but instead, another set joined me.

While the sink still runs, the water overflows to the floor, and I wonder what it's like to sleep in a bed, to feel safe, to be able to breathe? One day, I want a place like that, where no one knows where I live, a plush mattress I can sink into, into the deepest of sleep, where no one is after my money, where no one wants to see my blood spilt. I hear my mother downstairs, cupboards opening and closing, dishes clanking. She is still alive, for now.

I take my blanket and wrap it tightly around myself, push my curtains to the side, and open my balcony door. Then I sit out there, noticing the same car that has been there countless times, always here when I am home. I try to get a closer look at it, but I can't make out the person who sits within the confinement of their vehicle. The lights are turned off, and all I can make out is a small cloud from the exhaust pipe.

As the night grows darker, I watch all my neighbors from my vantage point, thinking how miserable people truly are around the holidays. Noreen buying her husband a Rolex, knowing he had an affair…She bought the watch with his money, a subtle "Fuck you." I peer into the Edens's backyard and see the grave like-hole still there. My mother told me it was for a possible soaking pool when I asked her about it. She brushed it off, but people don't just build small pools here to soak. They build Olympic pools surrounded by cabanas and topiaries. Where all things must be done big, soaking pools don't make the cut.

The other neighbors to my right are an exception to that rule. They thrive knowing everyone wants to buy them out of their small home and build a mansion in its place. They get off on the power of everyone wanting their land. They've always disliked us, and I don't blame them. I watch them through their window as they watch a TV show, sitting on opposite couches, ignoring each other, sipping on their evening decaf.

The night air slowly bites, the cold filling my lungs. I can see my breath as it leaves the warmth of my chest, fading into the night sky, reaching toward the stars. Wrapping my blanket tighter, I notice something slightly off.

My mother walks toward the car and looks around her cautiously, as if to check no one is watching her. She gets in the car quickly and drives off. Tanner never lets her leave the house after ten at night, not unless he needs her to run an errand for him.

I shiver, not from the cold, but because I am now alone, with him a floor beneath me. When my mother used to run to the store and I'd be home alone with Tanner, I was always terrified he'd hurt me more when she left, that if my mother wasn't there, he'd do unspeakable things to me. When my father started coming around more, it stopped, though, because Tanner had to put on a front. He'd threaten me and tell me he'd kill my father if I ever told anyone what he did to me. I kept quiet.

A loud bang goes off.

My ears begin to ring. The car parked across from my house drives off, its engine revving. A part of me panics, thinking my mother drove down the block and killed herself. I lean over my balcony to try to see if I can spot her car. Nothing. I rush toward my closet, throw on anything I can find, and run out the front door. Tanner's asleep on the couch in the living room. I leave the front door wide open, my dog running slowly behind me, barking. I call out my mom's name in case she can hear me, in case she is close by.

"Calista?" No answer. "Calista!"

I'm thinking the worst possible outcome. Not that she may be dead, but that now it's just me and Tanner. I sit down on the cold earth, the family dog lying beside me, comforting me. My mother would never leave home without the dog. It's her everything.

My bones slowly begin to ache. Maybe I'll just sleep outside tonight. I'd rather be judged by the neighbor than sleep inside the house with *him*. So I collapse at the park a block from our house. This will do. Our dog places his head on my chest and doesn't leave my side. It's true what they say about dogs—they are empaths, placed in this world to heal the broken.

As the earth begins to swallow me, my body is being shaken by my mother. She whispers to me softly.

"What are you doing?" she asks, concerned.

I sit up and rub the tiredness from my eyes, the dog licking my face to help me wake up.

"I went for a walk, and my body felt heavy."

My mother seems unphased by the strangeness of it all.

"Well, get up. The neighbors are going to gossip about this, and if it gets back to Tanner..." Her eyes drift toward the house.

It's a sad thing, really, that she doesn't want the neighbors to talk about us when they already do. They despise us—the large home, the heavy cash flow that really isn't even real. The perfect image of a family, but only because the wives in this area are too worried to talk about me, for fear the other wife will know things about their husband they don't want to know. My mother doesn't realize we are safe from judgement now because people are too afraid to know their own truth.

She helps me up, and we walk back to the house. Mom tries to hug me, but I pull away. I don't mean to, but sometimes, my body rejects her.

Before we enter through the front door, I stop and question her.

"Where did you go?" I ask, blocking the door.

"I had to run an errand," she says softly.

"An errand this late at night?"

"Yes, I needed to get some things in case we lose power. They are predicting a big storm soon but don't know when."

"So, you just went out at eleven at night, to get blankets and candles?" I'm not buying it.

"Yes."

"Show me."

"I don't need to show you." Her voice is no longer soft.

"I think you are lying."

"I am trying to keep us safe from the storm," she says, pushing me aside to walk into the house, our dog following behind her.

Part of me knows she's telling a half-truth because she is trying to keep us safe from a storm, just not *that* one. I tiptoe up to my room, reach for my notebook underneath the bed, and flip through the few pages I got done earlier. The pages are dry now, settled permanently in their home. I grab another pen and begin to write down more.

It would be nice to leave something behind in this world when I am long gone. I think that's why I've always been drawn to painting. While my body rots in a coffin, the colors on the canvas will be hung upon the walls, still full of life, the pigment never diming.

I'd like to be buried inside a painting, but at least I'll leave my soul in one.

TWENTY-ONE

VICTORIA – THEN

The last thing I want to do is meet Calista, but I have no other choice. It's bad enough to have to look at the woman who was always number one in my husband's eyes. Although I mothered his two other children, it was never good enough for him because people who live with regret can never get a good night's rest.

Passing by the neighborhood I know all too well, I see Calista's car just a block from her house. I park mine next to hers and get in. She looks tired.

Silence has no sound, but it's loud and deafening. I don't want to be the first to speak, and I know Calista doesn't want to be either. I look at her face, her bone structure far more beautiful than mine, Though I loathe her, I feel sorry for her. Her first love gone because of my greed, my desire to live a life I wanted since I was old enough to understand there was more to life. I sit in a confined space with a woman who could have been my friend but is instead my enemy.

"Thank you for meeting me today," I say, trying to make my words sound conniving enough to be sincere.

"Let's make this quick." Her eyes avoid mine.

"We aren't getting anywhere with the mediation. If the Brentwoods knew I was here, they'd…well…have me killed, most likely."

"And that's a bad thing, why?" Calista plays it off as a joke. She isn't good at it.

"Look, we need to figure out a proper agreement. I know you don't like me, and I get it. Getting knocked up by your husband, being a mistress, it doesn't make me look good in any light. I don't regret what I did, and you know that. I won't apologize for my actions because I'm fine with myself."

Calista's gaze is lost on the bruises along her wrists, so I stop talking. I've only had bruises like that a few times as a child, but never again. I made sure of it.

Taking a deep breath, I regroup. I need to calm down, need to try to be softer, have a different approach.

"Look, I'm sorry, okay? Not for that…I need you to stop prying. It could hurt my girls," I plead with her.

"Like you hurt mine?" she snaps.

I'm salting old wounds, and the stinging has never stopped for her, not in eighteen years.

"What do you want?" she asks.

"Look, if I make my girls agree to a certain amount, will you stop digging into some missing money?" I know it won't be that simple. Everything has strings attached. Nothing in life is without them. The earth is held up by bribes and deceit.

"Why would I do that? I know you are hiding something," she says bitterly.

The blood within my body begins to boil. I need to focus.

"Isn't it odd…" I begin, knowing this could end our conversation, knowing that once I accuse her, the gloves are off. I look at her, and she waits for me to finish what I'm going to say. "How Josh got worse after being at your home for dinner over the course of the last few weeks he was alive…Maybe you were in it for the long game, tricking him, slowly poisoning him. His surgery was supposed to be fool proof, make him live for at least ten years, if not more."

She leans over toward the passenger side and reaches for the door handle.

"Get out."

"No." The firmness in my voice is not enough.

"*Get out*," she repeats.

As I step out of the car, feeling the winter's air, she slams the door closed.

I know she's hiding something, just like me. We aren't that different. She tries to deny it, but it's true.

Nothing good happens late at night. I walk toward my car, grateful for the streetlights, and then sit inside, turning on the engine, letting my car fill with heat before driving home.

My ears begin to ring as a gunshot is fired at my car. I scream and duck. Another gunshot goes off, breaking my windshield. A small piece of glass hits my cheek, the smell of blood faint.

I hear a car drive off without getting a good look at it. When I sit up and stare at my shattered glass, fragments stare back at me, reminding me of what I've done.

Once I compose myself, I look around. All the people in the neighborhood are gathering outside, staring at my car, the bullet holes prominent. I hear people saying they need to call 911. They rush to grab their spouses. One woman says, "This thing never happens here," but it does.

The evening once meant for settling down is now meant for chaos. I drive off, hoping the police don't spot me on the way home. Just in case, I'll take the side streets. As I pass under the streetlights lining the sidewalks of all the suburban neighborhoods, I wonder if it was coincidence or if Calista decided to meet with me so she could finally get her revenge. It seems too easy for her. She doesn't have it in her, can't stand up for herself. Calista would never dare to fight back. She has always lost to me.

The shards of glass cut my legs when I move around in my seat, my mind thinking of who this could have been. I have made more enemies in my life than I'd like to admit. Pulling over into a McDonald's parking lot, I park and go inside to get a coffee. I sit down at the booth, the yellow and red décor inducing my anxiety.

The coffee slides down my throat, and I try to regain my composure. I try to think more accurately about who could have been behind this. Who wants to scare me? I can think of only three people: Calista, who isn't who people think she really is; the Brentwood matriarch; or Marla. I'm not sure which one is worse. The woman who wants to light a fire under my ass, to make sure I pay up for what I owe? I took something from her she can't ever get back…Or the Brentwood matriarch, as a warning sign to not give up their money, their wealth? The last thing the Brentwoods want is to lose their son's heavily guarded fortune. They like to keep tabs on all the money, in and out.

How have I gone from being on top of the world to fearing that I'll go back to where I came from. I'd rather a bullet strike me dead than go back there.

Growing up, I used to dream of a luxurious life. A mother who loved me, who picked me over the drugs she took, which ultimately ended her life. My father never came back when she died, and I spent the entirety of my childhood in the system. The old saying, "Fake it till you make it," was the motto I stood by and for.

No one would respect Victoria from Englewood, a poor girl who was orphaned as a result of Fentanyl. I did good in school. And the classes I wasn't smart enough in, I cheated my way through. No one bullied me because I bullied them. I beat them to it. I made do in my foster homes, knowing they got money for me being present, so if I laid low and stayed out of trouble, they'd keep me in their home long enough to re-invent myself.

One summer at the local pool, I met Tanner. He seemed lonely, not because he was a loner by choice, but because no one seemed to like him, his aura dark. He was gangly and awkward and was reading a book about success. I walked over to him and asked him it.

"Are you learning a lot?"

He looked up. "Yeah, here. Give it back to me when you're done." Tanner wrote his address inside the book, got up, and left.

I spent every day reading that book, studying every tip, memorizing every fact and the people who achieved greatness. The common theme was simple: know the right people, build connections, and take action.

I kept that book. I never gave it back, but I did pass by Tanner's house once to see where he lived. The house was large, but not over the top. The cars outside were expensive, but not luxury or rare. They could see the Brentwood estate from their home. Tanner was the same age as their son, but Tanner went to boarding school. Everyone else said Oaks Academy was for the troubled youth, but everyone who sent their children there denied it.

Truth be told, I figured I'd never see him again; he wasn't the kind of person you kept in contact with.

Over the next few years, I worked hard. Eventually, I got a scholarship, convincing the school I wanted to attend that I was the student they needed on their campus. I pictured a big life for myself—marrying a rich husband, having popular children, not that I loved kids that much. Nothing stood in my way. Other people wanted happiness, love, a simple life, to travel from time to time, but I wanted life's material luxuries. I wanted my name to be something. I wanted my parents to regret ever being how they were, even from the grave.

Coincidentally, I ended up at the same college as Tanner. He was studying business, and I was studying economics. We ran into each other once, but that was it for the most part, until graduation night when we ended up at the same party. He was more appealing after a few drinks.

Tanner was drinking from the bottle. I joined him, reaching to take a sip.

"To us," I said.

Someone snapped a picture of us together, handed me the polaroid photo, and walked away. I handed it to him.

"You keep it." I took another swig from his bottle.

After that, I wouldn't hear from him again until he had a business proposition for me a few years later. One he said would give me everything I ever dreamed of, and he was half right. People who are desperate can sense the other's thirst.

A policeman walks into McDonalds. I lower my head to not make contact with him, but he radios about the car out front. The last thing I need is a scene, for this to get back to the Brentwoods. Quickly, I phone Erik and tell him to come get me. I wait in the cheaply made booth, feeling the sweat gather beneath my body. It feels like forever.

When Erik pulls up, there are more policeman gathered around my car. I watch through the windows as they examine it, deciding what to do. Erik sees my car and hurriedly walks inside.

He slides into my booth, tired-looking.

"What happened?" he asks.

"Someone shot my car," I say, as if it were something normal.

"Are you all right?" He seems concerned.

"Yes. Can you make this go away, or?"

I hope he can work his wonders. All lawyers are scummy, but it doesn't matter how he handles it if he gets it done. He walks off toward the police, a few hand gestures and handshakes from the distance and I feel a sense of relief.

Erik comes back to the booth and grabs my hand. "I told them you were picking up something in Englewood, got followed, and it was a few stray bullets."

The cops know it happens often there. One by one, they pick up their late-night food orders and head out the door. I am in the clear.

I like efficiency.

Erik leans in closer and whispers, "Tell me what really happened." He's demanding some type of explanation.

"I met with Calista." I pause, "It's a no-go. If I go down, you'll go down, too, Erik. You're the only one who oversaw the trust, and you fucked it up, so if I sink, you sink." I keep my voice low.

Erik turns white, his skin matching the color of chalk, the kind that makes you cringe from the sound as a child, the texture bothersome on your hands.

We sit in the booth and pick at cold and soggy fries.

"Can you just drop me off at home? I need to get some sleep." I'm exhausted.

"Sure," he says, "whatever you need."

We get in his Porsche, a luxury to own a car like that, but for him, it's easy. He's paid in Brentwood cash, an endless surplus if you do the right things, like tax fraud. I foresee his run is almost done now, if things don't settle quickly. No one will hire him again. His name will be tarnished among the wealthy. I hope he's been saving, not spending his money recklessly. Money can run out, and that's what people don't understand. No matter the amount, if you make big, you tend to spend big.

Josh was never allowed to do that. His money was under tight management, like all the children. Forced to put on a perfect show. Humble but wealthy is the illusion his parents put on for their country club friends about their children when their dad was alive. On the other hand, they made it known they own everything and everyone.

When CeCe dies, it will be the happiest day of my life. Her rigidness doesn't scare me; it ignites me because one day, I'll take her place, whether the Brentwood family likes it or not.

On the drive home, I watch the sky begin to lighten. We pass by houses I used to dream of living in. It's hard to believe I got *almost* everything I wanted.

When we pull up in my driveway, all the lights are off. My children are sound asleep inside. They aren't the type of children who need me around. I made sure to raise them to be independent, to want the world. Though I may have hidden a lot from them, I never hid how cruel the world is. I want them to know that people will try to take advantage of them.

Although I feel alone these days, I don't necessarily miss Josh as much as I should. I loved him, but not enough for my world to come toppling down in his absence. It's a long game that I'm in, but Calista is trying to make it end abruptly. She needs to stop it before I do something about it. I walk to my kitchen and open the cupboard. It squeaks, but I am too lazy to fix things that are falling apart in our home. I have much bigger things to worry about.

The cupboard is almost empty of wine, but there are still two of the cheaper bottles left. I find my opener and uncork the bottle. Still, I don't bother with a glass; the bottle will do just fine.

The wine slides down my throat, soothing me. I walk upstairs, taking swigs, and head to my bedroom. I lie across the bed with my clothes still on and notice a few microscopic pieces of glass on me. Without bothering to pick them off, I take a few more swigs from my bottle to calm myself down.

I lay my head on the pillow and close my eyes, knowing I won't dream. People like me are only cursed with nightmares for all our sins.

TWENTY-TWO

JOSH – THEN

I'm sitting in an empty waiting room in one of those hospital gowns. Victoria pulled through on her promise, but even with how much I've tried to be a better person, this takes everything away. How will I ever be able to look at myself again?

Before my surgery, I had to meet with a few of my lawyers, in case things don't go as planned. Nothing does these days. I had to change my will, without Victoria knowing. I'll leave the trust the same, so she'll think it was a mistake. She won't notice that the trust and will don't match until it's too late. I don't want to die, but the doctors said that with this surgery, it's always a risk. In this case, twenty percent. I haven't been a worthy person, so it's only a matter of time until Karma does its thing.

My parents all had children with health issues. They are stone-cold, heartless beings, so it was God's way of saying you aren't untouchable after all. My brothers were born with diabetes, constantly having to pump themselves full of insulin, testing their blood before every meal, having to stick needles in their thighs. I wish I were as lucky as that. My sister was born with a cleft palette. She had to undergo extensive medical procedures to appear normal-looking, which is why she was so rude to Calista. Her lips were like an angel's bow, delicately drawn on her face.

At times, it felt like I got the short end of the stick. The doctors told my parents that, as I got older, my life expectancy would get shorter and shorter. I didn't want to die without experiencing everything. At times, I was selfish…

Actually, no.

Most of the time I was selfish, a total piece of shit.

When I turned eighteen, I didn't care anymore. Doctors said I probably wouldn't make it to my twenties, then that became my mid-twenties. I chose to live a wild life, not a full one. Looking back at it, I regret it all. I regret losing Calista. I regret the harsh light Ava must have seen me in when she was a child. I blame my family for making me pick and feel like a coward for having them be my scapegoats.

Growing up, we had to play the part of a perfect family. All the women at the country club worshipped the ground CeCe walked on. They wanted to be like her, dress like her, talk like her. My mother's accent is fake. She grew up in Queens. My father was a tyrant. The level of success he achieved was from robbing those beneath him.

The Brentwood name is built in blood. If you carry the name, you know that. We are who we are because my father did inside trading, and when his partner found out, the partner suddenly disappeared. Instead of getting reported and receiving possible jail time, my father was practically a billionaire. All my siblings and I know our father covered up his long-time partner's murder. My mother stood by his side. She is loyal to him, and she'd never stray. They were soulmates, which is ironic because they both lacked one.

My parents did a lot to get where they are today. Anyone who ever could possibly rob them of that no longer lives. We should miss our father, but none of the children do. My mother is too frail these days. Anything that's wrong cannot be done anymore. They lived a rich life of humiliating everyone to step ahead, but now, she sits comfortably in her home, sipping on tea and agreeing no more blood can be spilt because if anyone slips up, it could ruin everything. If only they knew.

Our childhood was not warm and loving. It was cold. If we wanted attention, we needed to do well in school, get proper markings, excel in sports, and be popular. Our parents wanted everyone to salivate over their offspring. If we did not live up to their standards, they'd take money out of our trusts, and we'd watch hundreds of thousands of dollars at a time slip from our future fingertips. In a world like today, a normal job won't help you live comfortably. Everything is too high in cost…Food, gas, just to live is to sell yourself to the cooperate world. Now add in being sick your whole life. A normal person would be left with nothing after every paycheck. The Brentwood children were not allowed to be normal.

My siblings didn't need the money like I did. My medical condition cost more than theirs. Although their problems were not cheap, they could live a lot longer with them. I, however, had to be loyal to my parents. They'd let me die if it meant not ruining their name.

I check the clock on the wall, growing impatient waiting for them to wheel me into a room and place my body on a cold slab of metal while they cut me open. The doctors will listen to classical music, treating my surgery like a game of fucking operation. I had to pay these doctors millions to do this. They had to sign hundreds of pages of paperwork, but in the contract, it didn't state what would happen if I lived or died. In surgery, and one like this, there is never a guarantee.

I grow more anxious, not sure what's taking them so long. Victoria dropped me off because she had to go get the girls and take them to school. She decided it was best we don't tell them anything, didn't want them to worry.

In case anything goes wrong, I left a note for my lawyer to give to Ava. Ava will know I wanted to take care of her. She'll know because the will and the trust don't match. Victoria never caught on because she sees life in dollar signs, not the fine print. I want Ava to know I'm sorry for everything; I've been a shit father. It's why I started to go to her house for dinners these last few years. I wanted to make up for the time I may not get with her.

Being sick has made me realize a lot, like the unspeakable things I put Calista through. When I'm alone for too long, I think about it, the nights I'd come home high off my ass on drugs or belligerently drunk. She was all alone, raising our child...*her child*. I'd have no recollection of it all, except for after, when I'd look at her, her beautiful eyes red and puffy from hours of crying, *crying that I caused*. The more I hurt her, the more I pulled away. Even when she was pregnant, I didn't have any regard for the child she was carrying, probably because I thought it would be a monster like me—the Brentwood curse, to be born in bad blood.

I wish I could blame everything on Tanner. His parents plotted hard to get him a job at my father's company, one of many he owned that I was forced into working at. Tanner introduced me to Victoria, but it wasn't his fault that I ruined my own marriage. Victoria was convincing. She embraced my darkness, wasn't afraid of it like Calista was. Victoria didn't try to fix me, like Calista did. If I never would have gotten Victoria pregnant, maybe things would have worked out for me and Calista. We always fought for each other, but I couldn't come back after something like that.

Now I'm here, waiting in this fucking hospital room to be sliced open, to have my organs spilling out of me while I lie naked on the table, powerless, finally like the rest of them. This is my Karma, for choosing my life over Calista's love.

Finally, a doctor walks into the room. I've been growing impatient being stuck with only my thoughts and life choices. He pulls out a manilla envelope and reviews information about me. It angers me how thick the envelope is, stuffed with pages, reminders that I am not like other people, that I am sick.

"Hello, Mr. Brentwood. I'm Doctor Cherry," the doctor says.

"Hello," I say, peeved.

He flips through the pages quickly, proof he doesn't care. I wouldn't care either if I were him. My mother could ruin his career, only my mother doesn't know what I'm doing. It was nearly impossible to get this money without anyone noticing it was gone. Victoria said it would be considered a donation, and she'd make sure the paperwork got filed properly. In exchange, I had to prove to her one last final time that Calista will get nothing if anything happens to me. She said it was her way of proving my loyalty to her. Victoria deserves that from me because my heart has always been with Calista, even when I was with Victoria. Calista deserved better than me. I just wish she knew she did. Victoria and I were made for each other, *as punishment.*

"The surgery will take about six hours on average. If we run into any complications, it could take longer," the doctor says.

192

I already know everything he's saying. It's been researched many times.

"Our anesthesiologist will be here any minute now. She'll brief you through the process, ask about any underlying medical conditions, medication issues, allergies, and then we will wheel you in shortly into the OR."

His eye contact is poor. My father raised his children to always look someone dead in the eye. It's how you command a room.

The doctor smiles at me for a flash of a second before heading out of the room. I wait as tolerantly as I can for the anesthesiologist. Taking out my phone, I send Calista a text message to let her know I can't make it to dinner this week, due to a work trip, but I'll call her when I'm back to reschedule. I bet when I die, she'll be the last thing I see, my last thought that runs through my synapses. My core memory is her walking down the hallway in high school, shy, quiet, but she chose to love me, something I'll never understand. I don't love myself. How could I?

The anesthesiologist walks in. She's a calculated type of woman, no free thinking going on in her head. She carries herself well, a walking textbook full of knowledge. I'd rather have her operate on me than Doctor Cherry. She knows what she is doing. I tune her out as she talks because I know I am in good hands with her. My father always said you know who runs the show before they even speak.

A few nurses walk into my room and take my blood pressure. They apologize for the painful grip of the device, but I've been in a chokehold since I could remember. They take my temperature, weigh me, and then wheel me off to the OR. As I lie down, being taken into surgery, all the fluorescent hospital lights blur together. It's a sight I've seen many times throughout my life, constant surgeries, but this one needs to work. I need to come out of this a better person, somehow.

The room they place me in is sterile. If my parent's room were a personality, this place would be it. The medical devices scattered among silver trays don't scare me like they should.

Through the curtains of the room, I can hear the doctors whispering.

"Did you have them sign your paperwork? We could lose our medical license for this, especially if he doesn't make it," Doctor Cherry's assistant says to him.

"Of course, I know that they are good for it. They will keep our secret," Doctor Cherry says confidently.

He is right. We take our secrets to our graves in the Brentwood family, our enemies buried right beside us, in case they can't be trusted. To lie with your enemy is to protect the family name, the family motto.

It doesn't matter what line of work you are in because no matter how good of a conscience someone has, money is money, and it's always been better to have it than to not.

A mask is placed over my face, and I count to eight before I'm slowly drifting.

I don't think of anyone.

I see no one I love.

I just see red.

TWENTY-THREE

ALLISON – NOW

Slowly, I begin to open my eyes. My head feels like it may explode. I look down and find both my hands tied together. It seems I've been sleeping in my own pool of blood on a cold concrete floor. My eyes begin to well with tears that scorch the cuts on my cheeks when they run down my face.

The room is silent, except for a pipe making a dripping sound. I hear no creaks from the floor above me, no muffled voices. I am alone, and everything is black.

My body hurts. Whoever hit me with their car must be worried I'd say something if I lived. There's really nothing more I can do but wait. My mother will wonder where I am if I don't come home soon, and Scott will be at my house to pick me up in a short while.

The longer I am trapped in darkness, my eyes begin to adjust to my surroundings. I see a plate close by me, a single sandwich on it. I inch my way toward it, but my body aches, and I'm overcome with a stabbing pain in my chest.

As I lie back down, the cold floor soothes my pain. I try to get some sleep, hoping that when I wake up, whoever put me here will realize they made a mistake, that I won't press charges or do anything, that accidents happen. They'll believe me. I'll make them.

My body is in anguish with every minor movement, and I begin to shiver. My stomach grumbles, but I cannot fathom eating right now. I wonder what time it is. How long have I been here for? Have days passed? Hours? Time goes so fast when the sun can kiss your face, drenching you in light, but in darkness, time seems to freeze.

Finally, I hear a sound. The floor begins to creak, and I look up, trying to trace where the steps are coming from. A door opens, and the hinges squeak.

Clunky footsteps make their way down, and I can feel their eyes land on me.

"Hello?" I say, praying for them to answer me back.

Nothing.

I try again.

"I won't tell anyone what happened, I swear. Please, just let me go. I think I need a doctor, and I—"

Before I can finish, a hand hits me across the face. My cheek stings. I fall back to the floor and start to cry in silence. My body begins to convulse as I hold back the tears.

Cold hands touch my face, and something is being tied around my head, a cloth of some kind. Not that it matters because it's too dark in here to make anything out. I hear the footsteps head toward the door, and it slams shut.

I think of all the people I love who may never see me again, and it makes me feel how final everything must have been. Trapped in solitude, I'm alone with my thoughts.

My mind begins to think of Ava and her wickedness, how maybe she deserved her end. Her neighbors all made her out to be this evil person ruining families, sleeping with married men, a troubled young woman, but what if they were lying, covering up for someone, paid off? Maybe all Ava and I have in common is our father, nothing more, nothing less.

The throbbing in my skull rocks me to my core. I can feel my blood drenching my clothes, and the smell of iron makes me sick. My ribs tense up and feel like I'm being sliced open. Is this what Ava felt like when she died, every breath she took slowly becoming her last? I don't want to share her fate; I don't even know who she was.

Trying to close my eyes once more, I pray that when I wake, I'm back in my bed asleep and this was all a nightmare, one that feels real, as a form of punishment for carrying the last name given to me at birth. I think of the teeth clinking around in the jar I shook earlier. How many more secrets are filled in jars? Whispers stashed away like forgotten toys.

My breathing becomes weaker.

When I wake up, everything is going to be okay. I know it will be. Nothing bad can happen to me—I'm a Brentwood, I remind myself over and over again.

My family is the bad thing to happen to someone, not the other way around.

TWENTY-FOUR

AVA – THEN

Christmas came and went. I avoided my *family* that day, never having been one for holidays. It just seemed like a waste of time to me, a holiday where family gathers. Usually, when Tanner falls asleep on Christmas Eve, I sneak down the stairs and give my mother a present, just the two of us, like how it should have been. This year, I made her a drawing, just one of her parents. I've never been great with portrait work, but I wanted to try for her. When she opened her present, she sobbed and placed the painting against her chest.

"I love it," she said.

Christmas Day, Tanner went to the movies. He always goes and sees a double feature, sometimes three.

This is the first time in my life there hasn't been a snowstorm for the winter season, and I decide to go for a walk since it's nice out, something rare during this time of year. I grab a light jacket, leash up Murphy, and head out, not bothering to wave to our neighbors. None of them like me. The rumors and gossip were placed down the chimney of everyone's home this Christmas, along with their gifts. If my mother knew what I had become, it would break her.

The neighborhood from this angle makes me feel equal to

everyone, no longer sitting high and mighty in my throne, looking down upon the people of this town and judging them for the lies and deceit they pretend don't exist. The people on this street are just as heartless as I am, all wanting to be successful, all wanting to show everyone what they have, when in fact, it's just nothingness.

My dog begins to pull me on our walk, eager to be outside. I focus on him, wanting him to know he is loved. We pass by all the houses I've been inside many times, houses that gave me money to support myself.

Every time my mother would give me a nice piece of jewelry to make up for the accidental life, Tanner would beat her, scold her. I could never wear anything in my jewelry box. It was beautiful but tainted. How could I wear something my mother suffered for? The emeralds I so longed to wear, the pearls delicate with grit, they never touched my skin once. They were memories, the cost too much to bare.

After I drop off my dog, I text Easton to see if he wants to go for a joy ride. I've been feeling suffocated in the house for this long. He's the only one who knows everything. I tried to tell Scott once, but he didn't want to listen to it. He said all families have their issues, and he'd rather not know my family's secrets.

I run inside the house to quickly change. My mother is asleep on the couch, so I write a quick note to let her know I'm out with a friend and I'll be back soon. She's been sleeping during the daytime lately, said it's because her schedule is messed up from the stress, but I know it's because she's afraid to sleep at night, to let her guard down while Tanner is in the house.

He's grown increasingly violent with every mediation, not getting what he wants, Bill breathing down his back in legal fees, suddenly wanting more and more, which is a heftier demand from the original scam they had going on. It didn't help that the Brentwood stock shot up even more this last month, the shares being at an all-time high, making the Brentwoods even more rich. How much is enough?

Easton shows up at my house. He knows not to ring the doorbell but sends a simple text. I rush outside and into his car. He locks the doors because he knows it makes me feel safer.

"Where to, little lady?" he asks, his hands on the wheel.

"I was thinking of renting a storage unit." I look out the window, staring at the house on Kenilworth as an outsider, thinking about how so many people pass by this house and wonder what it would be like to live here.

Soon, a new family can, when my mother and I leave this place, Tanner gone forever.

"What for?" Easton focuses his eyes on the road.

"Just to keep a few things in, that's all," I say, trying to not draw to much attention to it.

"How much does something like that cost? Can you afford it? Do you need me to spot you? I know college is super expensive. That's why I skipped it. Rather sell my drugs, keep a humble life." Easton reaches for the radio to turn on some music, soft enough so he can still talk to me.

"It's eighteen dollars a month. I just want to keep a few personal items in there. The dorms aren't that big, and I want to move some things from my bedroom into there, for safekeeping. Tanner's been on one lately." I try to look unbothered.

"You know, your mom and you can always hang at my place." His words are gentle, never pushy.

"I wouldn't want Tanner to hunt you down and shoot you with

one of his guns from his prized collection," I say, letting out a small laugh.

"On second thought..." Easton laughs with me.

I type in an address on his phone for a storage locker a few miles from the house. When I purchase a small unit, they hand me a small gold key. I hand the man at the desk two years upfront, paying in cash, and tip him extra.

The nice man walks me to my storage unit, with Easton slowly walking behind me. He takes one of his master keys and places it in the lock, fidgeting with it for a moment before the key makes a clicking sound. The man slides the door open, revealing a dimly light unit with a single florescent light pendant overhead that flickers.

"It's perfect," I say.

The man shows me where the light switch is and walks me through a few basic rules, each one I intend on breaking, as I imagine most people who have a storage unit do.

"Shit, you could hide a dead body in here, as long as you cover up the smell." Easton looks around at the hundreds of storage units, all with putrid orange-colored doors.

"Yeah."

Closing the garage door to the unit, I lock up with my key and feel a sense of relief now that I have this space, something I've never had before.

We head back to the car, and Easton suggests we get ice cream. I like that idea, things you aren't supposed to have when it's cold outside, things you shouldn't enjoy because it goes against the norm. We drive to the nearest ice cream parlor, the key firmly in my hand, leaving an indention on my skin. I don't realize how tightly I'm holding on to it. When I snap out of it, I place the key in my pocket. I'll find a safe place for it later.

Easton treats me to ice cream, and we sit and lick our cones in silence, enjoying each other's company. He's one of the only people I like. The other one was Scott, but he can't even look at me anymore. I've never felt so betrayed. Scott took me to get ice cream on our first date. I told him the only good flavor was vanilla because it's underrated. Everyone always says vanilla is boring, but the truth is, vanilla is more complex. It's hard to grow. The vine itself takes two to four years to mature, and its flowers bloom one single day of the whole year. If plants want to produce beans, they must be pollinated during that exact day. Nothing is basic about vanilla.

I should know better than to have loved someone who thought that.

For a second, I picture us laughing, licking our ice cream cones as it runs down the sides, covering our fingers in its stickiness. I snap out of it when I hear Easton talk.

"This ice cream hits the spot," he says, guzzling it.

I pretend to eat mine, but instead, it melts, spilling all over my hands. My mind seems to be trapped in the past.

I excuse myself to use the bathroom and rinse the ice cream off my hands, hoping the memories will fade within the sink's pipes. I wipe my hands dry and make my way back to Easton, where he's finishing up the last bite of his ice cream. He smiles at me, and it makes me feel better.

"You sure you don't want to stay at my place tonight?" he asks sincerely.

"I want to, but I need to do a few things with my mom later," I say.

"Well, let's get you home, then."

When we pull up to the house, Tanner's car is still gone. I walk inside. My mother is sound asleep on the couch, but she slowly wakes when I call her name. She sits up, rubbing her eyes, coming to.

"I'm so sorry. I slept horribly last night." She never sleeps at night, and she knows this. It's been like this most of my life.

"Are you ready to go through more paperwork for the lawyers?" I ask, wishing we didn't have to do this.

"Yeah, let me make us some tea." She rushes to boil some hot water.

I sit down at the kitchen table and, one by one, go through legal papers—documents of all the records of my father's will and trust, how many times it's been updated, which county it was filed in, his net worth when he died, and every receipt of donations that have been made. The words begin to blur together on the pages, like finding a needle in a haystack.

We sift through page after page, highlighting things. I can tell it bothers her, staring at all the money spent, when we were left with nothing. Every time she highlights something, I can feel it causing her pain. I do wish she'd have tried to fight back, but you can't get in the way when you are a small speck compared to the bigger picture.

Imagine being a young woman with a baby, being thrown out of your home with nothing but a diaper bag on your shoulder and a suitcase of everything you own. That wasn't the life she pictured for herself.

The doorbell rings, but we aren't expecting anyone. People don't bother us these days. I walk to the door to answer it, my mother in full work mode. It has been giving her purpose as of late, a reason to wake up, to take down the Brentwoods, to have a slice of their pie and eat it in front of them. That's all she's ever wanted. Her goal was never the money; it was revenge, for how they treated her and how they treated me.

I open the door, but no one is there. There is something tucked inside our mailbox.

An unsealed envelope.

I open it, standing barefoot on the cold stone steps leading into this hallowed fortress, and read it several times.

"Your days are numbered."

I look around to see if anyone is watching, peer my head further to see if the car that's been parked by our house has returned, but no one is around. The neighborhood is empty. The note should scare me, but it doesn't. The truth is, as much as I want to be a good person, I cannot take back the things I've done. None of us can.

"Who was it?" my mother says, her words muffled.

"It was nothing," I yell back, my words echoing down the hallway lined with my art, like a museum in Hell.

When I sit back at the table with my mother, I watch her read meticulously, making small notes between the margins of each line. She hands me another red pen, and I continue marking each page, checking every business to make sure they are real.

"Google everyone. Make sure they all come up as a legitimate company or charity," she says, passing me her tablet.

"Why can't the lawyers do it? Isn't it their job?" I'm becoming annoyed.

I google hundreds of places. Most check out right away, but some require minor digging. I check off each place from the list, until one won't show up...

Though I check social media to confirm, I still turn up emptyhanded. A renovation company called H2B Design ceases to exist.

"Mom, was Dad re-doing his house before he died?" I think she'll know more than me. They talked almost every day the last couple of years before he died.

"He wanted to, but it I don't think he ever got around to it."

I hand her the piece of paper, with the circled company.

"This place doesn't pop up, and there's a lot of payments, monthly, dating back a full year if not more," I say, confused.

"Don't tell Bill."

The fact she thinks I'd ever speak to that man willingly baffles me. I nod.

"What are you going to do with that information?" I ask, genuinely curious.

"I'm going to go see CeCe," she says, sitting up proudly in her chair.

My mother is going to make a deal with the devil. How she'll get past the gate, I have no idea. I haven't seen my mother smile like this in years—like for the first time, she's going to win—and I try to not take it away from her. So I keep my mouth shut because I tend to remind her how we ended up here in the first place. I need to stop letting her small cracks shatter her from the inside out. A heart is a fragile thing.

A headache strikes me right in my temple. My mother keeps a medicine drawer next to the stove, filled with Tylenol, Band-Aids, everything you could need in case of an emergency or sickness. Most people keep their pills tucked away in the bathroom, but ours is on display, like a spice rack.

Rummaging through each orange container, I can't seem to find the plain white one. I place each bottle on the counter, one by one, but nothing. The Tylenol isn't anywhere to be found.

"Did you check the upstairs bathroom?" she says, walking toward me.

"No?" My headache's growing worse. I head upstairs, desperate for medicine.

A few of Tanner's prescriptions are in the mix with my mother's. The label on all of his pill bottles have been removed, the writing on them nearly illegible. I open one of the bottles to see if any of them resemble Tylenol. It's my area of expertise, something I've been around for years now.

In one of the pill containers, there are round pills, the shade of a robin's egg. I know exactly what they are. The M on the pill is enough of a giveaway.

One pill, let alone two could kill someone.

I think I'm going to be sick.

"Did you find any?" Mom asks me.

"Yeah," I say, my headache turning to heartache.

I try not to think the worst, but it's too late.

I think Tanner killed my father. His plan has been set into motion.

My mother puts down her paperwork and walks to the couch. She is sitting soundly, knitting a blanket, and looks content. I picture our new life together in a nice cottage in the middle of the woods, away from society. It's a fantasy I have, but I snap out of it because living in a fantasy world is how you get stuck, trapped in dreams that will never exist. It's why I love to paint so much. My world I never got to have can live outside of my mind.

Sometimes, I wonder why I want to even help my mother because I do blame her for this life, as much as I don't want to think that way. I feel guilty wishing she was stronger, wishing we'd have been poor on the streets together, figuring out every meal as we went, figuring out how to make money to survive. I'd rather have struggled than to barricade my doors every night when I sleep, living in fear for my life. This is why most people hate all those sayings about hindsight.

My mother continues to knit, the needle piercing through the yarn over and over again, forming bits of a blanket that will probably never get finished. Tanner will come home in one of his fits of rage, scream in my mother's face, and she'll resort to a deep cycle of depression.

We have court next week. The judge decided mediation was no longer going to work. Tanner is out with Bill grabbing drinks, talking strategy, most likely. The talks with Bill determine what Tanner's mood will be like when he comes home. If the judge is leaning more in our favor, Tanner won't lay a hand on my mother. He won't belittle her. If the talk goes south, dishes are broken, and the screams become white noise to those whose windows are open around us.

Eventually, the sky falls dark, and I head upstairs to try to sleep. In the morning, we will intrude on the Brentwoods. Just in case I doze off, I lock my door and push the dresser up against it. I leave every window open in case I need to escape. It's second nature to me, like brushing my teeth before bed. My best friend growing up didn't believe me when I told her about everything. She stopped coming over after that, and all my other friends slowly after. Being alone is easiest for me.

Just a few more weeks and I'll be able to go back to my dorm room, a better type of prison cell, overly priced and moldy, like all places on campus.

My mind isn't tired, so I try to hush it by sketching. As I lay in bed with my sketchbook and an ink pen, I begin to draw a map of Kenilworth. I draw every home, connecting each driveway to the middle of the street. The more shaded the home in my sketch is, the more corrupt the people inside the home are. When I get to my house, it's black. I work my way toward the trees, but instead of leaves, I write secret messages just for myself, little notes on each branch, hidden within the trees. I tire my mind out with the tedious secrets every bush and tree has nestled between each branch and fall asleep holding the paper in my hand.

When I wake up in the morning, I walk toward my balcony, not to greet the day, but to inspect it, to make sure everything is as it always has been. Tanner's car is still not back in the driveway. He did not come home last night, which is a concern but at the same time a relief.

I lean against the railing, leaning as far as I can to see down the block. Everyone is nestled inside. I never want to live in a place like this again.

Eventually, after hunting the neighborhood, I take a shower and head out with my mother in her luxury car. Tanner bought it for her, a way to show the neighborhood we have money—if our house wasn't enough, that is. A matte-black G-Wagon. The mother I knew growing up was fine walking everywhere.

We sit in the car in silence, and I hope it stays this way throughout the drive. It's no more than a fifteen-minute commute to the Brentwoods from where we live. The saying, "Keep your enemies close," applies here, even though it was never intentional. Imagine living so close to people who wish you'd never been born. I never had the urge to even drive by it, so this will be my first time.

My mother doesn't speak on the drive there. I know she's trying to block out the pain of her never being accepted. Sometimes, I don't understand why she loves me. I'm a constant reminder of everything that slowly ruined her, a glass of wine spilt on a white dress, a cut you need stitches for, a scar that sticks out—that's what I am to her.

My mother pulls up to the telecom at the gate, sticks her arm out the window, and presses a button. She waits for a voice.

Nothing.

She presses it again. Her face begins to fall, not from the rejection, but because she wanted to finally stick up for herself. We sit at the gate for an eternity with no answer. This is the kind of family that has camera surveillance. They know we are here. I see the blinking red light on the camera. They enjoy watching us, probably the only family trait we share.

My mother reverses her car and speeds down the street, like she is trying to go back in time. I turn up the radio and let the music wash out my mother's thoughts. She'll take them down in court. It's been the only thing she's wanted to do since the day she married into that family. She wants to hurt them through their bank accounts, to find their deep-rooted secrets and expose them.

On the car ride back to Kenilworth, dread takes over my body. Every time I close my eyes to get some rest, I find my mind wandering to Tanner, thinking of all the ways he'll try to kill us. What if I'm not ready in time? What if I don't see it coming? I can't let him beat me to my own death. I want to die on my own terms.

That's something I've always known. Only, I will take my own life.

We pull up to the house and park in the garage. Tanner is sitting at the kitchen table, holding something in his hand. He motions for my mother and me to join him. I express no emotion, looking over my shoulder to see my dog sound asleep in his bed. Tanner would have tried to get rid of our dog by now, but he actually likes the dog, which doesn't fit the mold for a sociopath, but that's beside the point.

Tanner takes a deep breath before placing the piece of paper down in front of us with two pens.

"I'd like you to sign these, before court, so we know what you owe me for having taken care of you both for so long," he says.

Tanner hands us another binder, and within that binder is everything he's purchased for my mother and me. The list reads from diapers, to toothpaste, to tampons. I am appalled. What's left of my mother's heart is now broken. Money is a leash used to control people.

"Are you serious?" I jump out of my seat and continue down the list of items he purchased for me as I child—crayons, cough medicine, apple sauce. He's been keeping a log for what seems to be the last sixteen or so years. Someone wouldn't go through that amount of work, writing everything down, for no reason. This is proof I was a payout to him. He plotted to marry my mother, and it's in the form of a fucking grocery list.

He doesn't move an inch; his facial muscles remain neutral.

"Be grateful for what I did for you," he says.

"What, like kill my father?" I say snidely.

Tanner gets up from his seat and slams my head down on the table. My mother pleads for him to stop, that she'll sign it. She's hysterical, and I try to remain calm. I hear the scribbling on the page.

It's done. My mother caved. What else was she supposed to do? My head feels like it will burst like a balloon, pricked by a single thumbtack.

"You ungrateful little bitch, you'll sign this," he says, spitting on me.

The weight of his body hurts me, and I can feel my face turning redder. My neck strains like it's going to snap, like a child playing with a clasp on a necklace, moments away from breaking it.

"*Fine!*" I say, feeling his hands release me.

I know he can't kill me yet. I'll play his game.

So, I write my name down. He can have his stupid piece of paper, and he can get me to sign whatever he wants. But he'll be dead anyway. I will not let him kill me; I've been waiting for this moment almost my whole life.

"And stay out of my office, or I'll cut off each one of your fingers. Have I made myself clear?" he says.

My hand quivers, still holding the pen like it is attached to me.

He leaves the room holding the documents. My mother is silent. What is there to possibly say?

TWENTY-FIVE

CALISTA – THEN

This is all my fault. There is no way around it. I always think about the saying, "You made your bed; now you can lie in it," on days like today. The saying bothers me, though, because how do we know the bed we are making is with our enemy if we get fooled into silk sheets?

Ava is face down, Tanner putting his weight on her head, her cheeks turning an unsettling shade. I quickly sign the piece of paper, but that isn't good enough. He wants Ava's signature. I'm sick to my stomach that every single transaction has been documented. He declared himself our savior, the man who fed us and put a roof over our heads. We were nothing more than a bank account, slowly collecting interest in the form of Josh's death.

Tanner walks out of the room. Ava is shaking, but she walks calmly to her bedroom, her footsteps light on every stair. She moves her furniture in front of the door, to keep herself in and the evil out. The lines in the wooden floor over the last decade have shown her fear, even though she doesn't tell me. She's cold and distant. I hate myself because it is my fault. All of it.

There's no denying this house is not a safe place to rest, but all I can do is wait. The settlement is approaching quickly. I walk to the couch and continue to knit my scarf. My mind gets lost thinking about what Victoria said to me in the car. To be honest, Victoria has her reasons for thinking I killed Josh. I've been thinking about our confrontation, replaying her words in my mind. No matter what Josh did to me back then, I grew to understand his actions. Josh projected his frustrations onto me, which is never an excuse, but over time, I learned him.

With every new row I make in my scarf, my mind unweaves. What if Victoria tries to frame me for Josh's murder? When Josh died, we all assumed it was from the heart condition he's had since he was born. I asked for an autopsy report, but Victoria refused. Her reasoning was there was no need for one because everyone knew the cause, but I'm not so certain now. Victoria scheduled his meal service for him, cleaned for him, labeled his medicine. If you looked carefully at their relationship, it was as if she actually loved him.

No. She loved the weight of his last name more. To marry a Brentwood was the equivalent of getting into an Ivy league, but the marriage version.

The yarn snags. I try to fix the small piece poking out of the last loop. It irritates me. I'm able to recover the small section that was out of place, like how I've felt all these years. Background noise would help. I take the remote that sits on the end table by the couch and turn on the TV.

It's late enough in the evening to go back into Tanner's office. Ava doesn't realize there are sensors in there too, that before going too far in, you need to unplug it. The trick is to turn off all the lights and see where a small red flash comes from. If I let on to Ava that I'm searching for something, she'll want to help me, and I can't let her risk that.

The office is sterile, cold, and unwelcoming. I'm glad my photo is not hung up on his walls. I don't want to be his trophy anymore. There is nothing polished about me, just a caged middle-aged woman. There is no shine to me anymore.

The dog is whimpering by the door. I consider that a sign to grab my coat and take him for a night walk, to stop searching for the night. When I pass by each house, one by one, the streetlights go out. Crime is kept within the family in homes like these. Stopping at the Edens's house, I stare at their silhouettes in the window. I hope they keep their end of the bargain and don't back out. I need them. The dog pulls me toward Noreen and her husband's home. Whenever I pass by her on the sidewalk, she ignores me, but I'm not sure what I did to her. I count it as a blessing when someone makes it clear they don't want anything to do with me. It saves me from trying.

The air feels like it wants to snow, but it's being held back by Mother Nature. It's like she is waiting for the final ruling, that she is on *our* side. I walk the dog around the block twice before going back into my house. Ava is sitting on her balcony, watching people. She likes to know what she is getting into ahead of time. It's intrusive, but she's better off knowing.

The dog cozies up beside me on the couch. It's nice to have him here. He keeps me sane most of the time while Ava is gone at school. I'm grateful she came home for winter break, not that she has anywhere else to go. Ava doesn't seem to have any friends. Most parents would worry, but I get it. No one is as they seem, and having friends can make the loneliness feel worse at times.

To keep myself up, I continue knitting, repeating the same motion, stopping my hands from being idle, but my mind still wanders. A feeling of anxiousness overcomes me. I think of the re-occurring monthly payments on renovations, knowing nothing has been done to that house. I was in it right before Josh died. Victoria was out with her children, and Josh invited me inside. He said he had a gift for Ava and forgot it upstairs, asked if I could pick it up. I went for selfish reasons, to see how the woman he left me for decorated her home, how she kept it. I wanted to know what aroma the house smelled of. I always assumed it smelled like a basic cotton, the house full of neutral tones, no personality, just bland.

From the exterior to the moment I walked through the door, it was just as I pictured it, everything directly out of a Pottery Barn catalog—no personal touches. Josh always despised Pottery Barn. The thought of it made me laugh. Maybe that's why he was always coming over to our house the last few years.

The anxiousness runs through my veins. I get up from the couch, dig through my purse for my car keys, and head out the front door as quietly as possible, even though Tanner keeps me trapped here most nights, like a child with a curfew. I hate leaving Ava confined in this house by herself.

I'll be quick. At least, that's what I tell myself.

The car ride seems long, but my thoughts become the passenger. I pull up to the house I should have lived in with Ava and Josh. Maybe we would have had more children if things hadn't soured. I was pregnant with Tanner's child, but after he hit Ava shortly after we got married, I'm glad I made the choice I did, and I don't regret it. If that child had grown up to be anything like Tanner…

The world is better off.

If Tanner found out, though, I don't know what would have

happened to me. I dropped Ava off at school that day and drove to Gary, Indiana, a place where socialites and trust fund babies don't go. No one would know me there. Just an hour away from my house was like being in a different world.

The streetlights flicker, and I watch as they decide to stay on or not. Everything must rest at some point, including streetlights. I turn off my headlights and try to blend in with the dead of night. Somehow, I need to get into that house. I need to know.

The wind begins to howl, and my car begins to slightly rock back and forth. The whistling of the night makes my spine feel locked. I quietly get out of the car, zipping up my jacket and putting on my hood. At the garage, I check the small windows to see if any car is parked.

Usually, the girls go skiing with their grandmother and cousins the first week of January, I just don't know if Victoria went. I hate skiing.

Her car is parked inside the garage. She's home. She didn't go. I wonder if she wasn't invited.

After going back and parking my car around the corner, I decide to close my eyes for a bit. At least I'll be safe, sleeping in my car. I set an alarm on my phone for the morning, which is only a few hours from now, and then I'll wait for her to leave. People like Victoria drink too much and then go to a Pilates class early in the morning to feel better about themselves.

The rocking motion of the car from every gust of wind puts me to sleep. Mother Nature's gentle lullabies.

The sounds of suburban housewives' husbands rolling out the trash cans for garbage day wake me up. Turning my car on, I drive it closer to Victoria's house. Like clockwork, the garage door to her cookie-cutter home opens. She won't notice me. Victoria isn't someone who pays attention to anything or anyone but herself.

She speeds out of her driveaway carelessly, backing into her mailbox. She doesn't even realize it, but I'd expect nothing less from her. The house is empty now. I text Ava to check on her, but she's probably sleeping in. She stays up through the nights sometimes, like me. Nocturnal humans are the creation of pain and suffering.

A rush of adrenaline takes over my body the moment I step out of my car. I walk toward Victoria's home. She'll be gone for at least an hour, maybe two if she stops by the liquor store on the way home. Josh told me she'd been boozing a lot the last few months before he died. Being a Brentwood makes you want to drink. It's not for the faint of heart.

The closer I get to her house, the louder my heartbeat becomes. My chest begins to feel like it's being squeezed. I decide to check the backyard to see if the gate is unlocked. The front door has a ring doorbell, so I can't try that, and if a spare key is there, it would be pointless. I may as well call the cops on myself if I attempted something so moronic.

The wooden gate is one that unlocks on both sides. Although some designs are beautiful, they are often flawed, working in my favor. The backyard is unkept. The plants are all dead, the weeds have not been removed, and the pots have not been moved inside for storage. The backyard looks nothing like mine, but I can't afford to have idle hands. My mind is full of poison already. I always need to be doing something.

The French door in the back of their home needs to be washed. I check for a camera or a sensor, but there isn't one. I sigh with a sense of relief. People often forget that all doors are important. We have a sensor on our back door. Every time it opens, Tanner is notified. In fact, I can't do much without him knowing. All it takes is placing a magnet on the sensor, a simple trick most people wouldn't ever think of. A simple fridge magnet buys me the freedom I need every day, for just enough time.

The wind picks up, and a window slams open and closed. I wiggle the door handle to check if, by any luck, it was left open. It's locked. The backyard has no good hiding spots for a key, but there has to be one out here. She has two teenage daughters.

There is always a key in the backyard. The front is too risky because the options are always a potted plant or doormat. Backyards have more space, more opportunity for concealing. Nothing really stands out except a single piece of rocky tile that looks cracked. I take my foot and step on it. It's shaky. I bend down and pick it up, finding a single key taped to the bottom.

Finally.

The key fits perfectly into the door, and it clicks as I turn it in the lock. I'm in the villain's castle.

The house is the same as it was last time, nothing out of place, everything unlived in. A model home, if you will. I walk into every single room to see if anything has been changed since the last time I was here. The kitchen looks the same, nothing out of place except a glass of wine sitting on the countertop. When I was in this house last time, Josh was telling me about how much he hated the kitchen, how he wanted a home more unique, more him. The counters looked identical, the marbling exactly as I remember it, the cabinets white, and the stainless steel appliances large and obnoxious. Victoria doesn't cook, so like everything the Brentwoods own, it was all for show.

The wooden floors creak in the exact same spots as last time. Josh said it made him feel normal to have creaky floors. We laughed about it. The light leaks into the house from the windows. I make my way to the bedrooms. The carpet is new, but everything else is the same upstairs. The hallway is long and narrow. I'd feel suffocated if I lived here.

The first door to the left is Ashley's bedroom. I never went in their rooms the last time I was here, but when I stand there now, it doesn't look like anything that would cost thousands of dollars to upgrade. It's the same basic eggshell-colored walls. There is a canopy bed in the center of the room, with linen sheets. White, of course. There are tennis trophies on a few shelves, dance trophies, and a picture of Josh sitting on Ashley's desk, right next to another family photo.

I walk into the bathroom and notice nothing out of the ordinary. It's a Jack and Jill. Allison's room is next door. The French blue wall color makes me sad, reminding me of when Ava was little, when things weren't so bad. A time where things felt like I was finally keeping my head above water, after treading in the deep end for years. I sit on Allison's canopy bed, the white sheets slowly molding to my body. She has a photo of her dad on her desk too. They loved him. A different version, but still him.

When I get up from Allison's bed, I fix any indentations I left before making my way to her desk. I rummage through it and stop at something unsettling.

A photo of Ava from her balcony.

Hundreds of tiny needles poking my skin take over my entire body. How long has she had this for? Why has she been watching her? I open her desk drawer and find more photos of Ava. I take one, gently fold it up, and place it in my pocket. What kind of sick game is this? I look around and realize, though, that I am no better. I'm here, after all.

The last room upstairs is one I've always wanted to go in. A longing I wish I didn't have. The door slowly opens when I gently turn the handle, leading me to a room that hasn't been cleaned in months. There are piles of clothes everywhere and empty bottles of wine peeking out from under the bed, the bed Josh used to share with Victoria. The room has no light in it, except a single crack from the blackout curtain that wasn't entirely closed. It looks like Victoria has been isolating herself in her room for months. It smells like sweat and sins.

There is not a single picture of Josh in her room. I don't bother sitting on the bed, not wanting any part of Victoria on my skin. The closet light was left on, so I walk toward it and open the door. There are hundreds of pieces of paper in piles—receipts, things from the discovery that I also have in my possession.

There is a purse buried deep in the corner. No one stores a designer bag like that. Even I know this. I grab the bowling bag Louis Vuitton and lift it up. It feels heavy.

There must be thousands in cash…

I dump the money out and start counting it. Why does she need this much? Is she worried the Brentwoods will cut her off? Is this her winter stockpile? I notice something stuck in the corner of the bag and pull it out, the smooth plastic in my hand. It's a hospital bracelet.

I place everything back in the bag and take another look at the hospital bracelet. Maybe it was something she wanted to bury, something she was paid for. I'll take whatever ammunition I can get for this legal case. Anything and everything helps. I rummage through some more of her things. She got rid of all of Josh's clothes.

I'd have kept them; I'd have kept everything of his. I wish things had worked out differently.

I wish that every day of my life.

Everything else in her bedroom is as expected. Nothing updated here. The office is the last room upstairs. I let myself in and sit down at the desk, spinning around in the chair carelessly. There are more files about what a bitch I am. I read some dirt about myself, none of which is true, and laugh at their attempt to build a case on why the money should not be given to Ava. This Erik fellow is really outdoing himself. I go on the computer and open Victoria's emails. A crime, one I'm okay with committing. There's only one in there. Everything else has been deleted. It's unread.

"Secrets, secrets are no fun. You have one week, or I'll tell everyone."

There is no email address included, and it was sent from a third party. A simple rhyme has swayed my emotions from hatred to panic-stricken in a single click of a button. I need to leave, need to get back to Ava, having gotten enough of what I needed. There's enough to build my case in court about the renovations. How am I going to claim this? I hurriedly mark the email as unread and rush downstairs.

The front door opens, and I stop dead in my tracks.

Allison walks in, our gazes glued to one another. My heart is too afraid to beat. I reach for the picture of Ava that she took, folded up in my pocket and hold it up to her. She's been caught, as I now am. Allison blocks the ring doorbell and allows me to leave. A single photo just gave me all the power I needed.

Allison just learned it's important to not leave a trace because a slip up could cost you everything. Victoria is about to learn that too, and when she does, I'll be watching.

TWENTY-SIX

ALLISON – NOW

My stomach grumbles loudly every so often. It's the only way I can tell I'm still alive. The cloth covers my face, so I can't make out my surroundings. I don't really hear anything except for the occasional fast-paced footsteps and loud banging sounds here and there.

I think back to all those times I watched Ava in her house, sitting on her balcony, observing others from her castle, and I can't help but wonder if maybe, while I was watching her, someone was watching me. I tense up when I hear a door slam. Footstep after footstep gets closer to me, and I can hear the shuffling of the shoes.

"Hello?" I say, swallowing my fear.

Finally, a voice responds.

"Hello, Allison," a woman's voice says.

"Who are you?" I ask, trying not to raise any concern. I continue muttering, "I don't know how to address you…"

"You can call me Miss," she says.

I nod.

"Did I do something wrong?" I know even if I did, she wouldn't tell me.

"You didn't, but your mother did," the woman says, laughing, the kind that hides the pain.

"What do you mean?" I wonder if this has to do with the lawsuit, or worse, Ava's death. My head pain comes back full force from the stress. I need a doctor.

"What if I were to tell you your mother was a monstruous woman? Would you believe me?"

I hear a lighter igniting, and within seconds, there's a cigarette smell to accompany it. That isn't a smell I've ever liked—a woody type of scent mixed with carcinogenic poison.

"I can give you money. Lots of it."

"You see, that's where you're wrong. Your mother, she owes me a lot of money, has for almost the last year. For a rich family, you sure are cheap little bitches," she scoffs.

A cold piece of metal touches the back of my head. I know what it is. If it didn't soothe my aches, I'd have screamed at the thought of a bullet going through my skull.

"I can get you money, I swear. My mother, she doesn't control it. I do, and I just need to call our trustee, and..."

The woman is silent. She's listening. Her thoughts are loud enough for the both of us. This woman has no plan, except to get money. It's clear and simple.

"What does my mother owe you money for?" I'm hoping she can tell that I'm being sincere, that I don't know what is going on, that I've *never* known what is going on. Never once in my entire life have I known anything. My life and my half-sister's life were kept a secret from me. I was fooled into believing only what I was told, placed in a bubble that was never meant to burst, but when it did, it was like acid spilled over everything, killing anything in its path.

"Did you know Ava?" I ask the woman.

"Nope. Heard about her, though." The gun clinks back and forth against some type of metal now, maybe one of those cheap folding chairs?

I wish I could take this thing off my face. It feels like I'm starting to slowly lose my mind. I'll keep asking questions and buy myself some time. My mother will know I didn't come home. She'll call the police. My grandmother will give a reward, no questions asked.

"How do you know my mother?" I pray the story is long enough, just enough time to help me find a way out. The rope is slowly cutting into the flesh on my wrists.

"She grew up a few blocks from me," she says firmly.

"In Woodbridge?" I ask.

"Is that what she told you?" The woman laughs to the point she begins to cough. "Your mother was fucking dirt poor. She killed her daddy, you know that? She didn't bat an eye when her mother overdosed either. She was happy about it. A sociopath then and now."

My eyes begin to feel warm, and they swell with tears. The fabric around my eyes becomes damp when the tears roll down my cheeks.

"Did you know my husband is dead because of your mommy?" Her voice is filled with rage. "He died for nothing, absolutely nothing. It would have been one thing if your dad actually lived, but he didn't, so my husband died for no fucking reason at all." Her voice is getting louder.

I don't want to speak. I think of all those stories I used to read about people getting abducted and their captors brainwashing them into thinking their parents didn't love them anymore, or that their parents died, that all they have is them now. This has to be something like that. I'm choosing to believe this woman will tell me anything to get me on her side.

"You know, your daddy was a sick man. So your mother, she poached my poor family. She knew my kids were smart enough to go to college, but college is expensive. Life is expensive. He had surgery because of us."

I can hear her grief.

"My dad had a surgery to clean his arteries," I say, confused.

"Is that what that stupid bitch mother of yours told you?" she asks, livid. "Your mother bought my husband's heart, made a deal with him so our kids could have a better life than us...have a fresh start, and then your daddy had his surgery. He had my husband's heart put into your rich, entitled daddy's body, for what? Your daddy died, and we were told it would be almost fullproof. So what was the point of them both dying?" The woman starts throwing things around, screaming.

I try not to shudder in fear, but sudden movement causes me excruciating pain.

The woman gets close to me. Her warm spit slides down my face through the cover.

"Your mom, she owes me a lot of money, and if she doesn't get the rest of it soon, you'll be joining your daddy."

The woman gets up and walks up the stairs, slamming the door shut. I lie on the cold ground. That woman is telling the truth. My family kept an entire world from me. They hid things from my sister and me, like a sick treasure hunt that slowly reveals it's clues. The game didn't start until the day of the funeral. Ready, set, go.

The woman's words play in my head on repeat. *Your mother*

bought my husband's heart. As much as I don't want to believe her, deep down, I know she is right. My mother's been drinking a lot, wandering around late at night. She came home with bullet holes in her car last winter, thinking none of us noticed.

My mother is a murderer. My mother thought someone else's life was more valuable than another's. My mother used money to play God. *I hate her.* I hate her more than Calista did, more than Ava did. I hate her. I hate my father. How could they do this? How could they even follow through with it?

I think back to all those arguments they'd have late at night. We were supposed to be asleep, but I'd keep my door slightly cracked open, just to be able to make out bits and pieces.

The door opens again. This time, a softer pair of footsteps slowly walks down the stairs.

"Hello? Who is there?" My body is slowly failing me.

I feel hands on my face, the blindfold being taken off. When I open my eyes, they slowly adjust to the little light that is down here, in what I'm now gathering is an unfinished basement.

A girl about my age looks at me. Through my puffy eyes and tears, I can make out her heart-shaped face and milky white skin, her hair slicked back into a braid. Her teeth are crooked, and she's wearing an oversized T-shirt. She looks like a normal girl. I'd kill to be regular, a word people don't like, but it's a word I appreciate. Being a Brentwood isn't all it's cracked up to be.

"Don't tell my mother," she says, tense.

"Can you let me go?"

"I can't do that, but here, eat this." She hands me a piece of a clementine.

I take a bite of it, but as I eat, the juice stings the cuts on my mouth. I wince.

"Thank you," I say before pausing, trying to gather my words with my tired brain. I open my mouth but find nothing wants to come out.

She looks at me, waiting.

"I, I…Look, I…" I try to talk, but my eyes swelling with water makes me lose focus. "I didn't know, I swear. I can get you anything you want. Please, just let me go. Please. I'll help you ruin my mother if that will make you happy. I'll do whatever it takes. I don't want you to judge me for what she did," I wail.

"It's not your fault." The sadness in her voice hurts me.

"How can I make this right?" I ask, knowing there's no way.

"You can't." Her words are final.

I want to sink into the earth and let it swallow me whole.

"But money helps. It always helps. It makes things go away," she says. She isn't wrong. Money always makes things go away… disappear. "Your mother is on her way. She has the money."

"How much?" I ask, curious.

"Enough for us to not bother you again for a long time."

"I'm sorry." But I know it will never be truly enough.

"Don't be sorry. My mom sold my dad's soul for money too." And for a minute, it's almost like, in a distant world, we could have been friends.

She puts my blindfold back on, being careful to not touch any of my cuts. I don't deserve her kindness, not in any form.

I lie back down, hoping I can hold on just a little longer. After I close my eyes, my mind races back to Ava. I think of all the times my mother used to stalk her house when we were kids and she'd pretend we were playing a game. I think of the times my mother wished her family dead after my father's funeral. I think of her hatred for Calista. I think of the affair she had with my dad while he was married, and I know deep down, she harnessed so much hatred toward Ava that she killed her. It's all making sense now. My rose-colored glasses have been shattered.

If I get out of here, I'll turn her in. I'll make things right. I'll be better, I can do better. I need sleep, unsure if I will wake up again…

* * *

When I open my eyes, I'm back in my room, like nothing ever happened. A doctor is taking my vitals. There's an IV needle in my arm. My ribs ache, and my skull is bashed in. This is proof I wasn't dreaming

I shut my eyes tightly. Money fixes everything, except the truth. The truth always has a higher value than any dollar sign, at least to me.

TWENTY-SEVEN

VICTORIA – NOW

The clock sits on the shelf in the living room, taunting me. It flashes one in the morning. Allison is still not home. I haven't heard from her in hours. She always checks in, she's cautious, she doesn't do things like this. I reach for my phone, with the glass screen shattered into what looks like multiple spider webs. I've been restless these days.

Marla has been harassing me non-stop, sending me payment reminders. I've paid her off, I've given her every dime of what I owe her, I've paid my dues, but she has a hold on me. No one would believe her, I try to remind myself, but I know people live for a scandal, and the Brentwoods can't survive any more of those.

I thought that after the lawsuit got settled, everything would go back to normal. The girls would get their father's portion of the trust, and they'd get a monthly allowance I could monitor, shaving little pieces off the top for myself here and there as their provider…But no, Calista wanted to take money from me. I'm sure it gave her great joy to cause an issue with me and the Brentwoods. The thought of her coy smile makes me feel unwell. I bet she's rolling in her grave, or wherever the fuck she is, at the fact that I had to give her now-dead daughter money. The irony makes me want to pour myself another glass, but I've already had too much tonight.

I catch a glimpse of the clock again. How have only five minutes passed? I call Allison, but it goes directly to voicemail. I walk upstairs to wake up Ashley, my mini me, except a better version—prettier, even. Letting myself quietly into her room, I gently rub her back so she isn't startled. Ashley lets out a small whimper. She sits up slowly, yawning and rubbing her eyes.

"Do you know where Allison is?" I try to keep my voice relaxed.

"No, why?" She rubs her eyes again.

"She isn't home, and she didn't call or leave a note, so I thought she may have told you where she went. Go back to bed, okay?" I tuck her in, bringing the covers over her shoulders as she lies back down. This is as maternal as I get, but it's good enough for Ashley.

"If she's dead, I'll just be the richest one in the family, I guess," she says, half awake. She is my child.

My phone is glued to my hand, and I wait for a response from Allison, but as the night turns to morning, I fear the worst has happened. I stare at my phone and debate whether to get the police involved, but I can't risk them digging into our family anymore, not when CeCe is livid with me as it is for letting money slip away to Ava.

Erik and I were found out about our house renovation scheme. We had no choice but to settle. It was either that or be caught. I should have done a better job with the invoices. Contractors, if you find the right one, are just as shady as someone lying on their taxes, even though they can afford it. Erik told me his friend would write the receipts and bill me accordingly, but for a hefty fine. We could get away with it because CeCe and the rest of the Brentwoods don't come to you; you go to them. They said I could redo the house after

Josh died, to help ease the pain—All I ever did was that stupid fucking white carpet. I would sign the paperwork the contractor gave me, and he would take a large sum off the top. But somehow, Calista was able to piece things together. We were almost flawless in our approach. Erik made sure of it. Everything was monitored. It's how the fortune stays just that, a fortune.

I can't imagine what it is like to be in your late forties and everything you ever purchased had to be approved by your parents. Maybe I should have known that before I got knocked up on purpose by Josh, but I didn't realize the complications that would arise once I was married to him. I'm sure I would have still done what I did because I just didn't want to be who I was, and anything was better than that. To escape misfortune and poverty comes with fine penmanship when you sign a deal with the devil, and I had practiced what signature I'd use to write my name down hundreds of times.

My eyelids feel like burdens, and I pace back and forth in the living room. Maybe if I just close them for a few minutes, Allison will be home when I wake up…

A small bead travels down my neck, rousing me, and a cold sweat takes over my entire body. I gasp and grab my chest, breathing heavily, like my lungs are being crushed. Ashley walks over from the kitchen and looks at me like I'm a deranged. She brings me a glass of wine.

"Here," she says.

The red liquid slides down my throat, and I hope it will ease my anxiety and quiet my mind. I've tried every solution this last year, but this is the only one that seems to bite.

"She didn't text or call, in case you were wondering." Ashley heads out the door on her way to school. "Sarah's mom is taking me—you probably can't drive," she tells me, but in a condescending way, like I shouldn't be driving because I'm a bad mom.

I am a bad mom, and I don't really give a flying fuck about that. I didn't even mean to have Ashley, but Josh kept insisting we needed to give Allison a sister. At least Ashley turned out like me, so I'm able to understand her, even if she is a bit of a bitch. Genetics are strong in this family, but I hope killing people isn't a trait that gets passed down to my children. I can't handle any more stress. It's aging what little beauty I have left.

The second I inhale the rest of the wine in my glass, I call Erik. He'll know what to do. I call him twice, no answer. I try again.

Nothing.

He always answers my calls, always. He was fired as the Brentwood trustee, but I promised to give him a payout from the girl's monthly allowance for helping me with everything.

More time passes by, and I decide to call the police. I wish I didn't love someone I didn't even want, but now that I have her, I don't want to lose her. If I don't call, the world will label me as a bad mother for not taking charge of my missing daughter. The woman on the phone is monotone, asking me to repeat my emergency. She doesn't seem very interested, just does her job and tells me someone is on the way. I'm glad I never had to work after I met Josh. All the jobs in the world don't compare to having the power of status.

The police show up as I pound the last of my wine. They knock on the door, and when I let them in, they go straight to the living room, staring at my nice things. My white carpet that I *had* to have, my white walls that look as sterile as a hospital room, it makes them uncomfortable. If I weren't so distressed, I'd have enjoyed watching them feel displaced. I like to see how people react out of their element because I've spent decades of my life perfecting feeling comfortable in other worlds. I find it amusing.

"When did you last hear from your daughter?" the officer asks. He's an attractive, stockier fellow. I watch him taking down useless notes.

"Yesterday, I think?" This is going to make me look bad.

"You think?" The officer raises an eyebrow. He writes something down on his notepad and makes a face at me. He knows I'm drunk right now.

"If you stopped judging me, maybe you could do your job better." I regret calling them.

"We are just doing our job," The officer says.

His partner, a female about my age, with her hair slicked back tightly in a bun, stares awkwardly at me. She knows better than to speak to me. She knows I'm alpha, even though she is the one in uniform. That's what makes me alpha, that I don't need a uniform to be the dominant one, it's carved into my flesh.

"Look, my daughter, she's been under a lot of stress lately. She's been busy with school."

"Does she have a boyfriend?" the officer asks.

"No," I say sternly, but the truth is, I'm not sure. We haven't talked as much since everything happened, since she found out about her father's full life before I came into the picture. Somehow, she found out how I met her dad.

Ashley could't care less that I'm an adulterer. She was just excited she could by a Chanel purse with some of the money she got. Josh never liked her to have anything too expensive. He wanted her to have to earn it herself. After the funeral, Ashley said that suffering a trauma is like earning something you'd have to work really hard for, but I can't argue with that logic either.

"If I were you, I'd get some sleep, lay off the booze, and wait for her to come home. Text her friends, check her social media, call the school, and if she doesn't turn up, we will put out an ABP," he says, heading toward the door.

"You can't put out an ABP." I pause to think about the repercussions of the matriarch.

The officer turns around, confused.

"And why is that?" he asks, raising concern.

I need to think this through. Time to muster up some bullshit excuse. "Because…colleges. If they look her up, it will be all over the internet one day, and it will embarrass her. It's her future," I plead with them. The truth is, it isn't *her* future that could be jeopardized, but mine. CeCe doesn't allow this sort of thing. Allison would be better off dead, if that were the case.

The officers leave, slamming the door behind them. A picture falls off the wall, and the glass shatters everywhere. I don't bother picking it up. I couldn't care less . Pictures around here aren't for memories. They are for show.

Finally, the phone rings. It's from an unknown caller. I answer it, already knowing nothing good will come from a number that doesn't want to be recognized.

"Hello?" I say before anyone speaks.

"Why, hello there, Victoria. It's Marla. I just wanted you to know, since you haven't made your payments the last few months, I have your daughter. She's not doing so well, so if you bring me the thirty thousand to start…I'll give her back."

The white carpet starts to spin. I look down and throw up all over it. Fuck. To think I was concerned about the policemen's dirty boots a few moments ago.

"I'll call back in a bit to check up on you," Marla says.

How can someone have power like this over me? How could they control me? How am I letting them? I call Erik again, panicked. No answer. To think I ever slept with him, even out of spite for my husband, makes me irritated.

The bag full of money in my closet is drained. I have nothing left. All the kids' allowance has been spent on food, therapy, clothes, projects, the mortgage, and bills. There was nothing left over this month. They don't get their larger allowances until they are twenty-five. It's a Brentwood rule, and the biggest allowance comes in your forties—you'd think now that Cece's husband is dead, she'd have changed the rule, so her kids could be as obnoxious as her. For now, it's enough to get by and then some. My children are piggy banks you can't just break open. It pains me.

Hurrying toward my car, I reach inside my purse and dig for my car keys. Something sharp stabs my hand, making me bleed. The car automatically unlocks with the key in my hand, and I sit in the driver's seat, pulling down the mirror to fix myself up. I look horrible—haven't bathed in days, teeth stained from the wine I polished off earlier, my hair all wild. The engine makes too loud of a sound for my looming headache when I pull out of the driveaway. I'll have the money soon. I'll be quick.

The lines in the road blur together, but it's a short distance from my house, and I know this drive like the back of my hand. I used to do it every day after I would pick up the kids for school, and then we'd go play a special game. At least, that's what I told them it was called.

The scent of the air makes me feel sicker. I park my car and walk up to the house like I'm a realtor showing it to potential clients. I'm confident in my stride. No one will question me because I won't let them. I enter the key code to the lockbox and let myself into the Maples's home. For months now, I've been taking things slowly out of the house, so I hope there's something of value left. Marla's been breathing down my neck. A part of me feels selfish, and I can't decide if I'm doing this to save my own child or to save myself from my own crime. My past life could resurface at any moment. I tell myself it's for Allison, but I don't even believe it.

It's been a while since anyone's lived in this house. It's such a shame it sits here empty, but it works in my favor. I walk directly up the stairs, staring at the abstract artwork along the walls, not bothering with Ava's room. It would be like a lion licking the bones of its kill from months ago, just in case there may be something left. I've picked it over so many times for extra cash—pawned off her pearls and emeralds. I tried to scare Ava off with a letter, and now look at her, *dead*. She should have walked away.

I'm sure Tanner had a fit when she spent his money, but at least she had money to spend. He was all about status, so she had to have the best of the best, even if all his scams caused him to be in debt to dozens of people. A lot of people hate that man, myself included. If I had to do it all over again, I would still have picked Josh over Tanner.

Being in this house makes me feel like I won because no one is left standing. I get off on this thought, being able to lurk in this house with no one watching me. At the top of the stairs, I place my hand on the railing. I'm feeling a bit faint, but I know it's because I'm more drunk than I think. Stumbling toward Calista and Tanner's bedroom, I open the door to hell. A velvet sitting couch is next to Calista's armoire. I lay down on it, staring at the ceiling, feeling like a boat is rocking me back and forth. Sleep is really what I need, but I can do that after I find what I'm looking for.

In the overly sized closet—a second house on its own—I dig through her things, hoping something of Calista's will be enough. Her clothes are color-coordinated, and every purse looks like it's a knockoff. There is nothing of value to me in here. The closet is a wash. The doors to the armoire are a bit sticky, causing me to yank on them, I fall over, hitting my head on the edge of the bedframe, but I don't even care that I'm bleeding now. There's no time for any of this. Everything is on the line.

My stomach sinks. The armoire is empty, all her jewelry gone.

Who could have taken it? Ava is dead. Calista and Tanner were missing for months before she even died…Has someone else been in here? I go to her nightstand and start rummaging through everything, tossing clothes on the floor, underwear sprawled everywhere, bras scattered around me. Nothing, not even a La Perla set. Everything is cotton, basic, just like her.

My head is pounding. Without thinking, I open the curtains to let some light in. It's too dark in here during this time of year. Her neighbors are staring directly into the window as they sit on their porch having some tea. They see me. At least, I'm pretty sure they did, fuck. I need to get out of here.

In a rush, I close the curtains frantically and try to rummage through anything, just in case the neighbors call the cops. I get a whiff of my own scent. The smell of alcohol mixed with my own odor makes me cringe.

I try one more thing before giving up and being forced to go to CeCe's—Tanner's side of the bed. Unlike Calista, who only bought nice things for her daughter, he liked to own the real deal of everything, to show off what he had.

I open his dresser, find a simple wooden box, and take it. I know him, and I know there is something in here worth something. Not caring what state the room is in now, I decide to just let it be and get out. If my blood ends up in this room, so be it. The murder investigation is closed.

The town didn't want to be known for this. It was taken care of, ruled a suicide. No one will be searching for any more evidence here, and by the time they sell the house, they'll pay for someone to deep clean it before anyone moves in.

Crimes don't matter when the house is a hot listing. People love to live in a house where a girl died. It adds a rich backstory to the place. They do have a point—it's a great conversation starter.

Before I leave, I walk to the kitchen and stare at the table. I loathe it. The place where Josh would sit with Calista and Ava, laughing over mediocre cooking, while I would be home with my two girls, alone, having Erik please me because my own husband didn't want the life he was forced into. I walk over to the table and flip it on its side, watching the leg snaps. It satisfies me.

The doorbell rings, and I freeze, unsure what to do. I panic, quickly grab a knife from the butcher block.

In a hurry, I open the French doors, similar to my house but nicer. Her French doors have golden handles and engravings. I grab the wooden box and quickly walk deep into the foliage of what was once her backyard. Maybe it's the neighbors just checking in. I could tell them I'm a realtor, or a potential buyer and my realtor gave me the information, which isn't exactly a lie.

The garden is going to shit back here, and it brings me too much joy. Josh always used to talk about Calista's gardening skills, It was subtle. He never mentioned her name, but I'm not exactly dumb. I find a quiet spot behind a large tree. If someone peers into the backyard, they'll just barely miss me. I'm desperate to see if someone is in the house. Too many people have access these days—realtors, reporters, police, and me.

To ease my anxiety, I take the knife and attempt to pry open the wooden box while I wait. My hands are shaking horrendously, not from the nerves, but from the withdrawals. I jam the knife inside the crack over and over again, just enough to open it up. The wood goes flying all over in the backyard, but a Rolex stares back at me. I take a giant sigh of relief. This wasn't all for nothing.

The backyard doors open, and a man speaks.

"This backyard is wonderful. You could easily fit a pool back here…or two."

Gentle footsteps in the grass sound like they are getting closer to me. I begin to shiver but try to hold myself so my teeth won't chatter.

The door to the backyard closes. I let out a loud breath. I don't even know where Allison is, and I still need to wait for another call.

The backyard starts to feel haunted, like the ghost of Calista is here. In every life, she will follow me around like a shadow of guilt, but I ignore it. I check my phone and hope enough time has passed so I can go back in. Peering through the French doors, I see no one walking around so go to let myself back in.

The door is locked.

The cold golden handle laughs at me. I look around the yard for another way out and notice one of the tree branches that has fallen out of place. It doesn't match the tree it's next to. I gently lift its branches, revealing a cut-out to the neighbor's house. Poking my head through it, I notice they have a side gate, unlike this monstrosity, where you're stuck inside, like a ballerina glued to a five-year-old's jewelry box. I tuck the Rolex in my pants pocket and decide to do it. If I'm stopped, I'll tell them I was doing a showing and got locked out prepping for it. They'll know it couldn't be a lie because there have been a dozen showings a day from what my friend tells me—the last two buyers backed out, apparently they didn't have the funds and talked a big game.

Barely fitting through the hole in the fence, I make it next door. This backyard is empty, except for a new tree in their yard. The tree has probably taken root by now, small and fragile, but I'm sure it will hold on tight. Even trees want to be planted in nicer neighborhoods.

After running quickly through their yard to the side gate, I open it, not even caring if it makes too loud of a sound. I'm almost to my car, and I don't look back. When I get in my car, I drive off and circle the neighborhood endlessly, waiting for a call. This bitch is taking too long. She's toying with me, I know she is. Marla's blackmailed my family enough.

After another loop around the neighborhood, I see flashing red lights behind me—anything but subtle. I pull over to the side and wait for the officer to approach. Quickly, I pull down the mirror and fix my makeup. I look bad, but not bad enough for them to suspect anything. Putting the mirror away, I fix my hair in the reflection of the window, throw on sunglasses to hide my bloodshot eyes, and pop a mint. I'm fucked. I need to think fast. The sunlight reflects on the knife next to me, and I realize I brought it with me. I stash it as quickly as I can before staring directly in front of me, both my hands on the wheel.

The cop walks up to me and slowly knocks on my window. I smile, roll down the window, and pop my head out at him. He's attractive, black hair, late forties, a typical officer with a mustache, because of course.

"Did I do something wrong, officer?" I ask, playing dumb.

"We got a few calls from some neighbors that someone was circling the block. They said it looked suspicious."

Laughing playfully, I respond, "Better safe than sorry." I smile. "I'm waiting for my daughter to call me. She was going to the nurse's office to get sent home, but she hasn't called yet, so I've just been circling the block. In my day, if you wanted to leave school, you'd just leave school."

The cop laughs at this in agreement.

"If you're bored, maybe go to the school parking lot and play a game on your phone or something, like everyone else. Okay?" he says, giving me a warning. "It can be unsettling around here, since... you know...what happened with that family." Although, he doesn't seem sad. He seems like he wants to discuss it.

I can't help myself. I love to hear everyone's theories and stories about the tragedy, like I get off on it. God knows, it's been forever.

"What do you think really happened?" I make myself look

desperate for his response, and he leans over into my car. Shit, what if he can smell the booze on my breath?

"Do you really want to know?" he asks, playing with me, wanting me to say yes. Foreplay.

"Of course, I'm bored and have nothing to do until my daughter calls, so I'd love to hear your side of things. Pretty please!" The cologne he is wearing crosses my sense of smell. It's strong, too strong. I swallow my own vomit while he begins to ramble on.

"I think the girl…I think she killed her parents and felt guilty and then killed herself, or that her parents disappeared on purpose before her, came back, killed her, made it look like a suicide, and ran off with her inheritance…Because no one can find the money. It's still missing. It's like the suburban treasure hunt of our time. I hear it's millions, lotta people break into that house to find the *gold*, I've actually looked a few times myself, but don't tell anyone I said that."

The thought of all that missing money makes my skin crawl. I wish I was a snake and could shed my entire body. At least then I'd be able to sleep better at night. The Brentwoods tried to locate the money for months. It's just gone. No trace of it. That's all that stupid family talks about anyway, even though they have enough money to buy *anything*. They are suburban royalty, which is better than British royalty, if you ask me.

"How do you think she killed her parents, if it's your first theory?" I'm actually interested in what this moron has to say.

"I mean, she didn't look too strong, so I'm sure she had some help. But probably rat poison, or paint thinner. Apparently, she was an artist, but most artists have a few screws loose. Like uh, what's that artist's name…? The one with syphilis?" he says, racking his brain.

"Van Gough." Understanding what it's like to want to cut off my own ears right now…

"I heard that some of the cops got paid off to be quiet, though. They were able to retire. Half of them left after the case was closed… You didn't hear that from me, if anyone asks, but it wouldn't surprise me. The things people do for money these days."

"If the price is right," I agree, laughing.

He nods.

My phone finally rings, and I quickly apologize to the officer. "I'm sorry, I need to take this. It's my kid." My finger firmly presses the button to roll up the window, and I watch the officer back away from my car as I answer the phone.

"I have what you want. Where is she?" I ask, my blood boiling.

"She's at my boyfriend's house in Gary," Marla replies.

"Text me the address. I'll be there in an hour." I hang up and drive as fast as possible, thinking of all the things Marla might have told Allison, the things I'll need to find a way to lie about to her, to make her think it was all brainwashing. Allison will believe me. I'm her mother.

Marla is smart for not keeping Allison in Englewood. She knew I would look there. I can't believe I made a deal with the fucking devil. I married into a whole fucking family of them. If there was a God, He'd never help me. I'm on my own now.

I've always been on my own.

TWENTY-EIGHT

CALISTA – THEN

The lawsuit is finally coming to a head. All the evidence is compelling enough to make the judge lean in our favor—at least, that's what Tanner's scumbag lawyer keeps telling us—but all parties have been advised to try one last time to settle. Ava hasn't been home since the incident. She's been staying in her dorm mostly, she checks in on me every day out of guilt though. I miss the smell of her fresh paintings filling the house with toxic fumes. Tanner has only screamed in my face once since she left, blaming me for a high water bill after prepping my plants for their blooming season. We've had no snow still. It's been an unusual winter.

We have one more final mediation with the Brentwoods, and we settle. The judge won't need to rule anything if we can agree to it. The problem is this: if we do go to court, there's no way to know for certain that one side will win and the other won't. It's a fifty-fifty, which is why mediation is so important. If we can convince the other side to give us the money we are owed, we won't need to risk it all if the judge decides to not rule in our favor after all. Same with the other side. There's a lot to lose here. If we lose, we can appeal, but it's an ongoing cycle.

The office we walk into is cold, and the hairs on my arms stand upright, making each follicle hurt. Ava should be here any minute now. Tanner sits at the head of the table, looking smug. He's confident we will settle today, but he doesn't know that if we settle, it will be because of me. And he won't ever see that money. I've made damn sure of it.

Everything is ready.

Nothing will go wrong.

I've been preparing it perfectly, dreaming up his last breath in my mind.

The door opens, and Tanner turns his head toward it as Ava walks in. She ignores him. He pretends to put on a phony fatherly smile, but she flicks him off.

The judge walks into the room and takes a seat.

"Everyone ready?" he asks.

"Ready as ever," Tanner says, smiling.

The judge takes several minutes to look over all the paperwork, marking things, making notes, sighing here and there. I can't imagine going to law school, having the high honor of being a judge, just to have to deal with greedy people playing, "he said, she said." I'd rather be a housewife than a judge. At least it's honest work.

"Do you want to put in an offer first? So we can go to the other side with it immediately? Get the ball rolling…"

Bill stands up, adjusting his suit coat before addressing the judge. "We are firm at three hundred million dollars. We will not be going lower. That is one third of his wealth."

Tanner nods.

The entire room looks to Ava. I don't know what she is thinking. She is dressed for a funeral—tight-fitting black clothes, dark makeup—and looks tired. I know I've disappointed her in all my decisions, but soon, everything will be back to normal.

The judge heads back into the other room. An hour passes by before we get word of anything. The time feels even slower because not a single word is mustered. It's as silent as what I imagine being in space is like, where sound doesn't exist—eerily peaceful.

As I break away from staring at the wall, I see Tanner and Bill whispering to each other, strategizing. Bill doesn't know I've read every atrocious email he's sent. Nothing should ever be written down; everything must be oral arrangements only. Self-incrimination is a thing. *A good lawyer would know that.*

Ava stands up abruptly and asks Bill to leave the room. Bill makes it about him and says he's going to go check in on the other side, see what is going on. He grabs his folder and walks out the door, shutting it loudly behind him. It was intentional.

I worry what is going to come out of Ava's mouth. She's been a kettle of water left on high, waiting to scream for years. Ava looks at me, like what she is doing might not be the smartest thing, but I don't stop her.

"Tanner, when we win today—and we will—you won't get a dime of it. Nothing. You never will. You're a piece of garbage who preys on people who are already broken. When that Judge comes in here and they give us an offer, even if it's one million dollars, I'll fucking take it. Do you hear me? I'll take the smallest amount just to watch you die inside," she says, emotionless.

Tanner's face turns purple. He stands up from his chair and leans over the table, trying to control his rage because at any given second. the Judge can walk in.

"I've recorded the last few times you've hurt us, and **I've** put USBs in multiple storage rooms, told all my friends at college about you, so if anything should happen to us…I've done my digging too. You see, Tanner, I know people, lots of people. I know everything, like your little plan with Bill…Well, it's me who makes the final say, and the judge knows that." Ava takes a deep breath.

I'm proud of her, and I'm afraid for her.

Tanner storms out of the room. He's probably going to look for Bill. They are going to need to come up with a new tactic. I wish Ava had waited to say anything because what if Tanner acts early? What if he decides the money isn't important anymore?

The judge comes back in the room. Tanner and Bill are too caught up arguing to even notice.

"The other side has given an offer." The judge pushes a piece of paper toward Ava.

She looks at me, and I get up and lock the door. If Tanner and Bill try to come in, they'll be locked out, buying us mere minutes to think everything over fast.

"Mom, what do you think?" she says.

I've missed her calling me Mom. She usually calls me nothing these days, but the fact she needs me for this decision breaks me in the best way.

"Your father loved you very much. He wanted you to have this money. I know it from the bottom of my heart. He wasn't born bad. He was controlled to be bad. There's a difference. The will and the trust never matched because he was looking out for you. You deserve this money for everything you've had to endure. It's your choice if you think it's enough. If you ask for more, I won't judge you, and if you ask for less, I certainly won't judge you for that either." I fight back any tears.

The judge smiles at me. The door handle wiggles.

"There are some rules to this, though. If you agree to the money, you cannot, by any means, disclose the amount. You also must keep some of it in the stocks that the Brentwoods have. However, if you agree to pulling it all out as cash and not touching their stocks, you will get less after taxes, of course, you can do what you please with the money. If you don't, you will need a trustee to manage your money if you choose to keep it in the stocks, and the money can be revoked if you breach any of this. Is this clear?"

Ava nods.

"Will it be over then?" she asks.

I want to tell her it will only be just the beginning.

The judge excuses himself and walks back to the room to let them know we will consider their offer. Bill and Tanner come in, sitting in silence.

I walk out to use the bathroom. Ava follows me to get some coffee.

"Do you think that it's too much?" she asks.

"After what I put you through, nothing will ever be too much." I give her a hug.

She hugs me back, and it feels good to know, after everything, my child might still hold some love for me in her heart. All I ever wanted was to cloth her and feed her, but I had nothing. I had no one—no parents to help, no career of my own to help us pay for things. All I had was the hope that someone would love me for me and love the parts that came with me.

The table with the coffee and stale cookies faces the window toward the Chicago skyline. Ava walks toward it, pours herself some coffee, and lets the steam fade into the air while she admires the view.

I walk out of the common space and down the hallway to the bathroom. When I open the door, CeCe collides into me.

"Watch where you're going, you fool," she says.

In all this time, her disdain for me is unmatched. Victoria passes us, hurrying back toward the office. Her makeup is running down her cheeks, most likely because of Josh's vicious mother.

The only reason Victoria settled was because she had to. She got caught in a lie, and she had to convince her daughters to settle. Money was going somewhere, but I don't care where as long as I won. I see the matriarch for the first time in what feels like hundreds of years, and by the look of anger on CeCe's face, I won. An entire facial expression made of pure hatred toward myself means I am the winner.

I won.

I finally won.

I block her as she tries to push past me from the bathroom door.

"No," I say, proud to stand up for myself. "You listen to me, your son hated you. He hated your entire existence, and all he ever wanted was to be loved by you. He did anything and everything you asked to be accepted by you."

"Why are you defending someone who hit you, darling? Left you to starve?" she hisses.

"He didn't do that. You did."

"He had a choice," she says.

It hurts me because it's true.

249

CeCe tries to push her way past me again, but I force her back into the bathroom. She's older now, frailer, and she won't dare try me. I've been harnessing too much hatred from her for over a decade. I am a wild card.

"I am not afraid of you or your family. Your money is blood money. Your family secrets? I know them all, every last one of them. Josh told me everything," I say confidently.

A rush of blood fills my head, and the adrenaline in my body makes my skin burn. It feels good to finally tell her off after all this time. CeCe's been blocked off by iron rod gates and country clubs. She was unreachable and unobtainable…until now.

"You made him leave me, or you'd cut him off. He needed that money to live. You stole him away," I tell her. This time, I'm nearly pressed up against her body, so close I can feel her pulse speed up. I slap her, and the sound pleases me more than I can describe, my hand hot against her cold flesh.

She touches her face, shocked.

"My son valued his own life more than love. A trait that the Brentwoods have always possessed. Themselves over anyone. He'd do it again, I'm sure." She shoves me off her.

As CeCe walks out the door, I shout, "It's done. It's signed. I won!" A sense of joy takes over my body, making it all worth it.

CeCe turns around to get the last word, and I let her have it. "You will never truly win, because you are not one of us."

But that's a lie because I already have.

The walk back to the mediation room feels longer for some reason. I open the door, knowing in the next room over, Victoria is being verbally accosted by CeCe, her children witnessing the true brutality of the Brentwood name because this time, they are here to watch it.

Bill and Tanner are smiling. They know a deal has been made. Ava didn't tell them the amount, but Bill will need to know anyway, for legal purposes. The money won't come in for a few weeks. Time is running out. We will need to pay Bill his fees still, even after everything happens, just so he doesn't suspect anything. It makes me sick to give him a drop of the money, but it is what it is.

Ava seems relieved yet afraid. She knows it's only a matter of time until it's over for her, knows the darkness is looming now.

Ava smiles at me as she collects her things. I follow her to the front of the building, where her friend picks her up. Easton, I believe. I like him. He seems like good company, which is hard to come by these days. I'm afraid to go home alone to that house, but I have nowhere else to go—no friends, no family, nothing. I'm petrified that now everything is going through, Tanner may not want to wait to get rid of me. He just needs Ava now.

Maybe CeCe is right. Maybe I haven't won after all.

TWENTY-NINE

AVA – THEN

"Call me if anything goes wrong," Easton says, hugging me tight.

"I will." I know the moment I step through those doors, my life will change.

"You don't need to do this, you know? There are other ways."

But I'm already one foot out the car. I turn and look at him and smile.

"I got your back. You've always had mine," he says.

He's been there for me for so much already. I wish I'd never told him anything, but there's only so much turmoil I can handle on my own. Everyone knows a rollercoaster is much more fun when someone rides next to you. I scream, you scream. That's how I've been feeling lately.

The walk up the driveway feels different, more final. Easton drives off, and I stare at his car until it becomes nothing more than a spec. I've been sleeping at his house the last month. The dorms feel isolating. My mind doesn't work like the other students'. It truly is hard to be happy, and it's exhausting watching other people effortlessly smile. Never in a million years have I ever felt like that. I don't even know how to. My mind thinks a hundred little thoughts every second of the day, constantly running, *trapped*. Painting quiets me. My energy goes into each brush stroke.

The air smells dry, almost dusty. A snow is finally coming. Some people say you can't smell weather, but they are wrong. The keypad to the garage feels stiff. I open it and punch in the code to the garage, but it doesn't work. It's always been Tanner's birthday, an important day in history, only to him.

As I fumble through my purse, I can't find the house key. I must have left it at Easton's. My breathing begins to slow as I walk to the front door. This is it. The day is finally here. The money has been safely put in my name, I was supposed to wait until later. I opted out of the stocks and took the cold hard cash. Tanner doesn't know this. No one does except the judge from mediation, Bill was going to give him a cut for helping us out, so I decided to give him more for his silence. One million *cash* for a generous thank you.

I don't feel any different, just a bit more uneasy because Tanner has reached his end game. It was never about my mother or me, about him being a loving husband or a devoted stepfather. It was about the fact that my last name is Brentwood, and with a last name like that comes dollar signs, whether I was legally in the will or not. The only thing I learned from him was patience, to wait it out. We are playing the same game but with different outcomes.

The doorbell rings, and within seconds, the door is unlocked. Before I walk into the house, my mother points out that it's begun to flurry. She smiles. I've never seen her this excited for snow before. She always dreaded it growing up. Instead, she prefers her springtime, where everything that was hibernating can come back to life.

My mother rushes me into the house and hugs me.

Tanner is sitting at the kitchen table. He watches me, never breaking eye contact. My shoes are neatly placed by the front door, and I walk upstairs to my bedroom. Sometimes, I'm in disbelief I still have a room in the house, but appearances are everything. Even Tanner knows this.

When I told my mother I had to come back and pack up some more things, she told me she needed to have a long talk with me, so I figured just one last night here, *to take care of everything that needed to be done.*

It's a nice evening to open the French doors and let the cool air into my stuffy room. My mother brings me a warm cup of tea, and I take a sip of it to be courteous. She can tell I don't want to be bothered, so she leaves the room to give me some space. Something I appreciate.

Digging through my jean pockets, I reach for my storage key, incase anything goes wrong later. I tape it behind one of my paintings. As the tape tears, the ripping sound fills me with anxiety over the preparation of what could happen. I pull the handgun Easton gave me from my purse and put it under my pillow. I will wait for him to go to sleep... and tomorrow, I will sleep well—*the first time in years...*

* * *

A loud slam wakes me up.

I reach for my phone, but it's dead. The gun under my pillow is gone. My head is pounding, and I am surrounded by blood. The stickiness of it binds my hair together from my scalp.

I forgot. How could I have forgotten? I was so certain tonight wouldn't be like the others. The pain is excruciating. He wanted his prey injured before he attacked.

Everything is blurry when I head downstairs. The floorboards creak with every step. Another loud sound coming from the kitchen, and the noise stops. Rounding the corner, I see Tanner smashing things, holding my gun. My mother is still. She looks at me and glances toward the door, wants me to run, but I can't do that. Not to save myself, but because there is nowhere to run to. As long as he's alive, I'll never be still.

Tanner smashes a lamp with my gun. It shatters to the floor.

"What was she going to do with this?" he screams.

My mother stays silent.

"Was she going to kill me with this?" He laughs.

I need to grab anything I can find, catch him off guard. But I don't know his plan. I don't know which of us he wants dead first. Does he want my mother to suffer by watching her only child fade away, or does he want me to watch my mother die, filling me with rage, before my untimely death?

"Let's just have some tea. We can talk about this," she pleads with him.

"Tea? You want to have some fucking tea?" He violently points the gun at her.

"The neighbors will hear you," my mother says, trying to calm him down.

"We live in a fortress, a fucking fortress that I provided for you and your ungrateful bitch," he says maliciously.

The wind bellows like it's in pain, the sorrow too much to bear. I reach for the small sculpture by the entry way and grip it firmly. It feels like the metal is cutting through my hands. I run up behind Tanner and hit him in the head with it. He cries out in pain, rubbing his scalp, taking a moment to realize what has happened. The gun falls, and I run to get it, accidentally kicking it under the couch.

I panic and try to reach for it, getting on my hands and knees and trying my hardest to obtain it. The metal from the gun brushes against my fingertips, but I can't reach it. The dog begins to bark. Tanner gets up, full of rage, and kicks my dog. Murphy whimpers and runs away, limping. My mother screams, watching this happen to her, to us. The veins pop out of her neck. I've never seen her like this before. She talks like she lives in fear, and now it's spilling out of her mouth like a volcano that, after all this time, is erupting. *Everyone said it was inactive. People are wrong. They always are.*

The gun pushes further back behind the couch. I have it in my grip when Tanner yanks me by my legs and sits on me. He punches me over and over again, my face more numb with each blow.

"I'll start with you!" he says, spitting on me.

Through my blurred vision, I see my mother running to the kitchen.

I can hear the dog barking through the ringing in my ears. The blood is running down my face and into my mouth. I feel close to death, closer than I have ever been. I cough, choking.

My mother runs over and smashes him over the head with her tea kettle.

"Get off my fucking daughter," she says.

The weight on top of me lightens, and I try my best to sit up, but my ribs feel broken. Through my blurred vision, I see him holding his face, pacing back and forth, screaming in agony.

My mother quickly runs to the cabinet and grabs something from it, some type of herb. She puts it on a cloth and dampens it. What is she doing?

We don't have much time left. The clock is racing against us. My head is exploding, but all I can think about is the gun. I crawl to the couch and stick my hand under it one more time. If I don't succeed, it's over. Tanner's gun collection is in the basement. All it would take for him to win is running downstairs to grab anyone of those, but he wanted my gun. It had to be *my* gun. It's the kind of person he is. He likes to win when he's taking something from someone that is rightfully theirs.

I got it.

Tanner comes running at me. I point the gun at him. My mother comes up from behind him and tries to put the rag over his mouth, but he shoves her off him, like nothing more than a bug.

"I'll shoot you," I say, standing up as best I can. "I'll blow your fucking brains out, do you hear me?"

My mother's head is bleeding now. I watch her slowly stand up from the corner of my eye.

"I dare you," he says.

I point the gun at him.

"Admit you killed him," I scream.

"You already know the answer to that." He laughs.

"Admit it," I yell again.

"Fine, I killed him. Are you happy? I had to wait years to do it! That money is mine!" he says, his skin slowly blistering.

"Monster," I yell back.

"If you were going to shoot me, you'd have already done it," he says, so sure of himself.

My mother walks over to me. I'm covered in blood, the blood she created within my body, slowly pouring out of me.

"How?" she asks.

Tanner ignores her.

"How?" she says again, her mouth twitching.

"Why does it matter? He's dead, isn't he?" His words are empty.

"How!" She demands.

"I realized him coming over all this time would help me, help me plan the moment to swap out his medicine, *it was easy, too easy.* I just had to wait for the perfect moment where it didn't seem too obvious."

"Point that gun at him. Do not move," she tells me.

I keep my finger on the trigger, but it's hard to focus. I'm fading.

My mother leans into my ear and whispers something. "We can't let anyone hear the gunshots. Do you hear me? Wait for my signal."

She walks to the counter, puts something in a cup, and mixes it with water.

"Have him sit down at the table," she says to me.

With my gun firmly pointed at him, I motion for him to sit. My mother places three cups on it. Next to each cup is a scone. I'm not connecting anything right now. I don't understand what is happening. *Are we having a fucking family meal?* What is she doing? What if he lifts this table out from under us and grabs the gun? He won't hesitate. He can't afford to stall, and neither can we.

We all sit down at the table, the gun in my hand glued to him like macaroni on a fucking sheet of paper.

"Eat," she says.

We all take a bite of food. He doesn't break eye contact from me.

"Drink," she says.

We all drink.

Within seconds, Tanner is grasping for air, his body convulsing. I look at my mother and put the gun down. We sit at the table while watching him take his last breath. The sound is louder than any gunfire will ever be.

"You need to listen to me carefully," she says.

The dog runs over to us and licks my wounds. I'd cry, but I'm in shock. This is all my fault. I didn't barricade my door. I've been too busy watching other people to realize I needed to be more careful and watch myself. I just liked the idea of knowing everyone's business because no one could ever know mine. Tonight, I chose to stay at this house, to end him tonight by myself. I chose this, just as much as my mother did. I was supposed to be the one who killed him, but it was supposed to be in the early hours.

Maybe my mother is more of a Brentwood than I thought. I look at my drink and my scone and look back at her. Is it safe for me to eat this? Will I suffer the same fate as Tanner? Has she ever killed anyone before? It was so easy for her. I feel everything, and looking over at her, I can tell she feels nothing.

She begins to speak, but all I can hear is ringing, like a bell chiming the signal of victory. Then suddenly, I can't hear anything. Her mouth finishes moving, and she gets up from the kitchen table to open the door to the backyard. She walks toward a pile of snow and sits in it. There must be five feet of it outside. I watch her laugh so hard her belly hurts.

There's a dead body at the kitchen table, and my mother is laughing in the snow, the dog running out playing in it, his limp not even bothering him.

I don't understand, so I walk out toward the snow pile, sit down with her, and watch as she begins to make snow angels. Tanner's lifeless body is still slumped over in the chairs he had to have.

I make a snow angel with her. The coldness soothes my aches in more ways than one. We laugh together, and I understand that quote now: "The world changes when it snows."

THIRTY

CALISTA – THEN

This wasn't how it was supposed to happen. It was supposed to be simple, but how can murdering your spouse *ever* be simple? As I sit in the pile of snow, Tanner's corpse rots at a table where I spent too many nights being silenced over chicken or fish. I was going to put the poison in his food tonight, but then he found her gun before dinner was even ready. I let the snow soothe my soul for just a moment longer.

Ava is beside me, taking part in the comfort Mother Nature brought us. There isn't much time, though. The next part of my plan needs to be set in motion. I will need to explain it to Ava, and quickly, but it can wait another minute because the world is silent. People don't go out on nights like this, it's unsafe.

My body begins to shiver from the cold. I walk back into the house with Ava following me. She shuts the door.

"I will only repeat this once," I tell her.

Her gaze stuck on mine.

"Tanner has been waiting for the day Josh died, knowing you'd be left something. He had to keep us around, threatened to kill me if we ever left. We were bound to him, no matter what. What we did was self-defense and only that, do you hear me?"

I catch her eyes migrate toward Tanner quickly and back at me. She nods.

"Paul and Aletta, they are going to help."

Her face becomes a mask of confusion.

"Paul is a policeman," she says, and I can tell she thinks this is a bad idea.

"They told me what to do. They've been watching over us." I grab her hand, but Ava pulls it away from me. "We were waiting for the first snowstorm of the season. No one will be out. They are going to keep our secret for us. Paul has seen too many women die because they had no way of fighting back, no way to get help. Paul wants to help us. Aletta too." I hope she believes me.

"But at what cost?" Ava asks.

I'd like to think there would never be a cost to helping someone.

"Wait here, okay? Call no one. Do nothing," I tell her firmly.

I rush to the back door, run outside, past what was once my blossoming garden, and lift the branch separating myself from the Eden's yard. When I pound on their backdoor, within moments, I am let into their home, my blood-stained clothes and bruised face accompanying me. No words are exchanged. Paul grabs his coat and follows me back to my house.

My feet are frozen from the snow, my toes tingling from them going numb, but I'm grateful I'm alive. I am fortunate enough to still have those bothersome sensations.

"What do we do now?" I ask Paul.

"Wait until we get inside," he says softly.

At the back door, Paul looks through the glass at Tanner slumped over the kitchen table. Tanner's lips are a pale blue, and the blood has slowly drained from his face. We walk inside.

"Do you have gloves?" Paul asks.

I nod, run to the kitchen cabinet, and grab a pair of rubber gloves used for cleaning. I hand Paul a pair.

He clears his throat before speaking. "I can't have fingerprints. Both of yours are all over the house, but mine can't... We will drag his body through the snow. No one will see us, not a soul will be out tonight. The weather station predicted we are getting six more feet. We need to move quick. Put on warm coats, warm boots. We will be outside for a while. The snow piled on quicker than I thought," Paul says sternly.

Paul looks over at Ava.

"You are safe now," he says.

Ava breaks eye contact with him. She doesn't trust Paul, but she will need to.

All three of us drag Tanner's body through the snow. His body leaves a trail from our house to the Edens's house. I lift the branch to their yard, and one by one, we all pass, yanking Tanner through, just barely fitting.

Aletta rushes outside with shovels. All four of us dig until our hands are blistered. The snow is getting thicker, and it's hard to keep up when the weather is becoming turbulent.

We dig and dig until the snow is no longer blocking the grave. When we roll Tanner's body in it, the thud his body makes as it hits the earth satisfies me more than I'd like to admit. We fill it with as many bags of soil as Aletta has kept in her garage these last few months. *Waiting until it was finally time.*

We pack the dirt in silence until it's leveled with the rest of the ground. The snow will finish covering our crime. Tanner always hated nature, despised the bugs and the feeling of dirt under his nails, the uncleanliness of it all. He wanted to be cremated. I overheard him telling someone that once. Now, I hope worms eat his decaying flesh. It's the only solace I have.

We silently head back to our house, Paul and Aletta behind us.

Once we are all safely inside, I lock the back doors to the house, turn off all the lights, and light the fireplace. Picking up the kettle from the ground, I place it back on the stove to boil some water to make hot tea.

"How are you doing?" Aletta asks me.

"Fine." I'm not sure what the best answer is because the truth is, I'm overjoyed. Watching Tanner die gave me this type of energy I didn't know I could ever feel.

"We need to clean this entire house. Fix anything that's broken, wipe down anything. Ava, tomorrow, when you wake up, you will call the police," Paul says.

"Why me?" she says, confused.

"Because your mother is going away tomorrow. We are going to make it look like they are both missing. That way, your mother won't be a suspect, and no one will think you did it. The police will think someone abducted them. Make it seem like they are in danger. Tanner owes a lot of people money," Paul says.

I grab four mugs and begin pouring the water in each one, watching as the tea bags begin to float. They steep for a bit while I search for sponges and cleaning supplies to begin removing any blood left from this night.

"What if people think I did it?" Ava asks, puzzled.

"They won't because we will twist the narrative. We will let people have sympathy for you. You will come stay with Aletta and me during the holidays. We will be your family while your mother is gone. You'll be heart broken. After you report them missing, you won't be able to go back into that house for a while, *eventually* you will be allowed to grab a few things. At first, they will bring in a team to search the house for evidence. They won't be able to find much. They'll go through Tanner's office, and they'll find all the letters and emails about how much money he owed people, his scams. How his own family threatened legal action and then his brother suddenly died. They will need to interview dozens of people. The blame will be on someone else for a while, but no one will get convicted. Where there is no body, there is no crime. After time passes, you will go back into your house, you will pack up your things, and join your mother."

The mugs feel comforting in my hands, and I cup each one tightly before releasing it to Paul, then Aletta. I try to hand Ava a mug, but she rejects the offer. I leave my hands placed firmly around the mug, letting the warmth take over my body.

"When you pack your bag, you can't take much. It can't look like anything is missing," Paul says to me.

Aletta hands me a new ID and name and gives me a small sum of cash to get me by. "We can't have Ava take money out just yet because it will raise flags. This is from our savings. Ava will pay us back. Don't worry about it." Her eyes glisten from the tears she's trying to hold back.

As I take the ID from Aletta, Ava makes her way up the stairs toward her room. I follow her. She sits on her bed, staring at the blue walls, and I join her.

"It's a lot to process," I say.

She ignores me, just continues looking at the wall, staring blankly at it.

I sit with her in silence, but can tell she needs to be alone for a moment, I make my way back downstairs and sit on the couch, Aletta next to me. She places her hand gently on my back.

"You're one of the lucky ones now," she says. "Did you know that Paul is my second husband? My first husband, he wasn't so kind to me...Paul, he'd see me come to the farmer's market every Sunday with oversized sunglasses on. His dad was a produce guy. One Sunday, my sunglasses fell off when I went to pick up my basket that I dropped. You see, I had reported it to the cops many times, told my family, my friends, but no one ever helped me. Not until Paul did. That's why he became a policeman. He was on the inside, so he could get away with things. My first husband's funeral was lovely." Aletta grabs my hand and lets out the faintest smile.

From downstairs, Paul shouts, "We need to get started cleaning soon. Time is running out."

I wish I had more time with Ava. I wish it was just the two of us for a little while longer, like how it should have always been. I wish I'd listened to Josh that day of my wedding, but hindsight is just as deadly. It will drive you crazy to live in a state of constant wonder.

"In our new home, we can have any shade of blue you want," I tell her.

"I've been through every shade. There's really nothing left," she replies.

"Maybe a new color?"

"There was only ever one color for me."

We sit by the wall and stare at it together. I wish, more than anything, we could go back to the days of French blue.

I'll come back for her.

She follows me to my bedroom and watches as I fill a giant tote bag with some of my things. Nothing flashy, nothing that would give me away. All electronics stay here—no computers, no cell phones, nothing. I hate knowing I'll be out of touch for a while. It makes me nervous that the Brentwoods will soon know of a fable told by police officers and gossiping suburban housewives.

When I finish packing, I head downstairs. Aletta takes my tote to her house and leaves it there for safekeeping.

"Are we positive this is going to work?" Ava asks Paul.

"I'm risking my life on it," he says.

Her stress slowly dissipates into the warmth of our house, and the fireplace cackles.

Paul, Ava, and myself scrub the house. I've never been more excited to clean in my life. It's not just Tanner's death; it's my rebirth.

We clean through the night, except for Ava's room, because she needs to be bleeding in her bed for hours. When we are done, I take a long steam shower. I rinse off my body, lathering it with soap, feeling free. Then I put on sweatpants and head downstairs. I look at Ava, at my broken porcelain doll of a child who was once whole, and know that I took her purity away with my choices. I know I am responsible for everything that has happened and will happen. One day, I'll make it up to her. One day, we will have a new life together, a clean slate. She's always loved a blank canvas.

"Listen to Paul and Aletta, okay? They will coach you. They are going to take me to the airport. I won't call you for a while, but I'll let you know I'm safe somehow. When they get back, you will frantically run over to Paul's and pound on his door. Make sure you do it at eight in the morning, when all the moms are out taking their kids to school, walking the dog, or on their way to get coffee. Make sure people see you panic, make it grand. Be loud," I say to her.

She nods.

"I love you," I say.

"I love you too," she whispers softly.

I haven't heard her say those words to me since she was five. I'll hold on to that moment. It's the only thing of value to me.

Paul follows me through the back to his house. I watch as Ava stares blankly out the back door. She was dealt an unfair hand, but money makes everything better. She'll see. We can become new people finally. Money makes it easy to disappear, to start over, as long as no one is chasing us— as long as *he* isn't chasing us.

Aletta leaves the house every morning at six to go workout. We will need to wait for the plow to come first. People won't think it's weird if she's driving to the gym late. Hazardous road conditions make things more delayed.

I'll hide in her backseat until we get out of the area. Aletta will drop me off at a random location and will call me a cab to take me the rest of the way to the airport. Once this is done, she will drive to her gym to scan her card in, before seeing her family.

I'm to contact nobody unless it's an emergency. She hands me a burner phone and drops me off. I wear a hat that covers my hair and sunglasses to hide my face. After grabbing my bags out of the cab's trunk, I make my way inside the airport. Today is the first day of the rest of my life.

Ava will be okay. I know this time, I put my trust in the right people. It's the only thing I'm certain of.

A small bead of sweat drips down my neck when I go to security. They scan my ID and ticket before letting me through.

I sit down on the crappy chairs at the terminal, covered in grease and germs. The fabric is falling off, and none of the outlets work. I look over to see how soon we board. By now, Ava is frantically running to the neighbor's house, pounding on their door, saying she was asleep and was frantically beaten. She'll cry and tell them her attacker ran off, but her parents are missing. She can do this.

They announce that my flight is boarding. I wait in line patiently, eager to go. I walk through the jet bridge and step foot onto the plane. My seat is by the window, and I watch in awe as the sunrise turns to the softest shade of blue. I think about the day Ava was born. All girls who are born at the hospital I delivered at got a pink blanket to be swaddled in, but Josh wanted Ava to have a blue blanket. He insisted. "She needs a blue blanket," he kept saying over and over again to the nurse.

"Why?" the nurse asked him, genuinely curious.

I'll never forget what he said. He did many things wrong in his life, but that moment will stay with me.

"It represents love."

THIRTY-ONE

VICTORIA – NOW

I pound my fist against the metal on the gated door, keep pounding, waiting for Marla to show her hideous face.

Nothing.

"Open the *fuck* up, Marla!" I yell.

She's playing a game with me. I walk back to my car and grab the knife I tucked deep under my seat. Back at her door, I take the knife to try to pry it open. The door unlocks, and I quickly hide my knife, tucking it into my jeans.

"Hello, come in." Her face is smug. She's playing coy with me.

"Give me my daughter," I say, knowing I won't attract more bees with vinegar.

"I will, in a minute. I want to have a chat with you first."

Marla sits me down at her boyfriend's cheap plastic patio set for a kitchen table. She puts a glass of water down in front of me.

"You look tired, and you smell like booze. You drove like that? Can't take the trailer park out of the girl, right?" She wheezes when she laughs.

I scoot the glass of water back toward her.

"Give me my daughter, and I'll give you four months of money upfront," I say sternly.

"This isn't fun for you?" Marla asks sarcastically.

She walks toward the fridge and takes an apple from it. I watch her take a bite, the juice running down her face. She wipes it off with her arm.

"This is your fault...You didn't have a contract, so getting extorted for money...Well, dear, that's on you," she says with her mouth full.

"Are you fucking kidding me? A contract? You wanted what we did in writing?" I scream at her.

A younger woman runs in the room, concerned.

"Is everything okay, Mom?" she asks.

"This is the woman who took your daddy away. Just so you can put a name with the face, baby girl," Marla says, hugging her daughter.

"You are just as guilty as I am. You sold your husband out. You didn't care enough to tell him no, and now you are taking my money, my *kid's* money. You have more than enough for college. This is extortion, you dumb bitch!" I can no longer keep it under control.

I lunge across my seat and grab Marla, but she laughs. Her daughter looks terrified.

She should be.

"You know what's funny?" Marla says as I hold her shirt in my grip. "Is that I'm a better mother than you. My kids knew what I did. Yours had no idea. I guess that makes me better."

"What have you done?" I yell.

"I didn't do anything. I simply told your daughter the reason she was in my basement." Marla smirks wider.

Scouring the area, I look for a door that could lead to the basement. When I spot one, I run toward it. I want to get Allison and get out of here.

"Not so fast. I need payment before you can have your daughter back," Marla says, her voice stern.

Sticking my hand in my jean pocket, I reach for the Rolex. I pull it out and dangle it in front her face.

"This is a one-hundred-thousand-dollar watch. This is all I have. After this, we are done."

Marla rips the watch right out of my hand. "We will never be done," she says. Her spit lands on my face.

I reach for the knife buried in my jeans, and before I can control myself, drive it right through her heart. Her daughter watches in horror as the blood spills from her mother. Marla struggles and drops the watch from her grip. It falls, shattering the crystal. Marla's daughter runs to her side. She is trying to protect her…She's going to tell, I know she will. Her daughter won't let this go. I panic. No, I am *not* this person. I am not supposed to be in situations like this.

I need to protect my family at the cost of another.

Her daughter is covered in her blood now. It soaks through her clothes as she tries to stop the bleeding, but it's too late. It would take a miracle to survive something like that. Marla should have given me my daughter. She should have been done. Her greed is the thing that killed her, not me. I just twisted the knife, but she put it there.

"What have you done?" her daughter yells out, crying.

I say nothing.

"Help her, please!" she begs of me.

"I can't." I'm frozen, knowing there is no coming back from this.

The girl reaches into her pocket for her phone, and I panic. She begins to punch in the number nine, and I lunge at her to get her phone. It slides across the kitchen floor covered in blood. She reaches for it again. I tackle her, but she rolls over on me, the weight of her body on mine.

As I release her, she runs to the phone and enters in her passcode. She's panicking, and she's made the mistake of having her back turned. I take the knife out of her mother's chest and shove it directly into her. The daughter collapses to the floor. Her body makes a large thud when it hits the ground, the blood spilling out of her. I watch, like a child who just knocked over their glass of milk in the morning. A mess to clean up, but manageable. *Everything is manageable.* I need to keep reminding myself that all messes can be cleaned up.

The smell of the iron surrounding me makes me throw up all over myself. I know what I need to do. It makes me feel unwell, nervous.

My hands shake as I reach for the phone in my pocket. I send a text. This will all be taken care of.

The sink water feels nice against my skin. The blood falls off, and I watched my nightmare go down the drain, diluted with the water.

The cracked Rolex covered in blood sits there, teasing me. Was I ever going to let her have it? Was this my plan all along? Was this rage just sitting in my body, waiting to find an escape route this entire time? I try to convince myself I'm a good person, but I need to stop with the lies. I am not. It's plain and simple. I'll come back for the watch. I need to go check on Allison while I wait for whatever happens next.

The handle to the basement is locked. I search the entire house for the key, but no luck. It must be on Marla. Of course, it would be. I cover my hands in blood again and find the key safely tucked in her pocket. I clean my hands thoroughly and remove my shoes before walking down the basement steps. There's no light down here. It's dark and damp. Each step creaks as I walk down them.

"Allison?" I say softly. "Are you here?"

The faintest mumble comes from the corner. My beautiful daughter, lying on the ground, covered in her own blood. I sigh out of relief. If she died, how would I explain this all to CeCe? If she died, everything I just did wouldn't have been worth it. She's part of a legacy. I am the mother of rich children. Without them, I am just me.

Watching Allison suffer makes me feel what I already know.

I am a bad mom. A bad person.

A good mom calls 911. A good mom sacrifices herself. A good mom would call for help. A bad mom tries to cover it up and watches her daughter suffer in order to avoid penalty for the crimes committed. A bad mom gets away with everything. A good mom would hold her in their lap, stroking her hair, whispering to her that it is all going to be okay. I can do that last part. That's all I can do.

We need to wait until it's late out so all secrets blend in with the night. The evil slowly drips into the dimming sky, hiding the sun so sins can be kept quiet.

As I carry her up the stairs, I trip and fall. She cries in pain, and I apologize.

"It's okay. Just a few more steps." I comforted her to the best of my abilities. No, I've never shown her much affection, or Ashley, but they never seemed to mind. I place her on the couch and cover her with a blanket that's next to her. Then I walk to the kitchen and find any type of ice to place on her head and ribs. I step over two bodies on my way to help my own child. The two bodies I put there.

A sense of panic takes over me. What if her other children come home? What if her boyfriend comes back before they get here? I keep

274

watch at the door with my knife until my phone rings. My head is throbbing. It feels like it's splitting open.

I walk over to the Rolex and pick it up to rinse off Marla's greedy blood. Then, I place it on my wrist for safekeeping. Once it's fixed, I'll just keep it for myself. Tanner wouldn't want me to have it, so it makes me want it even more. That man had it coming. He really did.

A vibration from the phone snaps me back to reality, and I stop staring at the watch now comfortably at home on my boney wrist.

It says: "We are here."

I reply: "Go to the back."

When I unlock the back door, I look at Allison on the couch, holding on for her life.

A team of men all dressed in black walk into the room, holding buckets of cleaning supplies, each one strapped with a gun. I watch as they assess the area. CeCe walks in after them. Her black cloak clings to her body.

"We have a lot to discuss, dear." Her voice is cold.

For the first time in a long time, I'm afraid.

"Someone take my granddaughter home and have the doctor meet her there," she says, snapping her fingers.

"I can take her to the hospital now that you are here," I say uneasily.

"Nonsense. We have a mess to clean up…that *you* made. My assistant will do the rest," she says coldly. "How many family members are there? One more, three, six?"

"I think so. Maybe two or three more kids. This is the boyfriend's house."

"Well, I didn't think we'd be killing a whole family today." CeCe lets out a laugh.

It sends chills down my spine.

"You smell like a drunk," she says, looking at me, burning through my entire soul.

Josh hated her. I hate her too, but I am jealous to the point of admiring her.

Allison's body is gently lifted by one of CeCe's assistants. I'm not worried. She will be okay. At least, that's what I will tell myself.

"Clean everything up, find her other offspring, leave no trace, and then…burn it to the ground." She holds her hand up, gesturing to the sky.

Her words replay in my mind. *Burn it to the ground.* I watch CeCe take the knife out of Marla's daughter and place it in a bag.

She examines it. "Hmm, looks like one I have at home."

The murder weapon will be safer with her because she knows I'll owe her forever. That's more than just a knife; that's my entire future. CeCe is my owner now. Not that she never was, but this…this is the thing that is a physical metaphor for that.

The scrubbing begins. The soap begins to bubble, and the smell of bleach becomes too much. I watch them remove teeth, one by one, from the victims' mouths. The people who are helping CeCe are indebted to her, just like me, but I'll never see their faces because CeCe knows it's for the best. I watch her workers take care of my mess.

She snaps her fingers and signals for her driver to take us to her house.

"You are coming with me," she says, her voice colder than usual.

"I need to get home to Allison," I reply softly, not trying to talk above her.

"Allison has the best doctor money can buy." She walks quietly to her car hidden in the shadows, with her driver in front of us."

"I did this for the family," I say, knowing my fate.

"For the family? Is that right?"

We get into her Escalade, all black interior and exterior.

"I did what I thought you would have done," I say truthfully.

"Maybe I don't give you enough credit." CeCe closes the door behind her.

"I will always protect the family name because this name is everything to me, and I am lucky enough to be a part of it," I watch her remove her black gloves and Chanel sunglasses.

"You will never be a true Brentwood, as much as I appreciate your candor and efforts...A Brentwood must be birthed. You think you are a Brentwood because of the last name, but you are nothing more than someone my son married because he had no choice. Your children are the future of the Brentwoods, so we tolerate you, just like we tolerate the rest of the spouses of our children. Our legacy must remain intact, or it was all for nothing. You will never be *me*."

Her words sink into my flesh, *stinging*.

"But after tonight, you might be more than I thought. Not much, but just enough."

We sit in silence the rest of the car ride to her house.

THIRTY- TWO

CECE – NOW

Staring at the woman my son had to end up with makes me irritated. Victoria's bleach-blonde hair looks damaged, and her jeans are bursting at the seams. The fit is not right on her whatsoever. She looks unwashed, even beyond the blood-stained clothing. If she wants to play the part, she needs to audition for it better. I watch her as she sips on her coffee, her dirty hands touching my Flora Danica china, her lips pursed tightly as she takes another sip. Her fingernails have blood underneath them. She couldn't even clean herself up right.

Snapping my fingers, I signal for the housekeeper to escort Victoria to the guest room for a shower and fresh clothes. This catches her off guard, but I need her to look proper if we are going to sit down and chat. The housekeeper takes her hand, and off they go down the hallway filled with expensive art my husband and I used to collect. I wanted to sell it after he died, get a few better pieces, but I promised him I wouldn't. I keep my promises because he did everything for me, and I did everything for him.

Looking around at my beautiful estate, I know that it's blood that gets you places, not sweat. It's always been blood.

When I was growing up, everything was always leftovers from the restaurant my father worked at, scrubbing dishes by hand until his flesh was raw to the bone. It was always hand-me-downs from my mother's employers that she cleaned houses for. It wouldn't surprise me if they laughed behind her back when she was excited to take whatever they'd give her. I never wanted to wear it because I refused to be charity. Yes, I was always cold in the winter and sweltering in the summer. It was no luxurious life, and I had no four-thousand-dollar china to sip tea on in the winter, no housekeepers fanning me in the summer days when the air conditioning broke. I'd come with my mother to the homes she'd clean sometimes, and I knew I was born unlucky. Luck can change, though, but you need to force her hand. Luck has always been a woman.

It was sometime before my sixteenth birthday, I packed a bag and left my house. The sixties were a different time, where if you wanted to live a different dream, you just packed up your things and left. *Not just your name, but your family too.* I said goodbye to Queens and went to where the big boys played. A new last name, a new identity, a new everything. I didn't exist in the world until the day I left.

I played the part well, *too* well. When I met my husband, I taught him how to play the part even better.

I look around the house, the luxury I'm surrounded by, and I smile. Yes, I'd do it all over again, in this life and every life. No matter how many bodies I bury, as long as my sheets have a thread count of three thousand, I'll always be able to sleep soundly, I'll always be able to sleep soundly. *Your sins you commit must be worth it because if they aren't, it was all for nothing.* I told my children this, and that's the family motto.

I check my watch. Victoria is taking a long time. Washing blood off your body is quick. The longer you watch the blood fall off your skin, seeping down the drain, diluting its existence with something as simple as water, the more real it becomes. A quick shower like nothing happened is how you continue with your day to day life.

The truth is, in order to get what you want, no one else matters. I made sure my children knew that. The only one of them who remotely takes after me is my daughter, Vivian. She hates who I hate because she loves to copy me. Vivian will do anything for this family and anything for me because the life I gave her was impeccable. She is forever indebted to me, unlike my other imbecile sons, the ones who are still alive.

I miss the softness of Josh's soul, but I try not to miss him too much because I know it was my debt to the devil that took him from me. Each of my children were born with some health issues, as if Lucifer himself laughed at me every time a child came out of my womb. I stayed distracted with my work to not think about my children, born imperfect. It kept me from feeling sorry for myself. When they strayed and needed money for their health, I was able to keep them close. Some would say I forced my children to love me, but I say I made them respect me. They are one in the same.

The grandfather clock chimes. I am growing tired, waiting for Victoria.

I snap my fingers to signal more coffee and perhaps some biscuits to accompany it.

From down the hall, Victoria walks toward me. She knows she's wasting my time and I'm growing rather impatient with her. I need answers, need to know everything. The Brentwood name depends on her truths.

"Sit down," I say to her, watching her turn into a zombie-like state. She sits, and her gaze meets mine. It makes her nervous. I laugh. "I don't bite," I pause. "I only kill." I laugh, sipping on my drink. She smiles at me, but it's not real. I can tell.

"I would like a thorough play by play of why my housekeepers and security had to clean up your mess, and a rather foul one at that. If you tell one single lie, you will be done. I will see to it that my grandchildren will live here while you rot in a grave somewhere, and the money they receive from their trusts will be heavily monitored. You said you had good reason, so I'd like to hear it," I say calmly.

It makes her more nervous.

Victoria pauses before speaking, like she forgot how to talk. I wait for a moment before something resembling a sound comes out of her mouth. Victoria pauses again before clearing her throat to reform her words.

"We bought a heart for Josh."

My eyes widen. She did what? Behind my back?

"Well, Josh was sick, and he didn't think you'd go for it. He thought you'd rather him die than do something as heinous as we did. So...um, I bribed someone who needed money for her kids and bought her husband's heart." It's spilling out of her like the blood from that woman today. She continues. "The woman threatened us and was using the family name as leverage, so I had no choice." She finishes talking.

I can tell she has practiced this speech in her head, trying to justify what she did.

"Why did you not come to me sooner?" I asked, perplexed that she wouldn't think I'd take care of this for her, *for the family.*

"Because Josh didn't want you to know," she says.

I immediately am angered.

"You know, this isn't my first opening night on Broadway." I fix my hair as a piece falls into my face. "The men in this family are nothing without their women. Do you think that my husband got successful because of his ideas? No, it was me. It's always been me. My late husband, you see, lacked that driving force to conquer everything. He grew up with the nice family, the nice house, but he was a coward, until he met me. He needed pushing. He needed to see the future I saw for the name he had. I created the importance of the name. I wasn't born into it like he was, but I created a bigger version of who he was. He owed me his life. My husband was my puppet, and when I wanted something, I pulled the strings. Do you think that business partner of his was killed by my husband? No, he was killed by me. He was going to report my darling husband, who was trying to better himself. Insider trading isn't that bad because those who are willing to risk everything have always been rewarded heavily. Did you know there are good ways to kill people so they vanish entirely? You see, every tooth needs to be pulled, every fingerprint gone. A summer barbecue always needs a nice fire at the end of the night. My children, they suspected my husband was always the bad person growing up, but no one ever suspects the woman. They see us as weak. We run the show. You just ran it poorly tonight, but you ran it, nonetheless."

I take a sip of my drink and place the cup down over the plate. The slightest clink of the china satisfies me.

"You, you're the one who killed your husband's business partner?"

282

she asks eyes wide.

"But of course," I say with a smirk.

Reaching into my Hermes purse, I reach for the knife placed within a plastic bag. I set it gently on the table.

"This is mine now." I watch her try to hold back her vomit. "I own you, and if you so much as do one thing I disapprove of, you can choose prison or me taking this knife to your throat, is that understood?"

She nods. She fears me. Everyone fears me, and they should.

"Oh, and if you think of trying to blackmail me with anything I told you, think otherwise. There's no proof. Your tongue will be cut from your mouth before you even try," I tell her.

Victoria looks like she needs a drink, so I have my maid bring her one. I watch her sip on it. She doesn't wince once while she nurses it. This is her pacifier.

"On another note, I would like to show you my appreciation for your loyalty to the family name and thinking quickly, despite any repercussions. I admire that you called me. Only one other person in this family would have done that, and I want you to know that I thank you greatly for stopping any sort of pish posh." I walk over to Victoria and place my hand on her shoulder. The silk robe over the linen clothing she sits in feels lovely against my aging skin. I can feel the goosebumps on her shoulder even through the material.

She is mine now, forever indebted to me, like a prisoner begging to be saved from death.

Vivian walks into my tearoom, smiling at me. She gives me a rather large hug.

"You know, Vivian, dear, I think it's time we start treating Victoria more like one of us." I hold both of their hands at the same time.

Vivian's hair is neatly tucked in a bun, not a single hair out of place. Her figure is slim, her eyes almost black. She's uptight and proper. Vivian was raised correctly by me. She's a monster in a pencil skirt. A fantastic businesswoman.

"Mother, Victoria has always been one of us. She hates Calista," Vivian says, laughing.

"She proved herself tonight, though," I say, smiling warmly at Victoria. "If only you'd bought a more expensive heart, maybe he wouldn't have died."

Vivian looks confused.

"What are you talking about?" she asks softly.

"Oh, Victoria murdered a family today who tried to blackmail her, isn't that just grand? Who knew she had it in her." I take another sip of my drink.

"I'm just here to pick up a few things. I'll bring the boys over for lunch tomorrow." Vivian walks quickly into the study to grab a few books she needs to help her win her case.

A lawyer in the family has always proven to be beneficial. If only she were a trust lawyer and not like that dim-whit Erik, who cost us hundreds of millions out of pocket. I cannot believe my husband and I ever trusted him. He's lucky he's alive. He's been hiding. I'll find him, though. His days are numbered.

It's just Victoria and me sitting at the table now. The sun is starting to shine through the stained glass, casting a blush hue on her face.

"I should go check on the children, make sure everyone is okay," she says, her mind still processing everything.

As I reach for a scone placed on the table by my staff, I pause and smile.

"All three of them?" I ask, self-satisfied.

Her body turns a shade of white, like the roses in my garden.

"Do you think I'd let my son marry someone I knew nothing about? You possess qualities that I have. Wanting a better life, wanting everything you never had…I saw myself in you, which is why I made him leave Calista and be with you. Don't get me wrong, I would have preferred him to marry someone better, but, well, you know how it played out, *you got pregnant*. You are moldable, a better choice, and when we learned of his infidelities, I was almost thrilled to force his hand further away from Calista. So, tell me, how is your son?" Was it the young boy who accompanied Ava to my son's funeral? I pause for a moment to chew this exquisite scone, the blueberries bursting in my mouth, the sweetest vessels exploding.

From the look on her face, I have her. Mother knows all.

THIRTY-THREE

AVA – THEN

The sun starts to take over and begins to melt the snow from the storm. Slowly, it will be like none of this ever happened. Paul instructed me to go into Tanner's office, wearing gloves, and try to spread around some of his paperwork. Paul said it needs to look real, like a number of people could have broken into our home.

Paul said I need to do whatever it is quickly, and if I don't play my cards right, they will know, or suspect something.

Walking into the lion's den knowing he's been hunted and put to rest calms me. I pray no one suspects me. Digging through hundreds of pieces of paper, I crinkle up a few important ones and place them in trash. The police will look there. I position a few others in his paper shredder, as if he was in the middle of hiding his crimes when he was interrupted by something.

His office is enough proof alone for them to suspect a former co-worker or investor. He owed hundreds of millions. Tanner could have sold this house and paid off his debts, but it was a game to him, a long waiting game…Marry the woman with the last name of status, deal with her offspring, wait until the ex-husband died or kill him if it was taking too long, and then kill the mother and the daughter.

The first option would have been better, but some people see it as an investment. You aren't supposed to pull money out of your stocks. You need to let it sit there, grow interest, collect dividends. For eighteen years, I was his bull market.

There isn't time to dig through the safe, but if his passport is in there, I will want to make sure it's been taken, throw off the police more. After I type in his birthday, it opens with ease. I take the passport to find a hiding place for it, maybe in my mother's garden next to her favorite plants.

Rummaging through a few more documents, I come across one that is unsettling. A birth certificate. I flash back to the photo of Tanner and Victoria together. My head begins to pound, and there's a lump growing in my throat now. The only thing I can think about is their child. Where it is? *Who* it is? A part of me already knows. It's all making sense now.

The office is a disaster, ready to be searched. I quickly run up to my room and call for help as if none of this happened. The only memory I can have is my bleeding skull. No one came to me when I called for help.

I dial the numbers, the adrenaline causing my fingers to shake as I hit each number.

"Hello, 911, what is your emergency?"

"I'm...I'm bleeding," I muster the words.

"What is your address?"

"4525 Kenilworth," I say, my voice not even needing to fake the panic in it. I'm already terrified.

"Is anyone there with you? Are you alone?" the responder asks.

I don't answer and hang up.

Within minutes, the flashing lights of the ambulances, fire trucks, and cop cars circle the house below my balcony. I kept the doors open so I can watch the moment my life changes forever. Once it's been reported, it's real. You can't undo this. I was supposed to run to Paul's house, let people see me, cause a scene, but I just felt this would be more realistic, if I were that injured, there is no way I could go over there.

Paul and Aletta walk outside their front steps and pretend like they have no idea what is going on. The rest of the neighborhood follows suit. Everyone is probably enjoying this, gossiping, talking about how maybe I overdosed. Some of the wives are secretly hoping it's me who died, and at this moment, I almost feel the same. I don't know how to comprehend that I am finally rid of him. It doesn't seem real.

There's pounding on the front door, and when no one answers, the door is broken down. Finally, someone can see what goes on behind closed doors, even if the story isn't always right.

One by one, footsteps lead toward all the bedrooms, until they reach mine. There is no knock, just people rushing in, looking at all the blood on my bed, *my* dried blood. It will make sense to them when I tell the first responders I woke up in pain. They'll think I am unaware of my injuries, unsure of everyone else's conditions.

"Here!" a man yells.

I keep my eyes closed, try to play the part, except truthfully, my head is in excruciating pain.

An EMT opens my eyes and shines a light in them, checking my pupils.

"She's alive!" the man says. His stern hands checking for a pulse. "Possible brain bleed!"

288

They see blood everywhere. My blue walls stained.

We cleaned the entire house except this room. Everything was bleached, scrubbed, and picked up. We had to make it look convincing that I was asleep the entire time, the poor young woman covered in her own pool of blood, alone in her room, on one of the harshest winter storms in decades. *Left to die.* We did leave broken glass on the ground and made sure to make it look like it came from outside to inside. That's how you get caught, by slipping up on the smallest details. When you paint, you need to go over and over your drawing, fix any imperfection that an outsider will notice. The creator can be the only one to see the flaws, but not the bystander.

The paramedics rush me to the hospital. I know I can finally sleep now. I don't even need to fake it. I'm exhausted. I did my part. I just hope Paul's plan works. I hope he's not mad at me for changing the plan.

The sirens are loud, even from inside the ambulance, but I feel secure here. One of the paramedics even holds my hand. I almost feel guilty, him caring for me like this. It feels nice to be cared for. To feel protected.

A day or so has passed when I finally wake up. I'm surrounded by sterile walls, no decorations except for medical devices hung on the wall. A repetitive sound comes from the machine, drip after drip constantly coming from the IV bag. A nurse is taking my vitals when I open my eyes, and she smiles at me. She's young. She doesn't know what she's in for. Taking care of so many sick people can have a toll on someone. She'll run herself tired one day, but for now, she's happy to be here.

"Good morning, Ava," she says, with a smile on her face.

She's pretty. The doctors all probably flirt with her.

"You slept for over thirty hours! You'd be surprised what good sleep does for a body," she says with excitement, drawing my blood to check my levels. "If you are up for it, a detective would like to speak to you. If you aren't up for it, I can tell them to go away."

She feels bad for me. *I* feel bad for me.

I sit up, not even faking how achy my body is—like a car plowed right through me. "I'm fine." When I feel my head, I graze over dozens of stitches. Maybe I really did need to be here.

"Are you sure?" she says.

"I'm sure."

I wait for the detective to walk in. A hand grabs the curtain and pulls it back softly. A man in his forties, tall, tanned skin, pulls up a chair next to me. He doesn't seem like a detective. His authoritative tone never comes out. He's gentle, warm. Maybe it's an act. You know the saying. More bees with honey…

"Hello, Ava. I'm Detective Brown." He takes out his notepad and jots a few things down.

What could he possibly have to take note of without me even speaking?

"I was wondering if you have any memory of what happened a couple of days ago? Anything at all?"

"Are my parents here?" I try to sound confused. "Where are my parents?" This time, I make sure my voice has a slight frill to it.

The nurse is in the room with the detective, and they look at each other for a moment, like they are keeping something from me. But what I'm keeping is much bigger. Always be the hunter not the hunted, I remind myself over and over again. Don't break.

"Let's just focus on you right now. Can we do that?" he asks.

I nod, and he continues.

"Back to the other night. I need you to tell me what happened before you went to bed. Exact times, or close to exact would be appreciated."

I notice water next to me and wince as I reach to take a sip. The detective pushes it closer.

"I don't remember much. I came home and had some dinner with my mom, my stepfather…He was working, yelling on the phone. He's always in his office on the phone. I was exhausted. College has been hard, so I went upstairs. I took something to sleep, like melatonin or magnesium, whatever it's made of…and when I woke up, I was covered in blood. I felt this intense pain, but I must have passed out because that's all I remember." Tears stay trapped in my eyes, the officer sees the small swells forming.

"This is all very helpful, Ms. Brentwood," he says, writing some more things down. "Is there anything else you can remember about that night? Anything at all?" He seems hopeful, but he shouldn't be.

"It was like every other night," I reply, which is the first truthful thing I've said in a while. It *was* like every other night I'd stay in that house. Except this time, consequential.

"Thank you for your time." He smiles at the nurse as he heads out.

All I can think about is the birth certificate in Tanner's office and how I just now found it. Maybe he kept it as blackmail all these years. It wouldn't surprise me.

The nurse startles me when she hands me a cup of Jell-O. "Here you go," she says.

I don't touch it. I'm not hungry. And Jell-O is fucking disgusting.

After staring at cheap popcorn-white hospital ceilings, I am finally discharged the next day. No one comes back. No one mentions my mother and stepfather. Easton picks me up and takes me home. There is the signature yellow tape surrounding the house. Dozens of people swarm nearby, curious as to what's going on. My house was the bird feeder, and all the suburban housewives were like the squirrels, trying their hardest to feed, but it wasn't meant for them.

"Want me to come in with you?" he asks.

I can tell he's glad I'm okay, not in a romantic way, but in a real way.

"No, that's all right. I have to figure out a few things, and honestly, I could have slept forever in that hospital bed. I didn't realize how good sleep felt. How good it felt to be able to sleep without worrying."

"Save it for death. Plenty of it there." He says.

I walk toward my house, passing the yellow tape. A police officer tries to stop me, but I don't listen to him.

"Miss, you can't go in there," he yells. His voice just disappears.

Detective Brown is there, and he's calling order. He sees me, and we don't break eye contact. Paul is next to him. They are talking. Paul looks over at me and rushes over to give me a big hug.

He whispers, "I'm going to tell you your parents are missing. You are going to hyperventilate. You are going to make this entire room believe this lie." The second he lets go, I collapse to the ground, screaming and crying.

Detective Brown hurries over to me. He bends down at my level and rubs my back.

The tears roll down my face. Everyone thinks they are from my sadness, but these tears, these specific ones, are filled with joy.

Paul helps me up and guides me to the staircase. He sits me down on one of the steps.

"Where is my mom? Where is Tanner?" I ask, sobbing into my hands.

Detective Brown walks over to me and puts his hand on my back awkwardly.

"Are you sure you have no idea where your parents could be? If they had any enemies? If there is anything we need to know, now is the time to tell us." He tries to sound sweet and caring, but he fails.

"Tanner…I just…He…" I pause and grasp for air.

Detective Brown leans in closer. "He, what?" he asks.

"He owed people some money, but I don't know what for."

Just like that, the narrative was formed.

Daughter, sleeping soundly in bed, wakes up lucky to be alive. Mother is missing along with stepfather. Did they run away from someone who they owed money to? Were they killed? No one would dare think I had anything to do with it. The girl asleep in her bed, dying, bleeding out. If she didn't wake up and call for help, who knows what would have happened to her. How long will it be, though, until my mother and stepfather become the suspects? What if people think they tried to kill me for my inheritance and ran off? Or what if everyone thinks I killed them and cried wolf? Either way, for now, the first one is what they think.

Paul places his hand on my shoulder, not to comfort me, but to signal to me that I did a good job. I stare out the front door, watching officers walk in and out of the house. But I don't think about anything else except that birth certificate. Everything else is trying to cloud my mind, but I have other things to contemplate. I only regret Tanner dying because I need more answers. I hate that people take things to their graves, but this is something else I will one day take to mine.

"This is an official investigation into Tanner and Calista Maple," Detective Brown tells his colleagues. "This house is now under investigation. Everyone must treat this as a missing person's case or possible double homicide."

It's done. They will explore both options. The first one, were they killed. The second one, where they were the killers.

Paul tells me I should stay at his house for a while. He tells me I can go back in a bit for some of my things, once it has been gone through and logged as evidence. I need to get the key I left in my room, but it will have to wait. It might be best if I stays there anyways, for safe keeping, until things blow over . Paul says he'll take me to the store for some clothes to wear and anything else I may need in the meantime.

Detective Brown smiles at Paul. I can tell he's appreciative of his help with me.

I watch as the house of my nightmares is under a microscope. It's hard not to smile, finally watching it crumble to the ground, and I can't have a front row seat to enjoy it.

Paul and I head to the store to get a few things. He tells me to stay on my toes, that he doesn't trust it. It felt too easy. This isn't over yet.

THIRTY-FOUR

ALLISON – NOW

The orange hue from the neighbor's Halloween lights leaks into my bedroom, creating an ominous glow. I'm finally well enough to leave the house. My head no longer aches, my ribs only jolt me when I move too quickly, and my cuts are starting to scab over.

I knock on Ashley's door. She doesn't answer, so I let myself in. Ashley's sitting on her stupid poufy white chair, doing her makeup at her vanity. The light bulbs are bare and exposed, too bright for my eyes.

"Hi," I say softly.

She looks away from her vanity for just a second and then looks back at herself. A true version of my mother, which is odd, because Ashley is CeCe's favorite. Everyone knows it. Ashley does anything for CeCe, not out of fear, but because she worships her.

"How are you feeling? Mom said you fell down the stairs at a party, drunk?" she asks.

I ignore her question.

"Where are you going tonight?" I hope maybe she'll invite me with, any excuse to leave this house.

"A party some guy invited me. I'd bring you, but you look…" She's still focused on her own reflection.

"Like shit? I know. Thank you," I respond coldly.

If she found out our mother robbed a family of life and stole a man's heart, maybe she'd feel like shit too. But then again, maybe not. It's Ashley. She only cares about herself, her looks, and at times, our dead father. Ashley tries not to think about it, doesn't want that to define her. She has other goals in mind, like being popular and pretty.

I watch her from afar, even though she's right next to me. I grab my phone and see what Scott is up to. It's nice to have a friend who doesn't know about my life. Maybe he's free tonight. I send the text and notice I'm immediately left on read.

The garage opening can be heard from all the way upstairs. My mother is back. She has been spending a lot of time with CeCe lately. Mom's been over there almost every day since the incident happened, and she always comes back in a good mood, which is unusual. I walk down to the kitchen, she sees me and smiles, acts like nothing happened. Every time I try to bring it up, she redirects the conversation.

"Where were you?" I ask her, knowing the answer.

"Your grandmother's. We had dinner." She walks over to the fridge to open a bottle of wine. "You look healthy."

I want to take my phone and call the police, want them to take her away. I stare at her as she takes that first sip of wine, leaving her lipstick stain on the glass, as she does.

"Did you kill Ava?" I blurt out.

It catches her by surprise. I'm taken by surprise too.

"How dare you," she says to me. She didn't say no. She didn't deny anything. If someone were innocent, wouldn't they say so?

She takes my phone away from me and quickly goes through it.

"You're grounded." She takes another sip of wine.

"I know you did it," I say. "I'm going to tell." My words leave my mouth like light bouncing in the room.

"If you tell anybody what happened, so help me God…" she says.

"Tell anybody what?" Ashley reaches for a snack from the pantry. My mother brushes it off. "I was just yelling at Allison about not telling anyone what I used to look like with a perm, back in the 80s." She laughs.

Ashley is self-absorbed. She doesn't think much about anything, so it flies over her head. "I'm going to a party tonight. My ride is going to be here in a few. I won't be home until late."

The doorbell rings, and we watch her head to the door in her pinup Halloween costume. My mother doesn't dare mention to her how inappropriate she looks for her age. She doesn't mention to not drink, or to call her if there is a problem. She just lets her be. Ashley's the favorite, because CeCe thinks she's the future of this family.

I should be the one going to a party tonight. Instead, my world has been turned upside-down, my youth diminishing slowly, like vinegar on a stain. *Dissolving whatever is left of me.*

I grab my keys and run out the door. My mother chases behind me, but she isn't fast enough. She lets me go.

When I get to Ava's house, I walk to the front door but notice it's slightly open. I let myself in. The upstairs lights are on. In a dream-like state, I walk up each step, my body feeling like it's floating, weightless. The first time I've felt this way in what seems like forever. I keep thinking she's up in her room. *What if.*

The door to Ava's bedroom is open just a sliver. A light shines through, leaving a single line on the floor. I try to get a closer look at who is inside, but I can't make it out. It has to be her.

As quickly as I can, I push the door open and see someone I wasn't expecting.

"Scott?"

He panics and tries to make a run for it, until he notices it's just me.

"You had me there," he says, grabbing his chest and sitting back down.

"What are you doing here?"

"I just came here to think, you know?" He stares at the blue walls. "You know, they found one of my letters to her when she died, in her pocket. I got questioned a few times."

He tells me like he's wanting me to trust him. His hair doesn't look so golden these days, and his eyes look dim.

"But what are you doing here?" I ask, still needing answers.

Why does no one tell people the truth anymore? Why does everybody dance around the questions? The doorbell rings. Trick-or-treaters are laughing, and they press the doorbell again. We try to ignore it, but it's non-stop. It has me on edge.

"I'm just here looking for something." He turns it back around at me. "Why are *you* here?"

"I'm just trying to get to know my sister. If you haven't heard, she died," I say sarcastically.

When I tell Scott that, he doesn't seem to notice I said "sister." He doesn't even care I lied to him. At least, it seems that way. Maybe he didn't hear me, or maybe he just *doesn't* care.

I'm glad I don't have Ava's key on me. Something doesn't seem right. What if that's what he's looking for? What if all he's after is finding that missing key, the key that might hold all the answers, the key that holds all the missing pieces? I keep it tucked safely in my jewelry box at home. My dad got it for me. He said the ballerina reminded him of someone.

It was Ava. It was an exact replica of her.

Sometimes, I'd come home after school, and he'd be in my room with my music box open, watching the ballerina spin. He'd smile. I just thought he liked the sound, but he just was missing her. He was trapped in a life that was a mistake, a regret. *A music box.*

We sit on her bed together and stare at the wall. I try to act like everything is okay.

"Why did you break up with her?" I ask, convinced I see a small spec of dried blood on the wall.

"It's complicated." He isn't fazed that I know all these personal things about his life. Why doesn't he care?

"The town whore, sleeping with men for money, selling drugs, living in this princess world?"

"It's more complicated than that," he says. "She did things because she had to. I did things because I had to." He's not looking at me.

I keep my hand in my pocket, close to my phone, just in case.

"What could be more complicated than that?" I ask, perplexed.

"We have a long history, and I just thought it was for the best that we break up. My mom didn't like her." Scott walks over to her nightstand and plays with a few things that got left behind, the things people didn't want.

"My mom didn't like her either," I say with a small laugh.

"We should probably get out of here." He gets up and heads toward the door to leave.

"Yeah, you're right." I get up as quickly as I can, but I'm dizzy and fall back down on the bed.

Scott helps me up. "You good?" He seems worried.

We head down the stairs together, passing all her paintings, one by one. They are hard to miss. Beautiful reminders of what else is out there.

"Are you mad I lied to you?" I say.

We stop to look at the same painting on the wall, the one by the hallway toward the front door, a beautiful painting of what I imagine heaven looks like. Blue clouds swirled with golden flakes, the strokes so faint it looks as if nothing is there. But that's what Ava wanted people to think, that it was nothing on a canvas. Only those who deserve it will see its beauty. She liked to play mind games, from what I'm learning about her.

"I already knew about you and your family," he says, still lost in her painting. "I let you find me."

"Should I be worried?" I ask, my hand firmly on my phone still.

Through the door, we hear children yell, "Trick-or-Treat!"

The doorbell rings a few more times. Don't the children know, this house is where people go to die and souls are trapped amongst the stone? There is no candy here. Nothing sweet behind these doors.

"I'm not going to kill you, if that's what you are thinking," he says.

That doesn't sit right with me, the way it rolls off his tongue.

"I was just looking for something. Relax." Scott places his hand on my shoulder.

"What were you looking for anyways?" I'm trying to get an answer out of him once again, desperate to know.

"Don't worry about it."

"Look, I won't tell anyone you were here, if you don't tell anyone I was here?"

He smiles at me. I wish he wasn't so beautiful, so easy to believe.

A part of me wonders if he did it, if he is the one who dimmed her light. Maybe they got into some kind of a fight? Maybe he knew she had money, and he was in some kind of trouble. What if he has been searching for the murder weapon to dispose of? How often has he been coming here? I'm feeling dizzy again, so I sit down in the hallway. He watches me.

"Are you sure you're good? Do you want me to call someone?" he asks.

"There's no one to call," I say with sadness in my voice.

"No one?"

I nod.

Suddenly, the feeling passes, and I stand up on my own. We walk out the front door together. The neighbor is watching us from his porch. He doesn't wave or smile. The hairs on the back of my neck stand up, one by one, painfully.

"We probably shouldn't talk anymore," Scott says.

"What? Why?" I ask, confused.

"It's a reminder." He pauses. "I'm trying to move on, but I'm tied to her in so many ways."

If someone is trying to move on, why would they be in the house of their dead ex-girlfriend?

We walk to our cars, both sitting alone in them, watching the house, the neighbor watching us. Another car pulls up. The same man who was at my dad's funeral with Ava gets out of the car. I panic and duck.

He walks toward the neighbor's house and looks over his shoulder, as if he's being watched.

What is he doing there? The man walks into the neighbor's house, shutting the door quickly behind him.

Scott drives away first, but I sit a little longer, more confused than ever. I decide to call the police, so I reach for my phone and begin to dial the numbers. It's time to move on, I tell myself, punching each number into my phone.

Ava didn't kill herself. I can feel it in my bones. All that rushes to my mind is my mother and her lies…How Ava's neighbor said he knew nothing, yet I know he's lying… That boy that Ava used to hang with, and even Scott, who just breaks into her home…whenever.

Everyone is lying.

"Hello, 911? I'd like to report a murder."

THIRTY-FIVE

VICTORIA – NOW

CeCe cleaned up my mess. It's gone. I have finally become what I have dreamed of. *One of them.* Accepted. All it took was the loyalty to the family name. All this time, that was it. Action over words.

I sit in the tea room with CeCe and take a sip of my tea. It's disgusting, but I don't utter a word. My mind gets lost, looking at all her paintings in the house. One of them looks familiar, but I'm not sure where I've seen it before. The phone rings, and CeCe excuses herself. She nods to me as she leaves the room.

"Just a moment," she says, holding her hand over the mouthpiece of the phone.

I've never felt prouder to earn a spot at her coveted tea time. For her grandchildren, it was mandatory, but no one else, except her bridge club, was allowed to join. Calista never sat here. I have finally won. What people don't understand is that it's a game of achieving power. At some point, you need to put aside your moral compass, and if you don't, you've already lost.

No longer do I need to feel threatened or worried about CeCe. There is nothing left to dig up on me because she already knows.

My biggest secret was exposed to me last week, right here at this table. A child, born by mistake. It did no wrong. I just knew it would hold me back from the life I wanted. How could I be a mother then? I was with Tanner one night, when it happened. Years of a strange friendship, only because we shared a mutual obsession with a certain lifestyle. That was it. Too many drinks by the pool one night after a college party. One thing led to another. Nine months later I gave birth to a child. A boy.

I never named him. Naming him would make it real. To be honest, I've never even thought about him until CeCe brought it up to me. It feels like a lifetime ago because that's what it was, a life I buried. It never happened to me. It skips over in my mind.

The grandfather clock chimes, and it startles me. I snap back to it and brush the memory of my past under the rug, where it belongs. CeCe comes into the room with a grin.

"I found him," she says.

"Found who?"

"Your bastard child, of course," CeCe says coyly.

She takes a sip of tea, her pinky finger in the air. She taunts me with what she knows, savoring it, like the last bite of food on her plate.

"His name is Scott, in case you were wondering."

My heart sinks when I hear the name.

"He grew up around here. Nice adoptive mother, wholesome. His father died of cancer, brain."

Her voice doesn't sound the slightest bite saddened. Her words are calculated and cold as per usual.

"Shall we invite him over for some tea?" She asks, laughing.

There's nothing else to do but laugh with her. As I sip on my tea,

I know she did this to hurt me. I never cared before, but CeCe, she likes to know everything. She likes to make sure any secret someone has spills out of them, like blood out of wounded game.

"He used to date Ava," she says. CeCe has gone in for the kill.

Woman like her know where to stick the knife in someone to watch them squirm.

She tries to change the topic about my love life, what I've been up to these days, like two old friends catching up, but I know better than that. I know better than to tell her things that could be used against me. I'm sure she knows about my affair with Erik. I'm sure that's why he hasn't answered any of my calls. He's afraid. Erik hasn't pestered me about skimming money off the top for his help getting a failed organ.

Nothing.

Silence.

CeCe's maid brings her a photo album labeled: "Josh." She takes it and insists I scootch closer to her. CeCe flips through each page, talking about her son as if he were still here. For some reason, I grow uncomfortable with each page she turns. A part of me blames myself for him being gone, for getting the wrong heart, for taking away his last few months. I pretend to smile when she points to a photo of him in his little league outfit. What if she's playing a long game with me? What if none of this is real? She turns another page. It's his first wedding, the one to Calista, except Calista is ripped out of the photo.

"Don't mind that one," she says, laughing. "He just looked very good in this photo, and I didn't want it to go to waste."

I smile back at her.

Picking up the fine china, I drink my tea with caution.

"Shall we go golfing tomorrow?" she asks out of nowhere.

"I'd love that," I say. *I fucking hate golfing.*

"Lovely." She excuses herself from the table. "Follow me to the kitchen. One of my girls is making something, and I'd like to oversee it, make sure it's done right. You know how hard it is to find good help these days."

Following CeCe down the long hallways, ceilings fit for a palace, I arrive at the kitchen. Her chef is making cookies—a "family-ish recipe," she says, with a few twists. CeCe takes her finger and dips it into the bowl, trying the batter.

My eyes catch something unsettling in the kitchen.

A knife, just like the one I used to kill Marla and her daughter, sitting there, out in plain sight. The murder weapon, out in the open by the fucking fruit basket. But why is there a matching pair?

THIRTY-SIX

SCOTT – NOW

So many times, I have been back to that house, trying to find it, the missing piece, and every time, I come back emptyhanded. I can't take it anymore. Sometimes, I miss Ava and her laughs, the way she was so cynical, but her truths were just that. She had every right to be. This is my fault. I shouldn't have let it get this far. I have to live with myself now. The pain overwhelms me when I think too much about it. Sometimes, I want to cave and tell someone, but the world doesn't work that way.

Being together, lying for all those years, it wore me down. Her secrets were just as dark as mine, but we could never be together down the road. She hated the man I never got to know. I couldn't let her do that anymore.

In the rearview mirror, I see Allison's car still parked outside. My half-sister. If you look at us close enough, you'd see certain similarities—her skin almost as tanned as mine, her eyes with similar flecks of gold in them. She's too blinded to notice it. I think she may even have a crush on me. It's not her fault. She has no idea.

I think back to Ava's bedroom. Maybe I should have pretended to be surprised when she told me who she was, gotten up and started to argue with her, make it convincing, but to be honest, I'm tired. I've known who Allison was for a while, and when she went out of her way to find me, I had to play along. Flirt with her, make it seem like we weren't related. I needed to see what she knew, so I made it easy for her to find me. I've always been easy to find. It's just no one wanted to look.

The day I broke up with Ava, I watched the last of her light dim. She thought it was because of her sleeping around, the selling drugs, her shady behavior, but it was so much more than that. She could never know the truth. I had to let her think this was on her. I loved her. I really did.

We were sitting in her room, and I told her I couldn't be with her anymore. I'd never seen what it was like to destroy the last hope someone has. I couldn't tell her that of all these years of me being with her, I was trying to get closer to Tanner, just trying to figure out who I was, where I came from. I never expected to fall in love with her. She was a pawn that grew into so much more.

When I was much younger, I needed surgery and found out by accident my mother's blood type didn't match. They asked about my father, and my mother said, even if he was alive, it wouldn't match either. She never knew I heard her. I didn't want to break her heart. I just wanted answers.

My mom told me I was adopted sometime after that incident. I spent my summers working at the pool, saving up for a private investigator. My adoptive mother is the best, but I just wanted to know who I came from. Is that so much to ask?

Ava threw my love letters at me. She hit me over and over again while I shielded myself. She cried and screamed, but no one heard her in such a large house. No one ever heard her, except me. Now she had no one left. I made her feel like it was everything about her I no longer loved, but the truth was, I never stopped loving her. Her darkness, her talent, her hatred, made her uncommon. It was an accident how close we got. Everything was an accident. I didn't mean for it to happen.

As I drive off into the distance, I can still see Allison's car lingering, the headlights fading into nothing. Next, I drive to their home, watching Victoria through her kitchen window. I loathe her. She sits drinking wine alone at the table. Victoria looks uneasy. She takes a phone call, nervously pacing back and forth as she talks on the phone.

I hate her. At least, I want to. My mind is only filled with the things Ava told me. I never got to make my own opinions…They were made for me already.

THIRTY-SEVEN

ALLISON – NOW

An officer meets me outside Ava's home, the door slamming behind him. When he gets closer to me, I can read his badge: Detective Brown. He seems annoyed. The detective takes out a pen and paper and writes a few things down before speaking to me. I watch him scribble something, then lick the edge of his pen before going back to taking notes. He clears his throat.

"What murder are you talking about?" He looks at Ava's home.

"A lot of them," I say softly.

Through the corner of my eye, I see Ava's neighbor, Paul, watching me through the window. A lump swells in my throat. He wants me to see him.

"By a lot of them, what do you mean?" Detective Brown is bothered by my statement.

"Well, the girl who lives here, my half-sister, she was murdered... I think my mother may have...*killed her*. People who get that kind of money, they just don't kill themselves. It doesn't make sense. She could have done anything." The lump in my throat grows even more.

"Look, I'm sorry for your loss. We investigated every avenue, and they all pointed to no foul play. Ava, she had a lot of demons. We interviewed the entire block, and they all said the same thing. No one was surprised. Sometimes, money doesn't always buy happiness." He puts away his notepad.

Paul comes outside and sits on his front steps. Ava's friend doesn't leave the inside of the house. He stays put.

"My mother, she's done terrible things, though. I've seen it with my own two eyes. You need to believe me!" I start to scream at him.

"What mother hasn't done terrible things before? Let me guess, she grounded you? Took away your phone a few times?" He says, mocking me. "Look, it's Halloween. It's not funny to make prank calls. I suggest you go home." He puts his notepad back into his pocket.

Paul starts walking over toward Detective Brown. He greets me with a fake smile. I don't like him.

"Detective Brown, what are you doing here? More angry residences complaining about tee-peeing and egging houses tonight?" he says, laughing.

"This young woman was just leaving."

Paul signals for me to get into my car.

I don't drive off right away. Instead, I watch them through the window, pretending I am reading something on my phone. I have the windows cracked enough to be able to hear them, just slightly.

"She was saying that Ava was murdered," Detective Brown says to Paul.

"And...?" Paul asks.

"Everyone knows that she offed herself. Rich suburban girl with troubles, you know the drill."

"If she was murdered, who do you think did it?" Paul asks.

I pretend to keep texting in my car.

"You?" Detective Brown slaps him on the shoulder with a laugh.

Paul doesn't take kindly to his remark, and his facial expression changes.

"Lighten up, buddy. Retirement has made you stiff."

Paul pulls away from him. "Well, I need to get back inside. We are carving pumpkins."

Detective Brown shakes his hand and gets back in his car, then drives off.

I call my grandmother and decide to go spend Halloween at her home. Nothing is more terrifying.

The entire estate is decorated by her housekeepers. Immaculate spider webs cover the gates, and jack-o-lanterns span the entire property leading up to her door.

She's never liked holiday décor, but she does it to show up her neighbors. Everything she has ever done has to be more than someone else. It's a rule she expects us to live by.

The interior of her home has no Halloween décor whatsoever, except for bowls of candy here and there. She likes to keep appearances up from the outside, never the inside.

I walk the long hallways to the kitchen where she sits, being served caramel-dipped apples and a hot tea. She sees me and pats the chair next to her.

"Have a seat, dear."

Her hands are beginning to look like skeletons, age spots showing through her makeup. She's dressed up nicely for a last-second visit. My grandmother signals for me to have a piece of apple and puts the caramel dipping sauce in front of me.

"Go ahead. A few pieces won't do any damage to your cute little figure that you got from my side of the family, definitely not your mothers." She laughs.

"Grandmother, I have a question for you." I straighten my spine, sitting properly in front of her so she will take me seriously. "Do you think my mother is capable of murder?"

She doesn't wince. It seems as if it's a regular and ordinary question to ask.

"Everyone is capable of murder. Even you."

I watch her sip out of her expensive teacup. But I could never hurt someone. She is wrong. I reach for my cup and take a sip from it.

"Are you bothered by my answer? You look unwell." She signals for one of her maids to bring me a wet towel for my forehead.

They place it on me.

"I could never hurt someone."

"But you already have," she says to me.

What does she mean by that? Who is she talking about? She must have me confused with Ashley.

"I don't understand…" I say, unsure what she means.

"You hurt me by signing away a large sum of the family money to Ava," she says calmly.

"That's different. It's money. It's not a life."

"We think differently," she says coldly.

I eat the last of the apple slices and get up to cut myself another honey crisp apple.

"Sit down, dear. The maids can do that for you."

"It's fine. I can do it myself." I feel uncomfortable having people do everything for us.

I reach for a knife that's close by and start cutting up the apple slices, watching the juice pour out of the sides, getting the cutting board wet.

For a moment, I think about taking this knife and killing CeCe. I try to picture it, but I can't. She's wrong about me. I couldn't hurt anyone. Taking the sliced apple back to my seat, I place it down in front of us, but I'm not hungry anymore. I watch her take a piece and chew it slowly.

"Take another bite." She inches the plate toward me.

I do what she says, and as I chew, I spit the apple politely in my napkin. It has an iron taste to it.

"Something wrong, dear?"

"Nothing at all, grandmother."

The doorbell rings. The whole house can hear the chimes of the front door.

Within minutes, my mother is walking into the room. She greets my grandmother and takes a seat at the table. I try to not acknowledge her presence until my grandmother forces me to say something.

"Manners," CeCe says, and that's enough for me to snap out of it.

"Hi, Mom." Calling her my mother doesn't seem right anymore. It's hard to call someone your mother when you watched her slaughter people right in front of you.

"Should you tell grandmother, or should I?"

I look her right in her lost eyes.

"A Detective Brown called me. He says you went to the Maple house tonight. Is that true?"

"Yes," I tell her. "You used to stalk that house every day when we were little kids. It's a learned habit." I accuse her of being the cause of my obsession.

"You were there the day she died, were you not?" my mother asks.

CeCe is amused at this conversation. She bites into another piece of apple, but doesn't say a word, listening carefully. She always listens carefully. CeCe studies people, their body language, their desires, their needs. Then she uses everything against them. She said she made my grandfather fall in love with her before they were even introduced.

"I have no idea what you're talking about," I tell her.

"They could pin it on you, you know..." my mother says coldly.

"I didn't do anything!" I scream.

"That's not true."

I think back to that day. Could I be the reason she is dead? Can I not remember it because I blocked it out? Is everyone protecting me?

Think, think back to that day. What could they be talking about? I have no recollection of going inside.

I close my eyes and go through the day, every piece of that twenty-four-hour time period.

Nothing.

That's all I can remember.

Nothing.

But why?

THIRTY-EIGHT

AVA – THEN

9:00 am

Before I can bring myself upstairs, I stand in the kitchen and stare at the spot where I watched Tanner die. After all this time, I know what peace feels like. For months after it happened, people accused my mother and stepfather of running away after trying to kill me. Some people even thought I did kill them. Those people weren't wrong in a way. I watch the light outside shine through the window, giving a golden glow to a once colorless room.

I'm waiting for my mother. She said she'd be here by nine, and she's never late. It's been a long time since I've seen her. No communication except for what Paul tells me. "She's safe," or "she sounds good," keeping it short. I wish I could resent her for the life she caused me to live, but I can't. I understand her now. It took me a long time to get it, for it to click, but when it did, I wondered if I'd have done the same thing. We all survive differently.

The kitchen looks less glamorous, the appliances dusty. I walk toward a cabinet and get a glass. Nothing comes from the spout. I haven't kept up on payments. Fuck. I'll go to Paul's and get some water in a bit. I don't want to leave until she gets here.

The front door makes a shrieking sound when it opens. She's here. The footsteps grow closer.

My heart drops.

What is *he* doing here?

"Hello?" I say, puzzled.

He doesn't say anything right away, just stares at me.

"Hey."

"What are you doing here, in my home?" I ask, confused.

"I wanted to talk. It's been a while, and I just…I feel bad about how things ended, and I really do miss you. I swear I do, but I just… I need to know a few things." He runs his hands through his stupid golden hair, and I stand there stiff, my foot tapping again and again.

"Well, ask me," I say, not letting him walk all over me.

"Did you do it?"

"Do what?" I'm unsure what he means.

He gets closer to me, and I can feel his breath on my neck. The little hairs on my body stand up as he leans into me.

"Did you kill them?"

"No!" I shove him into the wall, but I didn't mean to push him so hard. "You need to leave!"

He gets closer to me again.

Click. That's the sound I heard. *Click…click…click…*my brain connecting the dots. The way he ended things with me, the way he left that day in a hurry, the sadness in his eyes…He couldn't even look at me. I was living with someone who didn't want me either. I feel dizzy.

"What are you talking about?"

But I know the answer—the images of Tanner and Victoria together, the birth certificate I found while going through his office a long time ago. I thought it was for blackmail, to save himself from a bad investment deal…to ruin a family as collateral for the money he owed. Something sick and twisted. Maybe he kept it so he could hold onto it in case his unwanted child became successful, or if he needed money, something like that. He didn't keep it because he had feelings. He never had feelings.

"It's why I can't love you," he says.

Nothing hurts worse than that, not being able to be loved by someone you chose.

"I need to get that birth certificate. I know you have it."

I don't want him to have it. I don't know how to tell him it's not even here. The cops raided this place.

"I don't know what you're talking about. The cops tore this place apart. Anything you are looking for, they probably have."

He gets closer to me. His lips rub up against mine, and he pauses. His breathing gets heavier, our breathing syncs, the uneasiness trapped between us.

"I know you always wanted him dead. I won't forgive you if I find out I never got to know my real father because of something you did. For all I know, you made up all these lies about him to fulfill your sad little artist girl tragedy of a life," he says maliciously.

His words kill me. I don't answer him because he runs off through the back door when he hears the front door open.

He wanted me alone.

-9:37 am.

Paul sees me standing in the hallway, the life drained out of my body.

"Are you okay? You look like crap," he states the obvious.

"Yeah, I'm good. Just thirsty. Our water is off."

"I'll be right back. I'll go run to the house and get you a couple bottles." He heads back out the door.

I walk to the couch and sit down, processing everything Scott told me, how he's the child of the two people in this world who I hate the most. The person who stole my father from me, the person who never wanted to be a father to me. If Scott ever finds out what happened, I'm afraid to think of what he may do to me. How could he not believe me? How could he say those things, *think* those things. Why after all this time is he so pressed on Tanner? Can't he just go talk to Victoria?

The love letters he wrote me, they mean nothing now. When I clean my room up later, I'll throw them all away. Except one, the first one, when everything was so new, when we weren't these people.

Paul walks back in the house, but this time, I can see his gun strapped to his hip. It startles me. Why does he have a gun with him? Was it always there? Did I miss it when he walked in because I was consumed with the news that Scott told me?

As Paul hands me a bottle of water, I carefully twist the cap off and take a sip.

"Thanks."

"So, think she'll be here soon? Or is she going to meet you at the storage unit?"

I never told him I had a storage unit? Did I?

"Here." I avoid the second half of the question.

We sit on the couch in silence. I check the time. It's going by slowly. Like the life I had growing up here. Every beating, every screaming match, time froze. Until the day it happened and time finally moved again.

Paul looks stressed. He never looks this nervous. I've seen him clean up a crime scene with assertiveness and precision, not a drop of fear in his body.

"I was wondering if you'd be willing to maybe give me a little money? I'm in a bit of a spot with the mortgage, and my wife, she's been ill recently. The medical bills are piling, and…" He stops.

Did Paul always want money from me? Is this why he helped me? If I don't give it to him, will he turn me in?

"Is that why you helped my mother and me?" I become defensive. "So we'd be indebted to you forever? So you can always have a small piece of the pie? Would you have helped us if it wasn't for that?"

I can feel my skin turning red.

"Get out!" I say, not thinking straight.

Why am I saying these things? Paul helped us. Paul is good. Why am I putting up my guard around him? He's never proven to be anything but kind. He risked it all for me. I spend time at his house when I couldn't go back here. When I had no one. Why am I becoming so defensive?

Paul doesn't try to say a word. Instead, he just leaves. As the door shuts, I regret yelling at him. He knows all my secrets; he's always known them. While I was busy watching everyone else, he was watching me. I'll get him some money later, I'll apologize and it will be water under the bridge. He's a dad, a *good* dad, he'll brush it under the rug.

I lie on the overly bleached rug that once had my blood all over it and close my eyes. Being back here is too much.

12:00pm

Easton's face comes into focus as my eyes slowly open. He pulls me up.

"I thought you were dead. You gave me a heart attack," he says, grabbing at his chest. "Is she here yet?"

"No, I don't think she's coming. She said she'd be here three hours ago. Should I be worried?"

"Nah, she'll be here. She loves you…She'll be here."

Easton sits on the couch. I relax in his lap, waiting for my mother. Easton strokes my hair to comfort me.

"Don't go spending your millions all in one place, now. Don't forget about the small people." He smiles down at me.

"Are you excited for your new life?"

"I feel like I won't get it, you know? Like it won't happen for me… "I feel his phone vibrate underneath me. He reaches in his pocket and digs it out. He puts his hand over the speaker as he answers it.

"Yo, I gotta take this. I'll swing by tonight to grab you and your mom, cool?" he says softly, heading out the door.

1:37pm

Still nothing from my mother. She isn't coming. I sit outside the front steps and watch everyone pass by.

The neighbors are talking amongst themselves about my return, staring at me as they walk their babies in fancy strollers, sipping on their coffees. Half these women wish I were dead because of the things I've done, but they've never known what it is to have to survive. Just because I lived in this house, just because I had a roof over my head, it didn't mean I was safe. It didn't mean the money was mine.

To work two jobs isn't enough to afford an apartment. It isn't enough to pay for school. They have no idea Tanner was broke, that he spent millions and millions trying to invest and become a billionaire, but that mindset, that's what really killed him, not me, and not my mother.

Greed.

I get up from the steps and walk around the block a few times. I pass by Erik, the Brentwoods' trustee lawyer, I'm certain of it. He's walking with someone I've never met before, but why is he in my neighborhood?

Something doesn't feel right, so I head back to my house and sit on the steps.

Erik walks by my house, making direct eye contact with me. I look away quickly. He must be here because he's trying to lock in a new client. Maybe he's desperate after his reputation got demolished in the lawsuit. All the shady rich people don't trust him now for making such a massive error I know my dad planned.

More time passes. The sky become shades of orange marmalade. I should probably go inside and start packing up the rest of my things. I quit college, it wasn't me. I tried to do what was normal, but I will never be *normal*.

My time here is limited, and I won't feel alone anymore. I go inside what used to be a house of demons, into what is now a house of ghosts.

I lock the door behind me.

I prefer the ghosts.

8:00pm

Packing up my things is harder than it seems. I'm still trying to

322

tape boxes together. There's a knock at the front door. My mother wouldn't knock, would she? I rush to open it.

"Detective Brown?" I say, confused.

"Can I come in?"

I signal for him to enter.

He takes off his hat and stands in the front entryway.

"I wanted to check in. I heard you were back. It's been a while, and I wanted to ask you a few questions, since we haven't talked in some time."

"How did you know I was in?" Maybe he was watching me this whole time?

"Paul and I ran into each other. He told me you were back. Good guy, watching over your dog for you while you were at school. I can't imagine how hard this has been on you. Being in this house would be hard on anyone who's going through what you have," he tells me.

Why did Paul bring me up? Was this his way of sending me a message? Was this a warning to me for lashing out earlier? It's not a secret that I'm home, but why was I even brought up? I focus back on Detective Brown.

"Is there a place we can sit down and chat?" he asks.

I lead him toward the kitchen.

"Something isn't sitting right with me, and I hope you can walk me through a few things." He's trying to be nice, but I know he's pretending. Detective Brown doesn't care about me. He cares about figuring out the crime, something to get a few pats on the back from his buddies.

I nod and go along with it.

"I've been piecing together some things. Can you tell me why you pulled out all that money the night before it happened? Were you paying someone off? Did you give your parents the money to help them escape Tanner's crimes? Where did you put all this money, it can't be traced."

I watch him as he slides a dried plant across the table.

"We also found these in your mother's garden. Deadly. Did you know that?"

I don't speak just yet. I need to sit there, play the confused girl.

Detective Brown then shows me the neighbor's cameras from across the street. He went to every single door for footage.

"No one came in or out of your house that night, which makes me think you had something to do with everything. A disgruntled daughter whose father died, blamed everything on your parents..." He trails off.

Stiffening my shoulders, I push the dried plant back toward him. "I don't know what you are insinuating, but I had nothing to do with anything. Tanner was up to no good. This has been made public. I had to pay off his debts," I proclaim, hoping my lies stick.

"The night before? Was there a deadline?" He's being smug; he thinks he has me.

"Unless you have a search warrant, I suggest you get out of my house. I've been through enough."

Suddenly, he leans into me. I can feel his breath, the warmth leaving his body, "My money is on that they are in your backyard. I'll be back tomorrow with a search warrant. People have been talking, Ms. Brentwood, and I listen."

I walk him to the door and slam it behind him, lock it once more.

He can tear up this house, this yard, but he won't find anything.

I need to make things right. I need to apologize to Paul.

Thou shalt love thy neighbor as thyself. More like, pay off thy neighbor to keep crimes committed a secret. I text Paul that I'd be happy to help him, that my behavior was unwarranted and that being home made me lash out. Paul doesn't respond. He'll see it soon enough. It was foolish of me to not offer him anything for everything he risked for my mother and me. Sometimes, I don't think clearly. I've never thought clearly, actually. My mind's always been thinking about ways to escape, ways to let out my pain. I don't think I've had a happy thought in a very long time. It's a learned behavior that I was stripped of.

8:27pm

I carry a few boxes upstairs and notice Detective Brown sitting in his car, watching me through one of the windows upstairs. I feel uneasy.

A car pulls into my driveway, and someone gets out, then walks toward the front door. I hear the doorbell ring, so I walk back downstairs. Who could it possibly be now?

But when I open the door again, the woman I hate most in this world stands in front of me.

"Victoria?" I feel like this is some kind of joke.

"Can I come in?" Her body language is off, and she looks afraid.

"Sure?" I say, curious as to what she's here for.

"Can we sit down and talk?"

"I'd prefer to stand…keep this short…if you don't mind." I enjoy being the one in power over her.

"Look, I need some of the money back. You can keep most of it. I just need some of it. You don't understand. If I can't pay someone back, she'll kill me or my girls. CeCe, she's on my ass to get it back too. There's a lot you don't know and…" she says, panicking.

"First off, CeCe has never been a grandmother to me. Second, maybe you deserve it. Maybe it's karma for ruining my family and making me grow up in this house." Telling her off makes me feel good. The high is addicting.

"Please, I'll pay you back. You don't understand!" she cries.

"Tell me what it's for, and then I'll decide." I like this power. No. *I love it.*

"I bought Josh a heart to live longer, okay? I wanted him to live longer. It came with a price tag." Victoria seems relieved to tell someone her secret.

For a minute, I'm taken aback. She risked everything for my father to live longer, only for Tanner, the father of her firstborn child, to destroy it, to take everything away from her, to make her into this groveling woman. Victoria wanted my dad to live, and he still chose his old life over his newer one.

"Can I think about it?" I ask her, knowing I won't give her a dime. She deserves everything she gets, everything she put my mother and me through.

"I don't have time for you to think about it," she squeals at me.

I laugh at her. It just slips out. She shoves me into a wall, and I shove her back. She starts to choke me; my neck feels like a balloon about to burst.

This is how I die. This is it.

Just as I have accepted death, waiting to see what the next journey holds for me, she lets me go. She stares at her hands. They shake, and she tries to stop it.

"I'm sorry!" she says, running out the door.

Detective Brown watches her. He's still there, hunting.

I go back upstairs and sit in my room, the room that has cradled me for most of my life, The room's walls that changed different shades through every phase. I walk to my balcony and take in my view one last time.

Detective Brown's car is now gone, replaced with a much more expensive one. I try to shake it off.

It's nothing.

Everything is done.

9:39pm

More time passes by, and I begin to pack up my belongings. I stare at the hundreds of different shades of paint tubes and think about all the colors in the world, all the different ways to see things.

My phone has no missed calls.

Nothing.

She's not coming.

I've accepted it.

I grab a few acrylic paints and open them up to see if they are salvageable. The luscious cadmiums and the sadistic crimsons.

I walk over to my painting to grab the key taped to the back of it, when

I hear a faint creak. Is someone there?

"Hello?"

No one answers. I try again.

"Hello? Mom?"

I leave my room grazing my hand against the door frame taking the brunt all those times. I hear the creak again. I walk to the front door.

Anxiety overcomes me. I locked it after Detective Brown left, but did I lock it after Victoria? I give the handle a slight jiggle, and to my relief, it's locked. The noise is just in my head, I'm sure of it.

I walk to the kitchen to get a glass of water, but when I turn the corner into the hallway, something sharp hits my side...

I'm trying hard not to close my eyes, but all I can see is a shadow-like figure. Though I try to reach my hand out, it doesn't come near me.

I'm feeling so tired.

I'm so cold.

10:03 pm time of death.

THIRTY-NINE

VICTORIA – THEN

9:42 pm

Nothing makes me feel more like shit than what I'm doing right now, sitting in a parking lot, crying, eating soggy fries and a shitty burger from McDonalds. I grab a flask out of my purse and take a swig. *One sip* won't hurt. I've been through a lot. I signed my soul away to the devil, and it's been like this ever since. Misery. But I'd do it all again because it's who I am. I can admit that.

As I put my flask away, I dig through my purse to find my phone. I need to call Erik and tell him I need his help. But even though I tear apart my purse and then my car, nothing. I spill my disgusting fries all over. I'll clean it up later.

"Shit!" I yell to myself.

The person next to me in the parking lot looks over at me, and I flick him off. I left my phone at that bitch's house. After a quick check in my car mirror, I fix my makeup and try to regain composure. I'll go back to the house and reason with her. It will be fine; it will all be fine. CeCe will forgive me. I'll pay Marla back, and she'll finally stop this ludicrous game of hers. And if not, I'll come up with another plan.

Within minutes, I'm back at Ava's house. I walk to the front door since it's cracked slightly open, just letting myself in. But I don't make it far.

Ava lies in a pool of blood. I rush over to her, trying to stop her from bleeding, but it's too late. She's gone, her skin just barely still warm. Her lips blue. Her eyes closed tightly. A knife so deep within her body, I don't dare move it. I'm too late. *The money is gone.*

I always wanted her and her mother to be dead, for me to be rid of them. Like a constant burden that I was always second to. I would never be loved how he loved them, his first true love, but for some reason, I feel nothing and everything all at once.

FORTY

ALLISON – THEN

10:15pm

Taking a deep breath, I muster the courage to get out of the car and just go talk to her. My therapist said I need some sort of closure. It might be good for me to get to know her. The lawsuit never gave us a chance.

I have a sister, a talented sister who I've watched silently, but I don't know her. Hopefully, I deserve to know her. Maybe she'd actually like me?

The door is left slightly open, so I let myself in.

"Ava, it's me. Allison. Can we talk?"

I wait for a response. Past the entryway, I see her on the ground, her mother holding her and sobbing silently. She's in too much pain to make a sound.

Calista begins hugging me, leaning on me. Blood is all over my clothes, her blood. Our blood. A blood we share.

I cry with her. I cry for someone I was never given a chance to know.

Her mother and I sit for hours, staring at her lifeless body.

We look at the knife penetrating her skin—the handle a dark shade of emerald-green with a gold lining around it.

1:39am

"Don't tell anyone I was here," Calista says faintly.

She drops me back at home, and I walk up to my bedroom. I sit on my bed, covered in blood, a beautiful shade of scarlet.

In the morning when I wake up, I walk downstairs, and my mother stares at me. I have no idea why.

FORTY-ONE

ALLISON – NOW

Sitting at the table with them makes me feel uneasy. I shouldn't feel like this around my own flesh and blood. Am I the reason Ava is dead? I can't be.

"Why do you think *I* killed her?" I ask.

The maids and chefs in the kitchen pause. They are paid well enough to keep quiet if they work for CeCe.

"Because you came home covered in her blood. Your grandmother was nice enough to donate to the North Shore Police Department as a thank you for all they do."

"You're making it up!" I say, standing up from the table.

"Sit down. *Now*," CeCe says.

I don't.

In a panic, I go to the counter and grab the knife resting on it, the knife with an emerald-green handle and a gold line on each side, used to slice both apples and flesh. As I hold the knife fiercely, I flash back to Ava, lying in the hallway, her blood pooled around her body.

I remember now.

I was there when she died.

This was the knife used to take her from me. In my grandmother's kitchen.

A trophy she kept, to prove she was and will always be the alpha. And sitting next to the knife was the matching set, the one my mother used to kill Marla, one she took from the Maple house. It was her who turned the house upside-down.

"What are you doing?" CeCe chuckles.

"I need answers. Did you kill Ava, Mom?"

Even saying the word "Mom" makes me sick to my stomach.

She looks over at CeCe and back to me.

"Allison, you were covered in her blood. I protected you," she says.

"That's a lie! The knife, the murder weapon, is in CeCe's kitchen!" I point to the knife I'm holding again.

"I had no choice," CeCe says, taking a sip of tea.

"What do you mean, you had no choice?" I yell.

I look at my mother, her face covered in shock that it was CeCe, not me. The fact my own mother thought it was me makes me even more upset. She was protecting me, but she should know I would never. My mother doesn't know me.

"The money. It didn't belong to her. It belongs to me. I gave up everything for wealth, a name. I was following your mother that night, I knew what she was doing, and decided to take matters into my own hands. She didn't deserve that amount of money. Erik paid for his mistakes with the mess he caused. That error simply won't do. You'll understand one day. Maybe not right now, but one day."

I look at my mother again. She doesn't say anything. She doesn't offer to take me home. She doesn't offer me a hug to console me.

The way she's looking at CeCe right now, that's the only look I needed to see. I'm going to end them.

I have another flashback as I'm storming out of CeCe's. It's of Calista holding me tightly, rocking me back and forth. More of a mother to me than my own in that moment. She's alive.

I need to find her. I run out of the house, sprinting as fast as I can to my car, and drive *through* the gates, breaking them.

The murder weapon is with me on the passenger seat. I need to find Calista.

Blasting music on the radio doesn't calm me. Instead, it sends me into a panic while I drive back to Ava's house. Her friend will still be there. I know it.

In a hurry, I blow through red lights. I can't waste any time. My tires screech against the perfectly paved road as I brake in front of her house, reaching for the knife. I get out of the car and run up to the neighbor's door, pounding on it. Right now, I don't care if I'm making a scene. I keep it up until a light turns on inside.

The door creaks open. No one is there to greet me. This doesn't feel right, but I have no other choice.

One foot in front of the other, I walk into their home.

Her neighbor sits by the fireplace, poking at it with a sticker. The embers slowly escape behind the iron grill placed in front of it.

"I know she's alive," I say softly.

He turns to look at me, but he doesn't respond.

"I need to talk to her friend, the one that was here earlier!" I say, my voice cracking.

He still doesn't respond. The silence is the loudest thing I've ever heard.

"Did you hear me!" I tell him again.

Footsteps. I hear footsteps.

When I turn my head, I see her, the beautiful, frail woman my mother hated.

"Hi," she says.

In an instant, everything I was going to say is gone. As I try to compose myself, I reach into my pocket and feel for the key. I hand it to her. She smiles, taking her cold hand and placing it on top of mine.

"You two were a lot alike," she says.

I walk out the door, my hand firmly gripped on the knife.

"Wait!" I shout, running toward her. "This belongs to you." I hand her the knife.

Calista takes it from me, her eyes fighting back tears.

"It was CeCe," I say gently, not knowing if I did the right thing in betraying my family, but are they really?

Calista takes the knife from me and puts it in her pocket.

"You can take it to the police," I tell her.

"The police think I'm dead, and if I show up, they will think I did this and ran away with my husband. The police will find a way to pin this on me. I need to stay dead, do you hear me? Can you keep my secret?"

I nod, hand her the keys to my car, and give her the gate code to CeCe's, not that she'll need a code now.

"You're already dead," I say, my body shaking.

Easton walks into the living room. She hugs him, and just like that, she's gone.

I sit down on a chair and notice Ava's dog. They were keeping the dog safe, her dog, this whole time, how did I notice it before? These people, they are good people. I've been learning what those kinds of people are lately. It's hard to recognize it when you grew up your entire life without seeing it.

"You did the right thing, you know, even if it doesn't feel that way," Easton says. "Where was the key? Ava told me about it, for safety purposes."

"Taped behind one of her paintings."

"Everyone always looks past the artwork. That's the real treasure. People can't find things when there are other shiny objects to distract them," Paul says.

"What's going to happen next?" I ask, unsure of my emotions.

"Everything."

FORTY-TWO

CALISTA – NOW

The gates are badly damaged when I pull up to the front of the house and park Allison's car.

I can't get what I lost back, but I *can* erase her. Them. All of it.

The door to the front of the house isn't closed. A sliver of light leaks from its cracks. When I let myself in, I ignore the grandness of this place. It feels so small when you've already lost everything.

It's late. All her maids and butlers have gone off to bed by now, but I know CeCe. I know she can't sleep well. Her sins keep her up most nights. Josh used to tell me whenever he'd get up in the middle of the night, she'd be there, drinking tea, staring off into the distance, like a zombie of sorts.

The hallways are dimly lit, and my eyes are slowly adjusting, but they need to hurry. I take a deep breath and walk toward a light to my left. There is a glimmer of florescence, and I know that's the room.

I peek around the corner and see her sitting there, toxic and frail. She's sipping on tea, the seat next to her empty. CeCe won't dare do the dishes. She'll wait for her maids to wake up and clear her table settings in the morning.

I knock on the doorframe. She's taken by surprise.

"Look what Hell dug up from the grave," she says, laughing.

I sit down across the table from her.

"I didn't invite you to sit," she says coldly.

I show her the knife. "Peculiar that this knife has been missing from my house, isn't it?"

"Things tend to go missing when the people who own them go missing themselves."

Just her voice sends me into a frenzy. "Let's chat."

"Well, I need to get my maid to make us some tea, then. We can't have a proper discussion without more tea."

I can't have her maid here. No one can see me here.

"I can make it," I tell her.

She seems appeased by me having to serve her.

I fill the kettle and wait for the water to boil. When I look up, I notice one of Ava's paintings is displayed right before my eyes. It was one of her least favorite paintings she said she did. It was of this little girl, the size of an ant, in a vast field, staring at a castle. When Ava painted it, she said the grass looked too stylized. The colors were all off, and it looked like a Monet knock-off mixed with a Disney movie. She hated it, but I kept it. I loved everything from her mind.

CeCe stole it and stole her.

The kettle steams. Once it finishes, I pour the boiling water into two cups and add tea bags to it. CeCe watches me as I do this. I bring the cups to the table.

"Here is a fresh cup," I say, handing it to her.

"What did you want to discuss?"

I watch her blow gently on the water to cool it down. Her lips pursed together makes me clench on the blade by accident and cut my hand. I feel the blood begin to pool.

"I'd like to know why you never liked me."

"Is this a joke, dear? What is the real reason you broke into my home?"

"The door was unlocked."

"I don't need a reason for never being fond of you. Mother's intuition," she says.

"'Mother isn't exactly the word I'd use to describe you."

I watch her take her fancy teacup to her mouth. She takes a sip.

"How does it taste?" I ask, standing up to pour my teacup out and put it in the sink.

CeCe starts coughing and wheezing, grabbing at her chest, but it's too late. She'll be gone soon. Victoria can fight against CeCe's other children now for money. They'll tear each other's throats out, and I'll watch from a distance.

"I'd kill you in this life and every life," I tell her, watching her eyes slowly dim as her heart stops. "That's for Ava."

I go to the stove and turn on the gas. She watches me, unable to do anything. She's in agony. It will be quick now, but she doesn't deserve that.

I take a match to my daughter's painting—it's been tarnished just being in this place—and watch as the flame from the match gracefully kisses the oils. It goes up in flames, the past burning with it.

Rushing as fast as I can, I run to the front door and head to Allison's car. I drive off through the gate and watch the fire blaze from a distance.

Somewhere, Josh is laughing.

Somewhere, he's proud of me.

I'm proud of me.

Before I can head back to Paul's to hide out for a little longer and gather my things, I make a pit stop. At Victoria's house, I dig through my purse for a pen and something to write on. All I have is lipstick and a napkin. This will have to do.

It reads: "You can have it all." A shade of red I never much enjoyed, but it might be my new favorite.

I drive back to Paul's house and sneak in through the back. Everyone is passed out when I get there. I walk to the living room, where Allison is asleep on the couch. She's wrapped in a blanket. I sit next to her, longing for my own daughter, blaming myself for everything. If only I'd have stood up for myself, if only I wasn't so afraid. I stare into the fire and think of CeCe's estate burning to the ground. Everything she's ever worked for, ashes.

I close my eyes tightly, but all I see is red...

The sun peeks through the windows. I must have fallen asleep. I look over and see Allison staring at me with a soft smile.

Aletta is in the kitchen, making breakfast. The sweet smell of milk mixing with flour fills me with joy. Paul is beside her, squeezing fresh oranges and straining the pulp. They look at each other and smile. I've always wanted that one simple thing in life—to grow old with someone, to make breakfast on a Sunday, flour on the floor, sticky juice on the counter, light beaming through the windows, proof you are alive. Instead, what I got was a first love filled with regret, a second husband who I thought was a safety net, and the loss of the one thing that mattered to me. I wanted so little, yet it was still too much to ask for.

"Sorry that I had the key to whatever it belongs to." Allison speaks softly and rubs her arms.

"Don't be sorry. You didn't know. You were trying to help her. It's what sisters do for each other."

Allison lets out a small smile.

Paul and Aletta invite us to the table, where we share what will be our last meal before I leave again. Paul called me when he noticed Allison kept going to the house. It was time I came back, for one last goodbye. We pass around the hot syrup to pour all over our food, indulging ourselves after several years that have felt like a multitude of lifetimes.

I cannot help but feel jealous in this home, that this was never supposed to happen for me. I've always lived in houses, but it's not the same thing. The two things couldn't be more far apart from each other—just as how Josh tried to replace us, his other children with both "A" names. *It was not the same thing.*

Allison hands me a plate of fresh fruit, her hand touching mine.

"Will you tell me about her?" she asks.

"I would love that." I say. "I have no idea where to start, so I'll start from the beginning, to when it wasn't always so bad, the quiet days when it was just the two of us, fingerpainting, baking cookies, the way she'd laugh and scrunch her nose." Yes, I'll start with that.

When the light fades away and the darkness fills the sky, Easton picks me up and drives me to Ava's storage unit. He was waiting for me this entire time, staying close by, just in case. Easton blamed himself for not watching her more carefully.

"I'll come back in a bit," he tells me.

I place the key in the orange garage door and lift it up. My heart sinks, and I fall to my knees, unable to balance myself on the axis of this earth. When I walk inside, I turn on the single Edison bulb and shut the garage door behind me.

She knew.

I think she always knew.

Duffels filled with money surround my feet, hundreds of them. Paintings and notebooks scattered everywhere, like she placed them in a hurry. Her story. Our story. I pick up one of the notebooks. Detailed with every moment in her life. Proof of everything. Her story shortened.

Ava never got to finish hers. She will never get the ending she was supposed to have. I left her. I left. *I* did this. I've always been on time for my daughter. if I had just not hesitated.

When I got to the airport, suddenly it was if my chest was caving in on me. I just couldn't get on the plane. I was frozen with thoughts of regret. My choices led to Ava having a traumatic childhood, I did this to her. *Me.* I thought she'd be better off without me, I had caused her enough damage. You can pick who your husband is, but your children cannot pick their father. I was ashamed. I was so afraid Ava was better off without me, but in the end she could make that choice for herself, I had to get back to her, I had to see her. I got on the last flight out when I finally got my mind right.

There's a letter attached to one of her paintings, the one that's covered in wolfsbane plants. I bend down and reach for it, holding it closely to my face to take in every word.

FORTY-THREE

AVA – NOW

If you're reading this without me, please know it's not your fault. None of it was. I don't blame you. I used to, but I know it's not your fault now. Please know that. Take this money. Have a fresh start, one where you are in control. You deserve a life of control, a life that is truly yours.

Sometimes, I felt like this was always the way it was supposed to be. I started preparing, which maybe I had a self-fulling prophecy, but something in me told me I was never going to make it. I think that's why I never felt normal, I never could understand others and blend in, no matter how much I wanted to. It's like those paintings I used to start and never finish. I became one of them.

I was never supposed to be here. I wasn't really made for this world anyways. Wherever I am, I'm safe now, somewhere where every house is filled with the brightest colors, the warmest tones, where shadows only exist to make things more beautiful. When you miss me, know I'm inside one of my paintings, dancing in the lavender fields that I never could quite get the color right on, or running my hands through golden barley. I'm more alive than I've ever been. I'm just alive somewhere else now, but it's your turn to live.

Live for you, no one else. How often do we get second chances? Almost never, so take this one. Take the money and do good things. Help others. Money can't change the past, but it can change someone's future.

I love you.

Printed in Great Britain
by Amazon